———————————— ★ ————————————

"What was Paul Mainwaring's daughter doing out here?"

The laugh was cruel. "A little high-class for pigs like us?"

"Don't give me any more of your overthrow bullshit right now, Donovan, or I might tell you to go to hell and I'll walk away. Don't forget, there isn't another lawyer in town who'll work with you."

I pushed him out of the way and grabbed a rusty rake. Awkward as it was, I managed to ease it under the blanket until I could gently lift it and set it aside. Because I knew her father, I'd seen her a number of times. Now, as she lay on her side, her profile was statue-perfect.

I hunched down. The wounds I could see were concentrated around her heart. There were six of them. Somebody had been very angry with her and had let a knife convey the rage. In books, beautiful dead women always retain some remnant of their beauty. Not so in real life. Heartbreaker that she'd been, now the skin was gray, and the tongue lolling out of the right side of her mouth looked lurid and sickly. Vivid blue eyes stared into eternity; even the dark hair was dusty and flecked with straw.

———————————— ★ ————————————

Previously published Worldwide Mystery titles by
ED GORMAN

SAVE THE LAST DANCE FOR ME
CROOKS, CRIMES AND CHRISTMAS
  "THE SANTA CLAUS MURDERS"
EVERYBODY'S SOMEBODY'S FOOL
BREAKING UP IS HARD TO DO
FOOLS RUSH IN
TICKET TO RIDE

BAD MOON RISING

ED GORMAN

WORLDWIDE®

TORONTO • NEW YORK • LONDON
AMSTERDAM • PARIS • SYDNEY • HAMBURG
STOCKHOLM • ATHENS • TOKYO • MILAN
MADRID • WARSAW • BUDAPEST • AUCKLAND

To my friends and saviors
Linda and Randy Siebels

Recycling programs
for this product may
not exist in your area.

BAD MOON RISING

A Worldwide Mystery/November 2012

First published by Pegasus Books LLC.

ISBN-13: 978-0-373-26822-1

Copyright © 2011 by Ed Gorman

Printed in U.S.A.

To the websites and e-groups that educate
and inspire those of us with the incurable cancer,
multiple myeloma.

"A hippie is someone who looks like Tarzan, walks like Jane and smells like Cheetah."
—Ronald Reagan

"Good morning! What we have in mind is breakfast in bed for 400,000."
—Wavy Gravy at Woodstock

"We are not about to send American boys nine or ten thousand miles away from home to do what Asian boys ought to be doing for themselves."
—President Lyndon Johnson

"There's a bad moon on the rise."
—Creedence Clearwater Revival

"Tin soldiers and Nixon coming…Four dead in Ohio."
—Neil Young's "Ohio" about Kent State

JESUS CHRIST WAS NOT A HIPPIE

In the summer of 1968, the good Reverend Cartwright, last seen setting himself on fire while attempting to burn a huge pile of Beatles records, purchased six billboards around town to make sure that believers and nonbelievers alike got the message that Jesus Christ had not been like hippies during his time on earth.

Three weeks earlier an eighty-six-year-old woman had written the local newspaper to defend our resident hippies from the slings and arrows of those who hated them. She said that given how the adults had screwed up the world there just might be a chance that these young people had some ideas worth listening to. Further—and you can imagine the bulging crazed eyes of the good reverend as he read this—further, as a lifelong Christian she was pretty sure that if Jesus Christ walked the earth today he would walk it as a hippie. Not, I assumed, in Birkenstocks, but you get the idea.

So now Reverend Cartwright was on the attack. Seeing the billboard I realized that it was in fact time for his radio show. Lately I'd been using it as my humor break for the day. For lunch I'd pull into the A&W for a cheeseburger and a Pepsi and sit in my car and listen to

*his show. It always opened with a tape of his choir—one
of the worst I'd ever heard—singing some song about
the righteous Lord and how he was going to disembowel
you if you didn't do exactly what he told you to do. Then
the reverend would come on. He always opened—as he
did today—with the same words: "I spoke with God last
night and here's what he told me to tell you."*

*I'd been hearing his show all my life. My father used
to listen to it on the days he wasn't working. He'd laugh
so hard he couldn't catch his breath at times. I'd be
laughing along with him as my mother would peek in
and say we shouldn't be wasting our time on a moron
like that. But then she didn't understand our weakness
for The Three Stooges, either.*

*Today, as I jammed extra pickles under the top of
my bun the reverend said: "If Jesus Christ was a hippie, as some local infidels are saying—then that would
mean that Jesus Christ would sanction what goes on
at the commune right on the very edge of our town. A
town I have personally sanctified to the Lord. If you will
support me with your prayers and your pledges I will
see that that commune is closed down and the infidels
driven from our midst."*

*His pitches for money were the dullest part of the
show and since he was obviously headed in that direction I twisted the selection knob looking for some news.
I counted three stations playing "Harper Valley P.T.A.,"
a song critics likened to a three-minute hillbilly version
of the novel* Peyton Place.

I found a newscast and quickly wished I hadn't. The

war the war the war. It had brought down LBJ and had returned to prominence Tricky Dick Nixon.

When I finished eating, I sat back and smoked a cigarette. Right then I felt pretty down, but nothing would compare to how down I would feel less than ten hours later.

PART ONE

ONE

"I AM JUST way too groovy for this scene, man."

If you were a teenager saying "groovy" you could get away with it. If you were a thirty-four-year-old Buick dealer all gussied up in purple silk bell bottoms, a red silk shirt and a gold headband, all you were was one more drunk at a costume party where everybody was dressed up as hippies. Or their idea of hippies, anyway.

"That's you all right, Carleton," I said. "Just way too groovy."

Wendy Bennett gave me a sharp elbow, not happy with the tone of my voice as the six-two Carleton Todd swayed over us, spilling his drink all over his hand. These were her people, not mine. Wendy Bennett came from one of the most prominent families in Black River Falls. Occasionally she wanted to see some of the friends she'd known from her country club days. Some of them I liked and surprised myself by wanting to see again. They were ruining my old theory that all wealthy people were bad. It just isn't that simple, dammit.

"Don't worry about ole Carleton," Carleton said, his eyes fixing on Wendy's small elegant breasts. We both wore tie-dye T-shirts and jeans, our only concession to costume. "I'm used to his insults. I was just in the TV room watchin' the Chicago cops beat up the hippies.

Your boyfriend here called me a couple of names in there." He opened his mouth to smile. Drool trickled over his lower lip. "But I called him names right back. If I was a cop I'd club every hippie I saw."

"Carleton, you're a jackass," Wendy said, steering me away before I could say something even nastier.

Don Trumbull's mansion sat on a hill in what had been forest, a bold invention of native stone, floor-to-ceiling windows, and three different verandas. At night the windows could be seen for half a mile. Now, like people in a play of silhouettes, human shapes filled the glass lengths, many of them wobbly with liquor.

"I'm proud of you."

We were on one of the flagstone verandas, the one that loomed over the downslope to the river. Moonlight glittered on the water and stars served as a backdrop to the pines that staggered up the steep incline of the far hills.

Men with Rotarian eyes drifted by, slightly drunk and silly in Nehru jackets. I wondered if they hated costume parties as much as I did. Tonight's fashions were dictated by all the slick magazine spreads about hippies, the problem being that the spreads featured Madison Avenue hippies. Collars so wide and droopy they looked like elephant tongues; medallions that would have suited Roman soldiers; and of course fringed leather vests for both men and women.

The hippies I knew really did live back to nature; dungarees for boys and girls alike and nary a Neiman-Marcus item among them. The musical *Hair* had become a hit signifying the sexual revolution that people talked about with disdain or envy. There were whispers that the revolution had inspired more than a few people here. Why leave sexual freedom to just the kids? The more we became a bedroom community for Cedar Rapids, the more modern parts of the populace became.

We sat on the edge of the flat stone railing and let the breeze have its way with us.

"I always wanted to be in a Disney movie. Did I ever tell you that?"

"No, not that I can remember." The Disney remark signified that she'd reached her limit for the evening. She generally got wistful then and I felt terribly protective of her.

"Not to be Cinderella or anything like that. But to be one of the animals that are always in the forest. They always seem so happy."

I was too much of a gentleman to remind her of Bambi's fate.

"No regrets. No fears. Just grateful to be alive and enjoying nature all day long." Then she giggled. "God, I just remembered what I said to Carleton."

"I'm sure he'll remind you."

"He's really not so bad."

"If you say so."

"C'mon, Sam, it's not that bad, is it? You like some of these people."

"Yeah, I actually do. But most of them aren't here tonight."

"It's summer. A lot of them are on vacation."

She yawned and tilted her perfect head back. When we went to high school together her name was Wendy

McKay. Because of the Mc in her name and the Mc in mine we sat together in homeroom where, eventually, she was forced to talk to me. She's admitted now that proximity alone had forced her to converse. We were social unequals. She was from a prominent family whose gene pool had endowed her with shining blonde hair, green eyes and a body that was frequently imagined when teenage boys decided to seek the shadows for some small-town self-abuse.

She married into the Bennett family believing that her husband loved her. Unfortunately, as she learned all too soon, he'd still been in love with a girl he'd known all his life. After he was killed fighting in Vietnam, it all became moot.

As we had both passed thirty, we didn't try to delude ourselves. She'd gone through a period of sleeping around and drinking too much. She'd ended up spending a lot of money on a shrink in Iowa City. I'd come close to being married three times. We wanted to be married; we even wanted to have a baby or two. But unlike me, Wendy wanted to go slow. So I kept my apartment at Mrs. Goldman's even though I spent most of my nights at her house, shocking numerous guardians of local morality.

"Am I drunk? I can't tell."

"A little."

"Damn. Don't let me do anything stupid."

"Why don't we make a pass through the house once more and then head home?"

I stood up and took her hand. She came up into my arms and we spent several minutes making out like eleventh-graders. I opened one eye and saw over her shoulder the couple who had appeared unheard on the veranda. I smiled at them as I eased out of the embrace. They didn't smile back.

"It doesn't do you any good to watch the tapes of those cops beating up the hippies," Wendy said as we passed through the open French doors and went back inside where three young musicians with long hair were playing guitars and singing Beatles songs. Somebody somewhere was smoking pot. As a lawyer and a private investigator for Judge Whitney, I had the duty to find and arrest this person. I decided to put it off for a few months. "You just get depressed, Sam." She didn't sound as drunk as either of us thought she was.

"She can't keep her hands off me," I smiled as we passed the new arrivals. Wendy swatted me on the arm.

As we joined the throng inside, she said, "Remember, don't watch those tapes again. You get too worked up." Then she hiccupped.

The networks were running tapes of this afternoon over and over again, the ones of Chicago cops clubbing protestors. The protestors weren't exactly innocent. They screamed "Pigs!" constantly; some threw things and a few challenged the cops by running right up to them and jostling them. There were no heroes. But since the cops were sworn to uphold the law it was their burden to control not only the crowd but themselves. Dozens of kids could be seen with blood streaming down their faces. Some lay unmoving on the pavement like the wounded or dead in a war. In the TV room of this mansion several men stood watching the tapes, their hands gripping their drinks the way they would grip grenades. When I'd been in there about a third of the men were against what the cops were doing. The rest wanted the cops to inflict maximum injury. One man said, "Just kill the bastards and get it over with."

For the next twenty minutes we circulated among the faux hippies. Most of the people we said goodbye to were cordial and even amusing, aware of the irony of middle-aged hippiedom. One man, a school board member I'd disagreed with on a few fiery occasions, even patted me on the shoulder and told me he agreed with me about the Chicago cops. "No excuse for what they're doing. I would've said something in the TV room but I didn't want to get my head taken off." I probably wouldn't be as fiery next time.

For a roomful of people dressed as hippies, most of the conversations sounded pretty square. The men discussed business; the women discussed domestic life and gossiped a bit. While Wendy excused herself to go to the bathroom—still hiccupping—I let a drunken city councilman tell me that he was going to start sending me all his personal legal business because "The big shots want too much money. You have any idea what they charge an hour?" Then, weaving around while he stood in place, he raised his drink, aimed vaguely for his face and said, the glass a few inches from his lips, "You don't have the greatest reputation but for the kind of stuff I'll be sendin' you it doesn't matter."

Wendy reappeared and rescued me. Her hiccups were gone. She looked around the largest of the rooms and said, "I wish there were more people from our class here."

"They aren't successful enough to be here. I only got in because you brought me."

"You're like my gigolo." She laughed but a certain dull glaze remained in her eyes. Where liquor was concerned she was the ultimate cheap date. A couple of drinks and she was at least semi-plastered.

"Let's try the front steps this time," I said.

"Huh?"

I grabbed a cup of coffee for Wendy. We sat on the front steps of the enormous house, enjoying the Midwestern night. Trumbull, the man who owned it, was the director of four steel plants. His wife was from here so they bought this place, turned it into a masterpiece and lived in it during the warm months. Florida was their home when the cold weather came. The drive that curved around the place was crowded with cars. We'd be long gone by the time most of them left so we wouldn't have any trouble getting out. But many people well into their cups were going to have some frustrating moments if they all tried to leave at once.

Wendy caught a firefly. She cupped it in her hand and said, "Hello, little fellow."

"How do you know it's a fellow?"

"Take a look."

In the shadow of her hand a golden-green light flickered on and off. "Yep, it's a fella all right."

She laughed and let him go. After her head was on my shoulder she said, "I know these aren't your kind of people, Sam. But remember, your kind of people aren't *my* kind of people, either."

"I thought you liked Kenny."

"I don't mean Kenny. I mean your clients. Some of them are really criminals. I mean bad people."

The front door opened behind us. Our haven had been invaded again. We could have kept on talking but we were self-conscious now. I got up and helped Wendy to her feet.

"Hope we didn't chase you off," a woman's voice said from the shadows.

"No. We were leaving anyway."

When we were out of earshot, Wendy said, "Very nice, Sam. You're really learning social skills."

"You mean instead of saying, 'Look, you sorry bastard, you ruined our whole evening.'?"

"Exactly." She clung to my arm woozily and kissed my cheek. "See, isn't it fun being polite to people you hate?"

"You're crazy."

"Look who's talking."

As we drew closer to my car, I slid my arm around her shoulders. We had our battles, but most of the time there was peace, something I'd never had much of in my past affairs. I'd started to believe what I'd heard a TV pop psychologist say, that some people liked agitation in their relationships. I'd just always assumed that was the way it had to be. But Wendy showed me how wrong I'd been.

Somebody called my name twice. I turned around and shouted back.

"There's a phone call for you, Sam," the female voice said.

I yelled my thanks.

"A client," Wendy said.

"Most likely."

"Poor old Sam."

"Poor old Wendy."

"I don't mind. Right now relaxing at home sounds better than this anyway."

A woman named Barbara Thomas was waiting for us on the porch. She was another one who'd skimped on costuming herself. A very flattering pair of black bell bottoms and a white flowing blouse. She'd been in our high school class and had married a lawyer. She was one of those girls who'd ignited many a speculative sexual conversation among boys. She'd always seemed aware of just how stupid we all were.

"Hi, Wendy."

"Hi, Barb. How're your twins?"

"Exhausting but beautiful, thanks. There's a phone in the den, Sam."

They stayed on the porch while I worked my way through the costumed revelers. The den was as big as Wendy's living room and outfitted with enough electronic gear to make me suspect that the owner of the house might be in touch with Mars. He was some kind of short-wave enthusiast. Four different kinds of radios and three different gray steel boxes that made tiny chirping sounds contrasted with the traditional leather furnishings.

I picked up the phone. "Sam McCain."

"Sam. It's Richard Donovan."

"You really needed to call me here, Richard?"

"Look, we've got a real problem out here."

Donovan was the leader of the commune. He brought rules and regs to the otherwise disorganized life out there. When one of his people got in trouble in town—usually being harassed for no reason by one of police chief Cliffie Sykes's hotshots—Donovan was the one who called me.

"And it can't wait until morning?"

"No." Then: "Look, I'm not stoned or anything and I'm telling you, you need to get out here right away."

The tension in his voice told me far more than his words.

"You're not telling me anything, Richard."

"Not on the phone. We've had run-ins with the feds before. They may be tapping our phone."

Paranoia was as rampant as VD among the hippies these days. The troubling thing was that some of it was justified.

"I'll be out as soon as I can."

"Thanks, Sam. Sorry I had to bother you."

If the trouble was as serious as it sounded, and if I got involved in it, I would certainly hear from my boss. Though my law practice was finally starting to make reasonable money, my job as private investigator for the judge was still half my income. And Judge Whitney, along with many other people in town (including a couple who kept writing letters about me in the local newspaper), didn't like the idea that I was representing the people at the commune. They wanted the commune and its hirsute folks to move to a different county. Or maybe, if God was smiling that day, out of the state. Judge Whitney didn't believe any of the ridiculous rumors about them—they were satanic and were summoning up the old bastard himself to turn the town into flame and horror being my favorite—but they did violate her notion of propriety, which had come to her down generations of rich snobs who felt that all "little people" were suspicious, period.

I had the feeling that whatever Richard had waiting for me wasn't going to change the minds of either the judge or the two people who kept writing letters about me.

On the porch Wendy and Barb were smiling. I remembered Wendy telling me that Barb was one friend who hadn't deserted her after her husband died in Vietnam, when she took up the bottle and inhabited a lot of beds that did her no good at all. Both women had warm girly laughs and the sound was sweet on the air, overwhelming the sitar music from inside. Oh, yes, somebody was playing sitar music now. I realize that not liking sitar music marks one as a boor and a likely warmonger and maybe even satanic, but I can't help it. Sitar music should only be played for deaf people.

"Oh, oh," Wendy said.

Barb smiled at me. "Wendy said you'd look a certain way if you were going to go see a client and dump her at home."

"'Dump,'" I said, "is a pretty harsh word."

"How about push me out of the car at a high rate of speed?"

They reverted to their girly laughter, leaning together in that immortal conspiratorial way women have of letting men know that they are hopelessly stupid. I could imagine them at twelve, merrily deflating the ego of every boy who passed by.

"I promise not to go over ninety," I said, lamely continuing the joke.

"Well, I'll have to let you two finish this," Barb said, as if I hadn't spoken. "My husband's in watching TV and before he loses all his clients I'd better get in there. He made the mistake of telling Walton from the brokerage that if he was ten years younger, he'd probably be a hippie himself. Walton didn't think that was funny. Then they started arguing about the cops beating up all those kids. You know how Walton is. He thought Ike was a Communist. And he was serious."

Wendy slumped against me as soon as Barbara got inside. "Whew. It just caught up with me. One minute I was sober and the next minute I was—"

"—drunk?"

"Again. That's the weird thing. I kind of sobered up but now—"

"Let's get going. I know this curve where I'm going to push you out. It'll be fun."

"Yeah, well, the first thing you'll have to do is help me to the car. I'm really dizzy. All that drinking I used to do. I must be out of practice."

She wasn't kidding. I had to half carry her to the car.

TWO

A MONTH EARLIER a gang of bikers had invaded the compound and smashed up the farmhouses and made several of the male hippies strip. For a few people in Black River Falls—anywhere you live there are a few people—it was a tough call. Who was more despicable? Drunken bikers or hippies?

The commune had a history. Shortly after the war two brothers decided to get a GI loan for a large farm they would work together. They built two modest clapboard houses about forty yards apart and proceeded to marry and raise their respective families. They were decorated warriors and popular young men who'd been raised on a farm in a smaller town twenty miles west of Black River Falls. Everything went according to Norman Rockwell for the next nine years but then, true to many of the stories in the Bible, one brother began to covet the other brother's wife. Well, in fact, he did quite a bit more than covet and when the cuckold caught his brother and wife making love in the shallow wooded area behind the outbuildings, he became so distraught he ran back to his home, killed their only child (a girl of seven) and then killed himself.

The survivors left the farm, the bank foreclosed and despite the efforts of a couple of other farmers to buy it

and lease it out to starter farmers who couldn't afford
the purchase price, the land refused to cooperate. There
was a scientific explanation for this, as a state agrono-
mist repeated to anybody who listened, but locals preferred the notion that the land was "cursed" because of
what had happened on it.

The hippies came two years ago. Twenty or so of
them stayed in the main house, the white one; another
fifteen or so stayed in the smaller yellow house. Some
of them worked in town; some of them raised a good
share of the food they ate; and a handful, from my
observation, were so stoned most of the time that they
couldn't do much more than tell you what they'd seen
in their last acid vision.

Peace and love, brother. Age of Aquarius. Brother-
hood of man. Every once in awhile stoned on nothing
stronger than beer, I'd get caught up in one of the many
rock songs that espoused those precepts. But then I'd remember Martin Luther King and Bobby Kennedy, both
of whom had died earlier this year, and I'd remind myself of how naïve it all was. There was no peace and love
in the slaughter of Vietnam or in the streets of bloody
Detroit or Los Angeles.

In some respects I felt sorry for the hippies. I understood in a theoretical way what they were rebelling
against. Our country was war-happy and our culture
was pure Madison Avenue. What I didn't understand
were the ways they'd gone about expressing their dis-
trust of society. I'd look at the babies they'd borne and
wonder what kind of lives the little ones would have.
The same for the sanctimony of their language. With-

out seeming to realize it they were just as doctrinaire as the straight people they put down.

Then there were the drugs, which was how I'd gotten involved with the hippies. Since no other lawyer in town wanted to deal with them, and since the public defender's office had only two attorneys who worked eighteen-hour days as it was, I decided to help as many as I could. Clifford Sykes, our police chief, was jailing everybody who even looked as if he could spell marijuana (something I doubt Cliffie himself could do).

Marijuana I had no problem with. But I couldn't see the social or spiritual benefits of dropping acid. I'd heard too many stories from the emergency room about young people who never quite recovered from their trips. In March two high schoolers had contrived a suicide plan and had, while acid fractured their minds, locked hands and jumped off Indian Point. They were skewered on the jagged rocks below.

These days chickens, cats and an arthritic old dog had declared the weedy yard in front of the larger two-story white farmhouse their private domain. A rusted plow and an old-fashioned refrigerator with the cooling coils on top sat on the edge of the yard, remnants from the farm before it had been deserted by the owners long ago. The enormous garden was in back. They were dutiful about keeping it plentiful. No matter how much pot, acid, cheap wine filled the night they were up early to work their land. They'd planted corn, carrots, beets, spinach, lettuce and cabbage. Using a battered wood-fired stove, they also baked bread. That was another surprise. One of them gave me a slice with strawberry jam on it one day and damned if it didn't taste good.

I snapped off the ignition key and slid out of the new Ford convertible I'd bought after my old Ford ragtop got too expensive to keep fixing up. Or maybe I got it to signal my father, who'd died three years ago, that in my thirties I was finally becoming the man he'd wanted me to be.

Now as I stood under the glowing span of moon and stars, a song by Crosby, Stills, Nash & Young began streaming from the main house. A breeze fresh as a first kiss made me close my eyes for a moment and ride along with it to long-ago summers when my red Ford ragtop and the lovely Pamela Forrest had been my primary concerns.

When I turned to look at the house I saw Richard Donovan coming down the steps. His father was a colonel in the Army and Richard had inherited his military bearing. Richard even had a uniform of sorts—blue work shirt, brown or black corduroy trousers. They were always clean. The girls usually wound up doing the laundry for the boys—the new "ism" feminism had yet to make its mark on this commune—but Richard did his own. I'd seen him hanging his own shirt and a pair of trousers on the clothesline one day. He told me he didn't trust anybody else to keep his stuff the way he wanted it.

In the windows on either side of the front door, faces watched us silently. Whatever had happened out here, everybody knew about it and they were waiting to see how I was going to react when Richard finally told me what was going on.

He was handsome in a severe, gaunt way. There was something of the Old West in the face, pioneer stock I suppose, and now anxiety filled the blue eyes and bulged the hinges of his jaw.

"We have an audience, Richard."

"They're scared."

"Of what?"

"Of what I'm going to show you. They're like little children. If I wasn't here this place wouldn't exist."

Nobody would ever accuse Donovan of being modest. Or having a sense of humor. He was the absolute lord and master of this place as well as the final arbiter. The first few times he paid me to represent him— he didn't seem to have a job so I wondered where the cash came from—he lectured me on how the country was going to be once the government "abdicated" and people like him took over. I didn't like him much and I suspected the feeling was mutual.

His gaze roamed to the tumbledown once-red barn downslope from us. In my high school summers I'd detasseled corn, the hottest and hardest work I'd ever done, eight a.m. to seven p.m. In temperatures frequently rising to one hundred. By noon you'd eaten your weight in bugs. At the end of the day, waiting for the bus to take us day laborers back to town, I'd always throw myself on any amount of hay I could find in the cooling barn and go instantly to sleep. This barn, however, looked as though it might collapse on me while I slept.

He nodded in the direction of the lopsided structure and started walking. The ground here was hard and lightly sand-covered. The voices from the watchers grew louder as the music stopped. Some of them were on the porch now. They knew a lot more about what was going on than I did.

The barn was within several yards of the woods and the woods were less than a city block deep. Behind them ran a two-lane gravel county road. High school kids wanting to raise some hell had gotten on the commune property by coming up this way. They waited till late at night when the hippies were asleep and a good share of them stoned as well. They smashed a few windows and spray-painted some swastikas on the houses. Donovan was the only one who confronted them. He jumped on the leader of the kids and broke his nose and arm. Cliffie Sykes had been persuaded to charge only the kids. But the parents of the boy who Donovan had hurt had now sued him in civil court. I'd handle the trial when it came up.

There was no door on the barn. Shadows deeper than night awaited us inside. Donovan stalked right in. I lost him for a few seconds. That's how dark it was. Then suddenly there was light in the form of a dusty kerosene lantern put to life with a stick match he blew out a second too late. He'd burned his fingers and cursed about it.

It was a conventional barn layout with stalls for animals and space for storing equipment. The haymow above us was accessible only by a ladder. The stalls were packed with boxes. This was a storage area. Since a good share of these kids—like some of the other hippies across the land—came from prosperous families,

I wondered if they'd brought along some of the goodies from the old days.

The smells ranged from old manure to wood soaked by decades of rain. A few brittle bridles hung from posts; horses had probably been commonplace. As had a leaky ceiling; ruts from tractor tires still gouged the dirt floor in places. Tin signs from the thirties had been nailed to the walls, pop and cigarettes and chewing tobacco and gasoline. This was a time trap; if you stayed here long enough you could probably hear ghost music from that era.

"Nobody here knows anything about this. I want to make that clear."

"I take it somebody's dead."

"Yes." His face was taut with sudden anger. "They'll probably be out here with pitchforks and torches when they find out."

"You're getting ahead of yourself. Calm down."

"Yeah, calm down. All the bullshit we have to put up with just trying to live our lives. You live in a shit-hole of a town."

He was already getting tiresome. "Show me where the body is." He looked as if he was going to start preaching at me again. "Now."

Donovan walked to a stall that held fewer boxes than the others. "Here." Then: "Superdog kept barking so loud I had to see what was wrong. He brought me over here. At first I thought he was crazy. I mean, who cared about these boxes? But then I took them down. I should trust our dog more."

The boxes were quickly stacked outside the stall. A

filthy brown blanket had been thrown over a human body. A small slender foot with a very white sock protruded from the bottom of the blanket.

I started forward but he stopped me. "I know who she is. She came out here a lot. The whole commune is in real trouble now. I wouldn't be surprised if one of the cops didn't kill her and plant her here to make us look bad."

"That's crazy."

"Well, right now crazy sounds pretty sane to me."

"Who is she?"

"The minute I say her name you'll know how much trouble we're in."

"Humor me. Who the hell is she?"

"It's Vanessa Mainwaring."

"What the hell was Paul Mainwaring's daughter doing out here?"

The laugh was cruel. "A little high-class for pigs like us?"

"Don't give me any more of your overthrow bullshit right now, Donovan, or I might tell you to go to hell and I'll walk away. Don't forget, there isn't another lawyer in town who'll work with you."

I pushed him out of the way and grabbed a rusty rake. Awkward as it was, I managed to ease it under the blanket until I could gently lift it and set it aside. Because I knew her father, I'd seen her a number of times. Now, as she lay on her side, her profile was statue-perfect.

I hunched down. The wounds I could see were concentrated around her heart. There were six of them.

Somebody had been very angry with her and had let a knife convey the rage. In books, beautiful dead women always retain some remnant of their beauty. Not so in real life. Heartbreaker that she'd been, now the skin was gray and the tongue lolling out of the right side of her mouth looked lurid and sickly. Vivid blue eyes stared into eternity; even the dark hair was dusty and flecked with straw.

I looked up at Donovan. "How many people were in this stall to look at her?"

"Just about everybody. Why?"

"You're not stupid, Donovan. You've never heard of a crime scene? The cops'll look for all kinds of evidence. People tramping around in here'll just make it tougher for them."

"Cliffie's a moron. He won't look for any evidence at all."

I pushed against my thighs to stand up and face him. "Cliffie's daddy hired a so-called police commander to do all the serious work. The old man got tired of everybody bitching about his son. The police commander's name is Mike Potter and he was a detective in Kansas City for six years before he had a heart attack and decided to look for a nice little nook to spend the rest of his career. He's good. And the first person he'll want to talk to is you. And one of the first questions he's going to ask is how many people tramped around in the barn after you found her body."

"You mean I was supposed to stop them?"

He wanted to argue. His question had been an accusation. "Who put the blanket on her?"

"I did."

"What time did your dog start barking?"

"Maybe an hour and a half ago. And listen—I'm not some zombie, man. I'm sorry she's dead. If that's what you're worried about. But I also kinda run this place, you know. I've got to worry about everybody else, too."

"Who did she know out here?"

"Everybody. She tried hard to fit in but most of the people didn't like her."

"Why not?"

He took the time to slide a package of Pall Malls out of his shirt pocket. He was stalling.

"Why didn't they like her?"

"Because of Neil, Neil Cameron."

I'd had to represent Cameron a few times. He had a temper. When townspeople hassled him he hassled back. "What about Neil?"

"She kind of jacked him around."

"He went out with her?"

This time he got a full one-act play out of lighting his cigarette with a stick match. "Some people said he was obsessed with her. When she broke up with him he just kind of—"

"Kind of what?"

He shrugged lean shoulders. "You know what it's like when you're dumped. You get crazy for awhile."

"Was he still crazy these days?"

He was good at evasion. "I don't know. You'd have to ask him."

"Where do I find Cameron now?"

"I'm not sure. His sister would know."

"Sarah Powers?"

"Oh, that's right. You handled a couple of cases for her, too."

Neil and Sarah had different last names because their parents were killed before the kids were even ten and different sets of aunts and uncles raised them.

"Sarah doesn't like you very much."

"Then we're even. I don't like Sarah very much, either."

She was one of the troublemakers out here. She'd been ticketed for parking the van in a No Parking Zone and had then screamed at the cop when he was making out her summons. Then she got in another screaming match with a check-out woman at one of the supermarkets, accusing the woman of overcharging her because she was a hippie. Two weeks ago she was in a record store telling all the customers that they should steal anything they wanted, that the filthy capitalists were ripping off the country and getting away with it. The owner of the store called me and said if I didn't remove her in five minutes—she had threatened to punch him if he touched her—he'd call the police. Fortunately, I'd been in my office and got there in time. The owner was a twenty-eight-year-old who fancied himself to be very counterculture. I wondered how he was feeling about things now that he'd heard Sarah's everything-for-free rap.

"Let me see the soles of your sandals."

"Why?"

"I want to check footprints. I need to eliminate yours and mine."

He wore tire-tread sandals, easy to identify. I checked my own, then began dragging the lantern low over the immediate area. There were numerous fresh imprints. "You said 'just about everybody' was in here looking. How many people would that be?"

"Well, not everybody's here tonight. I suppose fifteen or twenty."

"You should've sold tickets."

"Hey man, you'd be interested too, a dead girl in your barn. It's natural to be curious."

"Let's go find Sarah."

He put his fingers against my chest as if he didn't want me to move. He shook his head as if I'd said something he didn't agree with. "Look, I might as well tell you."

I shoved him away. "Tell me what?"

"About Neil." He sighed. "And Vanessa. They—she came out here the other night and he started screaming at her. We were all afraid he'd hurt her or something. Finally Sarah broke it up. She didn't want to see Neil hurt Vanessa. She and Van were good friends."

"So you think Neil killed her?"

"I didn't say that."

"Yes, you did." I wondered why it had come so easily from him. He'd been protective of everybody in the commune and then he set Neil Cameron up with a motive and a possible foreshadowing of the murder.

"I feel like hell telling you about Neil."

I almost smiled. He was a terrible actor. "Yeah, I can tell."

His eyes narrowed in the dusty gold of lantern light.

He was probably trying to figure out if there was any sarcasm in my response.

I walked to the rear of the barn. The doors hung askew and there was a wide opening between them. An average-sized person could walk between them with no problem. I went out and stood in the back. At this point the woods were close. A person who'd climbed up the hill from the road below wouldn't have had any trouble sneaking into the barn without being seen.

I went back inside.

"Let's go find Sarah."

I was glad to leave the barn, to enjoy the healing effects of the stars and the breezes of the night. I could see that at least six or seven people stood on the porch watching us. The music was off. Pot odor got stronger the closer we got to them. One of them was Sarah Powers, hands on hips, glaring at me. Before we even got there she snapped, "What's he doing here, Richard?"

"He's going to help us."

"You're such a child, Richard. He's here to get us in trouble and for no other reason." She had a tomboy rage that made her as formidable as a boy, forty pounds overweight, an unattractive round face and dark eyes that seemed to have only two expressions, contempt and rage. She tried to hide her own misery by taking it out on others.

"I want him off our land," she said as we walked up to her.

"Afraid you can't do that, Sarah. I'm an investigator for Judge Whitney. That gives me the right to arrest people and if you try obstructing justice, I'll arrest you."

"Thanks for inviting him here, Richard. You did exactly the wrong thing as usual."

"I need to talk to your brother."

"He isn't here."

"Where is he?"

"I wouldn't know."

"He could be in serious trouble, Sarah. Believe it or not, I'm trying to help him."

"I'm the only one who can help him. If he did what I tell him he'd never get in trouble."

"The police'll be looking for him as soon as they hear about this."

"A lot of people had reason to kill her. Don't try to shit me, McCain."

"A lot of people may have had reason to kill her but not a lot of people had the opportunity to kill her in your barn. That's the first thing the police'll jump on."

"C'mon, Sarah, help him."

"All you care about is this stupid commune, Richard. You don't care about Neil."

"He's my friend, Sarah. You're forgetting that."

"If he's your friend, what's McCain doing here?"

As she spoke, and for the third time, I saw her eyes glance at the small rusted Airstream west of the house. If he hadn't run away, that might be the place he'd choose to gather himself and plan what he was going to do next.

"Donovan, I want you to come with me. I want to check out the trailer."

"No!" There was pain rather than anger in her voice. She was protecting her brother.

"C'mon, Donovan."

ED GORMAN   39

She grabbed my arm. "You can't do this, McCain. He didn't kill her."

"Then he needs to tell the police that." I removed her hand from my arm. I nodded to Donovan and we started walking to the trailer. The group on the porch was still watching us. By now sweat was streaming down my chest and back. Despite our words I felt sorry for Sarah. She was right. Cliffie and the local paper would convict Cameron without a trial. The people who hated the commune would use the murder as a pretext for getting rid of it entirely.

The trailer had been left here by the farmer and his wife who'd tried leasing it the second time. They couldn't afford to fix up either of the houses to live in so they'd bought this old tin trailer. They'd left it behind with their dreams.

As we walked I said, "When we get done here, I want you to go to your house and call the police. Tell the woman on duty there what happened and tell her we need the chief to come out here with an ambulance. I'm going to guard the barn so nobody else gets in there."

I could hear her coming behind me. The ground was covered with rocks and pieces of wood, probably blown here in one of the many tornados the area had endured over the years. She was running. I shifted to the left, in case she'd already launched herself at me. But all she wanted, breathless, was to talk.

"He's in there, McCain. In the trailer, I mean."

"All right."

"But he's got a gun and I don't want him to do anything crazy. The mood he's in—he might try to kill himself."

I put my hand on her shoulder. "Look, Sarah, I'm not trying to be a hard-ass here. I just want Neil to talk to the police. We both know they're going to say he did it. If I was a cop I'd be inclined to say that, too. They had an argument. Neil couldn't deal with losing her. She was found in the barn. But the only alternative right now is that he runs away and if he does that he's in real trouble. He might be someplace where a trigger-happy cop spots him and kills him. Fugitive on the run. Happens all the time, Sarah."

Grief replaced anger. I took my hand away. I saw the youngster in her. Hers hadn't been a happy life, not looking the way she did. School kids could hurt you worse than bullets, with wounds that never healed.

"You don't give a damn about him."

"I'd like to see him clear himself if he can."

"You already think he's guilty and he isn't." Tears gleamed in her eyes.

"Good. That's what I want to hear him tell me. Now let's you and I go talk to him."

She glanced back at the people on the porch as if for reassurance. A shadowy male shouted, "Don't trust him, Sarah."

"He's wrong, Sarah. Right now Neil needs me more than ever. I'm the only legal friend he's got."

Donovan spoke quietly. "He's right, Sarah. You need to listen to him."

Grief became anger. "You want him to be guilty, Richard."

I had no idea what she was hinting at. "Let's find him, Sarah. Right away before things get any worse."

"How could they get any worse?"

"By not calling the police as soon as possible. If there's a long lag between the time I saw the body and calling them, it'll look very bad for everybody. Now c'mon."

"You better be telling me the truth about helping Neil."

"I am."

I turned toward the trailer. After half a minute she joined me and we set off. My shirt and trousers had sweated to me like a second skin. The alcohol kick from the party was long gone. The ground here was rough and rocky. I almost stumbled twice.

We were now ten yards away.

"I'll go ahead and talk to him. He's *my* brother."

"All right."

"You stay back here until I tell you to come in."

She was in a hurry now. I saw a silhouette of him, backlit by the sudden lantern light inside, watching her rush to him. Then the door squeaked open and she disappeared into the dim doorway.

I smoked. I smoked three cigarettes in the next twenty minutes. I could hear their voices but not their words. Sometimes there was the sharp noise of anger, sometimes there were sobs. There were even lengthy silences. I thought of all the things they were probably saying to each other. From what I knew of him, Neil probably wasn't about to turn himself in. But she would be pleading. I'd raised the prospect of him being killed by some overeager cop. I had the feeling that these were the words that had scared her into helping me.

A stray brown mutt came up and looked me over with big sweet eyes. Apparently she didn't like what she saw. She trundled away. I looked back at the houses. They were all in the front yard now, waiting to see what would happen. "In a White Room" was being played, but at a much lower volume than the earlier records. The heat and plain exhaustion were making standing difficult. I'd had a long day and now I was facing an even longer night.

The trailer swayed. Heavy footsteps. The door swung open. Sarah appeared. She half shouted: "Neil says you can come to the door and talk to him but you can't go inside."

"He's giving the orders now?"

"He's scared. You can't understand that?"

"He'll have to come out eventually."

"That's your problem. Right now you just get to stand in the doorway, all right?"

I had my .45. I'd talk to him in the doorway and then I'd go inside and get him. Apparently desperation had confused her. She assumed that I'd really put up with this and not make my move.

"All right, Sarah."

She stepped away from the trailer. She had her hands on her hips as I walked toward her. When I got closer she said, "Don't hassle him. He doesn't need to be hassled."

"Right."

"And keep your sarcasm to yourself. He's my brother." I wondered how many times tonight she was going to remind me of that.

I approached the door and she stepped aside.

"Remember what you agreed to."

"I remember."

Smells coming from the open trailer door almost gagged me. Several decades of filth combined to become a weapon. I started to stick my head inside but she got me before I was able to finish the move.

At the time I had no idea what she hit me with. Nor did I have time to think about it. My skull felt as if it had been cleaved in half. A headache that seemed to instantly shut down my entire body left me unable to defend myself when she yanked me backward and struck me with even more force a second time. I have no idea what happened next.

THREE

In high school Alan Nevins was inevitably called "Four Eyes" because of his thick glasses. We were friends because we read science fiction. I doubled up on Gold Medal novels of course, but since all the books and magazines we wanted could be found at the same drugstore—specialists in cherry Cokes—we always ran into each other. He was a relentless smart ass. He was also now my doctor. He'd taken care, good care, of my father in his last two years. He was Wendy's doctor as well. I was sitting on a bed in an emergency room cubicle while Alan sewed six stitches into the back of my head.

"He's too cute to die, Doctor. Is he going to make it?" Wendy said.

"Yes, he is pretty cute now that you mention it. But it's going to be touch and go," the good doctor said as he finished his work.

"Very funny, you two."

I hadn't planned on coming back to the hospital in which my father died for a long time. Years, hopefully. But here I was, as much confused as hurt. I had a ghost memory of being put in the flower power van out at the commune and taken here. The memory extended to clutching a phone in my hand and telling Mike Potter about the Mainwaring girl and where he could find her.

"Do you think an injury like this could change his personality, Doctor?"

"I'm afraid not. He'd have to be hit on the head a lot harder than he was tonight."

"I think I could arrange that."

I couldn't help it. I laughed, and when I laughed my skull cracked right down the middle again. I pressed my hands to my temples, as if I could crush the pain.

"Oh, I'm sorry, Sam," Wendy said, taking my hand. "You should've seen your face just then. No more jokes."

Then there were three of them. Mike Potter, in his police tans, had joined them. He was a short, wide, fierce-looking man who needed to shave three times a day. The mild, reasonable voice emitting from that baleful face always surprised people and put them at their ease, sometimes to their peril.

"How you doing, Sam?"

"I guess that Doc thinks I'll live."

"I know a lot of people who won't want to hear that."

"Another comedian."

He smiled. Of all Cliffie's gendarmes, Potter was the most streetable one. His years as a Kansas City homicide detective had given him a professional manner not usually seen on the streets of Black River Falls. He looked at Wendy and Alan. "I'd like five minutes alone with Sam here if you wouldn't mind."

"No problem," Alan said.

"If you're going to beat him, could we stay and watch?"

"I won't beat him right away, Wendy. But when

you hear him start screaming, feel free to come back and watch."

"This is like comedy night on *Ed Sullivan*," I said.

Wendy very carefully placed a tiny kiss on my forehead then disappeared with Alan. Potter went over to a coffeepot I hadn't noticed and poured himself a cup. He waggled an empty cup at me. I started to shake my head but it hurt too much so I just said "No."

He pulled up a chair next to my bed and sat down. His military tan shirt was sweated through in many places. "I think those hippies set a record for contaminating a crime scene in that stall where the girl was."

"You noticed that, huh?"

"They really that stupid?"

"Not stupid. Just—they were curious is all."

He set his coffee cup on the floor then yanked a package of Viceroys from his shirt pocket. I did the same with my own brand. His Zippo got both of us smoking.

"In case you're interested, the Powers girl had a thick steel rod stuffed into the back of her jeans. That's what she hit you with. She's a tough little cookie. Sort of mannish."

"I take it her brother escaped."

"That's what hitting you was all about. Give him time to get away."

"And nobody at the commune went after him?"

"They're not what you call upstanding citizens."

Most times I would have defended them. Right now I wasn't feeling gracious.

"You know this Neil Cameron?"

"Yeah. I defended him a few times in court."

"The boys at the station tell me he's a real bastard."

"He can be."

"Enough of a bastard to kill Vanessa Mainwaring?"

"I can't say."

"Can't or won't? He's your client."

"Can't. I haven't been asked to defend him in this case, anyway. And besides, I don't think you've got enough to arrest him. All you can do is bring him in for questioning."

"The chief thinks we've got our man."

"The chief always thinks that."

"He wants to see you, by the way. Tomorrow morning at your convenience. Which means as early as possible." He picked up his coffee. It was cooler now and he drank it down. He got up and carried the cup over to the sink. He came back and said, "You and Paul Mainwaring are friends, I'm told."

"Not really friends, friendly I guess you'd say. We agree on a lot of things politically and so we wind up at meetings sitting together and talking."

"Gee, the chief says you two are Communists."

"Does he still carry that photo of Joe McCarthy in his billfold?"

Potter smiled. "I stay away from politics. I hate them all. Anyway, you go see the chief first thing tomorrow, all right?"

"Sure."

"Sarah Powers is in our jail now and she'll stay there until somebody bails her out. I doubt the hippies can raise the money but maybe they'll surprise us." He went to the door and said, "Glad you weren't hurt, Sam. But those kids were bound to get in trouble. I suppose a lot of people have told you that."

"Just a couple thousand." To his back, I said, "Thanks, Mike."

He opened the door and stood aside as Wendy and Alan came back in. She watched him out and then closed the door. "He's so nice."

"He's so nice as long as he thinks you haven't done anything wrong. Then he's not so nice at all."

They came over to my bed.

With his acne gone and his style of glasses more fashionable, Alan had grown well into his medical whites. He had a red Corvette and a number of girlfriends. The only thing he lacked was hair. Two years from a bald pate for sure. He put his hand on my shoulder. "You're going to have your headache for at least twenty-four hours, maybe longer. I've given you some pills that will help. I'd say right now let's have Wendy take you home and make you comfortable."

"You did such a great job on Sam, Alan."

"I inflicted all the pain I could on him, Wendy. I did the best I could."

Wendy was of course delighted. She giggled.

"He's all yours, Wendy. Good luck. Sam, I gave her instructions on what to watch for and how to take care of you. She's got my card. I wrote my home number on the back of it. If anything changes, call me. Now I've got some really sick patients to see."

Just as the door closed, Wendy said, "I've never been in charge of anybody before. This'll be fun."

"A VISION," I SAID.

"I thought you might like that."

"Scrambled eggs, French toast, bacon, orange juice."

"Sit down and start eating before it gets cold."

"Thank you very much."

"How's your head?"

"Tolerable."

"How about the stitches?"

"Sting a little."

"I'll run some warm water on a washrag and hold it against your wound while you eat." She kissed me on the cheek. "So eat."

I ate. A window in her breakfast nook allowed me to glance outside at a backyard filled with the green green grass and the blue and red and yellow of various birds that were almost, but not quite, as beautiful as those in Disney animation. Wendy held the washrag against the back of my head for nearly fifteen minutes. She did this while sitting in a chair and drinking coffee and smoking Winstons. "Lady Madonna" played low on the radio.

"Do you remember me helping you to bed?"

"Vaguely. I was exhausted. And maybe I just didn't want to think about everything that had happened so I blacked out."

"Survival tactic."

"That sounds like something your shrink would say."

"He talks like that."

"You sure he's not trying to get you into the sack?"

"That was the last one. That's why I got this new one. And this new one looks very tame. He wears Hush Puppies. I'm pretty sure if you wear Hush Puppies you're faithful to your wife."

I hate laughing with my mouth full.

Then she said: "It's in the paper. They make you sound like a hero. How you suspected there was something wrong about that trailer and how you went to arrest Cameron and how his sister knocked you out."

There was a reason for the favorable treatment. A distant cousin of mine was now the editor. If Cliffie could rely on kin, why shouldn't I? But Wendy was only repeating what my mother, Mrs. Goldman my friend and landlady, and Kenny had told me earlier this morning when they'd called to see how I was doing.

"Well, we'll see how it plays with the people. Cliffie will say I got beaten up by a girl."

"Did I ever tell you that Cliffie groped me once?"

I had to speak around a large bite of French toast. "Cliffie did?"

"One of those Christmas dances for charity. Several years ago. Cliffie'd had plenty of eggnog. He grabbed me and dragged me to the dance floor. I swear that guy has six hands. Just when I was brushing his hand off my bottom he started dry-humping me. He even started kissing my neck. I was worn out after one dance. And I knew he remembered because every time he'd see me afterward he'd look away. This went on for a long time. Now he's back to ogling me. So don't worry about what Cliffie thinks. He's an idiot."

The kitchen phone was a bright yellow. It was affixed to the wall next to the counter space in the kitchen and its ring complemented the color. It trilled yellow. Honest.

I enjoyed watching her walk to the phone in her red

shorts and loose white blouse. A comely woman. When we were apart I could actually feel her sleep warmth. I considered that a very good sign.

"Hello." Then: "He's right here."

She held the phone out to me and when I took it she was nice enough to lean into me and kiss me on the cheek again.

"Are you all right? I was so scared reading about you. I've said a lot of prayers already. Oh—sorry. Good morning, Mr. C. I should have said that first I guess."

My secretary Jamie has come a long way. She still can't type but at least she catches about half her mistakes and retypes them over Wite-Out. The problem here being that she's a bit sloppy with the white stuff so that it tends to run down the page and smear some of the words below. But the fault is mine. I was forced to take her in trade from her father who couldn't pay the bill he owed me for representing him in court. She's cute and sexy and good-hearted as Bambi. Despite my attempts to explain why the lazy, shallow and self-absorbed love of her life Turk was bad for her, she went back to him after a long break-up Wendy and I had helped along. Turk had apparently interpreted their wedding vows to include his right to hit his wife, which he'd done on at least one occasion.

"Good morning, Jamie."

"I really like Wendy, Mr. C. You two should get hitched."

The "Mr. C" owes to the fact that the people on Perry Como's TV show call him "Mr. C." I know—my name doesn't begin with C. But as Jamie explained, "There's a C in the second and third letters."

"We're working on that, Jamie. What's going on?"

"The police station called and they said that Sarah Powers wants you for her attorney."

Days that began with surprises were not my favorite. Somehow the surprises were always bad. "All right. I'll stop there before I come in this morning."

"Oops. There's the other line, Mr. C."

I finished my eggs and a fresh cup of coffee while telling Wendy about Sarah Powers.

"Be careful she doesn't still have that steel rod. You sure you want to help her?"

"No."

"Then why do it?"

"Because there's nobody else who'll sign on. And she definitely needs help."

"You have a lot of other things to do."

"I just hate to see her in jail. She's sort of a sad case. In her mind she was just trying to help her brother."

"Why is she a sad case?"

"The ugly girl. The fat girl. The boyish girl. Easy to imagine how the other kids treated her growing up. She and Cameron lost their parents when they were still kids. She was defending the only real friend she's ever had."

"I hate to remind you, Sam, but you're still wincing from your headache because of her."

"Maybe I'm doing it just to piss off Reverend Cartwright."

She poked me on the shoulder. "Now there's a reason I can understand, Sam."

FOUR

"Hippies," Cliffie Sykes said. "I had my way we'd deport their asses."

"Sounds reasonable to me."

The police station was relatively new, thanks to a matching grant funded by the Sykes Foundation. Old man Sykes even sprang for some new Western-style uniforms. Now all the officers dressed like Cliffie, military tans and campaign hats. He had the usual state celeb political black-and-whites framed on the wall along with a melancholy painting of Jesus.

Behind him, the centerpiece of the office, ruling over all four dark green filing cabinets, the desk, the three-button phone and the family portrait was an outsized framed photo of John Wayne all dressed up as a Marine in his laughable propaganda movie *The Green Berets*. I preferred looking at the family portrait. Cliffie's youngest daughter suffered from spina bifida. When you saw how gentle and loving Cliffie was with her, you couldn't quite hate him for the bumbling, bigoted fool he was. You could dislike him but not hate him, though I was in a pissy enough mood to give him grief. While I didn't have a steady headache I did have attacks of sharp pain that forced me to close my eyes and grit my teeth. "You like 'em, don't you? You and friend Kenny, you guys

were beatniks and now you're hippies." I was here to
see Sarah Powers but as Potter had told me last night, I
needed to see Cliffie first—the mandatory endurance
contest I always had to survive.

"Kenny was a so-called beatnik when we were
juniors in high school. I never was. And neither of us
are hippies. I mean, if you want to get your facts straight
for once."

"Yeah, well, he still writes dirty books."

"He writes other things, too." I was counting on
Cliffie's disinterest in everything literary. He didn't
ask me to tell him exactly what those "other things"
were. In addition to paperbacks such as *Satan's Love
Slaves* and *Lesbo Lodge*, Kenny had now started writing for men's adventure magazines. You know the ones I
mean. The guys never have shirts on and they're usually
under attack by Nazis or killer dogs. Well, for that matter the women don't have shirts on, either, and they're
frequently attacked by Nazis and killer dogs. But the
women don't have scars all over their mostly naked bodies and they aren't holding machine guns. "Nazi Terror
Orgies" was one of Kenny's latest. This was not to be
confused with "Nazi Lust Prisons." Kenny had a very
good novel in him somewhere; he still wrote seriously
good short stories for himself. I had faith in him; his
wife Sue had faith in him. All we had to do was convince Kenny to have some faith in himself.

"I had my way, we'd put all those pornographers in
jail. And that goes for the Smothers Brothers."

Why correct him? The Smothers Brothers' politics
offended him—offended more than half the nation—

so their TV show had become a focal point for all the people who thought that the Vietnam War was just a dandy idea.

But this was just sparring and we both knew it. The main bout would start with something else, something he just couldn't wait to spring on me.

"I stopped by the Blue Moon Tap and told 'em what happened to you."

"Had a good laugh, I'll bet."

"Couple of 'em were laughin' so hard I thought they'd puke."

"Well, thanks for telling me, Chief."

"One guy had beer runnin' out of his nose he was laughin' so hard."

"I'll bet that was you, wasn't it?"

He glared at me. I'd found him out. Glare became glower and he said: "So a girl knocks out Sam McCain and the prisoner escapes."

He was saying that real men don't get knocked out by women. "I guess you could tell it that way if you wanted to."

"Oh, I want to, McCain. I really want to. All the crap I've had to take from you over the years. You and that g.d. judge of yours. All the b.s. about how you solved my cases before I did. And you with your law degree and the private investigator's license your judge made sure you got so you could snoop around. You damn right that's the way I want to tell it. And that's the way just about everybody in this town's gonna tell it. Hotshot Sam McCain tries to collar a killer and gets knocked out by a girl so the killer gets away. That'll look real nice in the state paper."

Before he'd mentioned the state paper his words hadn't had their desired effect on me. I knew that the people in Black River Falls who didn't like me, and the number seemed to grow every year, would have their fun. I'd be embarrassed and sometimes I'd get mad and sometimes maybe I wouldn't want to leave my office. But Wendy would help me through it and if I got lucky enough to look good on a few more cases, the story about Sarah smacking me with a steel rod would fade in time. Never disappear, nothing ever does; but fade. But now I imagined what the story would look like under a bold headline in the state paper. They had a photo of me a few years back following a trial I'd won. The trouble was I'd just gotten done tripping on a step in front of the county courthouse so my expression was that of shock and dismay when the photographer snapped his pic. Hapless was what I looked like; hapless.

Cliffie was taking such pleasure in my embarrassment I couldn't help myself. If he could be petty so could I. I realize that the thought of Sam McCain being petty—unthinkable. But—

I nodded to his framed melodramatic photo of big John Wayne in his Green Beret get-up. "You do know John Wayne was a draft dodger, don't you?"

"What the hell're you talkin' about? Some lefty crap you thought up?"

"Not crap, Chief. Facts. It's in several books. He decided against serving because he was afraid he wouldn't have a career when he came back—even though most other stars enlisted. So they trumped up some health problem and the draft board went along with it because they're part of Hollywood, too. So now you have big brave Duke calling war protestors draft dodgers. Kind of a hypocrite, wouldn't you say?"

"Just because it's in a book doesn't mean it's true."

"No, but people who knew him at the time agreed that it was true."

"Lefty crap."

"Which is the reason you always give for sending your officers out to harass the people who live on that farm. Because they're all 'lefties.' I thought we had an agreement you were going to lay off."

"I'll lay off when they start wearing shoes and having some respect for this country and cutting their hair so you can tell the boys from the girls."

"Yeah, that's a real problem, all right. I get confused all the time."

"You think it's funny. But it sure as hell isn't. A lot of people want to run 'em out on a rail. Reverend Cartwright says he can't sleep at night thinkin' of all the fornicating that's going on out there."

I couldn't help myself. I smiled.

"What's so funny?"

"Just thinking of Reverend Cartwright and all that fornicating. Must be driving him crazy." I stood up. "I take it we're through here."

"I don't believe a word you said about John Wayne."

"Up to you, Chief. But it's true. He was a draft dodger."

He waved me off. Then grinned. "You be careful

walkin' around town, McCain. There might be a teen-age girl lookin' for a fight. And you know how mean they can be."

There wasn't much point getting mad. I was going to be hearing a lot more of it in the days to come.

FIVE

HARRY RENWICK, a guy my father had bowled with, led me past several prisoners. Two of them were former clients of mine. One waved and one smirked. The smirker still owed me money.

I'd used the two interrogation rooms many times. Harry opened the first door. I went in and sat down at a bare table with four chairs around it. I didn't need to light up. There was about a carton of smoke still on the air from the last few interrogations.

"How's your mom doing, Sam?"

"Still trying to believe Dad's really gone."

He smiled. "Those World War Two guys, they always told us we had it easy in Korea."

It seemed more and more that the American Dream had turned into a war for every generation.

"Yeah, my dad could really get going sometimes."

"He was a great guy, Sam. One of my best friends. And he sure was proud of you." I'd wondered what was wrong with me after my father passed on. I never cried. I knew in the abstract I wanted to but somehow the tears never came. Now sometimes at odd moments I just wanted to let go. This was one of those moments, sitting here in an interrogation room where people were dragged to confess the terrible things they'd done—I just wanted to put my head down and wail for the father I loved so much. And who I'd never see again.

A knock on the half-opened door. Sarah Powers stood there in the two-piece maroon jail uniform. She looked heavy, pasty and angry. The only fashion accessory she'd been allowed were the handcuffs. A police matron nudged her inside.

Harry pulled a chair back for her. She sat down. Only when she was seated for a time did I see how fatigue had drawn crevices in her face.

The matron, a scrawny Irish woman, said, "I'll be right outside."

"You tell your mom I said hi."

"I sure will, Harry. Nice to see you." Then, whispering, I said: "This room bugged?"

Harry shook his head. "Not this one. The one down the hall."

After he was gone, Sarah said, "It was either you or a public defender. I didn't have any choice."

"You trying to flatter me?"

"Oh, go to hell, McCain."

"We're off to a good start."

Silence.

"How're you doing in here?"

Silence.

"You asked for me, remember? You keep this up, I'm going to walk out the door. You understand me?"

She raised her cuffed hands to her face and sighed. After she put her hands on the table again, she said, "There's a woman in my cell who left her baby in her car for three hours while she was in some dive seeing her boyfriend while her husband was home sleeping off a hangover. Thank God a cop came along and found the little baby. The woman was telling me that she shouldn't be in here. That she's actually a good mother. This is the second time she's done this. Then there are the two prostitutes. And the woman who embezzled money from the trucking company where she worked. Not exactly the kind of people I'm used to."

I took out my cigarettes and placed them on the table. I lighted two. I sat close enough to her to put one between her lips. "It's hard to smoke with those cuffs on."

She didn't thank me but her tone changed. It was as if she was suddenly too tired to argue. "Neil wasn't like this before he went to Nam. He was just a nice normal kid. But when he came back— They actually had to put him in a mental hospital for three months."

"Tell me how he changed."

I took the cigarette from her lips and moved it to a different angle. She inhaled deeply. "He'd always been kind of quiet. Got average grades. Never got in trouble. Wasn't a big reader but he loved going to movies. He went to junior college—this was in Des Plaines where we grew up—and he really liked it. He started getting interested in books for the first time. But then he got his draft notice. They didn't think junior college was good enough for a deferment so they shipped him off. He didn't write much and when he did, he didn't really tell me anything. He'd talk about the food and the local customs but nothing about how he felt or anything. In his letters he didn't sound the same anymore. I always figured he'd tell me everything when he got back."

"Did he?"

"No. But a kid he served with told me about something that happened to Neil over there. They were approaching this sort of hamlet—there were five of them—and there was firing from two of the huts. While four of them worked on the two huts, Neil swung around and checked out the other three. He heard noise in one of them and opened fire. When he looked in to see who'd been in there he found two little girls. They'd been huddled in the corner. His bullets had torn them apart. He said Neil was never the same after that. When they'd go into Saigon all Neil wanted to do was get drunk and start fights. My brother Neil, fighting? He might have been in a few shoving matches on the playground but that was the extent of it. And now he was always picking on bigger and tougher guys who were sure to hurt him pretty bad. You don't have to be a psych major to know that he wanted somebody to punish him, do you?"

Her shoulders slumped and she exhaled long and hard. Not even hatred can exhaust you the way love can. "He was that way when he got back home, too. He had nightmares that woke up the whole house. My biggest fear was that he was going to kill himself. And in a way he tried to. All the fights and two drunk driving arrests and confrontations with half the people he ran into. I thought when he met this girl Jenny he might come out of it at least a little ways. He cleaned himself up physically and cut way back on the alcohol. He was always decent to me. I think I was the only person he'd ever really trusted." I shifted the cigarette between her lips so she could comfortably take another drag.

"It went well for three or four months, with Jenny I mean. One night he even told me he was thinking about going back to junior college because she was going to enroll there for a year before going on to a state school. He even said they might get married. But then she started breaking up with him all the time. I couldn't figure out why. Then one day I ran into her at a restaurant in a mall and she told me everything. She was only nineteen and she just wasn't ready for the kind of commitment my brother wanted. She said they'd agree not to talk about marriage but then the subject always came up and he'd get angry and she'd get scared."

"Was he ever violent with her?"

"No. She said that wasn't what scared her. She had the same fear I did, that he'd take his own life. She was afraid to break it off completely because of that but she couldn't deal with Neil anymore, either. Then she said something that I've never forgotten. Neil told her that the only time he didn't have nightmares was when things were going well with them. Then I realized how dependent he was on her. She made him feel good again—much better than the Army counselor in Nam he saw who just kind of ran him through his office once a month. I sympathized with her. And Jenny was a sweet girl. She told me that she'd decided that the easiest way out was to go to the University of Illinois for freshman year and leave in a week.

"She went and that's when the trouble really started. He lost his job, he gave his best friend a black eye and he swung on a cop who was trying to arrest him for drunk and disorderly. He managed to escape and that's when he disappeared for awhile. I was the only one he contacted. He knew if he came back he'd have to go to county jail or maybe even prison and he said he couldn't do it. But I convinced him he couldn't keep running like that. I got him a good lawyer. He served six months in county in Illinois. After he got out he drifted to Iowa City and that's where he met Richard. Richard invited him to live at the commune. Neil got a job in town working at a discount store. I'd just graduated college and had free time so I came here to live in the commune and try to straighten him out. He'd already been seeing Vanessa Mainwaring. I met her a few times and liked her. I think Neil had learned about not pushing too hard. They seemed very happy together. Then they had this argument. I never knew what it was about. I guess they started shouting at each other on Mainwaring's front lawn and he came out and told Neil to go home. Apparently he'd liked Neil up to that point but you see somebody shouting at your daughter, you're going to defend her."

"How long after that was she murdered?"

"Two nights."

I asked the question she didn't want to hear. "Do you know where he is right now?"

"No."

"If you knew, would you tell me?"

"No. And please don't give me any speeches. I don't want to be the one responsible for the police finding him. I know he didn't kill her."

"Does that mean that you have proof?"

"It means I know my brother."

I said it again. "If he's on the run and they catch him and he won't give up, he might get himself killed."

"You think I haven't thought of that?"

Harry Renwick knocked softly twice then opened the door. "Time's up, Sam." He walked over to where Sarah sat. "We'll get you out of those cuffs."

The smile was unexpected. "He means once he gets me back to my cell."

"Best I can do, Miss."

"Tell Sykes that I'm officially her lawyer, will you, Harry?"

"Sure. He figured you would be. Oh—he's pretty mad about you saying John Wayne was a draft dodger."

"It's true."

"Yeah, I read that in the newspaper a long time ago. I decided I'd better not bring that up to the chief. You know how he feels about John Wayne."

Sarah Powers seemed lost. She glanced around the room. A man told me once that the only time he'd been in jail the whole experience was like a nightmare. This was county, not even hard time, and he only did thirty days for a drunk driving charge. He said all those prison movies were fake. They never dealt with how oppressive it was to be forced to live with men who had spent their lives cheating, stealing, beating people. And enjoying it. That was what scared him the most. The way they bragged about it. Then he said there were the smells. He said there were even men who laughed about the smells. I wondered if Sarah was having a similar experience here. Yes, the jail was new and yes, she obviously considered herself worldly and tough. But she was really just a middle-class woman terrified for her brother. And now, I suspected, terrified for herself.

Sarah Powers said, "I'm sorry about knocking you out."

I just nodded. I let her have one more drag.

Harry Renwick had good radar. "I'll keep an eye on her for you, Sam."

I think she would have hugged him if she hadn't had the cuffs on. Now she had at least one friend here.

SIX

Sunlight blasted me into temporary blindness as I walked from the station to my car. Only when I was halfway there did I see the three people standing two cars from mine: Paul Mainwaring, his daughter Nicole and Tommy Delaney. Delaney was a local high school football hero and former boyfriend of Vanessa.

He had a little kid's face—all red hair and freckles and pug nose—set atop an NFL body. In his black Hawkeye T-shirt you could see why he was so feared on the field. He started toward me but Paul Mainwaring himself put a halting hand on his shoulder.

The car I referred to happened to be a new white four-door Jaguar.

I usually found myself defending Paul Mainwaring. For all his work with the military and inventing things vital to war—he was a prominent military engineer—he had a true interest in helping the poor and had given thousands of dollars to the local soup kitchen and church relief funds. The irony wasn't lost on me; I'd always wondered if it was lost on him.

The face he showed now, as he broke from the group and walked toward me, stunned me. The white button-down shirt, the chinos and the white tennis shoes spoke of the preppy he would always be. The silver hair was disheveled for once. The sunken, bruised eye sockets and the unshaven cheeks and jaws revealed a man lost in not only despair but confusion. Even his walk was uncertain.

Tommy Delaney broke in front of him, aiming himself directly at me.

"Tommy, get back there where you belong."

Tommy gave me the practiced look that probably made even the toughest kids in high school run when he turned it on them. I just watched him as he fell into sulking. Behind him Mainwaring's daughter Nicole started sobbing and put her hands to her face.

I was embarrassed to be in Mainwaring's presence. I'd had the young man thought to be the killer of his daughter and I'd lost him because I wasn't clever enough to outthink a twenty-two-year-old girl. I wanted to say something but I wasn't sure what that would be.

"Paul, I owe you an apology."

He brushed it away. "It wasn't your fault, Sam. Don't listen to all this. I was in the Army for four years. Things just go wrong sometimes. The girl admitted that she struck you on the back of the head with a steel rod and knocked you out. I don't know anybody who could stand up to that."

I wanted him to repeat what he'd just said. I couldn't quite believe it after just one hearing. I was already known as the man who'd been outsmarted by a young girl. It was absurd—as Paul said, anybody can be felled by a steel rod smashing into your skull—but when you have enemies they work with what they're given. And yet the one who should despise me the most for my stupidity was telling me that getting smacked in the head was the reason I wasn't able to arrest Neil Cameron. Not because I was incompetent.

"I let myself down, Paul."

He extended his hand and we shook. I wasn't sure why we shook.

Then he offered his second surprise. "I want to hire you, Sam."

I allowed myself the luxury of a smile. "Right. I can see that. I come highly recommended."

"As I said, things happen. You've done some good work as a private investigator. And you know all the kids out at that commune. If anybody knows where Cameron might have gone, they do."

"I'm not sure they trust me."

"They trust you more than they do Cliffie. I've asked him a number of times to stop harassing them but all I get are those speeches Reverend Cartwright gives. All the marijuana and sex. By now Cliffie must've run every one of them in at least once. They certainly won't cooperate with him."

"I'm representing Sarah Powers, Paul. You should know that up front."

He blinked only once. "I didn't know that."

"That's why I think you should look for somebody else, Paul."

"She of course says Neil didn't kill Van."

"That's what she says."

"And you believe her?"

"In a case like this I only represent people I think are innocent. I want to find Neil and have him turn himself in."

"What if he's guilty?"

"Then he's guilty. If he's not, then I want to find the person who really killed Van."

"Then there's no conflict. I still want to hire you."

"I wish you'd think it over. I can recommend a few people in Cedar Rapids or even Des Moines. It might be better to let them handle it instead of me."

For the first time I saw resentment—anger—in the long, angular face. "You have a stake in this now, too, Sam. You need to prove to people you're not the fool they say you are."

He'd meant for his words to hurt. He'd succeeded. "I'll send a check to your office. I appreciate this, Sam." He spoke through a kind of pain I'd never had to deal with. "Maybe I'll call you tomorrow."

He turned and walked back to his people and his Jag. His daughter came to him and slid her arm around his waist. She tilted her head against his chest as he guided her to their car.

Tommy walked a few feet toward me and said, "Hope no girls beat you up on the way home, McCain."

"Get back here," Mainwaring shouted without turning around.

Of course Tommy gave me the famous soul-freezing evil eye before he did what Mainwaring said. I wondered what he'd look like if I was fortunate enough to back over him six or seven times.

A FEW YEARS AGO, before my secretary Jamie married her wastrel boyfriend Turk and bore him a baby girl as sweet as Jamie herself, I always checked out the clothes she wore. She had one of those stunning bodies you see on the covers of paperbacks, usually under the title *Teenage Tease* or some such thing. The wholesome pretty face only made her more appealing. These days I checked her for signs of bruises and cuts. In the first year of their marriage Turk had given her a black eye. I returned the favor by giving Turk a black eye. I'm not tough but I'm tougher than Turk. I also drew up divorce papers that Jamie refused to sign. She loved him and he would change, she said.

These days I had her solemn word that if he ever got physically violent with her again she was to tell me immediately. I made her promise on her mother's life. A good Catholic girl, she took such oaths seriously.

Turk still had his surfing band, probably the only one in landlocked Iowa. And despite the fact that surfing bands were now seen as wimpy and irrelevant. And he was still going to be on *American Bandstand*, though *American Bandstand* was fading fast. And he was still going to have several gold records. And he was still, when the time was right, planning to become a movie star. And he still didn't want to get a job because working conflicted with his songwriting and practicing. He couldn't even babysit his little daughter. That was left to Jamie's mother. These artistes, they need their time to create.

Today Jamie wore a sleeveless yellow blouse and a richer yellow miniskirt. She was easy to scan for bruises. I didn't see any. She also wore a pair of brown-rimmed eyeglasses. She'd started having headaches so I'd paid for her visit to an optometrist and then for the glasses. I still wondered about the headaches. I didn't trust Turk. Somehow in the course of our years together she'd become my little sister and I'd be goddamned if anybody was going to hurt her or baby Laurie.

Jamie's typing skills had improved marginally and she'd learned how to answer the phone professionally and take down information without mistakes. She gave me my messages and a cup of coffee. That was another thing she handled capably. Our new automatic coffee brewer. Me being me, I still couldn't make a decent cup of coffee, even with that new machine I'd bought at Sears on sale. But Jamie had triumphed.

As I went through my phone messages, I glanced up once and saw the way Jamie straightened all four of the framed photographs of one-year-old Laurie she had on her desk. Not that they needed straightening. But touching them brought her peace you could see in her face. At these times I always wanted to kill Turk. He should honor her for her sweetness and loyalty. Maybe I could get him convicted as a Russki spy and get him deported. After I beat the shit out of him.

SEVEN

IN GRADE SCHOOL we always swapped comic books. Kenny Thibodeau tended to like Superman and The Flash. I went more for Batman and Captain Marvel. In junior high we swapped paperbacks. Mickey Spillane and Richard S. Prather were early favorites though soon enough I discovered Peter Rabe and F. Scott Fitzgerald, among others. Kenny discovered John Steinbeck and Henry Miller. In high school I'd picked up on all the Gold Medal crime writers such as Charles Williams while Kenny had discovered Jack Kerouac and the Beats. At none of these junctures was it possible to predict what Kenny would bring to the table—literally the table in the booth at Andy's Donuts where I'd gone straight from jail—on this already hot and humid morning.

Baby pictures.

His daughter Melissa was two and a half years old. She wasn't just the center of Kenny's life; she was *all* of Kenny's life. Yes, he still wrote his soft-core sex novels and he still wrote his men's magazine "Die Nazi Die!" articles…but those he did almost unconsciously these days. Automatic pilot. His conscious attention was devoted to Melissa. All this was reflected in his attire. Not a vestige of the former Beat. Short, thinning brown hair.

Pressed yellow short-sleeved cotton shirt and pressed brown trousers. I mention pressed by way of introducing his wife Sue. As Kenny always joked, by marrying him Sue had inherited both a husband and a son. Kenny needed help and Sue, loving and amused, was there to provide it.

"This one's of Melissa and the cocker spaniel we got her last week."

Even though we had gone past picture number twenty I had to admit this one of Melissa in her frilly sundress leaning down to kiss the puppy on the head was pretty damned cute.

"And here's one—"

I held up my hand. "I don't mean to be rude, Kenny, but I've got a lot to do today."

For only a moment he looked hurt, then he grinned. "Yeah, Sue says I drive people nuts with my pictures. Just be glad I haven't invited you out to see the slide show I made of all the pictures we have of her."

"You have a slide show? Seriously?"

"With music." He sipped his coffee. "Don't worry, you'll get to see it one of these days."

"That sounds like a threat."

The timbre of his laugh hadn't changed since we were in fourth grade. "It is. But I'm sure you want to talk about the girl who got killed last night."

Kenny was the unofficial historian of Black River Falls for our generation. Every once in awhile he'd talk about this huge novel he was going to write someday, a kind of *Peyton Place* about our own small city. Despite his reputation for writing smutty books, people liked

Kenny and confided in him. He knew secrets nobody else did. He'd been helping me with cases since the day I'd hung out my shingle.

"Do you know anything about her?"

"I know one thing."

"What's that?"

"She's been seen with Bobby Randall on occasion."

"You're kidding."

"Wild child. Lot of trouble for her old man."

"Bobby Randall deals drugs."

"That's my point. A lot of trouble for her old man."

"I'm representing Sarah Powers. She's the sister of Neil Cameron, the guy everybody's looking for. They're both part of the commune. You ever hear of Bobby Randall hanging out at the commune?"

"Oh, sure. They had some real head-trippers out there for awhile. Right after Donovan and the rest of them came here. Randall was the only source they had so they dealt with him. But finally the head-trippers moved on. Randall still goes out there. I think he had something going with one of the girls at the commune for awhile but she broke it off with him for some reason. He's a heartbreaker."

I took a moment to finish my glazed donut. This coffee shop was one of the few small businesses that hadn't shriveled up since the new mall opened. The larger downtown stores had all moved to the mall, taking with them a good deal of traffic and thus business. The mayor had been frothy with reassurances that the mall would increase business for everybody because shoppers who'd trekked to Iowa City or Cedar Rapids would now be happy to shop here again. The younger people thought it was pretty cool of course. But the older ones—and the ones like Wendy and me, touched by a spiritual old age on occasion—saw it as one of those generational betrayals that are a part of growing up. The young betray the old until they are old enough to be betrayed by the next generation. I'm sure the good Reverend Cartwright has an explanation for such things.

"You hear much about the Mainwaring family?"

"Just that it's sort of gone to hell since Mrs. Mainwaring died and Mainwaring married again. I know the Mainwaring kids really don't like her."

"She's pretty exotic."

"Yeah, and from what I hear not a real warm person. But she went to Smith and worked on the Bobby Kennedy campaign and drives a Jag. I know you like Mainwaring but he's really a snob. And I still don't understand how a guy who makes stuff for war can pretend to be such a liberal."

"You think he's pretending?"

"Don't you?"

"I'm not sure. Maybe he's just sort of blind to himself."

"I don't trust him. I was in a peace march in Iowa City last month and I saw him on the sidewalk talking to a guy I was pretty sure was a fed."

"How can you tell?"

"Didn't you read that article in *Esquire* about how the feds who check out peace marches dress? Short hair, T-shirts and jeans. Hoover likes his boys to wear uniforms. And they all drive black Fords with black-walls because Hoover gets a deal on them."

One thing about Kenny—he'd never met a conspiracy theory he didn't like. "Maybe he's changed things because of that article."

"I doubt it. I admit I'm being paranoid but I still don't trust Mainwaring. I mean his *business* is with the federal government." He checked his wristwatch. "Melissa's at her grandmother's right now. I had to leave her there while I went to have Alan check on my blood pressure. He sure is a smart ass."

"You should've heard him last night when he was sewing me up."

"He was always like that." He slid out of the booth. "We were too mature to act like that as I remember."

"Right. All the times we both called his glasses Mt. Palomars. Real mature."

As if I hadn't spoken, he said: "I'll have some new pictures of Melissa next time I see you."

I wanted to ask if that was a threat or a promise but I was too mature to do it.

MY EARLY BOYHOOD was spent in the section just past the city limits called the Hills. This was where the poor white people lived. Even sociologists would have had a hard time defining the Hills because there were degrees of poverty even here. Depending on where you lived in the Hills, your home was either lower class livable or little more than a shack. If you lived in one of the shacks, which far outnumbered the tiny one-and two-bedroom homes, you saw a lot of the local gendarmes.

A fair number of men dealt in stolen property; a fair number of men couldn't seem to stay out of bloody fights; and a fair number of men let the bottle keep them from steady jobs. In the midst of all this the more reliable people like my parents and many others tried to carry on respectable lives. Kenny lived in one of the shacks but was saved and redeemed by his early interest in books. My mother and father were both readers, Dad with his pulps and paperbacks and Mom with her magazines (one of them, *The American*, carried Nero Wolfe stories frequently, introducing me to mystery fiction around age eight or so) and encouraged my brother and sister to be readers as well.

The worst part of my early life was when my older brother Robert died of polio. He had been, no other word, my idol, all the things I could only hope to be. When I got old enough I drove his 1936 Plymouth. My sister Ruth was sure that Robert visited her at night in ghost form. And I remember hearing my father half whispering to my Uncle Al that he was worried about my mother, that maybe she would never get over it and be herself again. We still went back to the Hills to lay fresh flowers on my brother's grave in the cemetery where Hills people buried their dead. In the worst of my depression after losing the woman I was sure would be my wife, I found myself waking one birdsong morning next to his gravestone. I had drunkenly confided in my brother—for that matter I'm not quite sure I ever really got over his death either—hoping he'd bring me solace.

Tommy Delaney lived in one of the small houses, this one isolated by the fact that it sat on a corner. Where there should have been neighbors on the west side of his place there were only three empty tracts. The city had made an effort to destroy the worst of the houses and shacks.

I heard the voices before I'd quite closed my car door. Man and woman; husband and wife. The ugly noise of marriage gone bad. There had been a time after Robert's death when my parents had gone at each other. As I later learned in my psych classes at the U of Iowa, this was not an uncommon reaction to the loss of a child. But their rages terrified my little sister and me. I'd take her to her tiny room and give her her doll and cover her with a blanket, anything to stop her sobbing. I'd sit on the bed till she went to sleep. They always promised, in whispers, that they'd never do it again. But they did of course. They were too aggrieved over the loss of their son not to.

The Delaney home was the size of a large garage but not as tall. The once-white clapboard was stained so badly it resembled wounds. The eves on one side dangled almost to the ground. The two cement steps had pulled a few inches away from the front door. In addition to the screaming, a dog inside started barking, explaining the dog shit on the sunburnt grass. But not even a dog could compete with the cutting words of the argument.

There was a rusted doorbell. I tried it. Somewhere, faintly, it chimed. Not that this deterred the screamers. Either they hadn't heard it or they didn't care that they had company.

The door opened and there Tommy Delaney stood,

massive in his Black River Warriors black T-shirt with
the familiar yellow logo. He wiped the back of his hand
across his eyes but he was too late. I could see he'd
been crying, the same way my sister had always cried
when our parents had played gladiators over the body
of their oldest son.

Then he suddenly stepped on the concrete stairs.
His weight was enough to make them wobble. I backed
down to the ground. He reached back and jerked the
door shut. That was when I noticed the tic in his left
eye. Kids respond differently to parental warfare. The
big tough football player had developed a tic. He'd probably developed other problems, too, ones less obvious.

He blushed. Blood went up his cheeks like a rising
elevator. "They're just havin' a little disagreement."
The tic got worse. Heavy fingers pawed at it as if they
could destroy it.

"How about walking over to my car? Maybe it'll be
easier to talk there." It wouldn't be—not with this battle
going on—but at least we wouldn't be right next to it.

"I don't know what you're doing here."

"I'm trying to find out who murdered your friend
Vanessa."

"You *know* who murdered her."

"I know who people *think* murdered her. That doesn't
mean they're right."

The baby face sagged in the brutal light of a ninety-
two-degree day. For all his power, he looked drained. I
doubted he'd slept much. "You stick up for the hippies.
I always told her not to go out there. I told her there'd be

trouble. Neil Cameron was crazy. You should read some of the letters he wrote her. He belonged in a bughouse."

"Tell me about the letters."

The tic had slowed some. I had to give his parents one thing—they had the strength of boxers who could go fifteen rounds easy. If anything, they were louder than ever.

"I only read a couple of them. But they were nuts."

"That doesn't tell me anything about the letters."

"Just the way he said stuff. That he'd kill himself if she didn't come back to him. And that they had this sacred bond that couldn't be broken. And that sometimes he stood on her street late at night staring up at her bedroom window and that he thought about just getting a ladder and kidnapping her."

His father shouted a particularly ugly word at his mother. Delaney glanced over his shoulder. When he turned back to me he resembled a little boy who had just heard something terrible but mystifying. Maybe his father had never used that particular word before. The tic got bad again.

"Sorry you have to listen to that."

"Yeah, why would you give a shit?"

"Maybe because I heard things like that for awhile myself when I was young."

"Yeah, well—" He swiped his hand across the tic again. But for the first time agitation left his eyes.

"You know the Mainwaring family."

"Not for much longer. I think Mainwaring's going to tell me he doesn't want me there anymore. He liked the idea of a football hero hanging around his place but I think the novelty's worn off."

He was smarter and shrewder than I'd given him credit for. "Were you in love with Vanessa?"

"What the hell kind of question is that? It's none of your damned business." Then: "For your information, I thought I was but when I saw how she treated me and every other guy around her, I just enjoyed the free ride and let her go her own way."

"What free ride?"

A smile loaded with malice. He angled himself toward the house where the spiritual murder was taking place. "The free ride of staying in a mansion where there was peace and quiet and eating better than I ever had. They even have a maid. All you have to do is say you want a Pepsi or a piece of pie and she goes and gets it for you. They even have guest rooms. It's like staying in a nice hotel. Mainwaring let me stay overnight any time I wanted to and I wanted to a lot."

I waited a moment before asking my next question. We just stared at each other. Then I said: "All I'm asking is one favor. I want you to think about who might have wanted Vanessa dead besides Neil Cameron."

"He killed her. You know it and I know it."

"I don't know it, Delaney. But I'd appreciate it if you'd think about it and give me a call." I handed him a card.

As he studied the card, the shrill got shriller in the house behind us. He shuddered. His entire upper body just shook for ten seconds or so. Then he sighed: "Maybe I'll think about it. Maybe not. Right now I've gotta get back in there before it gets any worse." He made a face. "I have nightmares he's gonna kill her sometime."

Then he was gone, trotting across the dead brown grass to the hell house.

EIGHT

"Was Jesus a hippie? I think not. Did Jesus smoke pot? Did Jesus listen to the Rolling Stones? Did Jesus burn the American flag? No, he didn't. And Jesus never said vile things about the Vietnam War, either."

Reverend Cartwright's midday radio show.

IT WASN'T REALLY a manor house but it tried to be, a three-story native stone building of twenty-five rooms, nine baths and two dining rooms, not to mention a fireplace that you could walk into. Not while logs were burning, of course. The home lay on fifteen acres of green trimmed lawn with gasp-inducing hedges and stone-edged ponds on which swans swam and pines of such sweet perfume you got dizzy. Behind the house was the bright red barn where Eve Mainwaring had the six horses she ran in her white-fenced three-acre domain. All four doors of the garage were open, revealing the fact that Mainwaring didn't think much of American car making. There was a Porsche, two Mercedes sedans and a Jaguar. All of recent vintage.

I'd called ahead. Mainwaring had told me to come around to the back veranda where he was having lunch. The day was well on its way to reaching the predicted ninety. From an open upstairs window I heard The Byrds' version of Bob Dylan's "Tambourine Man." As I looked up I saw a young female face, framed by long dark hair, watching me. The youngest of the Mainwarings, Nicole. She leaned back, out of sight.

Mainwaring sat beneath a large blue umbrella at a table of glass and chrome. He appeared to be staring out at the swimming pool. The water was blue and chemically fresh, no doubt. It was also empty.

I was still behind him when he said, "She always swam in the mornings. When it got cold she swam indoors. She rarely missed a morning."

I didn't have to ask who he was talking about. I walked across the fieldstone veranda and seated myself at his table. It was cooler under the umbrella. He wore a starched white short-sleeved button-down shirt, tan military-style walking shorts, white socks, white tennis shoes. Before him was a plate that held two halves of an English muffin and two poached eggs. One half of the muffin, covered with strawberry jam, had been nibbled on. The eggs hadn't been touched. They looked like the eyes of a comic monster. Next to his coffee cup lay his package of Chesterfields. "I don't eat breakfast. I run three miles and then have breakfast for lunch."

I wasn't sure what to say. Good for you or tell him how my day starts. You know, peeing and having a cigarette as soon as possible. But that doesn't sound quite as impressive as a three-mile run, I guess.

There were no amenities.

"I wanted you to talk to Nicole, Sam. But she and I had a disagreement this morning so she's up in her room sulking." He took a long drag on his cigarette. In the shade of the umbrella his silver hair didn't glow quite as much. "Eve will be joining us in a few minutes." He paused. His harsh blue eyes showed pain. "She was what we were arguing about, of course. Neither of the girls accepted her. They never gave her a chance."

"That's a tough transition sometimes. A stepmother."

"They never gave her a chance."

I was expected to agree with him.

"I see."

Then she was there, appearing in the French doors behind us, a sight rare even in the upper-class homes of our town. A maid, a real one, in a gray uniform and everything. White and fiftyish and from the looks of her, Irish. If she spoke with a brogue I'd suspect that we'd been transported into a sitcom.

"Will there be anything else, Mr. Mainwaring? I need to get going on the laundry."

"Marsha, this is Sam McCain. He'll be working with me for awhile. Have you had lunch, Sam?"

I lied. "I have, yes. But I'd appreciate some coffee."

"Why don't you bring us a fresh pot, Marsha?"

"Sure. Anything else, Mr. McCain?"

"No. But thanks for asking."

After Marsha had left, Mainwaring said, "You're like I was at first. Nervous about having somebody wait on me all the time. Marsha was Eve's idea. Ironically, the girls like Marsha much more than they do Eve."

I didn't correct the tense he was using. It was difficult to get it right when one daughter was alive and the other one was dead.

"Have you started work yet, Sam?"

A breeze carried the scent of the water in the pool. I was trying to say the unsayable. "I've been trying to get some background on Vanessa."

Paul Mainwaring's eyes narrowed and a bitter smile crossed his face. "Then you know she was something of a tease. Maybe even something of a whore."

Fathers aren't supposed to say that about their daughters. Other people say it and fathers say you're a g.d. liar.

"That's a little harsh."

"No, it's not, unfortunately. She was a very nice young girl even after her mother died. She was an A student, helped around the house and spent a lot of time making sure that Nicole and I were all right. I sent her to a counselor just to make sure that she wasn't hiding any deep problems. I was afraid that maybe she was really depressed but covering it up. The counselor said she was a remarkably mature fifteen-year-old and that she was dealing with Donna's death very well. All that changed when I brought Eve here and told the girls that I was getting married to her. They didn't even pretend to like her. We had the wedding here. The girls went somewhere else. Wouldn't come under any circumstances. In fact they stayed at their aunt's in Cedar Rapids for two weeks before they came back. And it was right after that that Vanessa started changing. It was very conscious on her part. She got into the whole hippie thing. Didn't wear a bra. I could smell the pot in her room. She also started bringing boys up to her room, something I'd never allowed before. I found some unused Trojans on her desk one day. She'd left them there on purpose so

I'd be sure to see them. She wanted me to see them. She wanted me to hurt me."

"What was Nicole doing all this time?"

This time the smile was fond. "Little Nicole? She did what she always did, followed her sister. She got the same clothes and listened to the same music and started spouting the same rhetoric. It was sort of sweet in an odd way. Vanessa would be going on about capitalism and how the pigs had taken over—I was of course one of the pigs. They used to be proud that I'd made my own way in the world and had become wealthy doing it. But now I was a pig. A liberal pig. But I was saying it was sweet—and it was. Vanessa had some idea of what she was talking about when she argued about the capitalist system. But Nicole—she was this innocent little girl with all these big words and big concepts and she had no idea what she was talking about."

"And where did Eve fit into all this?"

"Eve did the best she could under the circumstances, but obviously it wasn't enough."

The words had come from behind the sheer white curtains covering the French doors. Eve appeared in her jodhpurs and silk white blouse. Her brown leather riding boots gleamed. "I only listened for the last few minutes. I thought since I heard my name mentioned I might as well join you."

She was the sort of woman you saw in *The New Yorker* or *Town and Country*, ruthlessly fashionable and relentlessly beautiful in a cold, poised fashion. The one thing she couldn't control were the age lines that had begun to mar her elegant features. The closer she came the less intimidating she was. Her weapon's edge was being dulled by time. She understood this. She took the chair furthest from me to sit in, blonde hair gleaming in its chignon, a bit over-sprayed so that you'd be forgiven for mistaking it as a wig.

She reached over and took her husband's hand. "Thank you for sticking up for me, darling." To me she said: "This is why I married him. This is the worst moment of his life—even worse than losing Donna, I think—and he's still generous enough to defend me."

She talked in sudsy prose, like soap opera talk and I didn't like her at all. When Marsha appeared with our pot of coffee and two cups, Eve snapped, "Don't I usually have coffee with my husband, Marsha? You only brought two cups."

Marsha was wise. She wanted to keep her job. "I'll bring you a cup right away."

"And food. I assume you made lunch for me. I do need food, you know."

Marsha looked at me. She had no trouble reading the distaste in my eyes. It matched the distaste in hers. "I made roast beef sandwiches, a fruit salad, and a lettuce salad. I'll bring them out."

When she was gone, Mainwaring said, "She does her best, Eve."

"She's local. That's the problem. I wish you'd let me bring in somebody from Chicago."

"I know her husband. He works in my plant here. I couldn't face him every day if I fired her. Besides, I like her."

How strange it was, I thought, that Eve had managed to shift the conversation from the heartbreak of a young girl's murder to some goddamn maid problem—which wasn't a problem after all, Marsha being somebody I'd taken to right away. Apparently on an astronomical chart in the center of the universe you would find a planet named Eve.

"I'd like to get back to Vanessa."

"Of course, Sam. I'm sorry."

"So the girls and Eve didn't get along."

"Eve did everything she could."

"All right. But because of her—blameless as she was—" Her eyes pinched as I said this. Had she heard the slight irony in my voice? "Blameless as she was, Vanessa rebelled and started going around with too many guys."

"Sleeping with too many guys. You may as well say it, Sam."

"And taking drugs."

That froze both of them in their chairs.

"Where did you hear that?"

"I'm investigating, Paul. I see people. I ask questions."

"You may as well tell him, Paul. Vanessa was a dope addict."

She was a few decades behind in her drug slang but that didn't diminish the pleasure she took—and tried unsuccessfully to hide—in confirming what I'd said.

Paul's face grayed with her remark. I wondered if he was going to be sick. "If that's the way you want to put it, Eve."

But she was the dutiful and cunning wife. She took

his hand in both of hers and said—her first show of warmth—"Oh God, honey, that came out much harsher than I meant it. I'm sorry."

He was all forgiveness; color returned to his cheeks. "Oh, don't mind me. It's just a hard thing to face. You didn't mean anything by it." He eased his hand from between hers. His gaze was that of a teenager wistfully tending to his first love. "I don't know what I'd do without you, honey."

I remembered Donna, the mother of his two children. She'd been small, tending to plumpishness and very much a housewife and a member of such organizations as the PTA and the League of Women Voters. If Eve had a polar opposite, Donna had been it. Had Mainwaring spent his married life pining for the bed of a beauty? Or had he, with his money and his importance, decided that it was time he got a show woman for a wife?

"What did you and Vanessa argue about, Mrs. Mainwaring?"

"I wasn't aware that we *did* argue."

"That's being a little harsh, Sam. They didn't have arguments most of the time—they just sort of froze her out."

"I see."

"Is this how you conduct most of your investigations?"

"Now don't get your back up, Eve. He's just doing his job."

"Well," Eve said, "then he can do his job without me."

She was on her feet, all jodhpured and indignant.

"I'm sorry, Paul, but I'm not in the mood for this. Vanessa and I had our differences but that doesn't mean I didn't love her and consider her my own flesh and blood."

She had a line of shit that stretched from Iowa to Montana. But she was polished and just good enough at the acting to pass muster if you had the misfortune to be in love with her. Obviously the kids had identified her species as soon as they met her.

Katharine Hepburn had never walked out of a scene with more mannered disdain.

"I don't know why you had to make her mad, Sam. Maybe this isn't a good fit. I still can't believe my daughter's dead and now I've got my wife mad at me."

"I can quit or you can fire me. But the question I asked her was legitimate. You said yourself that she and your kids didn't get along. I wanted to get her take on things."

He leaned back in his chair and closed his eyes. "All the arguments I had with Vanessa in the last couple years. I wish I could take every one of them back." The purity of sorrow was now being tainted with remorse, making it all the worse for him. I said nothing. There was nothing to say.

Marsha appeared bearing a large glass tray. "Where's the missus?"

I wondered how Eve would like being known as "the missus." It didn't go with anyone who wore jodhpurs.

Mainwaring opened his eyes and sat up straight. "Eve had some business she had to take care of right away." The smile was strained. "This looks delicious, as usual. Thank you very much."

Marsha glanced at me for some explanation about why Eve had left so suddenly and why he'd been sitting with his eyes closed. I shook my head. She shrugged and said, "If you need anything more, just let me know."

"Thanks, Marsha."

After she was gone, Mainwaring said, "I'll handle Eve. She'll give me a raft of shit about you but she'll get over it. She's a very private person."

"I can always apologize to her if you'd like."

"No, no, I'd better handle it myself. She's very sensitive. Her parents were wealthy people who died in a plane crash when she was seven. She went to a convent school in Paris until she was nineteen and then she came over here and went to Smith. She eventually taught English Literature at Dartmouth. So she's very worldly. But she still gets defensive whenever the subject of the girls comes up. They made things very tough for her. And now you'll be investigating and bringing back a lot of bad memories for her."

I poured myself some coffee. "There's no other way to do it. Those memories will be important." I sipped the coffee. Marsha might be local but she sure knew how to make good coffee. "I have another question for you right now."

"You don't quit, do you?"

"I'd be wasting your money if I did."

"Fair enough."

"Do you know a young man named Bobby Randall?"

"That bastard. I threatened to kill him one night. I

had half a mind to do it, too. Right out on our drive he sold Vanessa some drugs. A small envelope. When I saw what was happening I ran out there. Vanessa stopped me from hitting him, otherwise I would've pounded him into the ground. All he did was smirk at me. That was when I lost control. I almost knocked Vanessa down getting to him but then she started screaming at me so I finally calmed down. That punk was still smirking."

"You didn't call Cliffie?"

"How could I? If I did, he'd arrest Vanessa, too. She'd never have forgiven me if I'd done anything like that."

He was a compromised man, beholden to both his children and the wife his children despised. Either way he moved, he was going to make somebody unhappy. There was a plea in his voice when he said, "And now I'm worried about Nicole. I don't want her to turn out the way Van did."

As MARSHA LED ME through the house and to the front door, she spoke softly. "I sure hope you can help him." She looked around. I knew what she was going to say. "His new wife won't, that's for sure." Now she put her mouth close to my ear. "I'm pretty sure she's happy that Vanessa's dead. Now all she'll have to worry about is Nicole."

I wasn't paying attention when I made my way to my car. I was sorting through some of the things I'd heard inside. When I focused on where I was going I was surprised to see Nicole sitting in my front seat on the passenger side.

I got in and closed the door.

It was always said that Vanessa was the beauty and Nicole the brain. Nice and tidy, but not true. Nicole was a nice-looking seventeen-year-old whose problem was acne. I went through a year of bad acne myself so I still had nightmares occasionally of waking up and feeling my face only to find that it was once again corrugated. She was kin to Sarah Powers, Neil Cameron's sister. Their high school years had to be hell.

Today she wore a white blouse and blue walking shorts. She held a can of Coke in one hand and a burning Winston in the other. "She's watching us."

"Who?"

"The bitch. Eve."

"How do you know?"

"See that window to the right of the east dormer?"

"Yeah."

"Watch the curtain. It'll move."

I watched. She was right.

"Why would she watch?"

"She always watches. Van and I always joked she was a spy." She made a face suddenly, leaned forward in the seat.

"Are you all right, Nicole?"

Her fingers touched her sweaty forehead. "It's just everything that's happening, I guess." She took a deep breath. "What were we talking about?"

"You don't get along with Eve?"

"You met my real mother."

"Yes, many times. She was a very good woman."

"Well, compare her to Eve and see why we hated her so much."

I didn't say anything.

A cruel smile. "I was listening to you on the veranda. The bitch even cut into you, too. She should've died instead of Van."

"Your father's in love with her."

"I know. That's what's so sickening. We met two or three of his lady friends, you know, after Mom died. They were all nice women. We would have been happy if he'd married one of them, but then Eve came along."

"How did they meet?"

"Some party in Iowa City. She was going out with this art teacher there. She dumped him right away, of course. Dad has a lot more money."

The way her fingers touched her ravaged face I could tell she'd become aware of me watching her carefully. But she'd misinterpreted why I was watching her. Beneath the scarring was an innocent, appealing face that made it seem impossible that she could be capable of so much anger.

"We used to plot how to get rid of her."

"Anything ever come of it?"

She smiled for the first time. "We were chicken." Then: "God, poor Van. I try not to think about it but it doesn't work. I barely slept last night." She picked up the cigarette she'd put in the ashtray. "I'd never say this to my father but I even feel sorry for Neil."

"You got to know him?"

"Sure. Dad liked him and Marsha liked him and I liked him. Eve didn't. She's such a snotty bitch. She always told Van she shouldn't go out with 'lower-class boys.' Van used to laugh about that. It's not like we're living in New York or anything. There are rich people here but it's not like there's this big deal when it comes to dating. Everybody goes to public school and goes out with everybody else." She put her knees up against the dashboard and slumped in the seat and tamped out another cigarette for herself.

I disagreed with her about the town not having a class system but I doubted that people talked about it as crudely as Eve had put it.

"And Van thought she was seeing somebody on the side." She lit her cigarette, inhaled, exhaled.

"That's a pretty heavy accusation. What made Van think so?"

"She said one time when Dad was out of town she caught Eve and the handyman looking guilty when they were coming out of that cabana by the pool. She said Eve hurried over to her and was real friendly. Eve's never real friendly."

"Who's the handyman?"

"You know a guy named Bobby Randall?"

Bobby Randall—handyman. I'd forgotten that. He was an excellent carpenter as well. "Yeah, I do."

"Well, he's real good looking and he knows it. Van—" She glanced out the window before speaking. "Van was into drugs. Heavy stuff sometimes. I stick to pot. Anyway, Van got her drugs from Bobby. He was always trying to get her into bed. She led him on; she did that a lot. People said she slept around and I guess that was true. But a lot of it was just kind of leading them on. Playing with them. She did it to hurt our dad. You know, because of that bitch Eve. I would've done the same thing probably if I didn't have—" She flipped her cigarette out the window and brought her knees down from the dashboard. "You know, my problems." The fingers of her left hand went—unconsciously?—to her cheek.

She opened the door. "The curtains just moved again up in Eve's room."

I said, "You've done a good job of convincing me not to like her. I didn't take to her right off but you clinched the deal."

She offered a slender hand and a smile. "Good. Then we're friends."

As we shook, I said, "We sure are."

Then, softly, she said: "Why couldn't it have been Eve instead of Van?"

She pushed out of the car and jogged back to the mansion.

NINE

"WOULD YOU LIKE half my sandwich, Mr. C? It's bigger than I thought it would be."

"I'm not really hungry, Jamie. Why don't you eat what you want and then stick the rest in the little refrigerator down the hall and then take it home tonight."

"Turk doesn't like leftover stuff."

Well, since you're supporting the family while Turk is loafing, he should be grateful for any food he gets. If I didn't care for Jamie as much as I did, I would have erupted like that five times a day, every time she unwittingly revealed how Turk took advantage of her. They'd broken up a few years ago because he'd had another girlfriend on the side. The marriage had been called off. But gradually she'd weakened under all his promises to be the man—or punk in my estimation—he knew he could be. Her parents couldn't pay for the small informal wedding so I made a present of picking up the tab. I also got her on a decent and low-cost insurance plan because I knew she'd be pregnant soon enough. She'd confided to me through tears—this when she'd discovered Turk's girlfriend—that Turk didn't care for rubbers. At that moment her period was late and she was terrified. The period came a few days later. I put Turk on the same insurance plan only because she pleaded with me. I had dreams of running him down with my car just to see how reliable the insurance coverage was.

"Aw, what the hey, Jamie, I'll take half your sandwich."

"I always like it when we eat together here. It's real homey."

Turk, you son of a bitch, if you ever hurt her again I'll tear your throat out.

The pastrami on rye she'd gotten from Goldblatt's deli down the street was excellent as always. We mostly talked about her baby. Jamie was starting a college fund that she was keeping secret from good old Turk because he "sometimes" tended to spend every cent in the house. She said that she wanted her baby to be a doctor or a lawyer—"just like you, Mr. C."

Then the two phone lines started buzzing and it was back to work.

Without quite knowing why, I called the Wilhoyt Investigative Agency in Chicago. This was a prominent firm that had recently helped bring down a powerful and corrupt politician who fought every civil rights bill that came up, despite the fact that he had a Negro mistress. He didn't seem to understand the incongruity. He must have thought he was back running the plantation.

My contact there was an older man named Pete Federman. He'd hired me four times to work on cases he was overseeing in Iowa City and Cedar Rapids. The checks were about double what I charged here. Federman had a cigarette hack and a lot of jokes about what it was like living under the burden of being a Cubs fan.

"You see the game yesterday, McCain?"

"Couple innings on TV."

"I'm taking a cyanide capsule with me next time I go. They screw up like they did yesterday, I'll just slide it under my tongue and that'll be that. The way my oldest boy's been carryin' on that doesn't sound all that bad anyway." Hack. "So what can I do for you?"

I told him about Eve. Gave him all the details about her background I'd managed to put together.

"If this isn't all bullshit she must be quite the doll."

I told him about Vanessa's death. "The girls couldn't stand her. After talking to her this morning it was easy to see why."

"Solid gold bitch, huh?"

"Yeah, and one who seems to enjoy the role."

"I'll probably need twenty-four hours on this. I take it you're on an expense account."

"Yeah."

"Then no discounts. For you personally I'd go twenty-five percent off."

"Hey, I appreciate that."

"You do good work, kid."

"Well, you do good work, too, Pete."

The big agencies had access to people and documentation all over the country. The starting point would probably be Dartmouth where she'd been a professor. They'd likely work backward from there.

I'd been talking on line one. As soon as I began lowering the receiver, line two rang. Jamie answered, "Sam McCain's law office." She sounded official as hell. She listened and then said: "He's right here, Commander Potter." She nodded to me. I picked up; she hung up.

"Hi Mike, what's going on?"

"You know that old Skelly station near the round-house? Been closed down for a couple years?"

"Sure. Why?"

"Well, somebody spotted Cameron there and I jumped in the car and found him."

"You bringing him in?"

"Yeah, Sam. But there isn't any hurry. He put a .45 to his head and killed himself."

PART TWO

TEN

THE STATION HAD been abandoned a few years after the war, the reason being that the ones in town were new and bright and easy to get to. This was a holdover from the early thirties, a two-pump station that sold only gas and oil, no car repairs. Kids had smashed out the windows and animals had used the drive as a bathroom. The front door had been chained shut. If you looked through one of the dust-coated front windows you could see a large movie poster advertising a Betty Grable film circa 1945 when Betty was already slipping in popularity.

Three squad cars and an ambulance were parked on the east side of the station. I pulled up behind them and walked to the back of the place where a green wooden storage shed was tucked into a stand of hardwoods. Potter was explaining to two uniforms how he wanted them to gather evidence, who would start where and so on. The ambulance boys leaned against the open rear doors of their big white box, looking slightly bored and taking it out on their cigarettes. As usual, the joyous birdsong reminded me that the so-called lower orders could give a shit about the travails of the plodding creatures that lumbered across their land. Nature presented them with their own travails.

Potter set his men to work and then walked over to

me. "I'd let you have a look at him but we're still gathering evidence. I wanted you out here so I could tell you firsthand what I saw when *I* got out here. He's in the back of the shed. He had a blanket and some sandwiches in a brown paper bag. Obviously somebody helped him. From what I could see, he didn't have any marks on his arms or hands or face. No signs of a struggle, in other words, in case you're thinking somebody killed him and then planted the gun in his hand. He fired a .45 above his right ear. The exit wound is a big bastard, bigger than usual. The doc is on his way. He'll be able to guesstimate when Cameron did the deed. Now I'm sure you have a lot of questions so if you want to wait around for a couple of hours—there's a pretty good burger joint about a mile from here—we'll probably have a lot more information for you."

"I'm sure your boss will take this as an admission of guilt."

"Right now I do, Sam. And if you can step back and be a little objective, you should, too. You'll say everything's circumstantial and it probably is but he was obsessed with the girl, she broke it off with him and he killed her. That's not exactly a new story. He hides out, he's afraid and probably sorry for what he'd done, and he kills himself."

"Where did he get the gun?"

"Where did he get the sandwiches and the blanket? Probably the same place."

"I'll get to see the blanket and gun?"

"As long as the chief isn't here. He's still pissed off

about your John Wayne crack. Being a draft dodger and all."

"Good thing I didn't tell him that Superman can't actually fly."

He shook his head and smiled. "You two really hate each other, don't you?"

"I don't hate him as much as he hates me."

"Yeah, I kind of figured that was the case." He waved to a squad car that had just pulled up. "Now I gotta get back to work."

I drove back to town. When I saw a phone booth outside a Howard Johnson's I pulled over. I had Paul Mainwaring's phone number scribbled in the small notepad I carry in my left back pocket. Marsha the maid answered.

"I'm afraid he's at the funeral home, Mr. McCain. The burial will be tomorrow. Mr. Mainwaring just wants to get it over with."

"Well, will you please give him this message, Marsha? The police have found Neil Cameron's body in a shed in back of that old Skelly station on the edge of town."

Her gasp—and it was indeed a gasp—surprised me. "Oh, my Lord."

"Are you all right, Marsha?"

"He was such a nice boy. I liked him so much."

She was reacting as if a close friend had died. "Did you know him pretty well, Marsha?"

"He was around here a lot. Sometimes Vanessa would invite him over but by the time he'd get here some other boy would have picked her up and taken her off. I cared for Vanessa but she was very cruel to boys sometimes. He'd look so sad I'd talk to him. Once in awhile if I wasn't busy and nobody else was around I'd talk to him for quite awhile. My own son is in his thirties and lives in Michigan with his family. I suppose I kind of adopted Neil a little bit. I know he was upset but I don't for a minute believe he murdered poor Vanessa—and you can tell that to Mr. Mainwaring for all I care—and I just can't imagine him killing himself, either. I'm sure you think I'm being naïve but those are my feelings."

"I'm pretty sure what they're saying is his suicide will close the case."

"Not for me it won't. Nobody'll ever convince me he did either of those things. Oh, there's the doorbell. People have been sending flowers to the house. I wish they wouldn't. We'll just have to drag them all to the funeral home and the church. You'll have to excuse me now."

By the time I got back to the Skelly station the onlookers and reporters had gone. Potter was standing next to a large metal box where his officers had been putting the evidence bags they'd been filling. Potter was talking to two of his men so I had time to scan the plastic bags. A quart of Hamm's beer, a half-finished sandwich of some kind, a pair of white socks with blood on the toe of one of them, a stadium blanket of deep blue with horizontal yellow stripes, a Greyhound bus schedule, a Swiss army knife and a small black flashlight. There were many more items beneath these but I assumed Potter wouldn't be real happy if he saw me pawing through his evidence bags.

"Any sign of a note?" I asked Potter when he walked over to me.

"No, but there might be a good explanation for that, Sam. Maybe he just didn't have anything to write with."

"It's still strange."

"It's strange if you *want* it to be strange. Otherwise it's as simple as my explanation."

I nodded to where the ambulance had been. "The doc say anything unexpected?"

"Just that it looked like a suicide. He wanted to get Cameron on the table before he said it officially, but he said any other explanation was unlikely."

"All the evidence in the bags—will his sister get his belongings at some point?"

"At some point, yes. I imagine this thing'll end at the inquest. So it shouldn't take long. He killed himself."

From what Sarah Powers had told me, Neil Cameron had been a confused and angry man after the war. The deaths he'd seen—and the lives he'd taken by mistake—had alienated him from not only others but himself as well. He'd come to rely on romance to redeem him but when that had failed him, failed him because of his own obsessiveness and possessiveness, he'd started getting into even more trouble than he had previously. Then he'd met Vanessa and became even more desperate. Some of these facts would make their way into the inquest. They would convince everybody present that he'd been a prime candidate for suicide. He'd murdered his true love because she wouldn't have him and then in remorse taken his own life.

"I'd tell your friends at the commune it's probably

time for them to move on, Sam. For everybody's sake, including theirs. I don't mind them as long as they don't break the law, but after all this the city council's going to be on their ass for sure. They'll come up with some ordinance to run them out or to make their lives so miserable they'll want to leave anyway. Might as well get it over with now."

"I'll talk to them. But Richard Donovan has a temper and he isn't afraid of much. I doubt he'll listen. And I'm not sure they should be forced to move anyway. If Cameron did kill Vanessa Mainwaring, he acted alone. The others didn't have anything to do with it."

"Just trying to help. I want a nice peaceful life. That's why I came out here. The hippies just seem to agitate a lot of people."

"And you know why that is, don't you?"

"The long hair?"

"All the sex. Everybody secretly wants to have as much sex as these kids have. But since they can't, they take it out on the hippies."

"You really believe that?"

I smiled. "Sometimes."

ELEVEN

THE FIRST TIME I ever heard Judge Whitney call Richard Nixon "Dick" and Leonard Bernstein "Lenny," I was under the impression that she was making up her so-called relationships with these two gentlemen. But then "Dick" Nixon came and stayed with her at her manse and "Lenny" Bernstein started sending her both birthday and Christmas gifts. There was also the fact that she certainly had the opportunity to meet with them because she took at least four trips a year to New York City where both men resided. She often said she could "breathe" in New York City, implying of course that she found our little city suffocating. She didn't try to hide her snobbery and maybe she didn't believe she was *being* snobbish. For a conservative Republican she was liberal when it came to civil rights and protecting the poor against the wealthy and she became enraged whenever a group of local idiots tried to have this or that book banned from the public library.

She was a remarkable woman given that she'd been married four times, no children, had managed to keep her looks even now into her sixties and, for good measure, had taught Barry Goldwater how to mambo. I'm not sure he *wanted* to learn how to mambo but the judge can be most persuasive at times. I know about the Goldwater tutorial because there's a black-and-white framed photo of it on the wall of her judicial chambers.

She's had her grief. Her deepest love was for her first husband who was killed in the Pacific when our troops were getting slaughtered there early on. Her fourth husband died behind the wheel of a new Lincoln Continental while drunkenly escorting his drunken secretary to a motel where they were known as frequent guests. This didn't help her own reliance on alcohol. Finally she checked herself into a rehabilitation clinic in Minnesota. She was now several years dry and a fervent attendee at AA meetings.

None of this had dulled her edge; nothing could. She was still imperious and after all these years I wasn't sure that I wanted her any other way.

She stood in the sunlight arcing through the tall, mullioned window of the old courthouse. In her crisp peach-colored suit, her Gauloise cigarette streaming soft blue smoke from her fingers, she might have been a woman in one of those magazines only rich people read. Staring out at a polo match or the arrival of a head of state.

Without turning to look at me, she said: "My friends at the club very smugly told me that Cliffie has the Mainwaring murder solved and ready for the county attorney. It's even worse this morning. By the time I got to my chambers, four different people told me that they'd read the local rag and apparently there's a quote from Cliffie—more or less in English—that he won't be 'outguessed' on this one. He also said that your friends, those dreadful 'hippies' as you call them, should be forced to leave town." Now she glared at me.

"I don't want that illiterate fool outsmarting us on this one, McCain."

"He hasn't yet."

"Dummies have dumb luck. Maybe he's right for once."

She crossed the room with finishing school aplomb and set her quite fine bottom on the edge of her desk, Gauloise in one hand, her glass of Perrier in the other. "If this Cameron boy didn't kill her, why did he commit suicide?"

"I don't think it was suicide. And I'm hoping the doc agrees with me."

"The 'doc,'" she scoffed. "Somebody brought him as a guest to the club one night and he got three sheets to the wind and started talking about how stupid Republicans are. At the club, if you can imagine."

"I wish I could've been there."

"You'll never set foot in our club if I have anything to do with it. You'd be worse than he was. You'd probably start giving your Saul Alinsky speech."

Saul Alinsky was the Chicago professor famous for teaching groups that were powerless how to organize and become powerful. These groups were always the outsiders, ethnic and political ones looking for justice. "He's one of my heroes."

"What's wrong with William F. Buckley?"

"Too prissy and too smug."

"I'll mention that to Bill when I see him next month."

"I have several other things you could tell him but you wouldn't want those words to come from your mouth."

A dramatic drag on the Gauloise: "So if he didn't kill her, who did?"

"Right now there are several possibilities. I wanted to ask you if you'd ever heard anything about Eve Mainwaring at your club."

She stretched her legs out, inspected them. Long and slender, perfectly turned. She had good wheels and knew it. "Personally I like her. She's a bit standoffish but that's only because when she first started coming there all the usual sex fiends started chasing her."

"Paul didn't object?"

"Paul wasn't around. God, that man travels more than LBJ. She usually came with one of the other club women."

"So you haven't heard anything about her?"

"That she sleeps around? Of course. I've heard it. But I don't believe it. I've talked to her a number of times. It turns out she loves Lenny's music."

"Ah."

"Don't think I don't know what's behind that 'Ah.' When I told her that Lenny was a friend of mine she was fascinated and wanted to hear all about him. I consider that a sign of intelligence and sophistication."

"So you don't think any of the scuttlebutt about her is true?"

"I most certainly don't."

"I don't suppose she's a fan of Dick Nixon, too."

Another momentary indulgence on her cigarette: "I wouldn't be crude enough to ask, McCain. That's something people like you would do. She did say, however—and I had absolutely nothing to do with this—that she didn't think much of Hubert Humphrey. I'll let you make up your own mind on that."

"She's supporting George Wallace?"

She slipped off the desk. "I've had enough of you for today. Now get busy. I want to put a stop to all this nonsense about Cliffie having solved the case."

"If I pull it off will you invite me to your club?"

She couldn't help it. She smiled. "They'd eat you alive, McCain. And they wouldn't laugh at even one of your stupid jokes. Now get going."

The main floor of the courthouse held what was called a luncheonette. For employees of the courthouse it was perfect for quick breakfasts, quick lunches and twenty-minute coffee breaks. Next to it stood a small stand run by a blind man named Phil Lynott. He'd gone to the Vinton School for the Blind back in the mid-forties and had been running the stand ever since. He sold newspapers, cigarettes, cigars and pipe tobacco. He was a rangy, balding man who wore dark glasses. He could tell you where every single item was. He could retrieve said item in seconds. Just about everybody liked him. One time a smart ass on a bet tried to steal a newspaper. A big defense lawyer who'd played tackle for the U of Iowa got the culprit around the neck and damned near choked him to death. Phil had had no such trouble since.

"Hi, Phil. Did Cartwright finally convert you?"

Phil laughed. "You know he's on in the afternoon now, too." He nodded to his small black plastic radio.

"Oh, goody."

"Whatever else you can say about him, he's great entertainment."

"...and so tonight in the park my flock will be presenting a one-act play called *Jesus Meets a Hippie*.

This is something the entire family will want to see, especially if you've got boys or girls who think they might want to grow their hair long and take drugs and fornicate before marriage. As I said to my wife just the other night, when I think of all that fornicating I just can't get to sleep."

Phil's laughter rang off the sculpted halls of the courthouse. "'Don't bother me now, honey, I'm thinking of all that fornication.'" He was still laughing when I pushed through the heavy glass doors and stepped into the ninety-six-degree afternoon.

"She's in the bathroom."

Jamie was whispering. And pointing. As if I didn't know where the down-the-hall bathroom was.

"Who are we talking about?"

"Shh. Not so loud, Mr. C. She'll hear you."

I seated myself at my desk.

"She came in real mad and then she just sat there and started crying. I don't blame her. If my brother committed suicide I'd be half crazy, too. I feel sorry for her." She was still whispering.

Sarah Powers walked in then. "Jamie said it would be all right if we talked." She stood in front of my desk. The anger Jamie said she'd come in with had probably depleted her momentarily. "I want to thank you for getting me out of jail. I probably owe you some bail money."

"No bail, Sarah. I told them I wouldn't press charges for you hitting me with that steel rod. And I convinced them you weren't being an uncooperative witness—that you didn't know any more than you were telling them."

"Well, I really appreciate it, Mr. McCain."

"I'm Sam. You're Sarah."

No smile; just a nod.

Jamie held up her bottle of Wite-Out, her lifeline to secretarial success. "I'm all out, Mr. C, I need to go get some more."

I knew she kept half a dozen emergency bottles in her desk. I was impressed that she'd devised such a clever way of excusing herself so I could talk with Sarah. Someday when I'm a little more successful I'll have an office with two rooms. I will stop people on the street to tell them about this and eventually two men in white will cart me off to the mental institution one town away while I'm babbling, "Two rooms I tells ya! Two rooms!"

"Good idea, Jamie."

"You want me to bring you anything, Mr. C?"

"No, I'm fine. Thanks, though."

Jamie stood up, that wonderful dichotomy of Teenage Babylon body and Donna Reed face. In her pink summer dress—something Wendy and I had bought for her on her birthday—she was a sweet young mother. Married, unfortunately, to a little rat bastard who considered Iowa a surfing state. Have you ever seen a cow surf? Neither have I.

When we were alone, Sarah said, "He didn't kill himself."

"Why don't you sit down, Sarah? You look exhausted."

"I know my brother. He wouldn't kill himself."

"You said you were worried he'd kill himself when he got strung out on that one girl."

She was still standing up. "I shouldn't have said that. Deep down I didn't believe he would have. And I don't believe it now."

I pointed to the chair. She finally walked back to the most comfortable chair in the place, the one I'd bought when the largest law firm in the city redid their offices and sold off most of their old furniture.

"He didn't commit suicide and he didn't kill her."

"I believe he didn't kill her. I'm not as sure about him committing suicide, though for some reason I tend to agree with you. I think he was murdered."

"You mean that?" She looked younger then, still and always the tomboy, but there was a childlike frailty in the dark gaze now as if she'd finally found a true friend. I could abide her usual anger because I could understand it but it was pleasant to see her almost winsome.

"There's something I got from one of the girls at the commune. Emma Ewing. She said that just before dusk she saw Bobby Randall's Thunderbird parked down by the garage. He was talking to Donovan. She was in the house for maybe twenty minutes, and when she came out again his Thunderbird was still there but she didn't see him anywhere."

"He comes there a lot?"

The eyes got shrewd. "Nobody told you?"

"Told me what?"

"A lot of us think he's got a deal with Donovan."

"What kind of deal?"

"Donovan says that we should only buy drugs from Randall. He said that right after we moved in. He says Randall's the only one we know isn't a narc."

"So he gets a cut from Randall?"

"We can't prove it but that's what we think. And you know Donovan went after Vanessa before my brother did. He was way hung up on her. He didn't go crazy like Neil but he started trying to sleep with every chick in the commune. He even hit on me a couple of times. I mean, guys don't hit on me unless they're really hard up."

"You've got to stop that. I do all right with women and look at me."

"There's nothing wrong with you."

"Oh no? I'm short and I'm not exactly handsome. It's attitude. I just pretend I'm this cool guy and sometimes it works. And that's what you've got to do."

"I'm scared of guys."

"Well, I'm scared of women."

"Really?"

"Absolutely. They're like this alien species. Just when you think you've figured them out a little bit they do something completely unexpected. And you're standing there looking like a fool."

She must have been restraining herself to a painful degree because suddenly she was sobbing, her face in her hands. I walked around the desk and stood in back of her chair. I put my hands gently on her shoulders and started muttering all the stupid things people mutter at times like these, a reminder of how difficult it is to really comfort anyone.

I reached over and snatched Jamie's Kleenex box from her desk. I handed it to Sarah. She plucked a piece free. It resembled a fluttering white bird in her fingers. She blew her nose but kept on sobbing.

When the phone rang, I took it on Jamie's desk. Paul Mainwaring didn't say hello. "I've sent you a check for a thousand dollars, Sam. That should be enough for your services."

"Way *too* much, actually."

"It's done. We have our answers. Now we can get on with our grieving. I appreciate your work on this, Sam."

"Shouldn't we wait for the autopsy?"

He wasn't angry; peeved was the word here. "Autopsy? We already have it. Vanessa was stabbed to death."

"I mean Neil Cameron's autopsy."

"What's that got to do with anything? Now I'm in a hurry here, Sam. As I said, I've sent you a check for a thousand dollars and I've thanked you for your work and I'm hanging up now."

"What if Neil didn't commit suicide?" I rushed my words, had to because he was about to put his phone down.

Peevishness was now anger. "He did commit suicide, Sam. That's obvious to everyone except you, apparently. I talked to Mike Potter. His opinion is that Cameron felt guilty about killing my daughter and that he knew he'd spend the rest of his life in prison so he killed himself. Even you should be able to understand that, Sam."

Yes, even you, Sam. Now quit picking bugs off yourself and begging for bananas and get off the damn phone!

"Potter hasn't seen the autopsy yet, either. Maybe he'll change his mind."

"Goodbye, Sam. I wanted this to be a pleasant little call because right now I'm losing my mind over my daughter's death and I need a lot of little pleasant moments. But thanks to you I'm all worked up again. Goodbye."

Sarah was dabbing her eyes with Kleenex. The sobs had given way to frantic sighs. I got myself a cup of coffee and said, "Where're you planning to stay?"

"At the commune, why?"

"Everything be cool there for you?"

"Yeah, except for Richard. He's pissed because all this is likely to get the commune shut down. That's the only thing he talked about. He didn't say anything about Neil being dead. I think he still hated him because of Vanessa."

"But Vanessa ended up doing the same thing to Neil that she did to Donovan, right?"

"The same thing she did to all her boyfriends. They'd get close and then she'd dump them. But Richard couldn't see it that way. When he'd drink he'd talk about how he'd still be with her if it wasn't for Neil."

"So it doesn't bother you to go back there?"

"The people there are more my friends than Richard's. They're tired of him. This Emma I told you about?" A fleeting smile. "She calls him The Overlord."

Jamie was back with two sacks. One was from the office supply store, the other from the deli. She placed the former on her desk and the latter in Sarah's lap. "They were having a special on ham and cheese on rye so I thought I'd get you one. I'll get you some Pepsi from the machine down the hall."

"She sure is nice."

"She sure is, Sarah. And so are you. I'm going to find Bobby Randall and meanwhile you're invited to stay in this luxurious office of mine as long as you want to."

Jamie returned just as I spoke. "Don't worry, Mr. C. I'll take good care of her. I'll show her some of Laurie's baby pictures." She beamed down at Sarah. "Laurie's my baby." I was surprised she hadn't already told our guest all about her. People who've been in my office for more than three minutes usually know the whole story by heart.

TWELVE

I'D BEEN TO Bobby Randall's place only once. Two years ago a woman who worked in the courthouse asked me to tell him to stop seeing her sixteen-year-old daughter. He was, after all, in his early twenties. His age made him prosecutor bait but she didn't want to press charges because, she said, her daughter, who was very much taken with the handsome arrogant Bobby, would never forgive her. The woman told me that she had nightmares of her daughter getting pregnant.

I'd seen Bobby around town. In his red Thunderbird he was hard to miss. His trail of heartbroken women provided tavern talk for other young men. Bobby was not beloved. In the words of the Everly Brothers, he was a bird dog. He seemed to take particular pride in sleeping with women who were affixed to boyfriends, fiancés and husbands. He had the looks, all dark curly hair and features that were almost pretty and swagger that would put my favorite draft dodger John Wayne to shame.

As I pulled into the alley where he had turned a three-stall garage into his workshop, I heard the competing sounds of rock music and circular saw. I pulled off the gravel onto blanched grass crosscut with tire tracks. This was the visitor parking area.

The doors were wide open, allowing in heat and flying kamikaze bugs. The set-up was impressive. Lighting was provided by overhead fluorescents. The walls were covered with shelving and pegboard that contained hammers, pliers, extra saw blades, screwdrivers and so many other things I gave up looking. He was cutting two-by-fours on a workbench big enough to play Ping-Pong on. He stood in T-shirt and jeans on a floor of wood that he'd covered with a linoleum-like surface. Everything was bright and new as if it would be used for a photo in a trade magazine. The one element that enhanced even the splendor of the workshop was the splendor of the blonde in the very tight Levi's cutoffs and braless pink T-shirt who sat perched on a stool in the corner. She held a long cigarette in one hand and a magazine in the other. Neither she nor Randall looked up when I entered because neither could hear me above the whine of the saw. The smell of freshly sawn wood took me back to the days when I was little and watched my father make wonderful things in his own tiny workshop.

When he'd shaved as much as he'd wanted to off the two-by-four he reached down for another board and that's when he saw me. His first reaction was anger. He changed it quickly to a smug smile. "I could have you arrested for trespassing."

"Who is he, Bobby?" She was the mythic mountain girl in all of Charles Williams' Gold Medal novels, pure animal sex and ravishing insolence. The voice didn't work with the body; cigarettes and booze and likely drugs.

"He's a nobody who thinks he's somebody because he works for Judge Whitney."

"That bitch. She put my brother in county for six months."

"You don't have any friends here, McCain." He lifted his saw and jabbed it in my direction. "So if I was you I'd leave right now."

"You could take him one-handed, Bobby. He don't even come up to your shoulders."

Bobby nodded to the blonde who was, for all her looks, a pretty nasty lady.

"She's got two brothers, McCain. She grew up watching them beat the hell out of each other. She knows about fighting. If she says I can whip your ass, take her word for it."

"How much dope were you selling Vanessa Mainwaring?"

That got us past the tough-guy talk.

The dark eyes narrowed in fear.

"A murder like that, the police are going to start looking into her background for the county attorney. The drugs'll come up and your name is going to be in the papers and on TV." It was bullshit but he was too dumb to know that. "You're going to find yourself up against some heavy-duty charges. Paul Mainwaring's going to see that you get put away for a long time."

The blonde started to say something but stopped herself. She had a scorching glare. I could almost feel my skin shrivel.

"The kind of business you're in, Bobby, you'll be lucky to get out in fifteen years."

"You bastard. You've been waitin' to nail me, haven't you, McCain?"

"You're wasting my time, Randall. I want to know how much dope she was buying and what kind."

"And then you run to the cops."

"Or that bitch of a judge." Blondie.

"Your Thunderbird was parked outside the barn where Vanessa's body was found."

He finally put the saw down. He made a show of flexing his bicep as he did so. Even in panic he had to peacock it. "So what?"

"Your car was there during the time the coroner said she was killed. So where were you?"

"You don't have to tell him nothing, Bobby. It's two against one. All we gotta say is he made alla this up."

"I just walked around the commune the way I usually do, McCain. I like the fresh air out there."

God had provided Randall with enviable skills—enviable to me anyway—as a carpenter and handyman. His law degree was apparently still in the mail.

"Mike Potter has checked all the footprints in the barn. He's accounted for all of them except two. I haven't mentioned you to him yet. But how would you like it if I went straight from here to a phone and told him to check out all your shoes?"

Even Blondie gulped when I said this. For just a second not even her cunning could disguise her apprehension. I wasn't sure what they were hiding from me but obviously I'd made both of them nervous.

"Let's go back to the dope. How much and what kind?"

"This is really bullshit, man. Like I said, I could charge you with trespassing."

"Yeah, you could. And I could always call Mike Potter. How about if we swap, Randall? You tell me about the drugs and I won't tell Potter anything if I believe you're telling me the truth."

"Don't tell him anything, Bobby. That bitch judge of his'll just put you in prison the same way she did Ronnie."

How could anybody as ravishing—and she was— as Blondie be such a bitch? And not exactly a bright one at that.

"I wouldn't listen to her, Bobby. She wouldn't be able to help you when Potter and the county attorney started snooping around. I can help you if you help me now."

"You back off, Dodie. I gotta be careful here."

Dodie? I had nothing against the name but somehow she wasn't a "Dodie." Dodies are cute and pert in my mind; this Dodie was a long-legged female swashbuckler who used sex and her belligerent mouth to get her way. Dodie?

Dodie slid off the stool and came up to stand next to Randall. She stood hip-cocked and spectacular. Just as long as she didn't open her mouth. "He's conning you."

"Maybe so but I want to hear him out at least. Why don't you go in and see about supper?"

"I want to stay here."

At this rate ole Bobby was soon going to get kicked out of the He-Man Club. You know, the guys who don't take crap off anybody, especially women. Dodie-with-the-unlikely-name was clearly in charge here.

"All right, but keep quiet."

"I'll keep quiet as long as you don't say anything stupid to this asshole."

When I thought about it, I could almost feel sorry for Randall.

"How long were you selling her drugs?"

He glanced at Dodie as if seeking her permission to talk. To me he said, "Six, seven months."

"How often?"

"She was one of my best customers. Every seven or eight days or so."

"You ever think maybe he's wired and you're talking yourself into hard time?"

"I'm not wired, Randall. And you're doing the right thing. What kind of drugs did she buy?"

This time he didn't look for permission. "Across the board. At least of the kind I sell. Pot, speed, coke, acid. Once in awhile I get weird shit like peyote or something. She liked acid. She loved tripping. The kids at the commune, all they ever want is pot and acid."

"You get to know her?"

Bobby Randall, cool cat and heartbreaker, blushed, which wasn't doing much for his image. The blooded cheeks told me that she had likely seduced him the way she'd likely seduced a lot of young men. He had to clear his throat to speak. "Talked to her a little bit."

"That better be all you did."

"Dodie, I already told ya nothin' happened."

"I seen her. And I seen the way you looked at her."

"Yeah, well, nothin' happened."

"Why was your car there so long last night?"

This time he didn't blush. He lowered his head and stared at the ground for half a minute. Then he looked up and said, "Remember, it's two to one. Your word against ours."

"You can relax, Randall. I think you're a scumbag but right now I could give a rat's ass about your drug

deals. I want to find out who murdered Vanessa and
Neil Cameron. So what were you doing there so long?"

"Don't tell him anything more, Bobby. He's got
enough to put you away already."

"None of this goes to the cops, right?"

"They'll nail your ass soon enough. They don't need
any help from me. I won't repeat anything we talked
about here today."

He pawed at his face, the same thing I'd been doing
to mine. Between the heat Dodie was exuding and the
temperature, Randall's garage was one steamy place.

"Me'n Richard—Richard Donovan?—we got a
deal. I give him a cut and he tells all his people to buy
strictly from me. I've been worried about cops so Richard agreed to let me put my stash in the barn. I was
unloading then covering it up. And I didn't see any
dead Vanessa."

"How did Richard act when you got there?"

He was in need of permission again. A quick glance
to Dodie then back to me: "Kinda nervous. That doesn't
mean anything. All the drugs I was hiding, I was nervous, too."

"Did you hide them in the front of the barn or in
the back?"

"Front. Richard had dug this deep hole then I had to
dig another one. Then we went to my trunk and started
loading everything into these Army ammunition boxes.
You know, metal and they'd lock real tight. Then we
pushed an old refrigerator over the holes we dug."

Sounded feasible but this was Bobby Randall. I
trusted him slightly less than I did Dick Nixon.

"I guess that'll be it for now, Randall."

"You happy, you dumb bastard? You just talked your way into prison."

"She's a sweetie, Randall. Make sure you keep her."

He sighed and shrugged. I gazed into the blazing eyes of Dodie Dear then I did some shrugging myself and started walking toward the alley. I got my last glimpse of his site. My father would have been overwhelmed by the entire arrangement.

I had just about reached the door when I heard Randall shout: "McCain, duck!"

I pitched myself leftward just in time to see a hammer flying toward the point where my head had been a moment ago.

"You better watch out for Ronnie and Donnie," she screamed. "They'll make you sorry you were ever born!"

And in this moment of Mountain Beauties slinging hammers at me, Randall shouted out the most preposterous thing of all. "Take a flier with you, McCain. In case you know somebody who needs some carpentry work."

Right next to the door was a straight-back chair with fliers piled on it. And damned if I didn't pick one up.

THIRTEEN

I HADN'T ASKED Bobby Randall about Eve Mainwaring. I was lucky he'd told me as much as he had, especially with Mountain Girl there. I doubted he'd talk about Paul's wife anyway. If his story was true about working with Donovan to off-load all his dope then he had a good excuse—as opposed to an alibi—to be out at the commune. And to spend so much time near the barn. Eve Mainwaring was another matter. I wondered—and he had to be wondering, too—what his carpentry customers would think of him if they knew that he was sleeping with the wife of a man who'd hired him as a handyman.

With his flier on my passenger seat I drove the twenty-eight miles to the Sleepy Time Motel, the just-far-enough-away concrete bunker where you went when you were too scared to try it close to home. Given all the sneaking around and close calls, adultery should be an Olympic sport.

On a summer afternoon when the sun bragged on how mean it could be, I wanted my old Ford ragtop back. And I wanted my father to be alive. And I wanted my mother to make a life for herself, not turn into one of the old ladies who spend most of their free time in church, arthritic hands entwined with rosaries, and memories their only comfort. And I wanted to convince Wendy to marry me, to take the chance at least a part of her knew was worth it.

The radio was still filled with responses to the police riot at the Democratic convention. Mayor Daley was denying he'd made any anti-Semitic remarks and the police commissioner just couldn't find a single thing his officers had done wrong. It was all the fault of the "anarchists." Somebody from the police union gave an even stronger defense of the cops. He talked about all the danger they'd faced that night, even though they were the ones with the clubs and guns and punitive rage. Never a mention about how we were feeding an entire generation into the bloody maw of an unnecessary war and how the president and the Pentagon lied every single day to the American people—the president worried about his place in history and the Pentagon not wanting to stop the flow of money to the great war machine Eisenhower had warned about as he left office. The kids weren't in the streets to have a good time—though some were I suppose—they were there to protest their lives being wasted on the lies of old men.

The Sleepy Time didn't resemble a hot sheet motel. It sat on a hill overlooking a leg of river and a picnic area on the bank. The colors of the office and the room exteriors were two shades of brown—the paint fresh—and the macadam was new. To the left of the office was a swimming pool where a lone young man practiced diving. It was too hot for tanning or sitting around to talk. The middle-aged woman behind the desk was California, tanned, freckled, pretty, her blonde hair streaked even blonder by the sun. Her energy and good nature were just short of aggressive. In her yellow blouse and long silver earrings she was well worth my attention.

"Let me guess." Alluring smile. "You don't want a room."

"You're a fortune teller."

"No. After twenty years in this business I'm just observant. The way you looked around on the drive and the way you came through the door over there told me that you weren't going to be a guest."

"Any guess why I'm here?"

"A cop or something like that. Which I think is cool. Breaks up the monotony. We're full up and everybody's behaving so I don't have much to do. My husband's in the hospital with back problems and my son's getting ready for his next swim meet so I'm all alone in here with my soap operas." Her teeth were luminous against her tanned face. "If you're not a cop you're a private investigator, and if you're a private investigator somebody hired you to find out about somebody cheating."

"You're doing most of my work for me."

"We run a respectable place. And a nice place. But we're not above letting our rooms to people who aren't married to each other. We make them pay full price for the privilege. That way we keep a reasonably suitable clientele. Not always, but most of the time."

"You ever had any trouble?"

"Oh, sure. But fortunately Frank, my husband, he was a Marine in Korea and he's kept in good shape except for his back. He's had to handle some angry husbands who've followed their wives here. And once there

was a homosexual man whose boyfriend followed him
here with a gun. Frank handles everything himself. We
don't want any unnecessary bad publicity. I wish he
was here now. My husband's the funniest guy I've ever
known. It's never boring when he's around."

I slid Bobby Randall's flier across the desk. She
smiled when she saw it. "Oh, yes, Johnny. So his real
name's Bobby?"

"Uh-huh. He's been here then?"

"I'd have to say no comment. The way politicians
do."

"What if I told you a man's future depended on what
I'm doing. An innocent man." It wasn't true but it sure
sounded good.

That sun-blessed face wrinkled in suspicion. "Who
exactly are you?"

I showed her my ID. "A young woman was murdered
in Black River Falls last night."

"Yeah. That was sure a bummer. But they've already
said that the guy who killed her committed suicide."

Time for another somewhat untrue statement.
"They're saying that to trap the real killer. Or anyway
the man they *think* is the real killer. He's a client of
mine. I'm trying to help him. I don't want to see him
railroaded into prison. I have a feeling you can help me
and nobody ever needs to know. Not even your husband."

That sand and ocean smile. "Now you sound like
some of our customers."

"So how about it?"

"Well—" She dragged out the word. "If you promise me you'll never use my name."

I used the three-finger pledge. "Scout's honor."

A nice surfy laugh. "Well, if you put it that way."

"So how about Bobby? He's been here?"

"Many times." A laugh. "Frank has a short list of men he calls 'living legends' and Johnny's one of them. I like Johnny better than Bobby if you don't mind. I had a bad experience with a Bobby when I was in high school. I hate people named Bobby."

"Sounds reasonable."

She laughed again. "Sarcasm. You and my husband would get along. He's always saying things like that. I know it's irrational but that's the way I am."

"So about Johnny-Bobby."

"Well, actually, our son Steve probably knows more than we do. He works nights and that's when Johnny usually shows up. He isn't exactly secretive, though. I mean the red Thunderbird."

"But you've signed him in yourself?"

"Oh, sure. Several times."

"I'm going to describe a woman. If you've dealt with her I'd appreciate you telling me."

"Wait a minute here. This is starting to make me very nervous." The good nature vanished. A surprising harshness was in the voice and blue eyes. "This is our livelihood we're talking about here."

"I already promised you there won't be any trouble."

"Uh-huh, that's another thing you have in common with my Frank. You're both bullshit artists."

"So you're just going to stop here?"

She made a fist of a tanned, freckled hand. The knuckles were bone-white. "Goddammit, I shouldn't have told you anything."

"Well, you've told me this much. How about just a few more questions?"

"Shit. How do I get into things like this anyway?" Then: "All right, goddammit, go ahead."

I described Eve Mainwaring in as much detail as I could remember.

"You mean Andrea Cummings."

"Good old Andrea. So you've dealt with her?"

"Just twice. Both times when she was with Johnny. Johnny should learn not to park so close to the office. I can see in the car windows. Andrea was sitting there waiting for him to come back with the room key. Listen, let me get Steve. I'll be right back."

She moved from behind the desk to the front door, quick and lithe, very healthy in the way of the middle-aged people you saw in advertisements shot on the beach. While she was gone I stared through the open door behind the desk. A black-and-white set played a soap opera. This one had everything. A man whose face was entirely wrapped in gauze, a weeping middle-aged beauty, and a sullen-looking hippie punk of sixteen or so. The beauty was shrieking at the punk that he had no respect for his parents. The punk just got more sullen and then pointed to the masked man. Then he shouted that she was his mom but the masked man wasn't his father, that his real father was a man she'd had a fling with. The masked man slapped his hand to his heart.

A monitor broke into ominous beeping. Take my word for it, the whole thing was one hell of a mess.

Steve had dragged on a red shirt and a pair of jeans. He was still scrubbing his hair with a towel. He had the same freckled exuberant air of his mother but not her good looks. He handled me with the skill of a politician. "Nice to meet you, Mr. McCain. Mom says you wanted to ask me about Johnny and Andrea Cummings."

"I also said your dad's not to know anything about this conversation."

Steve grinned. "You don't have to worry about that. I'd be in trouble with Dad for talking to Mr. McCain, too."

"The only reason I'm doing this is because McCain here says an innocent man could be accused of a murder."

"Just like a movie, huh, Mom."

Mom stood next to him, her proud smile possessive of her boy. "That's right, honey. Now go ahead and answer the man's questions."

"Your mother said you've checked Johnny and Andrea Cummings in a few times."

"More than a few times, in fact, Mr. McCain. Sometimes they're with each other and sometimes they're with other people."

"That's what I'd like to talk about. Andrea Cummings—can you describe some of the other men she's been with?"

"Well, over the past year I'd say there're probably five or six at least."

"He's got a good memory. He's a straight-A student."

"Oh, Mom."

"Well, it's true."

"She doesn't think that's embarrassing, Mr. McCain. Anyway, I can probably describe three of them because they've been with her a number of times. A couple of them were only out here once with her. Or maybe twice, but no more than that."

I took out my nickel notebook and wrote down his descriptions. Andrea-Eve was apparently no snob. One of the men was a handsome professorial sort, one was a tennis instructor from a nearby racquet club and one, the boy felt sure, was some kind of criminal. "He just had that look."

"He likes crime shows on TV."

"Could you be a little more specific about the criminal?"

"Well, for one thing he always wore short-sleeved shirts even in the winter and he had tattoos on both arms. A panther on his right and a tiger on his left. He had real hairy arms. I guess I associate tattoos with criminals."

"Was there ever any trouble?"

"I guess I don't know what you mean."

"Did other guests complain about noise—fights or screaming, anything like that?"

"Oh, no. They were always nice. Even the guy with the tattoos. If anybody was going to cause trouble, it was him."

"Did they ever ask you for any special favors? Like maybe getting them a bottle of liquor or something?"

"I'm not old enough to buy liquor."

The kid was a Boy Scout. He'd never heard of motel desk clerks who provided customers with bottles or babes. The Sleepy Time was a downright boring place.

"Well, the guy with the tattoos asked me if we had one of those machines where you could buy those things but I said no. It was kind of embarrassing."

I assumed he meant rubbers.

"When was the last time Andrea Cummings was here?"

"Just last week. With Johnny again. They didn't stay as long as usual and Johnny was in a hurry when he dropped off the key. He usually likes to talk."

"About what?"

"He usually talks about the Hawkeye football or basketball team, whichever one is in season. But this time he just tossed the keys on the counter and walked right out."

"I told you he had a good memory. Frank's the same way."

I closed my notebook and shoved it into my back pocket. I had already concocted a theory in the way of good private investigators everywhere. It was Eve-Andrea who killed Vanessa. Van learned about Eve cheating on Paul and threatened to tell her father if Eve didn't divorce Paul and leave. And since Van had confided in Neil Cameron about Eve, Cameron had to die, too, which Eve-Andrea accomplished by having one of her numerous lovers, probably the one with the tattoos, help her. See how simple things are when you have no idea what you're talking about?

"I appreciate your help very much, both of you."

As I started for the door, the woman called, "I sure hope the cops don't start hassling your man. I'm used to LA cops. They're the worst."

FOURTEEN

I was at Wendy's in time for supper. For once. Since it was so hot even with the air conditioning on we had one of those cold suppers that are often tastier than the hot ones. Slices of fresh watermelon and cantaloupe, a spinach salad with ranch dressing and slices of wheat bread that Wendy had made during the day. She said it was a beer night rather than a wine night. I didn't disagree. I drank a can and a half of Schlitz but was too full to finish the rest.

Wendy had allowed me to bring my cats from my apartment, the ones I was allegedly still keeping for the old friend of mine who'd gone to LA to become an actress. The last I'd heard she was married to a cop and living in the valley with their first child. Tasha, Crystal and Tess were thus mine. I told Wendy that they were my dowry.

The three of them sat on the far end of the dining room table watching us eat.

"Do you ever wonder what they're thinking about, Sam?"

"I know what they're thinking about."

"Oh, right."

"They're thinking how can a woman this gorgeous put up with a loser like McCain."

"That's funny. That's what *I* thought they were think-ing, too. They're very perceptive."

She sipped her beer. I liked to watch her wrists. They were delicately wrought and charming all by them-selves. Of course it would be difficult to date just a pair of wrists. People would talk. "God, you'd think Eve would be more careful."

"Maybe she's a nympho," I said.

"Nymphos are only in all those paperbacks you read."

"Well then she's super horny."

"Or something. Maybe she's going through the same thing *I* was when I was running around. I'm sure people called *me* a 'nympho,' too. But I wasn't married. I was only hurting myself and my mother and sister. She's hurting a husband."

"I wonder what kind of agreement they have about money. In case of a divorce."

"She wouldn't be in a position to say much if he just cut her off."

"Not unless there was some kind of cruelty going on, physical cruelty, and even then the judge would ask her why she hadn't reported it. He'd also tell her that run-ning around was no way to deal with marital problems."

All three cats looked toward the front of the house when the doorbell rang. Tasha yawned, indicating that she thought whoever had come calling was bound to be boring.

"I'll get it." She was up before I could offer to do it, giving me a prolonged gape at her smooth tanned legs in white shorts. The red cotton blouse accented her small perfect breasts. She was still talking. "You don't really think Eve killed Vanessa and the Cameron boy, do you?"

"It's worth considering, anyway."

When she got the door open, she said, "It's Kenny." She did her best to pack excitement into those two words. She still wished Kenny didn't write soft-core sex books for a living, but he'd won her over with his wife Sue and his daughter Melissa. I think she liked Kenny without quite approving of him.

"Hi, Wendy. I hope I'm not interrupting dinner."

"No, not at all. We're finished. Come on in and have some coffee." An afterthought: "Or a beer."

Kenny had been here many times to see me. He was careful with his cigarettes (Kenny was an ash-flicker and ashes on couches and chairs can mightily displease the hostess) as well as his language. "Coffee's fine," he said as he seated himself at the table. He was, in his words, "duded up." Starched white short-sleeved shirt with a red-and-black striped tie. And it wasn't a clip-on. I wondered where he'd been or where he was going. As Wendy was pouring him a cup of coffee, he said, "How much would you charge me to sue somebody for slander?"

"Are you serious?"

"Very serious."

"Who's slandering you?"

"From what I've been told, Reverend Cartwright is going to do it tonight in that moronic hippie play he's giving in the park."

"Who told you he was going to do it?"

"You know Mrs. Windmere from his church?"

Wendy laughed. "That old gossip? She used to help my mother clean house. We had to let her go because she made up these stories about what a sinful family we were. She even got Cartwright to show up one night and tell my dad that he was going to save our souls. My mother thought it was hilarious. My dad was so mad he grabbed Cartwright and threw him out the open doorway. I wouldn't believe a word she said, Kenny."

"How did you get hooked up with the Windmere woman, anyway?"

"I was having a cherry Coke at the Rexall fountain and she came up and told me that somebody was finally going to stand up to me. It took me a few minutes but then I remembered who she was. She was the old bag who chased me down the street one day. She kept screaming, 'Repent! Repent!' So here she was again. Of course I didn't have any idea of what she was raving on about. I was so embarrassed I could barely hear her anyway. You know how I hate scenes. All these people were standing around watching and listening now and then she said it: 'Reverend Cartwright has written you into his play. Finally a man of God is going to treat you the way you deserve to be treated.' Then she looked around at everybody and pointed to me and said, 'This man is a pronographer.'"

"'Pronographer'?" I said.

Wendy giggled. "Oh, God, that's right, Kenny. I forgot. Mrs. Windmere is always mispronouncing words."

"So I want to sue him."

"How about we wait until you see the show?"

He sat back in his chair, calm for the moment. "That's

what I wanted to ask you two about. I really don't want
to go alone. I even dressed up for the occasion so nobody could call me a hippie."

"Won't Sue go with you?"

"She would have, Wendy, but she doesn't want to
take Melissa out into all that heat. You know, with the
bugs and all."

"I'm sort of a baby myself, Kenny. I kind of like it
here, you know, with the air conditioning and all. And
the TV set and the indoor plumbing and the nice cold
beer. But I'm sure your friend and mine Sam would
love to go with you."

"Really? Damn it, Kenny, I don't want to go see that
stupid show. It'll probably be crowded."

"You really think it'll be crowded?" Wendy said.

"Sure. All of Cartwright's people'll show up and then
all the hecklers. Cliffie'll have a couple cops there to
keep the hecklers in line but they have a way of getting
heard no matter what."

"I don't want to remind you of all the information I
get for you, McCain. And I do it free gratis."

"Oh, that's right. You'd never want to remind me of
that, would you?"

"Maybe it'll be fun."

"Well, if you think it might be fun, Wendy, why
don't you go?"

"I miss out on all kinds of fun, Sam, and you know
it. And at my advanced age it doesn't bother me."

"If he slanders me, McCain, we can sue him for millions."

"He doesn't have millions, Kenny."

"Well, maybe we can at least get him off the air."

Knowing I was going to go, I said, "That's the first real incentive you've given me all night, Kenny. Let me change my clothes."

As I was closing the bathroom door, I heard Wendy say, "I knew you could talk him into it, Kenny. He's a pushover. But that's why we love him."

There's a librarian named Trixie Easley who sets up displays of old photographs from time to time. Generally these deal with our town from the 1870s to today. The pictures of the stage next to the bandstand in the city park are especially helpful for time traveling because in the various shots you see the town, the people, the clothes, the transportation and the plays themselves as they fade era into era.

For the dapper, for instance, homburgs gave way to straw boaters and eventually to felt hats such as fedoras. For women, hats ranged from bonnets to fancy straw to cloche to pillbox and variations thereof. The vehicles were equally interesting—from wagons to surreys to comic-looking early automobiles to family Fords to flivvers to the sedans of today. When I was young I'd look at the people in these photographs and think how easy life had been for them psychologically. There was always so much flag-waving and spirited talk about hardy souls and all that they seemed like a different species. But as I got older I knew that these mythic generations were just that, mythic. They trod through this vale of tears just like every generation. To confirm that truth all you have to do is read the newspapers and police reports of that time. I took ironic comfort in that fact; what did I have to bitch about when every generation had faced the same travails and terrors we have? And they didn't even have Walter Cronkite.

Downtown was bright and crowded. Cliffie had put several extra cops on the street. We had to park three blocks away. The air was turgid and hot. The sidewalks were full of people hurrying. Even from this distance we could hear recordings of Reverend Cartwright singing. He hawked his records along with his diet tip books and his collected sermons, you know, just the way Jesus did.

Wolf packs of teenagers filled the streets with their low-slung cherry bomb mufflers competing with the tinny voice of the good reverend. As we reached the edge of the tiny park I saw that my prediction had been accurate. Gathered close to the stage were the faithful, probably a couple hundred of them. This was strictly BYOS, bring your own seating. They sat on lawn chairs, blankets and even a few air cushions. Most of them had come family-size, wee ones as well as kids as old as sixteen or so. I had to wonder how many of the older ones had had to be dragged here tonight. Or maybe that was just my cynicism. Many of them could be just as sincerely devout as their parents.

Behind them were the smart asses. You could identify them easily by their cigarettes, long hair and smirks. Cops walked up and down in front of them, like Army sergeants assessing their men. Cliffie would have given them strict orders to take no shit whatsoever. He was probably right in doing so. Abhorrent as Cartwright was—not to mention stone insane—he and his followers had the right to watch the play in peace. Of course when I was a teenager I might well have been one of the smirkers out tonight.

While the smirkers weren't officially hippies—they got into too many fights to be all peace and love brother about life—a number of them affected hippie styles. Bell-bottoms, vests, tie-dyed T-shirts, and peasant blouses and long full skirts for the girls. A number of girls had come braless and that was all to the good. A new crew of them arrived in an elderly van painted with flowers and a peace sign.

The stage was long and flat, buttressed by folding metal props beneath. Behind it were heavy wine-colored curtains held up by thick steel rods. You could set up and take down the stage easily. Over the years it has been used by some actual celebrities. Kate Smith sang here pushing war bonds during WWII. Johnny Ray appeared here pushing for the polio drive, then the scourge of young and older alike. And most recently a local kid named Ryan Boggs brought his guitar and a three-piece combo here to sing his one-and-only hit song that had won him a spot on *American Bandstand* and *The Lloyd Thaxton Show.* He was riding a little too high one night in the Quad Cities when some loudmouth picked a fight with him. The guy swung on Boggs and Boggs hit him back. In falling down, the loudmouth hit his head on the metal edge of the footing underneath the bar and died. Boggs' record company decided that Johnny was not a "decent representative of American youth" and canned his ass. He now plays beer parlors.

The first person to appear on stage was a teenager dressed up in a long-haired wig and a tie-dye T-shirt covered in so many love beads he would probably suffer a neck injury from trying to support them. He wore jeans torn at the knees. He was barefoot. He came midstage. There were enough standing microphones to pick up just about every word. Music came up, sounding like Lawrence Welk playing something by The Doors.

The one thing the faux hippie was good at was portraying insolence. I wanted to slap the bastard across the fake beard and mustache. I knew tonight was going to be nothing but stereotypes, but nobody needed to make this town any more unfriendly to hippies. Even though the majority of citizens believe in live and let live, the aginners always spoke louder.

Subtle he wasn't. He pulled from his front pocket a twisted runt of a cigarette. "Tune in, turn on and drop out. Those are my words to live by. 'Scuse me a second." He lit the joint, inhaled deeply, held it, then exploded smoke from his lungs. "If everybody smoked a little dope, this'd be a cool, cool world."

The smirkers were nudging each other and grinning. The cops were giving them dungeon looks.

"I bet if Jesus was alive today he'd be smoking joints right along with the rest of us."

Now it was the turn of the followers to react. Some booed; others poked each other and shook their heads.

"And he'd be into a lot of things the squares don't understand. Like how everything should be free and how people like me should run the government and how this whole war thing is a complete lie. He'd be on our side."

More subtlety. The sound effects of lightning and thunder, the music quick-fading underneath. The whole stage shook. And then from behind the drapes a new character appeared, the Lord Jesus Christ himself. He was tall, he was bearded, he wore the flowing white robe of all the traditional paintings. The one difference was the face. Where Christ was usually portrayed in a sentimental almost sweet way, this Christ looked like he'd kill your mother for fifty cents. The broken nose, the long scar on the left cheek, the big fists dangling from the arms.

And then he spoke. He had the voice you'd expect from that face—rough, deep, threatening. He walked right up to the hippie and slammed his hand into the kid's chest, shoving him back a few feet. The hippie almost went down. "You've got some of your hippie friends here. Bring them out. I want them to hear this, too." He snapped his fingers.

While we waited the half minute for four other hippies—two girls, two boys—to appear, Kenny leaned in and said, "You know that bumper sticker: 'Jesus is coming and boy is he pissed'?"

My laugh was loud enough to attract attention, including that of the cops. Kenny was right. I had been raised to believe that Jesus Christ had been an understanding and forgiving man who helped the sick and the poor and the troubled. That was the Jesus I loved— whether he was merely man or son of God didn't matter much to me—and this cartoon travesty was perverse even for Reverend Cartwright.

All four of the new hippies wore wigs, meaning that they were the children of church members where long hair, among many, many other things, was forbidden.

"Now get this and get this straight. I'm going to tell you how to live the right way and unless you want to go straight to hell when you die, you better listen to me. You got that?"

The hippies all pretended to be terrified. They looked like bad actors in old silent films, hands over their faces as if trying to repel an attack, one of them falling to her knees and folding her hands in eager prayer. And they all chorused, "Yes, Jesus! Yes!"

"You know how in the Western movies there are towns that need to be tamed? Well, that's what you're going to do right here. And you're going to start right now. No more drugs, no more sex before marriage, no more pornography reading *or* writing and no more rock and roll."

They faked confusion, standing there in their bell-bottoms and tie-dyes and wigs, looking at each other in theatrical bafflement. Finally, the girl rose from her knees and said, "But how can we do this, Lord?"

There was a long pause filled with babies crying. A few of the smirkers were lighting joints.

"I am going to send one of my most loyal servants to the mountain the way it was done in Biblical times. There he will commune with me so that when he returns he will share my message with you. And from that message you will learn how to rid your town of the filth that stalks your streets."

The sound effects were better than I would have thought. Crackling lightning, deafening thunder.

And while it was startling the ears, the good Reverend Cartwright strode onto the stage wearing colorful

Biblical robes and carrying a staff. This was a very different get-up from the recent time when he'd set himself on fire trying to burn Beatles records. You had to admire him for trying again. Of course being Cartwright he stumbled as he moved to center stage.

He threw his hands wide the way he did when he healed people. His staff flew off stage right. And somewhere the kid with the tape recorder hit the thunder and lightning sound again.

"You heard the Lord. I will go to Pearson's Peak where I will wait until he contacts me with his word of how to bring this entire town to his ways. And I will broadcast my daily shows from there with a live remote so you will not have to fear for my well-being."

The smirkers were already laughing and shouting. "Pearson's Peak ain't a mountain!"

In case you allowed yourself to be misled by the Biblical use of the word "mountain," just as there is no ocean or surf in Iowa, just so there are no mountains. Pearson's Peak is a tall spot of red clay above the river road. It is approximately a thirty-foot drop to the pavement below. Many years ago, back when even the most elegant among us still used outhouses, somebody sarcastically named it after Pike's Peak.

This was typical Cartwright, the whole thing. His followers genuinely wanted to run the hippies out of town and no doubt Cartwright found them irritating. But this ham play and the word from the Lord was all to promote his radio show. I'm pretty sure Jesus never used a live remote, but then Jesus didn't have Cartwright's skill with self-promotion. Or confidence games if you prefer.

You see, Jesus ordered Cartwright to the mountain every year about this time. Cartwright did his communing inside a comfortable little trailer while all around him were booths offering religious pamphlets he bought in bulk at two cents each and charged $2.50 for. Then there were his self-published books, record albums, children's books and Jesus sweaters, caps and jackets. His church ladies sold burgers and hot dogs and pop at jacked-up prices. And every time he emerged from his trailer to speak to the two or three hundred people who'd gathered there, a plate was passed around. The shakedowns never ended.

He kept talking, or tried to. The smirkers kept shouting insults and laughing at him. Not even the cops walking among them could shut them up. Cartwright's flock turned on the smirkers and started chanting their own cleaned-up insults right back. Cartwright the mountaineer was drowned out completely.

And then finally, it broke. Whether the smirkers rushed the followers or the followers rushed the smirkers, it was hard to say, but somebody threw a punch at somebody and about a dozen bodies were entangled in pushing, shoving and throwing a few fists.

The cops rushed to form a broken line between the two groups. They shouted, too, for both groups to shut the hell up.

For the past few minutes I'd sensed somebody staring at me but in all the shouting I hadn't looked around. Now that I started scanning the people behind me I didn't see anybody taking any particular interest in me. These were the true onlookers. They'd come to the crash site just to check it out. They weren't followers and they weren't smirkers. I suspected that most of them in this blistering sweaty night were here for the yuks. This might well be more interesting than anything on at the drive-in (I'd checked and it was). I started to look back at the groups who were bringing the cops to understandable anger. But then peripherally I caught somebody waving. He'd quit waving by the time I'd started looking again. I was about to give up when I saw him lean from behind a tree and wave again.

Tommy Delaney, high school football player and tortured soul of his parents' many deadly battles, walked in my direction. I thought maybe he'd seen somebody behind me he wanted to talk to but then there he was putting out his hand.

As we shook he said, "I'm sorry I was such a jerk to you before, Mr. McCain. I ran into Sarah this afternoon and she told me you were a good guy and that I should apologize."

"I didn't know you and Sarah knew each other."

"Yeah. My uncle owns the used bookstore over on Main and Chandler. I used to work there sometimes. She was always coming in. She's a big reader." He had a shy smile. "We didn't get along at first. You know she can come on pretty strong with the hippie stuff. But eventually we got to be friends. I even took her to the movies a couple of times." Then he nodded to Kenny. "We sell a lot of your books there, Mr. Thibodeau."

"I wouldn't admit that to anybody, Tommy."

Tommy smiled but now his body tensed. Hands into fists, his eyes jittery. He gulped twice. He looked around at the melee that was calming down. He was going to tell me something. Then the tension and the anxiety drained from him and he said, "Well, I better get going. I—I'm not real popular with Mr. Mainwaring now. You know I've kinda lived there for the last year and a half. It was real peaceful there. But I don't think he wants me around anymore. I wanna see if I can patch things up. I hate to be—you know, banned from there for good or anything."

The sadness looked wrong hanging on the beefy teenager. He should be flattening players on the field or pouring himself a sloppy beer at a kegger or making it with a comely cheerleader in the backseat of a car. All that energy, all that popularity, all that raw strength— but now he was stooped again, bereft as an orphan in those Dust Bowl photographs of the Depression thirties. It wasn't difficult to imagine that he'd cried about this—or even that he might cry about it now, as soon as he was out of my sight.

"Did you want to tell me something, Tommy? I kind of got that sense a minute ago."

"Nah—I mean—" After a glance at Kenny and then at me, he said: "I just wanted to apologize."

He turned and left, quickly becoming a part of the crowd.

"I wonder what he wanted to tell you, McCain."

"Yeah, I wonder, too."

FIFTEEN

I WAS WORKING my ass off eating a bagel and reading the morning paper's version of the events that followed Kenny and me leaving the good Reverend Cartwright's play last night. Apparently things settled down enough for the program to continue. My favorite line in the story was: "According to most estimates, Pearson's Peak is not considered a mountain."

"Did you like the coffee this morning, Mr. C?"

"Great as usual." Jamie was sensitive about her coffee.

"I tried a new brand. I thought you might notice."

I put the paper down. "I was going to mention it the minute I stopped reading. Whatever brand it is, keep on buying it. It's terrific."

Her smile pleased me. I enjoyed seeing Jamie happy. Lately her blue eyes had lost their luster and her slight shoulders slumped. Between motherhood and her surfer-boy lazy bastard husband, she deserved to smile every once in awhile.

Which was when our door opened as if a pair of battering rams had been thrust against it. Jamie jumped in her seat, her hands covering her mouth, a sharp noise caught in her throat.

He stood in the doorway with his finger pointed at

me as if it was a weapon. "You son of a bitch." Then he glared at Jamie. "Get her out of here. And I mean now."

Jamie was already crying. I hurried around the desk. When my hands went to her shoulders I felt how rigid her entire body was. "Why don't you go somewhere for half an hour or so?"

"But where will I go, Mr. C?"

"The café down the street would be a good place. Get a donut and some coffee. It won't be as good as our coffee, of course."

She didn't laugh, just plucked a Kleenex from the box on her desk. And blew her nose; a hardy blow indeed. I helped her up from her chair, grabbed her purse and slid it under her arm.

All the time our guest stood there trying to restrain himself from attacking me.

"Will you be all right, Mr. C?"

"I'll be fine, Jamie. Now you go on and have a coffee break."

"But it's not even nine yet—"

"Get her the hell out of here and right now, McCain."

I walked her quickly to the door. Four steps across from the threshold she started to turn around to say something. I closed the door.

"You son of a bitch."

"You said that already, Paul."

After I was seated again, I said, "You could always sit down."

But Paul Mainwaring was seething. "I should tear your head off, McCain. But I've got stockholders and they wouldn't be happy about the bad publicity."

"Some people wouldn't consider it bad. They'd think you were a hero."

"That's just the kind of glib bullshit I'd expect from you." He was calming down enough to consider using the chair. He eyed it with great suspicion, as if it was about to attack him. "You've been asking a lot of questions that don't need to be asked. Dragging my family's name through the mud. I wanted you to find out who killed my daughter. But for some goddamn reason you started investigating my whole family." He was so angry he was spluttering.

"Sit down and tell me what you're so upset about."

In his blue golf shirt and chinos, he looked like any other millionaire playing hooky from the office. Except for the throbbing veins in his neck and temple. "I want you to stop right now. Period. And if you don't, I'm going to use every cent I have to make sure you won't have any business in this state again. I'm going to file a nuisance suit against you and leak all kinds of things about you to the press. There's a guy in Chicago who is famous for handling cases like this. He's destroyed a number of people. He doesn't care if he wins or loses the case as long as the other guy has to go on relief."

"Sounds like a nice fella. I'd like to meet him sometime."

His rage was back. He pounded my desk with enough power to cleave it in two. Or maybe three. "I'm sorry I ever had anything to do with you. I must have been out of my mind." Then he caught himself. "Twenty thousand dollars."

"Twenty thousand dollars. Nice round sum."

"It's yours if you give me a letter saying that you will never again work on the case of my daughter's murder and will never try to contact anybody even marginally involved."

"Correct me if I'm wrong, but you yourself just said you hired me to find out who killed Vanessa."

"You're not stupid, McCain. But you don't seem to understand that we know who the killer was. He took his own life. There is no more case. And there is certainly no reason to be investigating Eve. She's very upset right now and I don't blame her. Whatever she does with her life is her business. Do you understand that?"

Giving me the impression that he knew all about Eve's lovers. "Yes."

"Yes, you'll sign that document?"

"Yes, I understand why you're pissed and why she's pissed. But I was just trying to do my job."

"So you won't sign the document?"

"No, I won't."

He came up out of his chair with blood in his cheeks and spittle on his lips. "Then you're going to be very sorry. And if you ever approach my wife—or anybody in my house for that matter—I'll have you arrested."

There was no point in arguing. He needed to keep battering me with threats. He was exorcising the demons of a dead daughter, a faithless wife and now a minor private detective who could besmirch his reputation. Hating me made sense. He'd suffered more than anybody should have with the death of his daughter. I was only adding to his grief.

He leaned over my desk and jabbed a finger at me. "I thought you were a man of honor, McCain. But you had me fooled. You're just another grubby little opportunist."

Again there was no reason to defend myself. If I was an opportunist, I was a badly paid one. And even if I did manage to uncover the real murderer, nobody would be particularly interested past the usual twenty-four-hour time limit before another more interesting crime story came along. The trial would revive interest several months down the line but meanwhile I'd still be buying my boxer shorts at Sears and trying to find the station with the cheapest gas prices.

"You just remember what I said." But gone was the anger. In its place was only exhaustion. It was as if he, not me, had been the victim of his rancor. He even swayed a bit, like somebody who just might faint on you. His face was streaming with sweat and his shirt splotchy and dark in places.

As I watched him leave, he seemed to be a much older man than the one who'd come here maybe fifteen minutes ago. I heard his footsteps in the hall, slow, even shuffling, and then the exterior door open. It was several minutes before I heard his Jag fire up.

Jamie returned with a cardboard cup of coffee from the deli. She looked around as if Mainwaring might be hiding someplace, ready to pounce on her.

"He's gone."

"I was ready to call the police, Mr. C."

"I'm fine. He's upset about his daughter dying and it's affected his judgment, that's all. There can't be anything worse than losing your child."

"Oh, God, don't even say that. I look at little Laurie and I want to cry sometimes, thinking of all the terrible things that could happen to her. Sometimes I just want to lock us in a room and never leave so I can keep an eye on her all the time. But I have to go out. And Turk would help but he's, you know, busy with all his stuff."

Yes, too much to ask Surfer Boy to help with his child. I knew I'd soon be having one of those dreams where I separated Turk's head from his shoulders. I knew that broadsword would come in handy someday. Sam McCain, Barbarian.

I used line two to make several calls about pending cases, one in response to a bail bondsman who seemed to blame me for the disappearance of our mutual client.

"Sure, you don't have to worry, McCain. You get your fat fee one way or the other."

"Right. I inherited this stupid bastard from his brother who told me that while he did have a .38 in his pocket when the cops stopped him inside the supermarket, he wasn't planning to rob it. The only reason I took it is because the county attorney got way ahead of himself here. Even though this dipshit had a gun on him, it doesn't necessarily mean that he was going to rob the place. There's no evidence of that. I decided to help him out because I thought the law was overstepping. I got the county attorney to drop the robbery charge but he didn't have a license for the gun. And he had three priors."

A businessman's deep sigh. "I should've gone into the funeral business like my old man."

"I don't blame you. Getting to handle corpses all day is something I couldn't pass up, either."

A laugh rumbled from the phone. The guy was on the Pall Mall diet. "If you see this bastard, run him over for me, will you?"

"Will do."

As I was hanging up, line one rang and Jamie answered in her clear sweet voice and said, "One moment, please. I'll see if he's available." She put the line on hold and said, "It's Mrs. Eve Mainwaring."

Was she calling to tell me the same thing her husband just had—that I was to stay out of her life? I lifted the receiver and said, "Hello."

"I know my husband was at your office. I followed him."

"Any special reason you're following him?"

"Because he's not himself since Van died and I'm worried about him, what he might do. I was afraid—well, for some reason people don't seem to think he can be violent, he's so easygoing. But I've seen his violent side a few times during our marriage and he can be frightening. And I'm afraid I led him into something—Would it be possible to talk to you? Not at your office. Do you know where the Cotillion is?"

"Sure."

"How about eleven thirty? And don't worry, I'll pay your hourly fee."

"I don't care about the fee, Mrs. Mainwaring."

"We were introduced as Sam and Eve, let's keep it that way. I'll see you at eleven thirty."

As I hung up, I said to Jamie, "I'm going to eat lunch at the Cotillion."

"Petty cash I'll bet."

One of her many responsibilities was keeping track of the petty cash, never letting it get under fifty dollars. At first I'd been worried she might tell Surfer Boy about it. He'd find a way to con her out of some money. But one day, looking quite happy about herself as she dished out some money for me, she said, "It's a good thing I never told Turk about this. He'd be after me all the time if I did."

THE COTILLION WAS located on a small hill above the river. Before I reached it, I turned right onto a narrow road that hadn't been asphalted in years. I kept thinking about Tommy Delaney and the way he'd waved to me last night, as if he wanted to tell me something. I still wondered what it was.

This time when I pulled up at his white clapboard house that the casual eye might mistake for abandoned—if houses took on the emotional tenor of their residents, this one reminded me of a wound—there was no screaming, no sound at all except for a crop-dusting plane flying low and poisoning the air and the earth. In the backyard I saw Tommy shooting baskets at a hoop attached to a one-stall garage. He brought a football player's zeal to making lay-ups. He made three of them by the time I reached him. He was dribbling his way back to start again when he saw me approach. He pawed a right hand across his yellow high school T-shirt. His red hair was in his face, giving him the blunt sweaty

look of a big hearty animal. Only his blue eyes denied
the impression; he seemed to be afraid.

"Morning, Tommy."

"You're not supposed to be here, Mr. McCain."

"Oh? Why not?"

As he glanced toward the house I heard the back door
slam and in seconds a scrawny woman several inches
shorter than me stalked into view, her hands stuffed
into the pockets of her faded housedress. She was leath-
ery and intense and I imagined she could hold her own
with that sparring partner she'd married. If she'd had a
gun I would have been dead. "You get your butt off my
property and leave my son alone." To Tommy: "You go
on and get in the house."

He didn't bother to show embarrassment. Mrs. Hit-
ler had spoken and her word was so final it was like
arguing with wind or sunlight. He turned into a lost
puppy, all sunken shoulders and hanging head, tucked
the basketball under one arm and shuffled toward the
house as if he was going to be executed.

"If you're not off my property in sixty seconds I'm
calling the law on you."

I could see her as one of those hardscrabble prairie
women of frontier Iowa standing with a shotgun defending her roost and her children while her man was away.
Read a history of the frontier and you quickly learn that
women worked harder than men, that "a woman's work
is never done" had it right. Consequently, they were not
to be trifled with. As was the case with this scrappy,
wild-eyed woman.

"I take it you got a call from Paul Mainwaring."

"And so what if I did?" She stepped closer, squinting with a pirate's eye at the intruder. "You're no friend of my son's and Mr. Mainwaring *is*. He helped my whole family since my husband got injured down to the mill. And he's going to see to it that Tommy gets into college. Now you get your butt in that car of yours and get out of here."

Tommy Delaney was watching us from behind the soiled white curtains in the kitchen. He wanted to tell me something. I had no doubt of it.

"All I'm trying to do is find out who really killed Mainwaring's daughter. For some reason he doesn't want me to."

"He said you'd be talking crazy if you showed up out here. And he sure was right. I guess you don't read the papers, huh? That Cameron boy killed her because he was jealous she was seeing other boys. I'm just glad my Tommy got over her. He used to moon around here like a sick calf. I wouldn't say this to Mr. Mainwaring, but it seems to me that Vanessa brought a lot of this on herself. You can't flaunt around the way she did, have all these boys coming after you and treating them the way she did."

"She didn't deserve to die."

In the blue-sky morning, birds bursting from the green, green trees, a sun-scorched cow standing on a distant hill, the little prairie woman was quiet for the moment considering—or reconsidering—what she'd said. "I shouldn't have put it that way. Whatever she did, she didn't deserve to die for it." But pity was not anything to be indulged in. It weakened you. "But she shouldn't have lived the way she did. She made life hell for a lot of people."

I kept thinking about Tommy "mooning around like a sick calf." I needed to talk to him. He'd been part of the Mainwaring family. He might know something that I needed to know.

The phone rang inside. She didn't take her eyes from me. "That'll be somebody calling for me. But I'm gonna stand here till you get in that car and drive off. Now move. You don't have no business here and if you come back—or you try to talk to Tommy—I'm gonna call Mr. Mainwaring the way he told me to. And then you're gonna be in trouble. He won't fool around with you. He's got the money and the power to put you out of business. And those're his words. Now go."

Tommy came to the screen door in back and stuck his head out. "Phone for you, Mom." He wouldn't look at me.

She didn't have the same problem. She started toward me, stopped and scowled at me a final time. "Now you git."

I scowled right back but I got.

SIXTEEN

THE NAME COTILLION implies debutante coming-out parties and the type of fancy balls where Civil War colo-
nels made plans to deflower the local virgins later on
in the gin-crazed night. This particular Cotillion was
one of those modern glass-and-stone boxes that were
colder than any of the drinks they served. Its reputation
for excellent cuisine came, or so I had surmised, from
the fact that you paid a lot of money for very little food.
This is my small-town side, I know, and when I go out
to eat I don't want to gorge myself but I do want something more substantial than two inches of, say, steak
covered with oily sauce and topped with some kind of
vegetation that looks like a fungus. Not that it tastes
bad; it doesn't. The food is tasty, no doubt about it. But
even a mouse would ask for his money back when he
saw the size of the entrée.

But it is one of the local status symbols to be seen
dining here and the dearth of a substantial meal is often
explained this way: "This is how they serve food in
New York."

"You mean so tiny?"

"Right. Out here we're raised on meat and potatoes
and apple pie. We're used to stuffing ourselves. But this
is how people eat in the big cities."

I've heard this conversation, in various formations, for the five years the Cotillion has been open. If somebody dining here ever said, "You know, for what you get, this food is overpriced," the roof would collapse.

While I waited for Eve Mainwaring, I chomped on some breadsticks I'd swiped from the deserted table behind me. One of the waiters caught me. Instead of anger he flashed me the worst look of all, pity.

She arrived a few minutes after twelve. When people are late the least they can do is rush in out of breath and start their apologizing even before they reach the table. Goddesses are excepted from this rule. In fact I'm pretty sure there's a Constitutional amendment about that.

I'd managed to get a table along the wall that gave us moderate privacy. But I wasn't sure why I'd bothered. She did as much glad-handing as a politician ten points behind on the day before the election. She was chignon-ready with a golden linen dress and two-inch heels that gave her the air of importance she wanted. Given the heat, the other women here wore simpler outfits, comfort being at least as important as style. By the time she reached our table the public smile had become grotesque, as if it had been pasted on like a Groucho Marx mustache.

Like all good goddesses, apologizing was out of the question. She stood by her chair, apparently waiting for me to leap up and be a gentleman, but after she got over that foolishness, she yanked out the chair and seated herself. The smile still in place. "Do you have a match?"

"You want me to give you a hot foot?"

"Are you supposed to be funny?"

"My five-year-old nephew thinks I'm hilarious."

"I don't doubt that. Now be a gentleman and give me a light."

I pitched the matches across the table.

"You are really a disgusting little man."

"Do you want to hear what I think about *you*?"

She lighted her cigarette the way a Vogue model would—with that perfect angle of head—and then sailed my matches back to me. "I really don't give a damn what you think about me. I know you've been snooping and that's what I want to talk to you about. Or wanted to, past tense. I didn't realize till now that you're one of them."

"Martians?"

"Locals."

"The great unwashed. And you're right, I am one of them."

"Then this will be a complete waste of my time and yours. I came here ready to confide in you but now I'd never give you the time of day."

"You were late."

She sat back and stared at me. Then she began laughing. It was a very merry laugh and I liked it despite myself. The sound conveyed pleasure and irony. "God, is that why you're being such a jerk? Because I was late?"

"You owe me an apology." As soon as the words came out I realized how pathetic they were. An eight-year-old sulking because his feelings had been hurt.

She laughed again, damn her. "Well, then, we'll just have to do something about your little feelings being hurt, won't we? I happened to have had a flat tire and didn't feel up to changing a tire—which I've done many times, I assure you. I didn't want to ruin this dress which I like so I had to walk up to a house and ask the woman—one of the 'great unwashed,' as you said—if I might use her phone. She said yes. She was very sweet. I called the service station where we take our cars. The woman let me wait inside and even gave me coffee and a very tasty cookie. Chocolate chip, homemade, if you're interested. I would've called here and left a message for you but I thought the station would send a truck sooner than they did—both their trucks were busy at the same time. But here you were suffering for thirty-four minutes all alone and unloved, cramming breadsticks into your mouth. Flecks of which, by the way, are all over your tie and jacket."

Fortunately, the waiter appeared and I didn't have to respond to her. Her smile was always smug but now it was downright scornful. Before I could get a word out, she said, "I'll have a glass of white wine and this little fellow here will have a Coke. I'm sorry to see he's been sitting here all this time without ordering anything. They tried to teach him manners at the home but sometimes it's a slow process. We'll need more time to decide what we'll want to eat. And do you happen to have a bib he could use?"

The young waiter's face shifted from confusion to amusement and back to confusion. He wanted to smile about all her imperiousness but was that proper when the guy sitting across from her was from some kind of "home"? This could mean anything from cooties to frontal lobotomy.

After he was gone, she said, "I'm pretty sure that Paul will be joining us. He followed me here."

"Why would he do that?"

"He doesn't want me to talk to you."

"I hope he's calmed down some since he was in my office. He was ready for a net and the bughouse."

And then he was there and in the Cotillion. He was a celebrity. By now the restaurant was filling up with credit-card businessmen who recognized the most resplendent of the peacocks among them. Paul Mainwaring. Where his wife had made a ballet out of finding her table, Mainwaring moved relentlessly, flicking nods and waves to people, but never smiles. We both sat silently watching him invade us which he did with dispatch and economy.

"I don't want to make a scene here, McCain. Otherwise I'd pound your face in right now."

"And very nice to see you, too, Mainwaring. And thanks for sparing me the trouble of kicking you in the balls while you were pounding my face in."

The goddess, displeased, rolled her eyes. "Will you two shut up for God's sake? This is ridiculous. And by the way, Paul, I don't appreciate you following me around."

He pulled a padded brown leather chair closer to his wife and sat down. Then his hand went up like a spear and the waiter rushed for us as if summoned by not one but two Popes.

"The usual scotch and water, Mr. Mainwaring?" A slight tremor in the young voice.

"Of course."

To Eve, the waiter said, "All we have is a lobster bib, Mrs. Mainwaring. Would that be all right for this—" He eyed me as if I was road kill. "This little fella?"

"Oh, a lobster bib would be perfect."

He started to bow from the waist then caught himself. "I'll bring it back with Mr. Mainwaring's drink."

"Thank you so much."

Mainwaring's eyes had narrowed; his mouth was a bitter slash. The moment the waiter was out of earshot, he snapped, "You're still doing that stupid 'bib' gag? Isn't it about time you give it up, Eve?" He had shifted his wrath from me to his wife.

"Oh, that's right, forgive me. I apologize for trying to have some fun. That's against the rules, isn't it?"

"In case you've forgotten, my daughter is dead. I know you two didn't get along and most of that was her fault but couldn't you at least try to fake some regret?"

The first thing I tried to figure out was how sincere her tears were. They were silver and lovely against her perfect cheekbones, and even the single sob was just as startling as a cynic might say it was meant to be. But there was always the possibility that Mainwaring's words had had their desired effect and had actually surprised and hurt her.

Mainwaring sighed, glanced at me, shook his head, and leaned over to slide his arm around his wife's shoulders. Her head was down now. She was quiet. "Forgive me, Eve. I—I'm just confused and I'm taking it out on you. With Van gone—I don't need to deal with a scandal on top of this."

He put a big hand under her chin and raised her head.

The tears were gone from her cheeks but stood in her eyes. She used her starched napkin to dab her nose and then eyes. "And right in front of McCain."

"You were the one who wanted to meet him. I asked you not to." But his voice was sympathetic this time. He kissed her on the cheek.

She placed her hand over his. "But he already knows some of it." She inclined her head toward me as she spoke. "Maybe if we explained things to him—"

He was a man long accustomed to getting his way. Since things weren't going so well now he took his arm from her shoulders and sat there glowering. "Why don't we just get a microphone and tell everybody in the restaurant?"

"I was trying to be helpful, Paul. He's going to find out anyway."

"You think I'm going to sit here while you're telling him?"

Irritation was in her voice and eyes now. "You don't have to be here while I do it if you don't want to. Maybe I can persuade him to see things from our side."

"He's a private investigator who works for Judge Whitney. He's not exactly a good prospect for keeping a secret."

She looked directly at me and said, "Paul and I have an open marriage."

PART THREE

SEVENTEEN

So THERE WE had it. Open marriage was something I read about in *Playboy* and the kind of paperbacks Kenny writes. Sometimes you see brief stories about it on TV news but it's always reported as if the newsman is handling feces. Even the swankiest of people—despite the protestations that they love their spouse devoutly and are positive that sleeping around has no effect on the children—come off as selfish and decadent. What's wrong with these people? Haven't they ever heard of plain old all-American adultery?

The sexual revolution, which we heard about as often as we heard Pentagon lies about the war, had come to Black River Falls, Iowa.

"Well there, you've said it, Eve. Happy now?"

"Oh, sure, Paul. I'm delirious. Can't you tell?"

"Did your girls know about this?"

"What's that got to do with anything?" Mainwaring was ready for an argument.

"You said Vanessa changed after Eve came. I wonder if she ever found out about your arrangement."

"Not that I know of."

"We were very discreet."

"Look at his face," Mainwaring said. "He just can't wait to tell everybody he knows."

"You're right, Paul. I'm thinking of calling Walter Cronkite."

"I'm so damned sick of you. I wish I'd never hired you."

"Believe it or not, Paul, I'm not going to tell anybody. If your arrangement doesn't have any bearing on Vanessa's murder it doesn't matter. But I have to remind you that being discreet in a town this size is difficult. Your friends at the Sleepy Time got guilty and called you, but if they told me, how many other people did they tell?"

"I'll talk to them and they'll be damned sorry. Damned sorry. They needed money a few years ago and were overextended at the bank. I loaned them several thousand dollars at three percent. I can call that in any time I choose."

Again, Eve put her hand over his. "They're friends of ours, Paul. Keep that in mind."

"Some friends."

"I just want to ask one more time—"

Eve spoke before Mainwaring could. "The girls didn't know anything about it. We were very careful. They disliked me simply because I was trying to replace their mother. That happens all the time with widowers."

Not that it could have had anything to do with Eve's personality or the way she treated Marsha or her need to be number one babe in residence.

"Are we about done here?" Mainwaring had taken to drumming his fingers on the table. As chairman of the board he believed that when he was through talking the meeting was over. Who wanted to hear the prattle of lesser beings?

"We haven't eaten yet, Paul."

"Are you really hungry, Eve?"

She bowed her head slightly as if in prayer. I'd just demoted her from a fine actress to a ham. A very clumsy move. "No, I guess you're right. Van's dead and that's all that matters."

Suddenly soap opera actors looked pretty good to me.

"I told you what I'd pay you to write that letter, McCain. Twenty thousand. Now I want you to add a line about our marital arrangement. That you'll stay silent about that, too."

"I won't write it."

"Then you're a fool."

"No, I'm not. You'll just have to take my word for it. I won't tell anybody as long as it doesn't have any bearing on your daughter's death."

"Which means that you're going to keep on asking questions and putting your nose into things that aren't any of your business."

"That isn't my way of looking at it but yes, I still don't think the Cameron boy killed your daughter. And I don't think he committed suicide, either."

"I was hoping we were going to be friends, Sam. You're making that impossible." I wasn't sure what the word "friends" meant to her but I was probably flattering myself if I thought there was a hint of lust in her definition.

"Let's get out of here." Mainwaring had taken her arm and popped her out of her seat so that they were both glaring down at me accusingly. "If I see you anywhere around my property, McCain, I'm going to have you arrested."

"You're a very big disappointment to me, Sam," Eve said.

As soon as they started to leave, the waiter returned. "Aren't they going to eat?"

"No, but I am." I gave him my order. "Is there a pay phone nearby?"

"Just off the lobby."

"Thanks."

When Marsha answered, she said, "The Mainwaring residence."

"Marsha, it's Sam."

"You sound as if something's wrong."

"You didn't get this call, Marsha. I just had lunch with Paul and Eve—well, we planned to have lunch let's say—and they both made it clear that they don't want anything to do with me. So please don't tell them I called."

"All right. I won't."

"I appreciate it, Marsha. Is Nicole there?"

"She's up in her room. She's got a small TV up there and rarely comes down. This morning I brought her breakfast up to her."

"Does she have a phone in her room?"

"The girls each had their own line. I can't imagine what Mr. Mainwaring had to pay the phone company every month."

"Would you mind going up there and asking her if I could talk to her?"

"That's no problem, Sam. But you'll have to call her back."

"That's fine. I just don't want to be on the phone with her when Paul and Eve get back. They wouldn't be very happy to know she's talking to me."

"I'll hurry."

"Thanks again, Marsha."

"I imagine she'll talk to you. She told me she likes you. I'll be right back."

The wait was only a few minutes. "Here's her private number. She said she'd be happy to talk to you."

"Marsha, I'm sending you a Cadillac."

I could feel her smile through the phone. "I'd settle for a new Plymouth. My old one is wearing out. It's ten years old and needs a lot of help. It's sort of like me."

"You sure didn't look like it when I was out there."

"You sure can sling it, Sam. Good luck with Nicole."

While I dialed I thought about Paul and Eve Mainwaring. They had a secret worth keeping. Paul worked in a military environment and while generals likely had frequent orgies with various animals, the Pentagon made sure that these were classified as Top Secret as nuclear warhead locations. People with military secrets were blackmailed all the time. Mainwaring had opened himself up to that and to being tainted with the stigma of perversion if his behavior was made public.

When Nicole came on the phone, she said, "My father is going to be mad I talked to you."

"I know that. And he may well be on his way home right now. I had lunch with him just a few minutes ago."

"I don't give a shit what he thinks, Mr. McCain. I just said that to warn you."

"Is there a place we could meet around four o'clock?"

"I ride my bike up to Whittier Point a lot. There's a pavilion up there. I like to sit in the corner of it and read."

"That'd be great. Four o'clock, all right?"

"I'll be there."

I spent the next hour and a half in the office working on a probate case. Somewhere at midpoint the phone rang and Jamie said, "It's Commander Potter, Mr. C."

Potter said, "You won't like me after this call."

"What makes you think I like you now?"

"Very funny, asshole. Paul Mainwaring just left here and he's convinced the chief that you're to be arrested if you keep bothering people about his daughter's death."

"What would he arrest me for?"

"He'll figure out something. He'll haul you in and then you'll bail out and then he'll haul you in again when you start bothering people again. And so on. Why don't you save yourself and me a lot of trouble and just give it up?"

"Maybe because I'm on to something."

"Uh-huh. If you were on to something you'd have called me about it already."

"You make a lot of assumptions."

"Just give it up, Sam, because I'm the one who'll have to bring you in and that won't be fun for either of us."

"I can't do that, Mike."

"Well, then I can't keep from arresting you." And with that he hung up.

I went back to work on the probate case, more distracted than ever. Mainwaring was moving in on me now. As Potter had hinted, this was nothing more than harassment. But Mainwaring knew many powerful people in this state, including the governor himself. If Mainwaring wanted to call in some favors, he could. For relief I kept glancing at my wristwatch. An hour and a half before I drove out to Whittier Point. At least the scenery would change.

The probate case I was working on was ridiculous but modestly profitable so I'd taken it. When their old man died, leaving two thousand dollars and a shotgun to his daughter, his son came to me and said he wanted to contest it. This seemed curious to me because the son was a prominent psychiatrist in Iowa City. He'd grown up here with his old man and his sister. It was the latter he was after. According to him, the old man had always favored her. She got all the new clothes, all the money to go east for college and, more than anything, all the love and support because she reminded his father of his late wife. He was close to tears while he was telling me, biting his lip and twisting his hands. I felt like the shrink listening to a patient. I wouldn't be recommending his services to anybody I knew.

When I heard Jamie say, "Oh, hi, may I help you?" I raised my head and stared straight into the eyes of Sarah Powers. She and another girl stood in the doorway of my office, both looking nervous.

"Hi, Sarah."

"Hi." Sarah wore a blue work shirt and jeans. She

held a cigarette aloft with great delicacy, the ash at least half an inch long.

"Let me help you with that," Jamie said. Seconds later she slid an ashtray under the cigarette. Sarah flicked the ash and thanked her.

"This is Glenna, Sam. I wondered if you'd talk to us. Glenna knows something about what happened the night Vanessa died." Glenna was a thin, tall girl with blonde hair in a ponytail and quick, suspicious brown eyes. Her T-shirt read stop the war now!

"Sure. Come on in."

Jamie dragged an extra chair in front of my desk so both girls could sit. Glenna's buckskin, fringed shirt had to be damned hot on a day like this. When she sat down she leaned back and dragged a package of Winstons from the front pocket of her jeans. The pack was pinched by now so that when she got a cigarette out she had to straighten it up.

"Glenna just came to the commune a couple of weeks ago. She's a real good cook. She made a pumpkin pie last week that knocked everybody out. Plus she's got her college degree. But she dropped out of society just like the rest of us because it's all such bullshit."

That remark caused Jamie to show some interest in the conversation. She stopped her typing to listen. The remark caused me to force a somber look on lips that wanted to smile. The casual way so many of them said "we dropped out of society" had always struck me as funny. They shopped at grocery stores, they had cars that needed repairs, some of them had to pay light and gas and phone bills, and they weren't averse to going to doctors or free clinics. They'd dropped out of the parts of society they didn't like but they were very much still citizens.

"And she saw Vanessa go into that barn."

I straightened up. This required full attention. "What time was this, Glenna?"

"She says it was right after supper. She was going to the barn to see if this kitten had come back. She found this little black-and-white one—"

"Sarah, why don't you let Glenna talk?"

Sarah blushed bright as an autumn apple. "I'm sorry. But she's shy. She asked me to do the talking."

"I'm sorry. I need to hear it from her."

She took a deep breath. "She, uh, thinks you're like, you know, one of the pigs."

"Why, that's not true, Sarah. Mr. C isn't a pig. You shouldn't say things like that."

"If that's true, she should tell me I'm a pig herself."

"You're a pig," Glenna said.

"All right, now that we've got that established, how about telling me what you saw that night."

"I'm only doing this because I know Neil never murdered anybody. That's something only pigs do. Neil was transcendental and so am I."

"Good enough. So what about Vanessa that night?"

"I saw her behind the barn. She was arguing with Richard."

"You could hear them arguing?"

"No, but it was obvious. She sort of shoved him once and started to walk away but he grabbed her by the arm."

"They didn't see you?"

"I was over by that old silo. They couldn't see me in the shadows. Plus it was starting to get real dark."

"How long did you watch them?"

"Probably ten, eleven minutes, something like that. Until she ran inside the barn and he went in after her. That time I did hear them—at least, I heard him shout her name. I didn't want to get involved because Richard thinks we spy on him anyway. He can get real paranoid."

"Why didn't you come forward before?"

This time she took a deep breath. When she exhaled the sound was ragged, anxious. "I got in a little trouble in Iowa City. I'm on probation. I don't want to get hassled by the pigs again."

"What happened in Iowa City?"

"They can't take a joke is what happened in Iowa City."

"That doesn't exactly tell me anything."

"Go ahead, Glenna. Tell him."

"It doesn't matter, Sarah."

"Sure it matters. So please tell me."

"I puked into this bucket and then threw the bucket at a cop. I got vomit all over him. All we were doing was trying to take over this dean's office. This dean was a real pig."

The hell of it was she seemed to be serious. I wasn't sure how to deal with someone who didn't understand that throwing a bucket of puke at somebody just might be considered an aggressive and unlawful act. "Can't imagine why the cop'd be pissed off about that."

"I'm glad you never try to be sarcastic. I told you he'd be a pig, Sarah."

As I'd said so many times, most of the hippies I'd met over the past few years I'd liked. I agreed with them about the war, about the materialism of our society, about the alienation so many of us felt. Just as there were a few hippie haters in town, there were also a few hippie lunatics and right now I was sitting across from one of them.

"All I care about right now is that you'd be willing to testify to what you just said. Under oath."

"I don't think so."

"Hey, Glenna, you promised me you would."

"I said I 'might.' But I don't like this jerk. At all."

"Forget about him. He doesn't matter—no offense, Sam—what matters is that you're willing to admit the truth to the cops. And save my brother's reputation."

"Well, if I do it, that's the *only* reason I'll do it."

"That's all I care about," I said. "Sarah, I'll leave it up to you to hold her to this. The first thing I need to do is talk to Richard. This doesn't mean he killed her."

"See what I mean, Sarah? That's why I didn't want to come here. He's already making excuses for Richard. They're big buddies."

"She hates Richard, Sam. She thinks she should be running the commune."

Somehow that's not a surprise, I thought. But I didn't say it, of course, not with Rasputin sitting directly in front of me.

"He thinks he's so cool," Glenna said.

"She used to live with Richard."

"He doesn't believe any of the things he says about the revolution," Glenna said, managing to light a cigarette while saying this. "He has two credit cards."

"Maybe he needs them," Sarah suggested quietly.

"You think Lenin had credit cards?"

"I need to get out of here. I have some appointments. One of them will be to go see Richard. In the meantime, Sarah, I'd appreciate it if you'd make sure that Glenna is willing to tell her story to the authorities if need be."

"That's cool. Now he's not talking to me. He's only talking to you."

But Sarah was already dragging herself and Glenna to their feet and didn't respond. I think that she was as tired of Stalin's daughter as Jamie and I were.

"I'll talk to you soon, Sam."

"Thanks, Sarah. And thank you, too, Glenna. I appreciate you helping us like this." *You crazy bitch.* But of course that was a thought meant only for me, myself and I. Like Sarah, I had to abide Glenna's nastiness in order to ensure her testimony.

At the door, Sarah turned back and gave me a frown, a shrug and a nod toward Glenna, who was preceding her into the hall. I wished she would have drawn an invisible circle around her head, the way people do to indicate that somebody is nuts. But then Glenna just might have been packing a flame thrower and melted Sarah down on the spot.

After we heard the outside door open and close, Jamie said, "That woman scares me. And she shouldn't have talked to you the way she did."

"Well, she'll be helpful to us if Richard was involved as she claims."

"Turk thinks hippies should be put in prison. He says they don't contribute anything to society. And he says boys with long hair are nothing but girls anyway and make him sick."

Let's see. Turk the wife-abuser, Turk the willfully unemployed, Turk who lives off his wife's work, Turk the leader of Iowa's only surfer band, thinks hippies should be sent to prison. It seemed that the ones who hassled hippies the most were the bikers, the local thugs and the hillbillies from the Hills—you know, the cream of local society. No surprise that Turk was among them.

"I just say live and let live, like most people around here do."

As I was passing her desk, I bent over and kissed the top of her head.

"Gee, thanks, Mr. C." The blush just made her all the cuter.

I was about out the door. In fact I was one step over the office threshold when the phone rang. When I was four steps over the threshold and making my way to the outside door, Jamie said, "It's Mr. Federman. Do you want to talk to him?"

"Hey," he said. "I call at a bad time?" The people at the Wilhoyt agency were always polite.

"No. It's fine. Just real busy."

"Well I found out two things that might interest you. Eve, original name Sharon Carmichael, has been named in two different divorce cases by very unhappy wives. She has also been married to two wealthy older gentlemen. She got a small sum from one when he kicked her out for cheating on him and nothing from the other one because he threatened to send around the photos his private investigator snapped of her. Her name was variously Sharon Downes and Sylvia Tralins. I got this from two newspapermen. Just thought you'd like to know. Should I keep digging?"

"Definitely. I just wonder if Mainwaring knew about any of this."

He laughed. "The way you described how hooked he is—you think it would've made any difference?"

EIGHTEEN

THE COMMUNE WAS busy. Four or five people worked the sprawling garden, two two-man units were fixing drainpipes and a front door and two women were washing a van vivid with peace symbols in various colors. Grace Slick was urging people to violence (from her safe posh digs on the West Coast of course) and a dog was yipping his disagreement. I wanted to shake his paw.

As I walked to the front porch of the nearest house a few people looked me over and apparently decided I wasn't worth even sneering at. A Negro kid named Jim Ryan came out the front door carrying a toolbox. He was tall and fleshy but not fat. A few of the more ardent racists in town had hassled him many times. One time he decided to hassle them back. It turned into another case where Cliffie wanted to charge him but the county attorney's office said no, he'd just been defending himself. The good people of the town, who far outnumber the bad, wrote many letters to the newspaper talking about the "riffraff" that had picked on Ryan and given Black River Falls a name it didn't deserve.

Ryan had been one of those rare perfect clients—bright, quiet, amenable to following my instructions. Today he wore his "Power to the People" T-shirt and jeans. He smiled when he saw me. "Lot of people around here don't seem to like you much."

"It's the same in town, Jim."

He set the toolbox down. "I used to build homes in the summers. I collected a lot of stuff. You lookin' for Sarah?" He was talking loud, over Grace Slick.

"Donovan."

His dark eyes changed expression. "He's been in his room since early last night. He doesn't want anybody to bother him. I knocked once last night and he called me a bunch of names. Pissed me off. He's a nasty son of a bitch, way he runs this place. I'll be moving on pretty soon. Can't hack it here any more with him around."

"Any idea why he's holed up?"

"You're askin' the wrong guy, Mr. McCain. I never could figure him out except he's a jerk. I admit we need a leader here just to keep things running right. But we don't need an egomaniac."

A woman came out wearing a craftsman's denim apron. She must have been in charge of the music because it died just as I heard a "See you in the barn, Jim." She glanced at me. Her lips flattened into displeasure. She hurried on.

"Another admirer."

"They think you didn't defend us very well from all the bad publicity. Not all of them think that, not me and the majority. But some of them. They're lookin' for somebody to blame because they think maybe they'll all have to move because of some of the people in town. I kept tryin' to tell them that there wasn't anything you could do. But you know how stoners are."

"I guess I don't."

He grinned. "Sometimes they make me ashamed I enjoy drugs as much as I do."

The interior of the house had been cleaned up and painted. The furnishings in the front room came from the Salvation Army or someplace similar. The old stuff has faces—the weary couch, the tortured chair, the wounded ottoman. It was no different upstairs where air mattresses and sleeping bags ran three or four to a room. The smells ran to pot and smoke and wine and sex. A kitten so small she would fit in the palm of my hand accompanied me as I tried to find Richard Donovan. The walls of the hallway were colorful and baleful with posters of Che, Bobby Rush, Nixon, Southern cops.

My search ended at the only room with a closed door. I tried the doorknob and found that it was also locked. I knocked: "Richard, it's McCain. Open up."

So our little game began. I'd knock and he'd stay silent. I had my usual rational reaction to impotence; I kept rattling the doorknob. It would magically open; I just knew it.

Finally, he said, "I don't feel like talking. Just go away."

"If I don't talk to you, I'll talk to Mike Potter."

"Is that supposed to be a threat?"

"I've got a witness who saw you arguing with Vanessa right before she was killed."

The silence again.

"You hear me?"

"Yeah, I heard you all right and I bet it was that bitch Glenna who told you, too."

"Doesn't matter who it was. Now open up."

After a long minute he was in the doorway, shirtless, barefoot and sullen. He was doing a James Dean, his hands shoved deep into his pockets. From what I could see his room was clean and orderly, almost military in the precise way he'd laid it out. "So we argued a little. That's all it was."

"What did you argue about?"

"That's none of your business."

"I'm told she shoved you and started to walk away but you grabbed her by the arm. And then followed her into the barn shouting her name."

"You know the kind of lawyers my old man has access to? He'd take some bitch like Glenna apart on the stand."

"You're not convincing me you didn't kill Vanessa."

He leaned against the doorframe as if he might fall down if he didn't have support. His eyes went through three quick and remarkable expressions—anger, hurt, fear. "I shouldn't ever have hooked up with Glenna. She's psycho and I mean completely. Jealous of any girl who even looked at me."

"That why you broke it off with her?"

"I can't believe she still hates me. That was almost six months ago."

He took a minute to jerk a pack of Marlboros from his back pocket. He knew how to stall. He set a world record finding a book of matches in the other back pocket then getting the smoke lighted. "I had a little thing with somebody."

"Vanessa."

His body tensed at the mention of her name. "She and Neil were having problems."

"So you stepped in."

"She wanted it." The absolute lord and master of the commune was whimpering now. "I saw her in town one night and we ended up going to a movie in Iowa City. A French flick. She was a pretty cool girl for a hole like Black River Falls. Then we just started seeing each other—you know, on the sly." His gaze fell away from me. He got real interested in how his cigarette was burning. "I didn't want Neil to find out. I didn't want him to think I was moving in on his chick."

I forced the laugh back down my throat. "Yeah, you wouldn't want him to think anything like that."

This time his eyes tried to put burning holes in my face. "We were friends."

"You're a noble son of a bitch, no doubt about it."

He moved back, started to slam the door but I was too quick. In a past life I must have sold encyclopedias. I had my foot planted in front of said door and it wasn't going anywhere. "What happened when he found out?"

"Who said he found out?"

"Don't waste my time. Of course he found out. It's hard to sneak around in this commune or in town for that matter. Somebody must have spotted you."

He touched the fingers that held his cigarette to his forehead as if somebody had just driven a railroad spike into it. "Glenna followed me one night. She saw us and told Neil. He—" I wasn't sure if the shrug was meant to impress me or himself. "He was crazy. He threatened to kill me. Then I didn't give a damn about him anymore. And neither did Van. She was afraid of him in fact."

"Leading up to the night she was killed."

"What?"

"You still haven't told me what you were arguing about with her."

"You know every goddamn thing. How about you telling me?"

"That she didn't want to see you anymore and that there wasn't any point in bothering her the way you had been."

I wasn't sure if it was an illusion or whether his face had paled.

"That seemed to be the pattern. Whenever the guy got too close to her she got scared and walked away. And that's what happened to you, too, wasn't it?"

The scowl didn't work because he looked tired now. "You think whatever you want. But you better have some proof. Like I said, McCain, my old man has some very prominent lawyers. They'd eat you alive."

"I wouldn't go anywhere if I was you."

The scowl hadn't worked but he had more success with the smirk. "Sure thing, little man."

I withdrew my foot. The door slammed shut. I wondered how long it would take him to call his old man. The prodigal son returns home. In bad need of a big-time mouthpiece.

WHITTIER POINT WAS in favor when it was used by the kids of a grade school a block away. Then the grade school was consolidated with a larger school and

Whittier Point was left to lie fallow. The city kept the grass mown on the area around the large pavilion but all the playground equipment was gone. Without supervision the city would be asking for a lawsuit; hell, even with supervision there'd been lawsuits. Hot weekends families still trekked up here but on workdays it was often empty except for school-age lovers lost in their own obsession with each other.

Until nearly four thirty my only companions were quicksilver birds lighting on the empty picnic tables and two stray dogs who kept their noses to the cement floor as if uranium might be found under it.

For the first time I considered Richard Donovan a real suspect. Neil Cameron had been his rival for Vanessa. He'd been seen arguing with her not long before her murder. And he'd gone rich boy on me when I'd asked him if he'd killed her. Telling somebody you're going to get world-class lawyers to save you doesn't inspire confidence in your innocence.

And naturally I wondered why Nicole wasn't here yet. Maybe she'd changed her mind. Maybe she'd decided that she'd angered her father enough already by talking to me.

I got up and started walking around the area outside the pavilion. The birds had that day's-end sound and a cordial, solemn weariness seemed to settle on the trees and grass and the small lake just over the west side of the hill. There were moments when I wanted to be a kid again, hurrying home to my collection of paperbacks and comic books, the only realm in which I was really myself. My dad would still be alive and my mom and he would be laughing about something adult just as I entered the kitchen and asked when supper would be ready. I could even put up with my bratty sister whom I loved despite all my protests to the contrary.

Then I saw her.

The winding paved road ended up in a steep grade if you wanted to veer off and reach the pavilion. But she rode her ten-speed with energy and skill. As she drew near she waved; the gesture was girly and sweet. But then the front tire swerved and she was quickly dumped on the grass.

I ran over to her. She'd been thrown facedown but she was quick to roll over on her back with her arms flung wide. She was gasping for breath. Her eyes fluttered as if she might faint. I knelt down next to her and felt her racing pulse. Her breath still came in bursts and a whimper played in her mouth.

"I guess I should've taken the car." That she'd managed the sentence with such clarity reassured me she was all right. Still, it was strange that a girl of her age, in apparent good health, would be worn out to the point where she'd lost control of her bicycle.

I helped her to her feet and looked for any cuts or scrapes. She fell against me for a moment. I slid my arm through hers and walked her into the pavilion and sat her down. "I'm throwing your bike in my trunk and giving you a ride home. No arguments."

"They'll see us together."

"I'll let you off a ways before your estate."

"God, this is so embarrassing."

"It's still ninety degrees. Could happen to anybody."

"Our house isn't even a mile away." She touched her face. Body heat had emphasized the acne on her cheeks. Her white blouse was soaked in spots.

"I've got a cold Pepsi in the car that I've had about half of. How does that sound?"

"That sounds great."

She drank it in sips, which was smart. The drink relaxed her or seemed to. She leaned back and took one of those deep breaths that usually mean you're feeling better—even philosophical—about some problem. "I guess it was kinda stupid on a hot day like this." Then: "My dad *really* doesn't like you."

"That I know. But why did he kick Tommy Delaney out?"

She wiped her brow with the back of her tiny, corded hand. "Poor Tommy. I always liked him but I don't think anybody else did. Except Marsha. She told me one day how bad at home it was for him. His folks always argued and sometimes it got violent. I guess his whole life was like that. She said that was why he liked being at our place so much. It was peaceful and it made him feel special, you know, with my dad being so wealthy and all. The funny thing is, it was my dad who started inviting him over. He'd show him off to his friends. He always gave a speech, too, about how Tommy was going to put the Hawkeyes in the Rose Bowl. But Eve hated him. She thought he was a moron. And that was the word she used. She worked on Dad until he started to dislike Tommy, too. I guess when Van was killed he decided it was a good time to get rid of Tommy."

"Tommy's not handling it too well."

She fanned herself with her tiny hand. "That's what I figured. He really isn't some big dumb jock. He's real sensitive, you know? I think he was in love with Van for a little while but he was smart. He gave up right away. I mean it was hopeless. Then he fell in love with Sarah. Van wouldn't even listen to him when he was telling her that Neil was sorry for being so mad all the time and how much he loved her. Tommy felt sorry for Neil, that's why he stepped in. But I told him up front it wouldn't work."

"Why not?" But my question came automatically. I was thinking about Tommy being in love with Sarah.

"She wanted to humiliate Dad every way she could. And that meant being with a lot of boys. But I doubt she slept with more than one or two of them. She told me she hated sex because it reminded her of Dad."

"And this was all because your dad married Eve?"

"Well—" She perched herself on the edge of the bench. She pursed her lips, looked away for long seconds then said: "There was something else, too. But now it doesn't matter. Van's dead."

"Did this thing that doesn't matter anymore affect you the same way it affected Van?"

She inhaled deeply through her nose. "I really don't want to talk about it, all right?"

"It might help me."

"My dad said it's all over. That you're only out to embarrass him."

"At one time your dad and I were close to being friends."

"That isn't the way he remembers it."

There was only one way in. "Does Eve go out much at night—alone?"

Getting to her feet was an effort. She wobbled on the first two steps. I caught her wrist gently and eased her back.

"Please let me go. I really don't want to talk about this."

"I just asked you if Eve went out alone at night sometimes."

"What do you want me to say? Yes, she did."

"How about your dad? Did he go out at night alone sometimes, too?"

"Of course he did. And still does. He's an important man. He has to." She broke suddenly, hands to face, quick dagger of a sob. "You know about their arrangement, don't you?"

"Was that why Van hated him so much?"

This time she had no trouble standing. Or walking. She walked down the wall and finally seated herself on the low ledge at the end of it. She didn't say anything for a time. She wasn't crying now. She didn't even look upset. When she looked at me all she said was, "I need a cigarette."

I did the movie star thing and lighted smokes for both of us. I carried them down and gave her hers. She had her nice legs stretched out in front of her now. She was considering them. She didn't seem to have much pride in herself. I hoped she at least realized that she had perfect coltish legs.

She smoked eagerly. "How did you find out?"

"Right now that doesn't matter. How did you and Van find out?"

A bright smile. "We followed her. Private investigators. We wanted to get something on her. We thought maybe Dad would divorce her if we could prove to him she was unfaithful. And that was pretty easy. She went out with Bobby Randall several times. And we assumed there were others, too. It's funny how it worked out, though."

I waited until she was ready to talk again.

"Before we got to tell him, Van and I got the flu pretty bad. We were in bed because we were so sick. I was asleep late one night when Van came into my room. She was so sick she could barely talk. She said she'd started down the stairs to get some orange juice and then she heard something she couldn't believe. I was so groggy I wasn't even sure what she was talking about. She said that this party Dad and Eve were having tonight—the men were drawing numbers to see which one of them would sleep with another man's wife. I couldn't understand it at first. But Van wasn't just beautiful, she kept up on things. She said this was what they called wife swapping and she said Dad was having a great time. They were going to pair off then get together that weekend at Dad's house up on the river. It's three stories and sort of like a hotel. Then Van started crying. I helped her into the bathroom so she could throw up. She was that sick—sick about what Dad was doing. She got into bed with me—I used to do that to her when we were little. She just kept crying and I held her and rocked her and sometimes I'd cry too."

She turned and flipped her cigarette onto the lawn. "That was a couple of years ago and that's when she started running around. She'd never been like that before."

"Did Van or you ever confront your father about it?"

"Oh, sure. We could tell he was embarrassed. He promised he wouldn't do it anymore. We both wanted to believe him. But then after about a month or so he started going out alone at night the way Eve kept doing. We followed him. He went to the same motel Eve did. The women were wives of his friends. Van used to scream at him and threaten to kill Eve. She always said that Eve shouldn't ever have been allowed to live in the same house our mom did. I agreed with her completely. Completely." Then: "Pretty shitty, huh?"

"Pretty shitty." I don't know why I was surprised that the Mainwarings had lied to me about the girls not knowing.

"He said we'd understand better when we were older. But neither of us believed that. That isn't any way to live. It's like he's in his second childhood or something." Then: "I guess I'll take you up on that ride back home."

"You want to head back now?"

"Yes, maybe I'd better. I'm really wasted for some reason."

I remembered how she'd been in my car the other day, not at her best, either. But there were a variety of physical responses to loss and trauma.

"You feel up to walking now?"

"I'm not a baby." Sharp, angry.

"I was just offering to help."

"I know, it's just—I'm sorry. I shouldn't have snapped at you like that. I hate being bitchy."

"I can't imagine you bitchy."

Her whooping laugh was directed at me. "You're one of those guys Van always told me about—the ones who idealize girls. You don't want to be around me when I get bitchy. I was even worse than Van and that was pretty bad."

"Thanks for the warning. Next time I'll come armed."

A soft summer giggle. "Well, I didn't say I was *that* bad."

With that she shoved off the edge of the wall. "Thanks for everything, Sam. I really appreciate it."

I put my hand on her shoulder. "Let's go get your bike."

NINETEEN

THREE HOURS LATER I sat in a chair on Wendy's patio watching the day slowly fade into dusk. Wendy had given me a kiss, a beer and a promise that even though dinner would be late it would be something I really liked. She would meanwhile go visit her mother for no longer than an hour. Whenever her mom felt that nobody was paying her sufficient attention she had panic attacks designed to get her noticed. Since Wendy's sister lived in Portland, Oregon, it fell to Wendy to be the noticer.

Dusk is always a melancholy time for me and I've never been sure why. Sometimes I feel the loneliness that has always been my curse, a loneliness that nobody can assuage. Tonight for company I had Wendy's hefty cat Victor. He sat in the chair next to mine and swatted at everything that tried to assault his bastion from the air. He had yet to down a single firefly but he certainly kept trying.

I wanted to give myself up to the Cubs game that was just getting started on the radio. Misery loves company and nothing is more miserable than listening to the Cubs blow another season. But this was pre-game yak and so I was left to the dying day.

It would be nice to send my mind on vacation so that I could just sit here and be one with my surroundings but I was restless. I kept thinking about the night of the murder. None of the lovers Van had thrown over would have had a difficult time getting into that barn—there was easy access through the thin line of forest in the back. Anybody who'd followed her to the commune would have been able to swing wide and enter the barn without being seen.

I also thought about the effect Eve had had upon the girls. Imagine if you'd grown up with a sweet, attentive, understanding mother who died and was replaced by a stunning but vapid swinger. And even worse, that your father became a swinger, too. Hey, one Frank Sinatra is enough for this planet, man. Had Eve taken her vengeance out on Van?

Victor started purring when the back door opened, which meant his mistress and patroness had come home. She carried her drink on a blue cloth coaster over to Victor's chair and nudged him aside so that she could sit down. He went unwillingly. As soon as she was seated he jumped on her lap.

"Feeling any better?"

"Not really. So much up in the air."

"I ran into Mike Potter at the supermarket. I bought us some red snapper we can put on the grill tonight."

"He tell you I'm crazy?"

"More or less. And he's worried that you could get in serious trouble with the state if you keep pushing this."

"I just want to make sure we get the truth."

"I said that to him. He said, 'If Sam wants to waste his time it's up to him.' But he smiled when he said it."

"That was nice of him."

"How about a back rub on the bed?"

"Are you trying to seduce me?"

"Maybe. Or maybe I'm just trying to distract you. You need to take a break."

We fit just about perfectly as lovers. And when we finished, Victor was squatting on the bureau and watching us in the darkness scented with her perfumes and sachets and creams. We'd had an audience.

"I never did get that back rub."

"Too late, buddy. I'm going to grill us some red snapper. And you're going to set the table."

"This is just like the National Guard I go to once a month. Too many orders."

"Don't say that. They're talking about drafting you guys. I saw it in the paper this morning. You must've seen it."

"I'll start setting the table."

"So you're not going to talk about it?"

"They've been predicting that for two years now. I'll set the table."

I went inside and started grabbing plates, glasses, silverware and napkins. I was careful to limit myself to the second-best of everything. The plates had tiny chips and the shine was off the silverware. I didn't blame her. Her only real asset was this house she owned. She basically lived on the income from the trust her husband had left for her. It had been the largesse of a decent but guilty man. Not his fault that he'd fallen in love with one of the girls his bully-boy father would never have approved of. He'd married Wendy because he was fond of her and because his family approved of her family. The trouble was Wendy had been in love with him and had come undone when he'd been killed in Nam.

And Nam was on my mind now, as well. Not only because I opposed the savage meaningless war—Ike's "military-industrialist complex" warning coming true in spades—but also because our post commander at the Guard had given us notice that we might be called up. I'd lied to Wendy. Nam was in the offing. A number of Guard units had already been sent there. At the rate our troops were being killed the great dark god that was slaughtering the lives of soldiers and innocents alike was ever hungrier. It wanted more flesh and blood and many of the men in the Guard were at the right age for making patriotic sacrifices the chickenshit politicians could prattle about when reelection time came around again.

But talking about it with Wendy was difficult. Her husband had died over there. And that's what worried her, the cheap irony of losing her first husband and then her husband-to-be in the same war. I didn't blame her for the dread she faced in her nightmares but I also couldn't do anything about it. Maybe we'd luck out. Maybe we wouldn't be called up. But as General Westmoreland told more and more lies and more and more of our troops died, I didn't know how we would be spared.

She came in and opened the refrigerator. She slapped two pieces of red snapper on the counter and started preparing them for cooking. She was fast and efficient and fun to watch. She didn't say anything.

"You not speaking?"

"No, because if I do speak you know what I'll speak *about* and then neither of us'll feel like eating. You know how worried I've been about it. The story in the paper just made it official."

"Maybe it won't happen."

"Just let me prepare this fish and not think about anything else."

A good meal and two glasses of wine later we both felt momentarily invincible and loving. We sat in chairs on the screened-in back porch and held hands like high schoolers. Victor appeared and sat on Wendy's lap. The only music was the night itself, the breeze and the faint passage of cars and the even more distant sounds of airplanes approaching Cedar Rapids for landing. I felt old and logy and I didn't mind it at all. I even considered the possibility—combine alcohol and fatigue and you can come up with the damnedest thoughts—that maybe, just maybe, things were exactly as they appeared. Neil Cameron killed Vanessa Mainwaring because he felt betrayed by her. And then he killed himself. Judge Whitney wouldn't be happy with this because Cliffie would have won one. And even one would be too much for Judge Whitney. The Sykes clan represented all things evil to her.

"How about helping me clean up and then we go to bed?"

"Fine. As long as you can help me drag myself up from this chair."

"You were supposed to help *me*, Sam." She laughed. "God, we sound like we're eighty years old."

"Speak for yourself. I don't feel a day over seventy-five."

"I love this so much. It's so comfortable with you."

"Is that another word for boring?"

"What an ego. You just want a compliment."

"I love you so much because you're so 'comfortable.' Not exactly inspiring."

She giggled. "And because you're so exciting to be with and such a stud in bed and because all my girl-friends are jealous that I've been able to keep a heart-breaker like you interested in little ole me."

"Much better."

"*Now* will you help me clean up?"

I concentrated on the grill and she worked on the dishes. When I came inside she was just loading the dishwasher. "See, that didn't take long." She tossed me a towel. "How about you dry and I wash? I've still got these pots and pans to take care of."

The kinds of relationships I'd had with women in the past had been all sex and tension. Lots of breakups and makeups. There hadn't been time in all the grop-ing and battling to get domestic in any way. Wendy and I were already married in an informal sort of way. But sometimes I got scared it would all end for some terrible reason.

She jabbed me in the ribs. "You haven't seemed to notice but there aren't any more pots or pans to dry. You've been standing there with that last one for a cou-ple of minutes now. You must be thinking of something really fascinating."

"I'm just hoping this doesn't come to an end any time soon."

"You keep asking me to marry you and you say something like that?" She smiled and kissed me. "Look, Sam, I worry about the same thing. And that's why I just want to wait a little while. We're crazy about each other. I want to spend my life with you. But I just want to be careful about it." She took pan and towel from me and set them on the counter. "Maybe we'd better discuss this in the bedroom."

By the time we finished making love, neither of us had enough energy left for discussing anything. She fell asleep against my outstretched arm. The aroma of her clean hair was innocently erotic.

THE CALL CAME at 3:26.

The phone was located on the nightstand on Wendy's side of the bed—as was only right; it was *her* bed—and before I was completely aware of what was going on, she had the phone to her ear and was talking. She'd told me once that all the while her husband was in Nam, where he eventually died on his second tour, she had nightmares about the phone ringing in the middle of the night and a cold military voice telling her that her husband was dead. She told me that she woke up several nights to find the phone in her hand, a dial tone loud in her ear. She'd incorporated the nightmare into reality.

"It's Mike," she said, lifting up the Princess-style phone and planting it on my stomach. I took the receiver and listened. I asked him to repeat what he'd said, so he went through it once more. He said he was at the crime scene and that if I wanted to join him it would be all right. He said that Cliffie wouldn't be there; he'd called the chief but the chief felt that Potter could handle it. I could sense Potter's smile when he quoted Cliffie: "I think you've learned a lot from me since you've been here and I've let you handle a number of other things already. You just keep me posted—the morning's soon enough." This was the first time I'd heard Potter draw down on Cliffie. But it was late and the scene he was at had to be a true bummer.

"What's going on?" Wendy whispered. Since I was still talking to Potter, I held up my hand to wave her off.

"I'm on my way, Mike."

Wendy had slipped into the bathroom. I heard her pee and then start brushing her teeth. If the National Dental Society or whatever it was called wanted to give a trophy (a big shining jewel carved into a tooth) to the person who brushed her teeth the most times a day, Wendy would be their choice. Seven, eight times a day and that doesn't count flossing.

I got a light switched on and dressed. I used one of her hairbrushes to batten down my own dark mess. I was lighting a cigarette when she came out wearing a ragged old robe she liked. She managed to look tousled, sweet and very sexy.

She came over and took my cigarette from me. She inhaled deeply; exhaled in a blast. She held up a finger. "One more." After she finally gave me my smoke back, she said, "Mike sounded shaky. What's going on?"

"Tommy Delaney," I said, "hanged himself earlier tonight."

TWENTY

CUE THE RAIN.

Halfway to the Delaney residence a hot, dirty summer rain shower started pelting my car. I had the radio turned up to KOMA in Oklahoma, still my favorite station. In the middle of the night this way the signal was stronger than during the day. A bitter anti-war song seemed right for this moment. I kept lighting one cigarette from another. I resented all the snug people in their dark snug houses as I passed street after street.

All the natural questions came to me. What had Tommy Delaney wanted to tell me and then backed away from? Was this going to be another murder disguised as a suicide? Had he left a note explaining everything?

The Hills had never looked better, the darkness a mercy to the crumbling houses and sad metal monsters parked curbside, all cracked windshields and rusted parts and political bumper stickers for men who had only contempt for the owners. The closer I got to the Delaney place the more lights I saw in the small houses. The people inside would have heard the sirens and seen the blood splash of emergency lights pitched across the sky. Most would have stayed inside; after all it was raining now and who wanted to get wet. But the vampires among them would have shrugged on raincoats and trudged out. Pain, misery, death awaited them and this was a tasty brew that would give them a fix of the life force they sought.

The local press was already there. The cops had shunted them to a corner of the action. A beefy part-time deputy stood next to them to make sure they didn't stray. I parked next to the ambulance and walked over to where Mike Potter was giving orders to another part-time deputy. The crowd numbered somewhere around thirty, not a sell-out crowd but not bad for a rainy four a.m. show that wasn't in 3-D or Cinemascope.

The air smelled of wet earth, exhaust fumes from all the vehicles, and a cancer ward's worth of cigarette smoke, my own contribution included. Two squad cars sat together shining their headlights on the front of the garage. The door was down so all I could see was the blank white wood with rust snaking down from the roof. Above the door was the basketball hoop where I'd seen Tommy Delaney shooting baskets that day.

As I approached Potter I heard a scream from inside the house. The piercing agony of it stopped me as I think it stopped everybody who heard it. I'd been surveying the scene the way an investigator would. The scream forced me to survey it now as a simple human being. No doubt one or both of the parents had found their son hanging from a crossbeam in the garage. A madness would set in. They would blame themselves, they would blame him and they would blame existence it-self, a ramble scramble of rage and grief and even more rage. I'd worked with enough social workers to know how suicides like this played out.

Potter said, "I'd stay away from his folks if I was you."

"They mentioned me?"

Rain pattered on his police cap. "According to her, her son was a nice, easygoing kid until you started pestering him about the Mainwaring girl."

"That's bullshit."

He had a flashlight the size of a kid's baseball bat in his hand. "C'mon, I'll take you into the garage."

On the way in, I said, "Did you hear me? What she said is bullshit. I came out here twice. Twice. That's hardly 'pestering' him or whatever she said. In fact I'm pretty sure he wanted to talk to me about something."

"Then why didn't he?" The cop guarding the side door stood aside as we approached.

"How do I know why he didn't."

"But you're sure he did? He sent you some kind of mind message?"

The sarcasm ended the minute we stepped inside. The hard-packed dirt floor, the rain and cool air streaming through the glassless window frame in back, the smells of gasoline, oil, dirt, now joined with vomit and feces. Somebody had run the only car outside so that the police could bring in all the necessary equipment to nail down every aspect of the suicide.

The way Tommy's mouth was twisted, it was almost as if he'd been smiling when death had taken him, a grotesque smile that seemed fitting for his end. He wasn't twitching, anyway, twitching the way he'd been with his folks screaming behind him in what was likely their ongoing marital war. I remembered the tic in his left eye and the forlorn, beaten tone of his voice. Their voices would have been with him as he'd looked for shelter and solace somewhere else. The Mainwaring home would have provided that.

All he wore was his jeans; no shirt, no shoes. Puke streamed down his chest and his right foot had been splashed with his runny feces.

"He left a note."

"Let's talk outside."

Potter raised his eyes, studied Tommy for a time then looked at me. "Yeah, outside."

The rain was backing off to a drizzle and the action was slowing down to the point that some of the ghouls, soaked, were wandering home. The hardiest of them would stay to see the corpse inserted into the ambulance.

I felt somebody watching me and when I looked to my left I saw Mrs. Delaney hiding behind a kitchen curtain. Even from here her hatred was clear.

"I got on a ladder and climbed up and looked at the ligature marks, Sam. No doubt about this one as far as I'm concerned. He definitely killed himself. The ME'll examine him and make absolutely sure it's suicide."

"I didn't have any doubt about this one."

"Why not?"

"For one thing, the little time I spent with him he struck me as a pretty sad kid."

"Hell, he was a football hero."

"Not when you heard his parents shrieking at each

other. I stood on the front lawn and heard them. Tommy was coming apart. It was like shell shock. And that came from years of listening to them trying to destroy each other. The other thing was he wanted to tell me something—at least that was the impression I had. But he could never quite do it."

"Any idea what it was?"

"No. But he knew a lot about the Mainwarings."

He lighted a cigarette now that the rain wouldn't soak it. The smoke smelled good in the chilling air. "That note he left, he apologized to his parents for taking his life and asked them to pray for him. And then he said that he never had any luck with women and that he just couldn't go on."

"And that's all?"

Before he could answer, the back door screeched open and barked shut. I saw her coming at me. Nuclear warhead. No confusion about who she wanted and what she planned to do.

Potter saw it, too, and stepped in front of me. "Mrs. Delaney, I asked you to please stay inside."

She pointed a witch finger at me and screamed: "He killed my Tommy! He wouldn't leave him alone! Tommy was scared of him! Tommy'd be alive if it wasn't for him!"

"Please, Mrs. Delaney—please go back inside. This isn't good for you or your husband."

But it was great for the living dead, the remainder of the group already pushing their way toward the garage. Drama was almost as good as blood.

She flung herself at Potter, trying to get her hands

on me. "He should be the one who's dead! He should be the one who's dead! He killed my Tommy!"

Paralysis. I couldn't move, speak. I was afraid of what I might have done to contribute to Tommy's suicide—maybe he felt pressure to tell me something but was afraid to and my contacting him scared him—just as I was afraid of her. All that anger, all that sorrow. I wanted to say something to comfort her but anything from me would sound blasphemous now.

"Just let me tell him to his face!" She dove at Potter but a stocky, balding man in a Hawkeye T-shirt came up from behind her and put big workingman hands carefully on her shoulders and began the inch-by-inch process of extracting her from Potter's body.

He just kept saying, "C'mon now, honey; c'mon now, honey," the way you might to a small child you were trying to soothe. Soft words, loving words. Hard to imagine this was the same man I'd heard battling this woman when I came here the first time to talk to Tommy. This time he was saying the right thing in the right way.

When he finally drew her to him, she folded herself into his arms and wept. He put one of those big hands on the back of her head and began stroking her gently. This made her weep even more.

This time the paralysis wasn't just mine. Potter stood in place, too, just watching her collapse into her husband's keeping. Not even the ghouls said anything, or moved. I thought of a documentary I'd seen about a tiger cub born dead and the mother trekking the corpse nearly a hundred miles across scorching dusty Africa. Not wanting to ever give it up. Mr. Delaney showed that kind of ferocious protectiveness as he slowly guided her back toward the house. He kept muttering his mantra. She clung to him with a desperation that made them indivisible.

Potter said, "Nothing with kids. And Tommy was a kid."

We'd had this conversation a number of times, how he could handle just about anything but death scenes involving kids or young people. He said he'd seen too many such scenes in Kansas City. He never elaborated on any of them.

Then he got brisk and officious. He wanted to wrap things up. The ME could get here and give his benediction and then everybody—except one unlucky uniform—could go home and catch what remained of sleep before the six-thirty alarm clock.

The remaining ghouls began to fade. A light went on in a back room. Shadows against a cotton blind. A piercing sob then silence. The light went out.

"I hope this is the end of it," Potter said. Irritation was clear in his eyes and voice. "No more murders or suicides. My wife keeps reminding me that we moved out here to take it easy. Now my migraines are back, I'm downing a bottle of Pepto a day and I'm constipated."

"Pepto constipates you."

"I know, but it's either that or having heartburn that damn near knocks me out."

I stared with great longing at my car. It would take me away from here. I would be back in bed with Wendy. In the morning the sunlight would be golden and pure and maybe we'd make love in it and then have breakfast on the back porch and Wendy would be sweet and fetching and for a time I wouldn't have to think about everything that had happened in the past few days or whether Wendy was going to marry me sometime soon. Or if my National Guard unit would be called up for the war that was a farce and a cruel joke on the American people.

"You be sure and keep me posted if you hear anything," Potter said.

"I will."

As I walked to my car I saw Mr. Delaney in one of the kitchen windows watching me. I almost waved. Instinct. But in this instance waving would be more than slightly inappropriate. I got one quick good look at his face. He seemed to hate me as much as his wife did. Maybe more but he couldn't express what he was feeling the way she did. He just stared.

In my car I snapped the radio on. Then right back off. Wrong to listen to the radio somehow. Instead I smoked and drove fast. Very fast. I didn't go back to Wendy's, I just drove. It was one of those robotic driftings I went through occasionally. Wasn't aware of where I was driving or what I was seeing. Just driving, the act itself lulling me into a state where nothing mattered but the present moment—my fortress against any kind of serious thought.

The first time I became aware of where my car was taking me was down on D Avenue where the Burger Heaven and the second-run theater used to be. There'd been a used paperback store there for awhile, too. And a tavern where they kept their pinball machines in front so teenagers could play them and not get carded or thrown out. It was all gone now. A supermarket and a new Western Auto took up most of the block. No comfort in those.

Wendy was asleep on the couch in her pajamas when I came in. The TV was on and snowy. Victor dozed on the armchair. I went into the kitchen and got myself a beer and sat down in the breakfast nook.

She came in soon enough. "I tried to wait up for you." Sliding into the booth across from me.

"You should've stayed in bed."

"You ever think I was worried about you?"

"If you're so worried about me why don't you just say you'll marry me?"

"Boy, you're in one hell of a mood."

"If you say so."

"All right, I'll marry you. You set the date."

"Are you serious?"

"Yes. I've been thinking about it. We love each other and even though I'm scared about it I don't want to ruin everything by putting it off. I just realized that if you ever walked out the door I would be miserable for the rest of my life."

"Well, probably not for the rest of your life."

"Goddammit, you're in a bad mood. I tell you I love you and that I want to marry you and you just keep on bitching about things."

"Well, I'm happy about it. Of course."

She was out of the booth before I could say anything more.

"Go to hell, Sam. I don't want you in my bed tonight. You take the couch."

Then she was gone. It hadn't done me any good to take Tommy's suicide out on her. I gave it twenty minutes and then went into the dark bedroom and told her how much I loved her. She laughed and said, "I was wondering when you'd show up. Now get into bed."

TWENTY-ONE

I WAS IN court the next morning. A divorce case. By the time of the trial I'd come to pretty much hate both of them. Selfish people who'd forgotten that they had two very lonely and frightened little girls to take care of. He'd told me, quite earnestly, that as soon as the papers were signed it was "Nookie City for this guy." There are men who could have pulled it off and made you smile along with it. He wasn't one of them. He was, I suppose, good-looking in a big-guy sort of way but he was as vain as a starlet, always combing his hair and watching his biceps pop in his short-sleeved shirts.

One time when he was in my office, I went to the john and came back to find him sucking in his gut and putting the moves on Jamie. She was wily enough to say, "My dad wears the same aftershave you do." A thirty-eight-year-old self-described stud ("Hey, chicks dig me and Elaine could never understand that, the bitch,") being compared to a God-only-knows-how-old Granddad-type? He got back to business, which meant running down his ex some more and winking at me every time he mentioned "chicks." Number one, I hate people who wink and number two, his winks looked like tics.

The judge, a man who had no time for Judge Whitney

or me, called me to the bench and leaned over and whispered: "Am I right in thinking that these two are among the biggest assholes who've ever appeared before me?"

I nodded. "Thank you."

He settled mutual custody on them and ordered both of them to take parenting classes. They sputtered and spluttered and called "outrage" in the middle of which the judge brought the hammer down, stood up and left.

"Parenting classes? Who does that asshole think he is?"

"Maybe you'll meet some chicks there." I grabbed my briefcase and got out of the courtroom fast so I wouldn't have to talk to him anymore.

The sun was so hot at ten thirty I had a science fiction image of people staggering down the sidewalk and falling into the street, their hands waving desperately in the air like drowning victims. I smoked a cigarette and took my time getting back to the office. I passed at least six people who told me how hot it was. I wouldn't have known that otherwise.

My office is located in the rear of a building that has been many things up front. The current tenant who took the front section and thus eighty-five percent of the entire place was an auto parts store.

I walked alongside of the building and when I turned I saw Jamie sitting on the steps leading to our office. She had tears in her eyes. She smoked a cigarette and sniffled. When she saw me she just sat there. No signal of recognition.

"What're you doing out here, Jamie?" I said.

"He told me to sit out here."

"Who's he?"

"Mr. Mainwaring."

"What the hell's going on?"

Her blue eyes shone with tears. "I just did what he told me, Mr. C. He scares me."

"So he's inside now?"

"Uh-huh."

I took her hand. "It'll be all right. Why don't you take an early lunch and do a little shopping?"

"Will you be all right?"

"Never better."

"I really don't like him, Mr. C."

"I don't either. But now he's my problem, not yours. Now go have some good food at the deli and put it on the office account."

"Are you sure that's all right?"

"Well, I've talked to the owner of this here law office and he said it was fine with him."

She was picking tears off her cheek with a little girl finger. And now she smiled. "I always tell people you're the funniest man I've ever known, Mr. C."

I didn't have to walk all the way into my office. He half dived out of it to grab me before I reached the threshold. He used his size to shove me hard against the hall closet. "Where is she? Where did you send my daughter?"

He'd become a grotesque. The blue eyes were crazed and the words were cries. Drool trickled from the left side of his mouth. He was slick with sweat and it wasn't from the heat. And then his hands reached for my throat. I tried to push off the closet door but he was too quick.

I could feel the fingers on the sides of my neck. I had just enough room to knee him in the groin.

He didn't fall down, he just went into a crouch. He turned away from me so I couldn't see his misery. Even in this situation he was a man of great pride.

I went into my office and sat down at my desk. I pretended to be fascinated by all the pink phone slips waiting for me. He was resourceful. In less than a minute he started groaning out insults. "I'm going to see that you're in prison for a long time, you little bastard." And: "If she dies, you'll be an accessory to murder."

That one got my attention and bothered me. "What the hell are you talking about?"

"At least own up to what you did, you slimy son of a bitch." The voice was stronger now and he was out of his crouch. As he came through the door he winced with every step. But his rage was as good as several shots of bourbon. "I don't know how you could ever be so god-damned irresponsible. I knew you were dirt, McCain, but she's a seventeen-year-old girl."

He sank into Jamie's chair. His ferocity was wearing him down. He stretched a hand to her desk as if for support. The next sound was a wail. "He'll kill her."

"Paul, damn it. Look at me. Tell me what you're talking about."

"You know damn well what I'm talking about. She's going to have an abortion because you told her to."

"Paul, that's crazy. I didn't even know she was pregnant."

"Oh, sure. I suppose you didn't see her yesterday afternoon, either."

"Yeah, I did see her. And what we talked about most of the time was how she and Van learned that you were doing the same thing Eve was and that you were in a wife-swapping group. And how much she and Van hated it."

"Don't put the goddamn blame on me. This is your fault. She's looking up some butcher who'll abort her. She doesn't know about sleazy things like that. That's your territory. You and your great friend Neil Cameron. He's the one who seduced her."

I had my elbow on the desk. Now I rested my head on my hand and took a deep breath. There are moments when the brain can't—or refuses to—comprehend and process all the information it is presented. Pregnant. Abortion. Neil Cameron. My voice sounded mournful. "What makes you think she's looking for an abortion?"

"She told Marsha she was having one and was driving over to see some guy. This was about twenty minutes ago."

"Oh, God."

"No shit, huh? Finally sinking in, McCain? Maybe having second thoughts about what you told her?"

I slammed my fist so hard against the desk top that I numbed my hand. "I didn't know she was pregnant and I sure as hell didn't tell her to get an abortion. Do you understand that?"

For the first time clarity came into his eyes. The lunacy waned. "Then who told her about this abortionist?"

"I have no idea. And even if I get around with low-lifes sometimes, I don't know anything about an abortionist in Black River Falls. There was one but he's doing time in Fort Dodge."

Wailing now. "Then where is she?"

"Shut up for a minute."

I grabbed the receiver and started dialing. Kenny answered on the third ring. At this time of day he'd be working on his portable typewriter slamming through "Cannibal Warriors of the Third Reich!" or something similar.

"Yeah?" He did not like being interrupted.

"I've got a big problem here, Kenny, and I'm really in a hurry. Is there anybody you know of who's peddling abortions these days? I know it's been quiet since Thompson got sent up to Fort Dodge for killing that girl."

"Supposedly there's some guy in Milburn. His name is Windom or something like that. I don't know that for a fact. But I heard it from one of the kids who always comes out here to get his copies of my stuff autographed."

Even Kenny was a star of sorts. "That's all you know?"

"Yeah, I'm sorry, that's the best I can do."

"Thanks, Kenny. That's a start anyway."

Mainwaring was on his feet. "What did he say?"

"Milburn. Some guy named Windom. But he says the only way he heard it is that some kid who wants his books autographed told him."

"People want that trash autographed?"

This coming from Mr. Open Marriage and Mr. Wife Swap. But now wasn't the time to respond.

We took his Jaguar. Milburn was fifteen miles away.

We both smoked. Any time we pulled up behind a car or truck Mainwaring leaned on the horn as if he thought they'd be so afraid that their vehicles would just take flight and clear a path for us.

"If he laid a hand on her, I'll kill him."

"First of all, we don't even know that he's the guy. So it would make sense to stay a little cool until we find out."

"You don't give a damn, she's not your daughter."

"No, but believe it or not, I like her and I don't want some butcher cutting her up."

All I got was a snarl.

Despite the heat, autumn could be seen in the hills, the tips of trees burning into golds and browns and reds and that scent of fall on a few vagrant breezes. For all the stupendous colossal magnificence of the Jag, the damn air conditioning wouldn't work so we had the windows down.

Milburn runs to maybe fifteen thousand and is known mainly for the Pioneer Days celebration it throws on Labor Day, complete with costumed people and a lot of artifacts from the middle of the last century. It gets a lot of state press and some big national advertisers sponsor a good share of the expenses.

As we entered the town limits I had the feeling that the place was a big old dog lying on its side in the boiling heat. The shopping district which ran four blocks showed a lot of empty parking spaces and only a few people on the sidewalks. A tractor was ahead of us at a stoplight so Mainwaring went into one of his rants about how hillbillies should be shot-stabbed-set on fire for getting in the way of the movers and shakers who by divine right were running this planet. Since (A) farmers aren't hillbillies and (B) I'm pretty sure that there had to be some hillbillies in my bloodline dating back to the early 1800s, I started thinking about shooting-stabbing-setting *him* on fire.

Finally I saw a Sinclair station and said, "Pull in."

He swept the beast onto the drive and I was out the door, him shouting, "What the hell are you doing?"

I like gas stations. The smells of oil and gas and the clang and clank of the guys working on cars in the garage. I like good old gas station conversations, standing around and saying nothing much with a Pepsi and some peanuts and a cigarette with some other guys who are also saying nothing much. This time all I wanted was a phone book which, in the case of Milburn, was about as thick as a comic book.

The middle-aged guy in the green uniform who came out of the garage wiping his hands on a rag looked like the man to ask. "Can you tell me how I'd find Sullivan Road?"

"Sure. Easy to get to from here. You go down two blocks to the Woman's Shop—big store right on the corner—and you turn right and go straight for—let's see—eight blocks. Maybe nine. Anyway, Sullivan Street is off that road there. You'll see a street sign."

"Thanks."

"We don't see many of those around here."

He meant the Jag. "Yeah, but the air conditioning doesn't work."

He had a great Midwestern grin. "You're kidding."

"'Fraid not. Well, thanks."

"You took long enough," Mainwaring said when I got in the car.

"Shut up and listen."

"I'm not used to people telling me to shut up."

"Tough shit. Now listen."

I gave him directions. They were easy to follow but we went through the honking again. I wanted to find Nicole, too, but without a siren on the Jag other vehicles just weren't going to shoot up on lawns to get out of our way.

Sullivan Road was where houses went to die. Most of the homes were built in the twenties from what I could see, two-story white clapboards adjacent to garages not much bigger than closets. Porches leaned and chimneys toppled and shutters hung crooked. On a few of them you could see porch swings that hung from only one chain. The cars were also old, blanched colors and monster rust eating its way across the length of the vehicles.

"This is just the kind of place I expected it'd be," Mainwaring said.

"We're looking for 1724."

"Some rathole."

"We're on the 1600s now."

"If he's touched her I'll kill him."

"You already said that. There's 1702."

"There's her car!"

The way he grabbed the door handle I thought he was going to leap out of the car before he even slowed down. There was a space across from Nicole's silver Mustang. Mainwaring pulled in. I had to grab his shirt as he tried to vault from the car. "We don't know what we're walking into here. So let me handle this, you understand?"

"Take your hand off me. This is my daughter you're talking about."

"Yeah, well if you're so concerned about your daughter, then we go in there cool and calm." He was so pissed I reasoned that the only way to get his attention was to shock him. "What if he's operating on her? He hears us breaking in and he slips and makes a mistake? You want to be responsible for that?"

His eyes closed tight. An anxious breath. "Oh, God, my poor little Nicole."

"I'll handle things. All right?"

"All right."

"Let's go."

The white picket fence around the scorched grass leaned inward, in some spots so low it was only a few inches from the ground. The gate was missing. The walk to the door was cracked into jagged points. A variety of animals had used the east side of the lawn for a toilet. Apparently the right side didn't have any toilet paper.

Mainwaring dragged himself now, as if afraid of what lay ahead. He must have been still thinking of the image of the abortionist's tool slipping when he heard our invasion. He muttered to himself but I wasn't sure what he was saying.

In the short distance between the car and the screenless screen door I was already soaked with sweat. We were going to hit ninety-four today according to the dubious wisdom of the weatherman.

There was a bell but I stuck my hand through the frame of the screen door and knocked. The neighborhood was quiet. The loudest sound was the power mower we'd passed about half a block away.

I knocked again. This time a male voice behind the door said something. Then the man who I assumed owned the voice did a foolish thing. He went to the east window and edged the dirty white curtains back and looked out. Straight into my face. I jabbed a finger at the door. The curtain dropped back.

Just to annoy him I knocked again. This time he opened the door, a short, heavyset man who had more hair on his body than a papa gorilla. A white T-shirt only emphasized the thick hirsute chest and arms.

"Help you with something?"

Mainwaring's strength was sufficient to hurl me off the low doorstep and grab on to the hairy man with enough force to drive him back inside so fast I didn't have time to quite understand what was happening. I piled through the doorway right behind him. By now Nicole, who was seated on a badly soiled light blue couch, was pounding on her father's back as he bent over to smash his fist again and again into the hairy man's face. The man was on his knees. His face was already bloody.

I pushed Nicole aside so I could slam my fist into the side of Mainwaring's head. But he had true madness on his side. He was gone into a realm where only murder would satisfy him. Prisons are filled with men like him, men who pay for a single explosive moment with long stretches behind bars.

The hairy man was crying and pleading. Mainwaring didn't stop hitting him until I kicked him so hard in the back of his left knee that he slowed and turned just enough for me to hit him almost square in the face. The hairy man was smart enough to slide away.

Nicole was back on the couch, sobbing now, sounding as crazed as her father, striking her fists against her thighs again and again.

I shoved Mainwaring toward her. "Take care of your daughter."

Dazed, he stumbled toward the couch and sat down next to her. He still didn't know what to do. He just sat there, still trapped in the vestiges of his rage. Then she surprised both of us by throwing herself into his arms and finally he was her father again and he held her and began crying along with her.

I followed a trail of blood dots on faded linoleum to a small bathroom where the hairy man was splashing water on his face and cursing with a good deal of eloquence.

"That son of a bitch is gonna be payin' me a lot of money by the time I get through with him."

"Are you Windom?"

He whipped around and glared at me. "No, I ain't Windom. Windom moved about four months ago when me'n the missus moved up from Anamosa. She's at work and this is my day off from the railroad." He put a hairy paw to his nose. "This look broke?"

I stepped closer. "Doesn't look like it but I'm not a doc."

He was still trembling. So was I for that matter.

"I'm gettin' me a lawyer."

"I don't blame you. I'll help you find one. I'm Sam McCain." I put my hand out and he shook after hesitating. Blood bubbled on the left side of his mouth. "You need to go to an emergency room and get checked out. What's your name, by the way?"

"Ryan. Nick Ryan."

He grabbed a towel. Wiping his face he winced. "Bastard is lucky I didn't have my glasses. I can't see much without 'em." Finished drying his face he said, "She ain't been here but maybe fifteen minutes and I didn't know what the hell she was talking about. She said she was in trouble and didn't I know what she meant. Then she started cryin'. If the wife was here she woulda known what to do but you know how it is when women cry—especially a young one like her—I just got her a bottle of pop and an ashtray. Young kid like that, I felt sorry for her. Then her old man busts in and tries to kill me. What's this Windom s'posed to have done, anyway? This is the second girl come here since we moved in."

"He supposedly performed abortions."

"I'll be damned. I don't go for that, you know. Catholic."

"You go to the ER and they can bill Paul Mainwaring."

"Who the hell is Paul Mainwaring?"

He squinted at me when I laughed. "A very important guy. Just ask him."

"Well, I hope he's rich because I'm gonna sue his ass off. We need to fix this place up, that's why we got a deal on it. Place we had in Anamosa was real nice but then the job shifted down here. I make a good living."

"I've got an uncle on the railroad. He makes a lot more than I do."

"Yeah? Whadda you do?"

"I'm a lawyer."

This time the laugh was on me. "You should work for the railroad like your uncle. Honest work."

"Believe me, I've thought about it. Now let's go back to the living room."

I led the way. Mainwaring was helping Nicole to her feet. I said, "You owe this man a sincere apology. And you're going to pick up his ER tab. And unless you can make some kind of settlement, he's going to sue your ass off."

"He's an abortionist."

"Now you've slandered him, too."

"I told you, Dad, Mr. Ryan's been very nice to me. He didn't know what I was talking about when I said I needed help."

Mainwaring's eyes roved from hers to mine. "This is true?"

"No, we're making it up because we're all scared you'll go crazy again. Now apologize to him and then give him a ride to the ER and then come to an agreement about how much money you're going to give him." I glanced at Ryan. "I'm his lawyer."

"That's a surprise."

"I'll drive myself home, Dad."

"Can I trust you?"

"How about you? Can I trust *you*?" This was one

of those questions carrying a load of history with it—
Eve, open marriage, wife swapping and alienating his
two girls.

"Just go straight home."

"You're forgetting something," I said to him. "I don't
have a car here. I'll have to ride with Nicole."

She took the keys from her purse, zipped the purse
shut and then looked at me. "Maybe you should drive,
Sam. I'm still shaking."

"Just hope that Mr. Ryan doesn't have any serious
injuries, Mainwaring."

"Oh, great, now I'm the villain."

"Yeah," I said, "as a matter of fact, you are." If I'd
been a sadist I would have used the moment to tell him
what I'd learned from the Wilhoyt investigators about
his wife. But as much as I disliked him, he had more
than his share of grief. I didn't want to add to it.

Nicole, in her peasant skirt and blouse, led me out
of the Ryan home. As we walked to her car she said,
"Maybe he's learned his lesson. Maybe he'll change."

I didn't want to give her odds on that but I said,
"Yeah, maybe."

I drove at about half the speed Mainwaring had a
bit earlier. For a time neither of us spoke. "Van and I
used to play a game. We used to sit in the back of the
car when Mom and Dad would take us someplace and
look out the back window at license plates. For weird
ones, you know. One time we saw one that read 'I'm
cute.' We laughed about that the whole way to Cedar
Rapids." Her voice was wistful but pained.

After a time she said, "He wants to send me to my

aunt's house till I have the baby. Then we'll adopt it out. That's what he says now, though. I'm trying to imagine having a baby and giving it away."

"You want to go to your aunt's house?"

"Yeah. Even Sarah said I should go away, I mean before she told me about Windom. She said I should go away to school for a year. Try to forget everything."

"She told you about Windom?"

She patted her face as she sometimes did. Maybe she was hoping that her acne had magically disappeared. I used to have moments like that—daydreams—about being taller. "She's my best friend. When I told her that Neil and I snuck around and saw each other for a month—and then I told her I was pregnant—she said I should see this Windom and get an abortion and go away to school. And try to forget everything. I think the whole thing made her mad. She said that Tommy was going to beat Neil up for her but she stopped him and said she'd take care of it." Then, "Poor Tommy. He was kind of a little boy in a lot of ways. But he was so sweet." Her eyes glistened. "And Van and Neil—it's just all so screwed up."

"You don't hold anything against Neil?"

"I want to but I can't." Her gaze was distant now. "I knew he was with me just to make Van jealous. I even told Van about it. But she didn't care. She thought it was funny. She didn't know I was p.g. though. But it was my fault as much as his. I always saw all these really handsome guys around Van. I guess I just sorta wanted one for myself. You know, with my face and all. He was a lot of fun, too. Took me places and made me think about things I never had. He was brilliant. He really was."

"You need to see a doctor right away."

"I know. I've been afraid to go. I'll probably go to Iowa City where nobody knows me."

"Fine."

"You know, I have a little crush on you. Not a big one. But a nice little one."

"Well, that's funny because I have a little crush on you, too. Not a big one. But a nice little one." Her laugh made us both feel better.

I pulled up next to my car in the small lot behind my office building.

She reached out and took my hand. "I hope I see you again."

"Me, too. And for what it's worth, I think you're wrong about not meeting any more handsome guys. I have the power to see into the future and from what I can see there're a lot of them waiting to take you out."

"I sure hope you're right."

I slid out of the car and started toward my door. Behind me she said, "Thanks for everything, Sam."

By the time I reached the commune a hot rain stormed across the prairie with mean intent. Humans and animals alike rushed to shelter. Lightning walked the land on glowing spider legs and thunder shook the earth. I pulled as close to the houses as I could and then started my own rush to get out of the rain.

With everybody inside temporarily the voices were almost as loud as the music, this time the Beatles' best album, *Rubber Soul*. I had to use a fist on the door to get any attention. A white kid in something like dread-locks came to the door. I told him who I wanted to see and he gave me a thumbs-up. Maybe in a past life he'd been a WW1 ace.

I took one of the two broken-back metal chairs on the porch and had myself a smoke. The laughter from inside was clean and young and I felt envious of them. Crazy and pretentious as some of them were, at least they were questioning the conventional wisdom of growing up, entering the nine-to-five, and setting aside money for your funeral when you turn forty-five.

I watched the rain drill the flower power bus and the other wrecked-looking vehicles. A sweet dog face could be seen underneath the bus, all wide-eyed and floppy-eared.

Then she was there. "God, this rain doesn't even cool things off, does it?"

"I wonder how old Cartwright is doing up there waiting to hear from God."

She took the chair next to me. "Sometimes I feel sorry for him, Sam."

"I would if I didn't know he was such a con artist. Hair tonic and diet crap and all that."

In her denim work shirt and jeans she was tomboy comfortable and purposeful. That was my impression, anyway. Except for the eyes. She couldn't hide her anxiety. I guessed she knew why I was here.

"Mainwaring and I followed Nicole this morning. She was under the impression she was going to have an abortion."

The old confrontational Sarah scoffed at me. "You're

not exactly being subtle. As far as I'm concerned, I gave her good advice and I don't give a damn if you like it or not. I've seen too many girls her age ruin their lives by getting pregnant."

"So have I. But that's not what this is about."

She leaned away from me. "Oh? So what's 'this' about?"

"I think you know."

She was quick, starting for the door before I got out of my chair. I'd never get her out of the ruckus inside. But then she turned and came back. I had the feeling she was as surprised by her move as I was.

She sat down again. I started to speak but she held up a hand for me to stop.

"I can't get over Tommy killing himself."

"Why do you think he did it?"

"Because of me. Because he was in love with me."

"And you weren't in love with him?"

She dropped her head, was quiet. "I loved him enough not to marry him."

"I don't know what you mean."

She sat back and ground the chair around so she could face me. "He wanted to run away and get married. Not even finish high school. I told him he was crazy but Tommy—Tommy got obsessed easy. Plus he just wanted out of his house. He used to cry like a little kid when his parents had had one of their battles. I hated them for what they'd done to Tommy. But I still wouldn't ruin his life by marrying him right now. I told him he should take one of the scholarships—he had three or four colleges offering him full rides because he was such a good football player. If we got married his life would be ruined. I loved him too much for that."

"So Tommy killed himself because you wouldn't marry him?"

"I don't like your tone there. You trying to say I'm lying?"

"Not at all, Sarah. I believe you. But maybe there was another reason Tommy took his life. In addition to you not marrying him, I mean."

"Well, then I sure don't know what the hell you're talking about."

"I'm talking about him knowing that you killed Neil after you found out that he got Nicole pregnant. You knew Neil had killed Vanessa but you decided to keep his secret. But then when Nicole told you about her pregnancy—" I tried to take her hand. She slapped mine away. "Nicole told me how angry you were when she told you about sleeping with Neil. But I noticed you didn't speak up for Neil quite the same way even before you found out about Nicole. It wasn't anything obvious but your tone definitely changed. I knew then that you were sure that Neil had killed Vanessa. I can't read your mind but I think it was probably then you realized that your brother was out of control and that he was going to keep right on doing what he'd always done. I cut him a lot of slack for what he saw in Nam, Sarah, but I suspect if you're honest you'll tell me that he was always this way growing up, smashing things and smashing people. That's the way it was, wasn't it?"

"You don't have any right to talk like that. I thought you were my friend."

"I am your friend, Sarah. I care about you. I just think you'll feel better if you tell the truth. There's been too much lying already."

She raised her head and stared at the ceiling of the porch. A whimper became a small sob. "He was my brother. He'd had a hard life. I loved him."

"I know you loved him. But you saw that he needed to be stopped. And when you found out about Nicole— You decided you didn't have any choice. You killed him and tried to make it look like suicide."

She picked up my package of Luckies from the arm of my chair. I handed her my matches. When she got her cigarette burning she handed them back.

"You don't know any of this for sure."

"I do now. And you know it, too."

"He attacked me."

"I don't believe that but it'll make a good defense."

"I don't want you for my lawyer anymore."

"That's a good decision."

"I thought you were my friend," she said again.

"I am. That's why I'll get you the best criminal defense attorney I can."

"I don't have any money."

"It can be worked out." I had no idea how at the moment but there on that porch at that moment it was the right thing to say.

"I didn't plan on doing it."

"All right."

"Don't you believe me?"

"Yes. But you'll have to work this through carefully with your lawyer."

She exploded from her chair as if she'd been blasted out of it. She stalked to the east end of the porch and lowered herself onto the railing. She inhaled hungrily. The tip of the cigarette was an evil little red eye. "You don't know what it was like with Neil. All our lives. He was always in trouble. He was in a fight or he'd stolen something or he'd smashed up something. I used to feel sorry for him because I loved him so much. He always said that people wouldn't accept him for who he was and that's why he was always in trouble. He was just paying them back. For a long time I believed that. But when he got into so much trouble in the service—"

"You mean what you told me about Saigon?"

"No. When they got back stateside he started stealing stuff from the other soldiers. Watches and jewelry they'd bought for their girlfriends and wives. One of them caught him at it and Neil nearly killed him. They had him see a shrink. The shrink said that he should get a dishonorable discharge but no time in the brig. He came to my little apartment off campus. He was so angry about things he scared me.

"He'd always taken advantage of people before— I was able to see that then—and he got some kind of thrill out of stealing and fighting and conning people. But I thought that with everything he'd gone through— I thought maybe he'd want to straighten out for the first time in his life.

"And at first when he came to the commune he was really laid back. Really cool in a way he'd never been before. I'd see him out back of the barn planting along with some of the others and I'd get tears in my eyes.

I really believed that God had granted him another chance. Neil always laughed when I told him that I prayed a lot. But I didn't care. I kept right on praying for him. And everything was fine until he fell in love with Van. She was so beautiful I couldn't blame him. But by then Nicole and I were friends and she told me how Van used guys to hurt her father. She wanted to humiliate him by being a whore. I tried to tell him that but he just accused me of being jealous. I just couldn't deal with him anymore."

She was more silhouette than person perched there on the railing. I said, "But you knocked me out so he could escape."

"I was afraid for him. I was thinking maybe he really did kill Van. I didn't want him to go to prison."

"But then you couldn't take it anymore when he got Nicole pregnant."

She flipped her cigarette into the air, a blazing rocket ship against the moon-bright night. "Nicole is a kid. That's why I liked her right away. She's kind of innocent. We had lunch in the city park one day and she brought along a bunch of Archie comic books and talked about how Veronica reminded her of Van in a lot of ways. I laughed about that for a week. She was like this goofy little kid sister I never had. And when he got her pregnant—he couldn't at least have used a rubber?"

I stood up. "Don't tell me any more. We need to get you that lawyer first. I'll start calling as soon as I get home."

"You going to take me in yourself or have the cops come out here?"

"You got a preference?"

She came over and slid her arms around me. "I'm really scared." She seemed to fight her tears at first but then she was crying so hard her fear and sorrow came in great spasms.

We said very little on the drive back to town. There wasn't much point in talking I guess.

TWENTY-TWO

I'D GONE TO law school with David Brunner. He was now a prominent criminal defense attorney in Chicago. You can correctly assume he was a whole lot smarter than I'll ever be. I explained the case to him and told him that we could cover his fees. The largesse was coming from one Paul Mainwaring. As Marsha explained to me over the phone, Nicole was near a breakdown worrying about her friend Sarah. Mainwaring had saddled her and her sister with a sneering, duplicitous wife and an open marriage so he now saw that he needed to save his daughter. Marsha also told me that Paul and Eve had had two warring days of shouting at each other and that Eve had suddenly packed three suitcases and had taken a room at the Drake in Chicago.

Brunner was in the middle of a trial but promised he'd have one of his assistant attorneys on a train within two hours, which he did. John Silverman was in my office by late afternoon. I briefed him and then took him to the police station to meet Mike Potter and Cliffie. Potter and he got along in a reassuringly professional way. A way that was spoiled when Cliffie came in and began to pontificate about the case and warn John that "out-of-town lawyers" never did well in Black River Falls. He also reminded me several times that he said from the beginning Neil was the killer. Potter and Cliffie left us then to wait for somebody to escort us to a room where we could talk with Sarah. "I can't fucking believe that guy," Brunner said. Twice. A mild reaction compared to some when Cliffie was the subject.

The good Reverend Cartwright was presently housed on the fourth floor of the Protestant hospital where he was making a fraudulent saga of being struck by lightning. He had been pronounced fine by the emergency doc and fine by his own doc but the Rev insisted he was suffering from terrible but unspecified health problems that only hospital rest could cure. He bravely broadcast from his hospital bed where he announced a "Fund Drive for the True Friends of Jesus." He said that God had told him he would recover at the same rate that money poured into church coffers. He never runs out of gimmicks and damned if most of them don't work.

Four nights after taking Sarah to the police station, I got home late and weary. I'd been in court all afternoon and the central air there had worked only intermittently. Everybody in Court B was in a surly mood, me included. During lunch assistant prosecutor Hillary Fitzgerald stopped on the step where I was eating my burger from the courthouse menu and said, "I feel sorry for your client, McCain. I've never seen Judge Hammond this nasty. Your guy is facing a DUI and I think Hammond is going to give him the chair." She had a winsome smile.

When I was coming up to the house, I saw that something was wrong. I hadn't been able to contact Wendy by phone. Now the lights were out and the house had a deserted look. Where had she gone?

Her car was in the two-stall garage. Had a friend picked her up?

I hurried to the back door and walked inside. We never locked up until we went to bed.

Refrigerator thrum. Air conditioner whoosh. All those inexplicable sounds of a house talking to itself.

Downstairs empty. Upstairs—

I went straight to our bedroom and there with the bloody sunset filling the window like a wound she lay in a tight fetal position in the center of the bed. Her blue walking shorts and white blouse were badly wrinkled, something she would ordinarily not have allowed.

The bedroom décor was all hers, of course. And it was very feminine with a canopy bed, a doll collection, a dressing table, enough perfumes to enchant a sultan, and three stacks of fashion magazines from her high school years. I knew this because one night when she was depressed she sat in a chair in the living room with several very old issues, going through them with great interest. I asked her about them and she said, "That was the last time my life was simple. Back when I used to sit next to you in homeroom."

I knew she was aware of me because the sound of her breathing came sharper now. But she kept her eyes closed. When I saw the envelope on the hardwood floor I reached down to pick it up.

"Don't look at it." Her eyes were still closed; she hadn't moved.

But I did pick it up. I knew what it would be of course. Her mood told me that.

"We're going to Canada."

"No, we're not, Wendy."

Then she was not only sitting up she was hurling herself off the bed and standing in front of me.

"Well, you're sure as hell not going to Nam, I'll tell you that. I lost my husband over there; I'm not going to lose you the same way."

"I have to go, Wendy. It's my duty. Other guard units have gone."

"Don't give me any patriotic bullshit. I don't want to hear it." I took it as significant that she wasn't crying. Her fury wouldn't allow for any softer expressions of pain.

I reached out for her but she jerked away. "Don't touch me. I can't believe you're just going to go along with this."

"What the hell choice do I have, Wendy?"

"Go to Canada. Or say you're a pacifist. Or say you're queer. Some goddamned thing. You're a lawyer, Sam. Start thinking like one."

She was doing me a kind of favor. By having to deal with her I didn't have to deal with my own feelings—fear and anger just like hers—that would be mine when I was alone.

"And think of your mother, Sam. How's she going to take this? She needs you just the same as I do."

I knew better than to touch her. "Listen, honey. Why don't you fix us a couple of drinks while I wash up?

Then we can sit on the patio and talk this through a little more calmly."

"Don't give me your calmly bullshit, Sam. That's what you always say when you can't think of anything else." Then she waved me off. "This is making me so crazy. I'm like I was after my husband died." She looked crazy, too. Then, "I'll go make some drinks."

In the upstairs bathroom I washed up and as I did I studied my face in the mirror. I knew what she meant about those old magazines. My face had been very different back then. If I survived the war it would change even more and probably not to my liking.

I'd been taking my time in the bathroom until I heard her weeping downstairs. Great harsh gushes that must have burned her throat.

I hurried up then. I needed to be with her for both our sakes.

* * * * *

REQUEST YOUR FREE BOOKS!

2 FREE NOVELS
PLUS 2 FREE GIFTS!

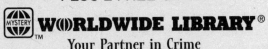

W⊕RLDWIDE LIBRARY®

Your Partner in Crime

FAMOUS FAMILIES

ReaderService.com

Manage your account online!

- Review your order history
- Manage your payments
- Update your address

> ### We've designed the Reader Service website just for you.

Enjoy all the features!

- Reader excerpts from any series
- Respond to mailings and special monthly offers
- Discover new series available to you
- Browse the Bonus Bucks catalogue
- Share your feedback

Visit us at:

ReaderService.com

REQUEST YOUR
FREE BOOKS!

2 FREE NOVELS
FROM THE SUSPENSE COLLECTION
PLUS 2 FREE GIFTS!

YES! Please send me 2 FREE novels from the Suspense Collection and my 2 FREE gifts (gifts are worth about $10). After receiving them, if I don't wish to receive any more books, I can return the shipping statement marked "cancel." If I don't cancel, I will receive 4 brand-new novels every month and be billed just $5.99 per book in the U.S. or $6.49 per book in Canada. That's a saving of at least 25% off the cover price. It's quite a bargain! Shipping and handling is just 50¢ per book in the U.S. and 75¢ per book in Canada.* I understand that accepting the 2 free books and gifts places me under no obligation to buy anything. I can always return a shipment and cancel at any time. Even if I never buy another book, the two free books and gifts are mine to keep forever.

191/391 MDN FEME

Name	(PLEASE PRINT)	

Address		Apt. #

City	State/Prov.	Zip/Postal Code

Signature (if under 18, a parent or guardian must sign)

Mail to the **Reader Service:**
IN U.S.A.: P.O. Box 1867, Buffalo, NY 14240-1867
IN CANADA: P.O. Box 609, Fort Erie, Ontario L2A 5X3

Not valid for current subscribers to the Suspense Collection or the Romance/Suspense Collection.

Want to try two free books from another line?
Call 1-800-873-8635 or visit www.ReaderService.com.

* Terms and prices subject to change without notice. Prices do not include applicable taxes. Sales tax applicable in N.Y. Canadian residents will be charged applicable taxes. Offer not valid in Quebec. This offer is limited to one order per household. All orders subject to credit approval. Credit or debit balances in a customer's account(s) may be offset by any other outstanding balance owed by or to the customer. Please allow 4 to 6 weeks for delivery. Offer available while quantities last.

Your Privacy—The Reader Service is committed to protecting your privacy. Our Privacy Policy is available online at www.ReaderService.com or upon request from the Reader Service.

We make a portion of our mailing list available to reputable third parties that offer products we believe may interest you. If you prefer that we not exchange your name with third parties, or if you wish to clarify or modify your communication preferences, please visit us at www.ReaderService.com/consumerschoice or write to us at Reader Service Preference Service, P.O. Box 9062, Buffalo, NY 14269. Include your complete name and address.

REQUEST YOUR FREE BOOKS!
2 FREE NOVELS PLUS 2 FREE GIFTS!

HARLEQUIN®

INTRIGUE®

BREATHTAKING ROMANTIC SUSPENSE

YES! Please send me 2 FREE Harlequin Intrigue® novels and my 2 FREE gifts (gifts are worth about $10). After receiving them, if I don't wish to receive any more books, I can return the shipping statement marked "cancel." If I don't cancel, I will receive 6 brand-new novels every month and be billed just $4.49 per book in the U.S. or $5.24 per book in Canada. That's a savings of at least 14% off the cover price! It's quite a bargain! Shipping and handling is just 50¢ per book in the U.S. and 75¢ per book in Canada.* I understand that accepting the 2 free books and gifts places me under no obligation to buy anything. I can always return a shipment and cancel at any time. Even if I never buy another book, the two free books and gifts are mine to keep forever.

182/382 HDN FV54

Name   (PLEASE PRINT)

Address   Apt. #

City   State/Prov.   Zip/Postal Code

Signature (if under 18, a parent or guardian must sign)

Mail to the **Reader Service:**
IN U.S.A.: P.O. Box 1867, Buffalo, NY 14240-1867
IN CANADA: P.O. Box 609, Fort Erie, Ontario L2A 5X3

**Are you a subscriber to Harlequin Intrigue books
and want to receive the larger-print edition?
Call 1-800-873-8635 or visit www.ReaderService.com.**

* Terms and prices subject to change without notice. Prices do not include applicable taxes. Sales tax applicable in N.Y. Canadian residents will be charged applicable taxes. Offer not valid in Quebec. This offer is limited to one order per household. Not valid for current subscribers to Harlequin Intrigue books. All orders subject to credit approval. Credit or debit balances in a customer's account(s) may be offset by any other outstanding balance owed by or to the customer. Please allow 4 to 6 weeks for delivery. Offer available while quantities last.

Your Privacy—The Reader Service is committed to protecting your privacy. Our Privacy Policy is available online at www.ReaderService.com or upon request from the Reader Service.

We make a portion of our mailing list available to reputable third parties that offer products we believe may interest you. If you prefer that we not exchange your name with third parties, or if you wish to clarify or modify your communication preferences, please visit us at www.ReaderService.com/consumerchoice or write to us at Reader Service Preference Service, P.O. Box 9062, Buffalo, NY 14269. Include your complete name and address.

HIDIR12

UNION GÉNÉRALE D'ÉDITIONS
8, rue Garancière - Paris VIᵉ

Abélard et Héloïse, *Correspondance* (texte traduit et présenté par Paul Zumthor).

René d'Anjou, *Le Livre du cuer d'amours espris* (texte établi et présenté par Susan Wharton).

Anthologie des grands rhétoriqueurs (texte établi et présenté par Paul Zumthor).

Anthologie des troubadours (texte établi et présenté par Pierre Bec, édition bilingue).

Robert de Boron, *Le Roman du Graal* (texte établi et présenté par Bernard Cerquiglini).

La Chanson de Roland (texte traduit et présenté par Joseph Bédier).

La Mort du roi Arthur (texte traduit et présenté par Gustave Jeanneau).

Lancelot, Roman du XIII⁺ siècle, tomes I et II (textes présentés et traduits par Alexandre Micha).

Pierre Michault, *Œuvres poétiques* (texte établi et présenté par Barbara Folkart).

Christine de Pizan, *Cent ballades d'amant et de dame* (texte établi et présenté par Jacqueline Cerquiglini).

Poèmes d'amour des XII⁺-XIII⁺ siècles (texte et mélodies choisis, présentés et traduits par Emmanuèle Baumgartner et Françoise Ferrand, édition bilingue).

Poèmes héroïques vieil-anglais [Beowulf, Judith, Maldon, Plainte de l'exilée, Exaltation de la Croix] (texte traduit et présenté par André Crépin).

Poèmes de la mort (texte établi par Jean-Marcel Paquette, édition bilingue).

Le Roman d'Apollonius de Tyr (texte traduit et présenté par Michel Zink).

Le Roman de Renart, tomes I et II (texte traduit et présenté par Micheline de Combarieu du Grès et Jean Subrenat).

Théâtre comique du Moyen Age [Les Malheurs de Babion, le Jeu de la feuillée, le Jeu du pèlerin, le Jeu de Robin et Marion, le Garçon et l'aveugle, le Dit de l'herberie, la Farce du cuvier, la Farce de maître Pathelin, le Franc archer de Bagnolet, la Moralité de l'aveugle et du boiteux] (texte présenté et traduit par Claude-Alain Chevallier).

Le Voyage de Saint Brandan par Benedeit (texte et traduction de Ian Short, introduction et notes de Brian Merrilees).

LA CHÂTELAINE
DE VERGY

Textes établis et traduits
par
René STUIP

Ouvrage publié avec le concours
du Centre National des Lettres

*Série « Bibliothèque médiévale »
dirigée par Paul Zumthor*

© Union générale d'éditions, 1985
ISBN 2-264-00668-4

AVERTISSEMENT

Lancée au sein de la série 10/18, cette collection a pour but d'offrir à un très large public des moyens d'accès direct à la culture du Moyen Age. Elle répond ainsi à une demande sensible, en France et à l'étranger, depuis quelques années, demande dont témoigne aussi bien le succès des thèmes et images médiévaux dans des domaines comme le cinéma, la télévision ou la bande dessinée. Jusqu'ici plusieurs obstacles gênent, pour les non-spécialistes, cet accès direct : ils tiennent à la fois au mode d'édition et aux difficultés propres à la langue médiévale.

D'une part, diverses maisons d'édition littéraire ont publié en traduction un petit nombre des textes où s'est exprimé le Moyen Age ; mais la traduction seule, par l'inévitable modernisation qu'elle implique, dénature plus ou moins l'original, et peut en fausser la compréhension, en empêcher la perception juste.

D'autre part, plusieurs maisons d'édition de caractère universitaire publient des collections de textes originaux, dignes de toute confiance sur le plan historique, mais destinées de façon spécifique à l'enseignement et à la recherche, et pourvues à cette fin d'un appareil, parfois considérable, d'érudition.

Un facteur accroît ces difficultés, que rencontre tout amateur des choses médiévales : parmi les très nombreux textes que nous a légués, en manuscrit, le Moyen Age, seul un nombre assez restreint a été l'objet d'éditions multiples, de rééditions et d'un effort de diffusion qui l'a mis en vedette. Or, le choix de cette

5

« élite » de textes n'a souvent été dicté que par d'anciennes routines, sinon par une idée préconçue et conventionnelle de la civilisation médiévale; il demande à être élargi.

La collection Moyen Age vise à surmonter ces obstacles, tout en faisant bénéficier sa clientèle des avantages que comporte le livre de poche. Elle se limitera toutefois, en principe, à procurer des textes qui furent écrits en ancien français, sans s'interdire d'en présenter parfois qui le furent en latin ou en occitan ancien. Tous les volumes de la collection donneront le texte original, accompagné, soit d'une traduction (littérale et uniquement destinée à permettre au lecteur de le déchiffrer sans peine), soit (s'il s'agit de textes plus récents et relativement faciles) d'un lexique des mots rares ou désuets. Texte et traduction seront établis par des médiévistes qualifiés, selon les meilleurs méthodes philologiques; mais ils seront publiés sans appareil érudit ni notes critiques qui pourraient alourdir la lecture. Une introduction fondée sur les recherches les plus récentes présentera le texte en le replaçant dans son contexte historique et culturel.

Quant au choix des textes qu'offrira la collection, il sera dicté par une intention de découverte, par le désir de guider les lecteurs, soit vers des secteurs moins connus mais révélateurs de la civilisation médiévale, soit vers des œuvres majeures mais qui aujourd'hui encore restent introuvables, faute d'éditions, ou le sont devenues faute de rééditions. Dans la mesure du possible on fera alterner la parution de textes plus anciens (XIe-XIIIe siècles) et de textes plus récents (XIVe-XVe). Les textes courts seront regroupés en anthologies centrées sur un genre, un thème ou un style.

L'ÉDITEUR.

DRAME À LA COUR DE B.

« Drame à la Cour de B. » aurait sans doute fait la manchette des journaux si les événements décrits dans les textes édités ici s'étaient produits de nos jours. Certains hebdomadaires auraient publié « toutes les photos », et bientôt on aurait eu des articles prétendant divulguer « enfin toute la vérité sur les meurtres à la Cour de B. ».

Que s'est-il passé ? Une duchesse, jalouse de n'avoir pu obtenir les faveurs d'un jeune noble, révèle à l'aristocratie de B., lors d'une fête à la cour, l'amour secret qui lie ce jeune noble à une châtelaine. Les deux amants se tuent, et la duchesse jalouse est mise à mort par son mari qui, lui aussi, a joué son rôle dans ce drame.

En réalité, l'histoire, telle qu'elle a été décrite dans *la Châtelaine de Vergy,* n'a probablement jamais eu lieu sous cette forme : les personnages sont inventés. Cette fiction littéraire du XIIIe siècle a joui d'une grande popularité : il nous reste encore une vingtaine de manuscrits qui conservent une rédaction du premier texte en vers, il existe aussi des traductions médiévales en néerlandais et en italien, et le nom du personnage principal se retrouve dans

nombre de textes littéraires du XIVᵉ et du XVᵉ siècle.
Certains manuscrits sont illustrés : parallèlement, au
XIVᵉ siècle, on fabrique des objets en ivoire comme
des coffrets et des peignes sur lesquels sont sculptées
les scènes les plus importantes du drame ; on représente aussi l'histoire sur des fresques à Florence et
sur des tapisseries.

A la fin du XVᵉ siècle on voit paraître une version
en prose : *L'Istoire de la Chastelaine du Vergier et de
Tristan le chevalier*. Le chevalier anonyme du texte
original reçoit alors un nom, et certains points restés
plus ou moins obscurs dans le premier texte sont
expliqués. Vers 1540, paraît une version dialoguée
en vers, agrémentée de gravures sur bois. Toujours
au XVIᵉ siècle une grande dame (Marguerite de
Navarre, la sœur de François Iᵉʳ) reprend l'histoire
dans son recueil de nouvelles, *L'Heptaméron*.

Dans cet ouvrage nous ne parlerons ni de la
traduction italienne de Bandello qui est basée sur la
version de Marguerite de Navarre, ni de la traduction française du texte de Bandello par François de
Belleforest en 1580, ni de cette pièce de théâtre de
l'extrême fin du XVIᵉ siècle, *Radegonde, duchesse de
Bourgogne* (tragédie en 4 actes et en alexandrins) du
Seigneur du Souhait, qui date de 1599 et qui s'inspire
probablement soit de Belleforest soit de Marguerite
de Navarre.

Nous ne parlerons pas non plus de toutes les
versions, françaises ou étrangères, publiées après le
XVIᵉ siècle ; l'histoire de la diffusion du texte et des
altérations qu'on y a apportées, surtout au XVIIIᵉ et
au XIXᵉ siècle, reste un problème à part.

Nous présentons ici les quatre textes indiqués plus
haut, et qui sont autant de versions différentes de *la
Chastelaine de Vergi*, nom que l'on donne au texte
rimé du XIIIᵉ siècle, datant de 1230-40 environ et qui

8

a été copié au moins une vingtaine de fois jusqu'au xvɪᵉ siècle.

Dans la seconde moitié du xvᵉ siècle, l'on met en prose le texte versifié relativement sobre du xɪɪɪᵉ ; ce procédé à la mode redonne une jeunesse à bien des textes anciens du xɪɪᵉ et du xɪɪɪᵉ siècle devenus trop ardus. Comme bien d'autres textes ayant subi les mêmes changements, le nouveau texte est appelé « histoire », *L'Istoire de la Chastelaine du Vergier et de Tristan le chevalier*. Lettre et esprit de ce « nouveau-né » diffèrent considérablement de la version originale.

Une troisième version a été conservée dans un petit livret datant probablement des années 1530 (vers 1540 ?) ; le texte a maintenant la forme d'un dialogue versifié, avec par-ci par-là quelques lignes en prose qui annoncent le contenu du passage suivant. Ce livret semble être destiné à un public de lecteurs ; c'est déjà le petit format (68 mm sur 96 mm) des livrets populaires. Nous y trouvons 15 gravures sur bois.

La dernière version que nous présentons ici est l'adaptation de Marguerite de Navarre ; dans son *Heptaméron,* la Châtelaine de Vergy forme le sujet de la nouvelle 70. Marguerite a voulu donner un ton moralisateur au texte ; ceci est encore accentué dans la discussion qui suit la nouvelle.

L'ordre des textes édités est chronologique. Nous commençons par le texte original en vers du xɪɪɪᵉ siècle, puis donnons la version en prose du xvᵉ. Tiré une première fois dans une édition de luxe à 50 exemplaires en 1888, et édité une seconde fois dans une revue régionale peu connue, en 1927, ce texte est pour ainsi dire toujours ignoré. Il sera suivi du texte de l'édition de 1540 qui n'a jamais connu (à notre connaissance) les honneurs d'une édition moderne. Vient ensuite le texte bien connu de Marguerite de Navarre.

Chaque texte sera précédé d'une brève introduction ; les trois derniers textes sont accompagnés d'un glossaire, le premier d'une traduction. Des notes ont été ajoutées à chaque texte pour rendre compte des changements que nous avons apportés au texte tel qu'il se trouve dans nos sources.

Nous remercions François Suard, Karine Huchet, Francine Melka-Teichroew et Tanja van Tuyn de l'aide précieuse qu'ils nous ont apportée dans la préparation de ce livre.

LA CHASTELAINE DE VERGI

INTRODUCTION

C'est sur un arrière-plan courtois que doit se lire
ce texte du XIIIe siècle : en effet le milieu culturel où
il est né est essentiellement celui de la cour, avec
tous ses raffinements de mœurs et de manières, et
avec les charmes de ses habitations. Dans notre texte
même nous en trouvons des reflets : ainsi nous
pouvons constater que les contacts entre le duc et le
chevalier sont de nature à permettre à ce dernier de
fréquenter la cour et de s'entretenir en privé avec la
duchesse ; il y a des fêtes auxquelles assistent les
nobles de la région, dans le palais ducal qui abrite
entre autres une « salle » et les appartements de la
duchesse ; l'on mange et l'on danse ; la Châtelaine a
sa demeure dans un parc voisin et elle a cédé à la
mode : elle a son petit chien.

C'est une vie agréable et douce qui est décrite
dans notre texte ; il n'y a pas de grande aventure, il
n'y a que cette histoire d'amour. Il s'agit d'un de ces
récits brefs si nombreux à l'époque : Fabliaux, Lais,
contes d'animaux, textes brefs d'un tout autre genre,

mais destinés probablement, tout comme *la Châte-laine de Vergy*, à un public courtois.

Dans la littérature de l'époque (deuxième moitié du XIIe et première moitié du XIIIe siècle) nous rencontrons souvent le motif de l'amour courtois, forme spéciale « de ce respect de la femme qui caractérise la courtoisie et marque un changement profond dans la littérature et dans les mœurs » (Frappier 1973 : 12). Dans la littérature en langue d'oc et dans certains textes du nord (en langue d'oïl) l'accent est mis sur le service d'amour, par lequel l'amoureux s'ennoblit moralement. En servant bien sa dame il obtiendra finalement sa récompense, c'est en tout cas ce qu'il espère. Il s'agit alors d'un amour qui lie un jeune homme à une dame d'un rang supérieur ; elle est souvent mariée. C'est ce dernier trait qui explique la nécessité de tenir cet amour secret.

On a depuis toujours eu tendance à établir des rapports entre *la Châtelaine de Vergy* et certains lais du XIIe siècle, *Lanval, Graelent* et *Guingamor,* parce que l'on y retrouve en partie les mêmes thèmes ou les mêmes motifs. C'est surtout le rapprochement avec le *Lanval* de Marie de France (vers 1170) qui a retenu l'attention ; là aussi il s'agit d'un jeune homme amoureux importuné par la femme de son seigneur qui l'accuse ensuite d'avoir voulu la séduire ; dans les deux textes le jeune homme trahit l'amour secret. Mais la façon dont, dans ces textes, les deux thèmes sont élaborés, est bien différente. Marie de France laisse une certaine liberté à ses personnages : elle semble les suivre, s'associer à leurs aventures. Dans *la Châtelaine de Vergy,* l'au-teur dirige de main de maître les actions et les paroles de ses personnages : il ne leur laisse aucune liberté. Leurs actes semblent venir d'eux-mêmes, mais l'enchaînement logique et la structure de l'action montrent bien qu'il n'y a rien d'imprévu pour l'auteur, aucun des actes n'est laissé au hasard, tout est pensé, pesé. Dans *la Châtelaine de Vergy* les protagonistes meurent tous (on pourrait expliquer le départ du duc pour la Terre Sainte comme une mort sociale), tandis que dans *Lanval* la fin est heureuse, ouverte sur l'avenir (les amants partent ensemble pour Avallon, le pays des fées). La *Châtelaine* comporte un enseignement, l'auteur nous avertit dès le début du texte de ce qu'il faut faire et ne pas faire en amour : il ne faut pas découvrir ses secrets (vv. 5-8) ; ce conseil est repris à la fin par ces mots :

> Et par cest essample doit l'en
> s'amour celer...
>
> (941-2).

Il s'agit donc pour l'auteur d'un *exemplum,* court texte moralisateur ou didactique, concentré ici sur la nécessité de cacher l'amour. Cela se comprend fort bien d'ailleurs si l'on se rend compte de la nature de l'amour entre la Châtelaine et le chevalier : c'est probablement un amour adultère. Quelques indications dans le texte (vv. 32-39, 704-708) suggèrent en effet que la Châtelaine est mariée. Le caractère présumé adultère de l'amour qui est plus ou moins acceptable dans la littérature courtoise de l'époque, ne le sera plus pour les remanieurs du xve et du xvie siècle, qui feront de la Châtelaine ou bien une jeune fille ou bien une veuve.

L'auteur de notre texte indique dès le début qu'il s'agit d'un amour courtois, car il emploie un des termes consacrés (« fin'amor » et dérivés) dès le vers 12, parle d'une sorte de contrat entre les deux amants (« couvenant ») au vers 23, et mentionne à plusieurs reprises dans l'introduction (vv. 1-42) la nécessité de cacher cet amour. Son public aura compris dès le début du texte à quel type de complications il pourrait s'attendre. Lorsque, vers le milieu du texte, l'auteur décrit (ou plutôt évite de décrire !) la nuit d'amour de la Châtelaine et du chevalier, nous retrouvons la notion de « fins amans » (v. 437) dans un passage qui explique que ce type d'amour n'est pas pour tout le monde : seuls le connaissent et le comprennent ceux qui veulent vraiment s'adonner à Amor. A la fin du texte (à partir du vers 934) on nous rappelle encore une fois la nécessité absolue de cacher l'amour.

La grande popularité dont jouit *la Châtelaine de Vergy* s'explique par le sujet (fort goûté d'un public aristocratique), et par le caractère artistique et littéraire de la mise en œuvre de motifs communs comme la femme de Putiphar, la mort d'amour, la tombe commune des deux amants, par la référence implicite ou explicite à certains genres lyriques (aube [vv. 448-458], jeu parti [vv. 268 et ss.], la chanson du Châtelain de Coucy [vv. 295-302]), caractères qui rappellent des textes comme *Lanval, le Lai des deux amants, Pyramus et Tisbé, Tristan et Yseut, le Roman de la Violette, le Roman de Guillaume de Dole.*

L'anonymat des personnages a fait croire à l'un des premiers éditeurs du texte qu'il s'agissait d'un roman à clef ; il avait même réussi à identifier les protagonistes, vivant au XIIIe siècle (Raynaud 1892 : 152-53). Ces identifications sont rejetées depuis longtemps déjà comme trop fantaisistes. D'autre part cet anonymat relatif des personnages principaux a sans doute été l'une des causes du changement du nom de la Châtelaine : elle est « de Vergy » dans les manuscrits les plus anciens, mais dès le XIVe siècle nous trouvons une erreur de transcription qui montre que le verger où elle habite l'emporte sur le nom géographique de Vergy (Côte-d'Or). C'est le copiste du ms. *F* (Paris, B.N.n.a.fr. 4531) qui écrit :

> Et cil en plorant li a dit   337
> Jaim vostre nieche du vergier
> Sire je vous dirai issi
> Jaim vostre nieche du vergi   340

S'apercevant de son erreur le copiste biffe le vers 338 et écrit ensuite le vers correct (339), qu'il fait suivre du vers qui révèle le nom de la dame aimée : DU Vergi, et non plus DE Vergi. Nous retrouverons le nom « la Chastelaine du Vergier » dans la plupart des transcriptions ou adaptations tardives.

Le texte a été conservé dans une vingtaine de manuscrits (du XIIIe au XVe siècle) et sous la forme des remaniements que nous avons vus ; d'autre part on trouve dans la littérature des XIVe et XVe siècles de nombreux renvois à la Châtelaine de Vergy comme à l'exemple d'une amante loyale (voir Raynaud 1892 : 155-58). Il y a eu aussi des traductions médiévales du texte en moyen néerlandais et en italien. Il existe de plus une dizaine de coffrets en ivoire, datant probablement tous du XIVe siècle, où nous voyons représentée l'histoire de la Châtelaine, et une suite de fresques, également du XIVe siècle, dans le Palazzo Davizzo Davanzati à Florence. Peut-être faut-il ajouter encore à ces représentations de l'histoire de la Châtelaine une valve de boîte à miroir, reproduite par Koechlin, 1924 (pl. CLXXXVIII, no. 1118 A). Nous y distinguons un couple dans un jardin : à gauche une femme portant une couronne, un petit chien à ses pieds ; à droite un homme qui s'avance vers elle. C'est un des moments privilégiés de l'histoire, représenté aussi dans quatre manuscrits (cf. Stuip 1970 : 34). Il est vrai pourtant que cette scène, détachée de tout contexte, pourrait renvoyer aussi à l'adieu de Tristan et Yseut.

Populaire encore au xvᵉ et au xviᵉ siècle, comme nous l'avons déjà fait remarquer, l'histoire de la Châtelaine semble être oubliée au xviiᵉ siècle. Dès le xviiiᵉ nous la retrouvons : en 1722 le Comte de Vignacourt fait éditer à Paris un texte remanié : *La Comtesse de Vergi. Nouvelle historique galante et tragique.* A partir de ce moment le récit des amours de la Châtelaine et du chevalier a de nouveau sa place dans la production littéraire en France ; il est vrai que l'on fait parfois un mélange de notre histoire et du *Roman du Châtelain de Coucy et de la dame de Fayel.* Ce regain d'intérêt se traduit peut-être aussi par le fait que, au xviiiᵉ siècle, on a réalisé plusieurs copies de manuscrits où se rencontre notre texte. En 1779 « la chastelaine de Vergy » a été « mise en roman » par Legrand d'Aussy ; la première édition du texte en ancien français, de la main de Dominique Méon, date de 1808. Il faut attendre la fin du xixᵉ siècle pour avoir une première édition scientifique, celle de Raynaud (1892).

Là présente édition (comme celle de 1970 d'ailleurs) diffère des autres par le choix du manuscrit de base ; tous les éditeurs ont choisi le ms. *C* (Paris, B.N.f.fr. 853), un grand recueil de textes parmi lesquels se trouve *la Châtelaine de Vergy.* Etant donné que le ms. *C* (de la fin du xiiiᵉ siècle ; il représente l'un des deux grands groupes de manuscrits de *la Châtelaine*) n'a pas été très important dans la tradition du texte et qu'il en existe déjà des éditions courantes (Raynaud-Foulet, Bédier, White-head), nous avons voulu donner le texte d'un autre manuscrit, lui aussi de la fin du xiiiᵉ siècle et qui joua un rôle important dans la tradition du texte.

Dans cette édition nous avons suivi fidèlement le

texte de A (B.N.fr. 375). La division en paragraphes repose sur l'emploi des capitales dans le manuscrit, sauf dans le dernier cas (entre les vers 933 et 934). Les changements que nous avons cru devoir apporter en certains endroits du texte sont basés sur la comparaison de quatre manuscrits : A et E (B.N.fr. 2136) du premier groupe, C et Go (B.N.n.a.fr. 13521) du deuxième groupe ; ils ont été rassemblés après le texte et la traduction. La traduction n'a aucune prétention littéraire ; sa seule fonction est d'aider à comprendre le texte original.

Pour rétablir, lors de la lecture, le rythme du vers octosyllabique, il faudra prononcer le *e* féminin. Dans les cas assez nombreux où un *e* final ne s'élide pas devant un mot commençant par voyelle, nous avons surmonté ce *e* d'un tréma. Le tréma marque également, à l'intérieur des mots, une nouvelle syllabe.

ex. : U-ne-ma-nie-re-de-gent-sont   v. 1

quë-uns-ce-va-liers-tant-proi-a   v. 21

qu'il-se-üst-qu'a-l'eu-re et-au-jor   v. 24

La langue du ms. A présente des traits picards qui, à première vue, pourraient dérouter un lecteur non averti. Signalons donc, à titre d'exemple, les mots suivants :

avenra : adviendra
baisie : baisée, embrassée
biau : beau
castelaine : châtelaine
cevalier : chevalier
chou, çou : ce (forme accentuée)
chius, cius, cis : celui (-ci)
cocie : couchée

17

dou : du
fisent : firent
irie : fâchée
jou : je (forme accentuée)
le : parfois *la*
leu, liu : lieu
sanlant : une graphie de *semblant*
u : ou, où.

Remarques bibliographiques

Editions principales :

G. Raynaud, *la Chastelaine de Vergi,* dans *Romania*
XXI (1892) : 145-193, et Paris, 1910 (coll.
C.F.M.A., 1 ; 2ᵉ éd. revue par L. Foulet, 1912 ; 3ᵉ
éd. 1921 ; 4ᵉ éd. 1963).

F. Whitehead, *la Chastelaine de Vergi,* Manchester,
1944, 2ᵉ éd. 1951.

R. E. V. Stuip, *la Chastelaine de Vergi,* édition
critique du ms. B.N.f.fr. 375 avec Introduction,
Notes, Glossaire et Index, suivie de l'édition
diplomatique de tous les manuscrits connus du
XIIIᵉ et du XIVᵉ siècle. Paris/La Haye, 1970.

L. A. Arrathoon, *la Chastelaine de Vergi.* A new
critical edition of the text with introduction, notes
and an English paraphrase. Thèse, Princeton
Univ., 1975.

Etudes (en ordre chronologique) :

Nous ne mentionnerons que les études citées dans
l'introduction et quelques autres études récentes.
Pour les études parues avant 1969 nous renvoyons à
notre édition de 1970.

18

P. Zumthor, De la chanson au récit : « la Chastelaine de Vergi », dans *Vox Romanica* XXVII (1968) : 77-95. Aussi dans Paul Zumthor, *Langue, texte, énigme*, Paris, 1975 (p. 219-36).

J. Frappier, *Amour courtois et Table ronde*, Genève, 1973.

J. Ch. Payen, « Structure et sens de la Chastelaine de Vergi », dans *le Moyen Age*, 2 (1973) : 209-230.

L. A. Arrathoon, « The Châtelaine de Vergi. A structural study of an Old French artistic short story », *in Language and Style*, VII (1974) : 151-180.

J. Rychmer, « La présence et le point de vue du narrateur dans deux récits courts : Le Lai de Lanval et la Châtelaine de Vergi », *Vox Romanica*, XXXIX (1980) : 86-103.

Une étude très intéressante et qui établit les liens entre les coffrets en ivoire et le texte de *la Chastelaine de Vergi* est :

B. Schmolke-Hasselmann, « " La Chastelaine de Vergi " auf Pariser Elfenbeinkästchen des 14. Jahrhunderts. Zum Problem der Interpretation literarische Texte anhand von Bildzeugnissen », *Romanistisches Jahrbuch*, XXVII (1976) : 52-76.

Voir aussi le catalogue de l'exposition de Paris, *les Fastes du Gothique*, 1981 : 173-75 (n° 128) pour une photo du coffret d'ivoire venant des collections du Louvre, et R. Koechlin, *Les Ivoires gothiques français*, Paris, 1924 (3 tomes).

Et ci aprés de le castelaine de Vergi

Une maniere de gent sont   (f. 331 vo b)
qui d'estre loial samblant font
et de si bien consel celer
qu'il se convient en eus fier ;   4
et quant vient quë on s'i descoevre
tant qu'il sevent l'amor et l'oevre,
si l'espandent par le païs
et en font leur gas et leur ris.   8
Si avient que cius joie en pert
qui le consel a descouvert,
car, tant com l'amors est plus grant,
sont plus mari li fin amant   12
quant li uns d'els de l'autre croit
qu'il ait dit ce que celer doit.
Et sovent tel mescief en vient
que l'amor falir en convient   16
a grant doleur et a vergoigne,
si comme il avint en Borgoingne
d'un cevalier preu et hardi ;
et de la dame de Vregi,   20

20

quë uns cevaliers tant proia
que la dame li otroia
par itel couvenant s'amor
qu'il seüst qu'a l'eure et au jor   24
que par lui seroit descouverte
leur amors, qu'il i aroit perte
et de l'amour et de l'otroi
qu'ele li avoit fait de soi.   28
Et a cele amour otroiier
deviserent qu'en un vergier
li cevaliers tous jors venroit
au terme qu'ele li metroit,   32
ne se mouveroit d'un anglet
dessi quë un petit chienet
verroit par le vergier aler,
et lors venroit sans demorer   36
a sa cambre ; et seüst bien
qu'a cele eure n'i aroit rien
fors la dame tant seulement.
Issi le fisent longement,   40
et fu l'amors douce et celee,
que fors eus ne le seut riens nee.

Li cevaliers fu biaus et cointes,
et par sa valour fu acointes   44
dou duc qui Borgoigne tenoit,
et sovent aloit et venoit
a la cort. Et tant i ala
que la ducesse l'enama,   48
et li fist tel samblant d'amors
que, s'il n'eüst le cuer aillors,
bien se peüst apercevoir
par samblant, qu'ele amast por voir.   52
Mais sanlans qu'ele l'en feïst,   (–c–)
li cevaliers sanlant n'en fist
que poi ne grant s'aperceüst

qu'ele vers lui amour eüst, ₅₆
et tant qu'ele en ot grant anui
qu'ele parla un jour a lui,
et mist a raison par mos teus :
« Sire, vous estes biaus, et preus, ₆₀
ce dient tuit, la Diu merci !
Si avriiés bien deservi
d'avoir amie en si haut leu
qu'en eüssiés honor et preu, ₆₄
que bien vous serroit tele amie. »
« Ma dame », fait il, « je n'ai mie
encore a çou mise m'entente. »
« Par foi », fait ele, « longe atente ₆₈
vous poroit nuire, ce m'est vis.
Si lo que vous soiiés amis
en un haut liu, se vous veés
que vous i soiiés bien amés. ₇₂

Cil respont : « Ma dame, par foi,
je ne sai mie bien por quoi
ce me dites, n'a coi ce monte.
Mais je ne sui ne rois ne conte ₇₆
qui si hautement amer doie,
ne je n'en sui mie a deus doie
d'amer dame si soveraine
se je bien i metoie paine. » ₈₀
« Si estes », fait ele, « se devient ;
mainte plus grans mervelle avient,
et autele avenra encore ;
dites moi se vous savés ore ₈₄
se je vous ai m'amor donee,
qui sui haute dame honeree ? »
Et chius respont isnellepas :
« Ma dame, je ne le sai pas, ₈₈
mais je vauroie vostre amor
avoir par bien et par honor ;

mais de cele amor Dius me gart
qu'a moi n'a vous tort cele part   92
u la honte mon signeur gise,
qu'en nul foer në en nule guise
n'enprendroie tel mesprison
comme de faire desraison   96
si vilaine et si desloial
vers mon droit signor natural. »

« Fi ! », fait cele qui est marie,
« dant musart, et qui vous en prie ? »   100
« Ahi ! », fait cil, « dame, merci !
Bien le sai, mais itant vous di. »
Cele ne tint a lui plus plait,
mais grant corouç et grant dehait   104
en ot au cuer, et si pensa :
s'ele puet, bien s'en vengera ;
si fu ele forment irie.
La nuit quant ele fu cocie   108
jouste le duc, a souspirer
commença, et puis a plorer.
Et li dus errant li demande
qu'est ce qu'ele a, et li commande   112
qu'ele li die maintenant.   (-d-)
« Certes », fait ele, « j'ai doel grant
de ce que ne set nus haus hom
qui foi li porte, ne qui non ;   116
mais plus de bien et d'oneur font
a ceus qui leur traïteur sont,
et si ne s'en aperçoit nus ! »
« Par foi, dame », çou dist li dus,   120
« je ne sai pour coi vous le dites,
mais de tel cose sui je quites,
qu'a nul foer je ne nourriroie
traïteur, se jou le savoie. »   124

« Haés dont », fait ele, « celui
(sel nomma) qui ne fina hui
de moi proiier au lonc du jor
que je li donnasse m'amour.   128
Et me dist que mout a lonc tens
qu'il a esté en ce pourpens ;
onques mais ne le m'osa dire.
Et je me porpensai, biaus sire,   132
tantost que je le vous diroie ;
et ce pert estre cose vraie
qu'il ait pieça a chou pensé :
de ce qu'il ait ailleurs amé   136
nouvele oïe n'en avon.
Si vous requier en gerredon
que vostre honneur si en gardois
que vous savés que il est drois. »   140
Li dus, a qui semble mout grief,
li dist : « J'en venrai bien a cief,
et mout par tans, si com je quit. »
A malaise fut cele nuit   144
li dus, onques dormir ne pot
pour le cevalier qu'il amot,
qu'il croit quë il eüst mesfait :
par droit que s'amour perdue ait ;   148
et pour ce toute nuit villa.
L'endemain par matin leva,
et fait celui a soi venir
que sa feme li fait haïr,   152
sans ce que de riens ait mespris.
Maintenant l'a a raison mis,
seul a seul, n'en i ot k'eus deus :
« Certes », fait il, « c'est grans doleurs   156
quant proece avés et biauté
et il n'a en vous loiauté.
Si m'en avés bien deceü,
que j'ai mout longement creü   160

24

que vous fuissiés de bone foi,
loiaus a tout le mains vers moi,
que j'ai vers vous amour eüe.
Si ne sai dont vous est venue 164
tels pensee et si traïtresse
que proïe avés la ducesse,
et requise de druerie.
Si avés fait grant tricerie 168
que plus vilaine ne puet estre :
issiés errant hors de ma terre,
que je vous en congié sans dote
et la vous vé et desfent toute. 172
Si n'i entrés ne tant ne quant, (332 ro a)
que se je des ore en avant
vous i pooie faire prendre,
sachiés je vous feroie pendre. » 176

Quant li cevaliers chou entent
d'ire et de mautalent esprent,
si que tuit li tranblent li menbre,
que de s'amie li remenbre 180
dont il set qu'il ne puet joïr
se n'est par aler et venir,
et par repairier u païs
dont li dus veut qu'il soit esquis. 184
Et d'autre part li fait mout mal
ce qu'a traïteur desloial
le tient se sires, et a tort.
Si est en si grant desconfort 188
qu'a mort se tient et a traï.
« Sire », fait il, « pour Diu, merci !
Ne creés ja ne ne pensés
que j'onques fuisse si osés ! 192
Ce que me metés a tort seure
je ne pensai ne jour në eure,
s'a mal fait qui le vous a dit. »

25

« Ne vous vaut rien li escondit »,   196
fait li dus, « que point n'en i a.
Cele meïsmes conté m'a
en quel maniere et en quel guise
vous l'avés proiie et requise,   200
comme traïtres envious.
Et tel cose deïstes vous,
puet estre, dont ele se taist. »
« Ma dame a dit chou qu'il li plaist. »   204
« Ha ! », fait cil qui mout est maris,
« ne vous i vaut li escondis ! »
« Riens ne m'i vaut que j'en deïsse...
Si n'est riens que jou n'en feïsse   208
par si que j'en fuisse creü,
que de ce n'i a riens eü. »
« Si a », çou dist li dus, « par m'ame ! »
cui il souvient mout de sa fame   212
qui li ot dit un grant savoir,
— dont quide bien quë il soit voir —
c'onques n'oï que nus parlast
que cil en autre liu amast.   216

Dont dist li dus au cevalier :
« Se vous me volés afier
par vostre loial sairement,
que vous me dirés vraiement   220
ce que je vous demanderoie,
par vostre dit certains seroie
se vous avriiés fait u non
ce dont j'ai vers vous sopeçon. »   224
Cil qui tant convoite et desire
a jeter son signeur de l'ire
qu'il a envers lui sans deserte,
et qui redoute cele perte   228
comme de guerpir la contree
u cele est qui plus li agree,

respont que tout sans contredit
fera ce que li dus a dit,   232
qu'il ne pense ne ne regarde   (–b–)
de ce dont li dus se prent garde.
Ne s'en seüst pas apenser
ce que li dus veut demander   236
de riens fors de cele proiere.
Le sairement en tel maniere
l'em prist li dus, et cil l'en fist,
et li dus maintenant li dist :   240
« Sachiés par fine verité
que, ce que je vous ai amé
ça en arriere de fin cuer,
ne me laisse croire a nul foer   244
de vous tel mesfait et tel honte
comme la ducesse me conte.
Ne tant ne la tenisse a voire,
se ce ne le me feïst croire   248
et m'en meïst en grant dotance
que j'esgart vostre contenance,
et de cointise et d'autre rien
a coi on puet savoir mout bien   252
que vous amés, u que ce soit.
Et quant d'aillours ne s'aperçoit
nus, qu'amés damoisele u dame,
je me pens que ce soit ma fame,   256
qui me dist que vous la proiés.
Si n'en puis estre desvoiiés
que je cuiç qu'ensi voist l'afaire
por riens ke vous me sachiés faire,   260
se vous ne me dites c'aillors
amés, en tel liu, par amours,
que m'en laissiés sans nule doute
savoir ent la verité toute.   264
Et se ce faire ne volés
comme parjur vous en alés,

hors de ma tere, sans delai. »
Cil ne set nul consel de soi,   268
que le gieu a parti si fort
que l'un et l'autre tient a mort :
que s'il dist la verité pure
— qu'il dira s'il ne se parjure —   272
a mort se tient, s'il mesfait tant
qu'il trespasse le convenant
qu'a sa dame et a s'amie a,
qu'il est seürs qu'il la perdra   276
s'ele s'em puet apercevoir ;
et s'il ne dist au duc le voir
parjures est et foimentie,
et pert le païs et s'amie ;   280
mais dou païs ne li causist
se s'amie li remansist,
que sour toute riens perdre crient.
Et pour çou qu'adés li souvient   284
de la grant joie et du soulas
qu'il a eü entre ses bras,
si se pense s'il la messert
et se par son mesfait la pert,   288
quant o soi ne l'en puet mener,
comment porra sans li durer ?
Si est en tel point autresi
com li castelains de Couci,   292
qui — au cuer n'avoit s'anui non —   (–ç–)
dist en un ver d'une cançon :

Par Diu, Amours, grief m'est a consirer
du douç soulas et de la compaignie,   296
et des samblans que m'i soloit moustrer
cele qui m'ert dame, compaigne, amie.
Et quant regart sa douce courtoisie
et les dous mos qu'a moi soloit parler,   300
comment me puet li cuers u cors durer ?

Quë il ne part ? Certes, trop est malvais !

Li cevaliers en tele angousse
pense se le voir en conoisse,   304
u il mence et laist le païs.
Et quant il est ensi pensis
qu'il ne set li queus li vaut mius,
l'euwe du cuer li monte es eus   308
por l'angousse qu'il se pourcace,
si li descent jusqu'en la face.
Li dus quide que soit tel cose
que reconnoistre ne li ose.   312

Lors dist li dus isnellepas :
« Bien voi que ne vous fiés pas
en moi tant comme devriiés.
Quidiés vous, se me disiiés   316
vostre consel priveement,
que jel deïsse a nule gent ?
Je me lairoie avant, sans faute,
traire les dens l'un avant l'autre ! »   320
« Ha ! sire », fait cil, « merci, sire !
Je ne sai que je doie dire
ne que je doie devenir,
mais je vauroie mius morir   324
que perdre chou que je perdroie
se le voir dit vous en avoie.
Que s'il estoit de li seü
que l'eüsse reconneü   328
a rien qui soit u mont vivant... ! »
Lors dist li dus : « Je vous creant
sour le cors et l'ame de moi,
et sour l'amour et sour le foi   332
que je vous doi sour vostre homage,
que ja en trestout mon eage
n'en ert a creature nee
parole nule racontee,   336

ne samblant fait, grant ne petit. »
Et cil en plourant li a dit :

« Sire, jel vous dirai ensi :
j'aim vostre niece de Vergi,   340
et ele moi, tant c'on puet plus. »
« Or me dites donc », fait li dus,
quant vous volés c'on vous en coevre,
set nus fors ke vous dui ceste oevre ? »   344
Et li cevaliers li respont :
« Nenil, creature du mont. »
« Et », fait li dus, « ce n'avint onques ;
comment i avenés vous donques,   348
ne comment savés liu ne tens ? »   (–d–)
« Par foi », fait cil, « sire, par sens
que je vous dirai sans riens taire,
quant tant savés de nostre afaire. »   352
Lors li a toutes acontees
les venues et les alees,
et la convenance premiere,
et dou petit cien la maniere.   356
Lors dist li dus : « Je vous requier
quë a vostre terme premier
voelliés que vostre compains soie
d'aler o vous en cele voie,   360
que je voel savoir sans aloigne
së ensi va vostre besogne ;
si n'en savra ma niece rien. »
« Sire », fait il, « je l'otroi bien,   364
mais qu'il ne vous griet në anuit ;
et sachiés, jou irai anuit. »
Et li dus dist qu'il i ira,
ne ja ne li anuiera,   368
ains li sera soulas et gieu.
Entre eus deus devisent le lieu
u assambleront tout a pié

si tost comme il fu anuitié, 372
quë assés pres d'illoec estoit
u la niece le duc manoit.
Cele part tienent lor cemin,
tant qu'il sont venu au jardin, 376
u li dus ne fu pas grant piece
quant il vit le cienet sa niece
qui s'en vint au bout du vergier,
tant qu'il troeve le cevalier, 380
et grant joie fait au cienet.
Tantost a la voie se met
li cevaliers, et le duc laist.
Et li dus aprés lui s'en vait 384
pres de la cambre, au plus que puet :
illoec s'areste et ne se muet,
— d'un arbre mout grant et mout large
s'estoit couvers con d'une targe — 388
et mout entent a lui celer.
D'illoec vit en la cambre entrer
le cevalier, et vit issir
sa niece et contre lui venir 392
hors de la cambre en un prael ;
et vit et oï tel apel
com ele li fist, par soullas,
de salu de bouce et de bras. 396
Si tost com ele le coisi
de la cambre mout tost sali,
et de ses biaus bras l'acola
et plus de cent fois le baisa 400
ains qu'el feïst longe parole.
Et cius le rebaise et acole
et li dist : « Ma dame, m'amie,
m'amors, mes cuers, ma druerie, 404
m'esperance et tout quanque j'aim,
sachiés de voir que j'ai grant faim
d'estre o vous si comme je sui,

car pieça avoec vous ne fui. »
Ele redist : « Mon douç signor,   (332 vo a)
mon douç ami, ma douce amor,
onques puis ne fui jor në eure
que ne m'anuiast la demeure !   412
Mais ore de riens ne me doel
quant j'ai o moi chou que je voel,
et vous estes sains et haitiés :
que li tres bien venus soiiés ! »   416
Et chius dist : « Et vous bien trovee. »
Tout oï li dus a l'entree
— de la cambre si pres estoit —;
sa niece a la vois quenissoit   420
si bien, et a la contenance,
quë il est tous hors de dotance,
et si tient de chou la ducesse
que li ot dit a menteresse.   424
Et mout li plaist : or voit il bien
que cil ne li a mesfait rien
de ce dont il l'a mescreü.
Illoeques s'est ensi tenu   428
toute la nuit, endementiers
que la dame et li cevaliers
dedens la cambre en un lit furent,
qui sans dormir ensanle jurent,   432
a tel joie et a tel deport
qu'il n'est raisons que nus recort
— c'on le dïe ne quë on l'oie —
s'il n'en atent avoir tel joie   436
quë Amours a fins amans done,
quant sa paine li gueredone.
Car cil qui tel joie n'atent,
së il l'ooit, rien në entent,   440
puis qu'il n'a a Amor le cuer,
que nus ne saroit a nul foer
combien vaut a tel joie avoir

32

s'Amours ne li faisoit savoir : 444
ne teus biens n'avient mie a tous,
car cë est joie sans corus
et soulas et envoiseüre.
Mais tant y a que petit dure, 448
— c'est avis a l'amant qui l'a —
ja tant longes ne duera ;
tant li plaist la vie qu'il maine
que, se nuis devenoit semaine, 452
et semaine devenist mois
et mois un an et uns ans trois
et troi an vint et vint an cent,
quant verroit au definement 456
de la nuit, ains qu'il ajornast,
si vauroit il qu'il anuitast.
et en tele pensee estoit
cil qui li dus atendoit, 460
car ains jour aler l'en convient ;
et s'amie o lui a l'uis vient.
La vit li dus au congiet prendre
baisier donner et basier rendre, 464
et oï souvent souspirer
et au congié plaindre et plorer,
que plouré i ot mainte lerme ;
et si oï prendre le terme 468
du rasambler en tel maniere. (–b–)
Li cevaliers d'iloec arriere
s'em part, et la dame l'uis clot,
mais tant comme veoir le pot 472
le convoia de ses biaus ieus
quant ele ne pot faire mius.

Quant li dus vit clore l'uisset
tantost a la voie se met, 476
tant que le cevalier ataint
qui a soi meïsme se plaint

33

de la nuit : si com il a dit
trop li avoit duré petit.   480
— En tel pensee et a teus dis
fu cele dont il ert partis,
a qui il semble pour la nuit
que fali ait a son deduit,   484
ne dou jour ne se loe point. —
Li cevaliers en itel point
est de pensee et de parole.
Quant li dus l'ataint si l'acole   488
et li a fait joie mout grant,
si li a dit : « Je vous creant
que tous jors mais vous amerai,
ne ja mais ne vous meskerrai,   492
que vous m'avés voir dit de tot
et ne m'avés menti de mot. »

« Sire », fait cil, « pour Diu, merci !
Et por Diu vous requier et pri   496
que cest consel celer vous plaise ;
perdue aroie et joie et aise
et morroie sans nule faute,
se je savoie ke nul autre   500
ice savoit, fors vous sans plus. »
« Or n'en parlés ja », fait li dus,
« sachiés qu'il ert si bien celé
que ja par moi n'en ert parlé. »   504

Ensi s'en sont parlant venu
la dont il estoient meü.
Et ce jour, quant vint au mangier,
moustra li dus au cevalier   508
plus biau samblant que n'avoit fait ;
et tel courouç et tel dehait
en ot la ducesse, sans fable,
qu'ele se leva de la table,   512
et a fait samblant par faintise

34

que maladie li soit prise.
Et li dus, quant il ot mengié
et bien lavé et festiié, 516
si va la ducesse veoir,
et la fist sour un lit seoir,
et a commandé que nului
ne remegne laiens fors lui. 520
On fait errant çou qu'il commande,
et li dus tantost li demande
comment cius maus li est venu,
et que çou est qu'ele a eü. 524
Ele respont : « Se Dieus me gart,
je ne m'en donnoie regart,
ore quant au mangier assis,
que gringneur sens et plus d'avis 528
n'eüst en vous ke je n'i vi, (–c–)
quant vous tenés plus cier celui
que je vous ai dit qui porcace
qu'il a moi honte et despit face ! 532
Et quant vi que plus biau samblant
li feïstes que dedevant,
si grant doel et si grant ire oi
quë illoec demourer ne poi. » 536

« Ha ! » fait li dus, « ma douce amie,
certes, je ne kerroie mie
ne vous në autre creature,
quë onques par nule aventure 540
avenist çou ke vous me dites.
Ains sai bien qu'il en est tous quites,
n'onques n'ot pensé de ce faire,
tant ai apris de son afaire, 544
si que ne m'en enquerés plus. »
Atant d'iloec se part li dus,
et cele remaint si pensive
que jamais, tant com el soit vive, 548

une eure a aise ne sera
devant que plus apris avra
de ce dont li dus li desfent
qu'el ne li demande noient.   552
Mais ja ne l'en tenra desfense,
car en son cuer engin porpense
qu'ele le porra bien savoir
s'ele se soeffre jusqu'au soir,   556
qu'ele ait le duc entre ses bras :
ele set bien k'en teus soulas
en fera — ce ne dout je point —
mius son voloir quë en tel point ;   560
pour cë adont atant se taist.
Et quant li dus coucier se vait
a une part dou lit s'est traite :
sanlant fait que point ne li haite   564
que li dus o li gesir doie,
qu'ele set bien çou est la voie
de son mari metre au desous,
par faire sanlant de courous.   568
Pour çou se tient en itel guise
quë ele mius le duc atise
a croire qu'ele soit irie.
Pour ce, sans plus, qu'il l'a baisie   572
li dist ele : « Mout estes faus
et trecieres et desloiaus,
qui me moustrés sanlant d'amor,
c'onques ne m'amastes nul jor.   576
Et j'ai esté lontans si fole
que j'ai creü vostre parole ;
souventes fois me disiiés
que de loial cuer m'amiiés.   580
Mais hui me sui aperceüe
que j'en ai esté deceüe. »
Et li dus dist : « Et vous, de quoi ? »
« Ja me deïstes vous, par foi »,   584

36

fait cele qui a mal i bee,
« que je ne fuisse si osee
que je vous enquesisse rien
de ce que vous savés or bien. »   588
« De quoi, suor, savés vous, por Dé ? »   (–d–)
« De ce que cil vous a conté »,
fait ele, « mençongne et avoire,
qu'il vous a fait penser et croire.   592
Ne de ce savoir ne me caut,
que je pense que petit vaut
a vous amer de cuer loial,
quë onques, fust u bien u mal,   596
mes cuers riens n'en vit ne n'en sot
que ne seüssiés ausi tost.
Et or voi que vous me celés,
vostre merchi, les vos pensés.   600
Si sachiés ore sans doutance
que jamais n'avrai tel fiance
en vous, ne cuer de tel maniere
con j'ai eü ça en arriere. »   604

Lors recommença a plourer
la ducesse, et a souspirer,
ains s'esforça quant qu'elle pot.
Et li dus grant pité en ot,   608
qui li a dit : « Ma bele soer,
je ne sousferroie a nul foer
ne vostre courouç ne vostre ire.
Mais sachiés, je ne voel pas dire   612
ce que volés que je vous die ;
si faites trop grant vilenie. »
Ele li dist isnellepas :
« Sire, ce ne me dites pas,   616
que je voi bien a cel samblant
qu'en moi ne vous fiés pas tant
que celaisse vostre conseil.

Et sachiés que trop m'esmervel,   620
c'ains n'oï ne grant ne petit
conseil que vous m'eüssiés dit,
dont descouvers fuissiés par moi.
Et si vous di en boine foi :   624
ja en ma vie n'avenra. »
Quant cë ot dit si reploura.
Et li dus le racole et baise,
et est de son cors a malaise,   628
si que plus ne se pot tenir
de l'aventure regehir.

Puis si li a dit : « Bele dame,
je ne sai que face, par m'ame,   632
que tant me fi en vous et croi
que celer cose ne vous doi.
Sachiés, et itant vous en di,
que se je sui par vous traï   636
vous en receverés la mort. »
Et ele dist : « Bien m'i acort ;
estre ne poroit ke feïsse
cose dont vers vous mesfeïsse. »   640
Cil qui l'aime por çou la croit,
et quide que verités soit
de ce que li dist, puis li conte
de sa niece trestout le conte :   644
comment aprist dou cevalier,
et comment il fu el vergier
en l'anglet u il n'ot qu'els deus,
et con li cienés vint a eus,   648
Et de l'issue et de l'entrée   (333 ro a)
li a la verité contee,
si qu'il n'i a de riens teü
quë il ait oï ne veü.   652
Et quant la ducesse l'entent
quë il aime plus bassement

qui de s'amour l'a escondite,
morte se tient et a despite.   656
Mais ains de ce samblant ne fist,
ains otria tout, et pramist
au duc a si celer chele oevre
que s'ensi est qu'el le descoevre,   660
quë il la pende a une hart.
Et si li est il ja mout tart
de celi parler qu'ele het
des icele eure qu'ele set   664
qu'ele estoit amie a celui
qui li a fait honte et anui :
pour itant ce li est avis
qu'il ne veut estre ses amis.   668

Si aferme tout son porpens
que s'ele voit ne liu ne tens
qu'a la niece le duc parot,
qu'ele li dira ausi tost,   672
ne ja ne celera tel cose
u felonnie avra enclose.
Mais ains en liu n'en point n'en vient
tant que la Pentecouste vient,   676
que ce fu la feste premiere
que li dus tint sa cort pleniere,
si qu'il envoia partout querre
toutes les dames de la terre,   680
et sa niece tout premeraine
qui de Vergi ert castelaine.
Et quant la ducesse la vit
tantost tous li sans li fremist,   684
con cele du mont que plus het ;
mais son corage celer set,
si que plus biau sanlant li fait
c'onques nul jor ne li ot fait.   688
Mais mout ot grant talent de dire

çou dont ele a u cuer grant ire ;
et la demeure mout li couste
por ce jour de la Pentecoste.   692

Quant les tables furent levees,
en a la ducesse menees
les dames en sa cambre o soi
pour eles parer en recoi,   696
pour venir cointes as caroles.
Lors ne pot garder ses paroles
la ducesse, qui vit son lieu,
ains dist ausi comme par gieu :   700
« Castelaine, soiiés bien cointe,
car bel ami avés acointe. »
Et cele dist mout simplement :
« Je ne sai quel acointement   704
vous pensés, ma dame, por voir,
que talent n'ai d'ami avoir
qui ne soit du tout a l'onnor
et de moi et de mon signor. »   708
« Je l'otroi bien », dist la ducesse,   (-b-)
« mais vous estes bonne maistresse,
qui avés apris le mestier
dou petit chienet afaitier. »   712

Les dames ont oï le conte
mais ne sevent a coi ce monte ;
o la duchesse s'en revont
as caroles que faites ont.   716
Et la castelaine remaint ;
li cuers d'ire li torble et taint
et li mue trestous u ventre.
Dedens une gardereube entre,   720
ou une pucelete estoit
ki as piés dou lit se gisoit,

40

mais ele ne le puet veoir.
Ou lit s'est laissie chaoir   724
li castelaine, mout dolente ;
mout se plaint et mout se demente
et dist : « Ha ! Sire Dius, merchi !
Que puet çou estre ke j'oï   728
ke ma dame m'a fait regret
ke j'ai affaitiet mon cienet ?
Ce ne set ele par nului,
ce sai je bien, fors par celui   732
que j'amoie, et traïe m'a !
Ne pour riens ne li deïst ja
s'a li n'eüst grant acointance,
et s'il ne l'amast sans dotance   736
plus ke moi, qui il a traïe ;
bien sai quë il ne m'aime mie
quant il me faut de convenant.
Dous Dieus, et je l'amoie tant   740
comme riens peüst autre amer,
ne ne pooie aillors penser
en nule eure, ne jor ne nuit,
car c'ert ma joie et mon deduit,   744
c'ert mes delis, c'ert mes confors,
c'ert mes soulas, c'ert mes depors.
Comment a lui me contenoie
de penser, quant je nel veoie !   748

Ha ! amis, dont est ce venu ?
Que poés estre devenu,
quant vers moi avés esté faus ?
Je quidoie ke plus loiaus   752
me fuissiés, se Dius me conseut,
que ne fu Tristrans a Yseut.
Plus vous amoie la moitié,
se Dius ait ja de moi pitié,   756
que ne faisoie moi meïsmes :

41

onkes avant, ne puis, ne primes,
en penser, en dit ne en fait,
ne fis petit ne grant mesfait   760
pour choi me deüssiés haïr,
ne si vilainement traïr
comme a nos amours depecier
pour autre amer et moi laissier,   764
et descouvrir nostre consel.
He ! las, amis, mout m'esmervel,
que li miens cuers, si m'aït Dius,
ne fu onques vers vous itius :   768
que, se tout le mont et neïs   (c–)
et ciel et tere et paradis
me donnast Dius, pas nel preïsse
par convenant que vous pardisse.   772
Que vous estiiés ma rikece
et mes soullas et ma leeche,
ne rien grever ne me peüst
tant comme mes las cuers seüst   776
que li vostres de riens m'amast.
He ! fine Amour, et qui pensast
que cil feïst vers moi desroi,
qui disoit, quant il ert o moi   780
et je faisoie mon pooir
de faire trestout son voloir,
qu'il ert tous miens, et a sa dame
me tenoit il de cors et d'ame ;   784
et le disoit si doucemant
que l'en creoie maintenant.
Ne je ne quidaisse a nul foer
qu'il peüst trouver en son cuer   788
envers moi courouç ne haïne
pour ducesse ne pour roïne,
qu'a lui amer m'estoit si bien
qu'a mon cuer prendoie le sien.   792
De lui me pensoie autresi

qu'il se tenoit a mon ami,
toute sa vie et son eage,
que bien connois en mon corage : 796
së avant morust, tant l'amaisse
quë aprés lui petit duraisse,
qu'estre morte o lui me fust mius
que vivre, si ke de mes oeus 800
ne le veïsse nule fois.
Ha ! fine Amour, est ce donc drois
quë il a ensi descouvert
nostre consel ? dont il me pert, 804
qu'a m'amour otroiier li dis,
et bien en convenant li mis,
quë a cele eure me perdroit
que nostre amour descouverroit. 808
Et quant j'ai avant perdu lui,
ne puis aprés itel anui ;
que sans lui por qui je me doel
ne puis vivre, ne je ne voel, 812
ne ma vie ne me plaist point ;
ains pri Diu ke la mort me doinst
et que, tout ausi vraiement
comme j'ai amé loialment 816
celui qui m'a ce pourcacié,
ait de l'ame de moi pitié ;
et a celui qui a son tort
m'a traïe et livree a mort 820
doinst honnour. Et je li pardon.
Ne ma mort n'est se douce non,
si m'est avis, quant de li vient ;
et quant de s'amour me sovient, 824
por lui morir ne m'est pas paine. »
Atant se tut la castelaine,
fors k'ele dist en souspirant :
« Dous amis, a Diu vous commant. » 828

A cest mot de ses bras s'estraint,   (–d–)
li cuers li faut, li vis li taint,
angousseusement s'est pasmee,
et gist pale et descoulouree   832
en mi le lit, morte sans vie.
Mais ses amis ne le set mie,
qui se deduisoit en la sale
a la carole, u danse et bale.   836
Mais ne li plaist riens quë il voie
quant cele a qui ses cuers s'otroie
ne voit point, dont il s'esmervelle ;
si a dit au duc en l'orelle :   840
« Sire, qu'est ce ke vostre niece
est demouree si grant piece
que n'est as caroles venue ?
Ne sai se l'avés mise en mue. »   844
Et li dus la carole esgarde,
qui de ce ne se prenoit garde ;
celui a soi par la main trait
et droit a la cambre s'en vait.   848
Et quant illoeques ne la troeve
au cevalier commande et roeve
qu'en la garderobe la quiere,
car il le veut en tel maniere.   852
Et cil qui l'en sot mout bon gré
est en la garderoebe entré,
ou s'amie gisoit enverse
ou lit, descoulouree et perse :   856
cius a trouvé le cors tout roide.
Le bouce li baise, qu'ert froide,
et au sanlant ke li cors mostre
voit bien k'ele est morte tot outre.   860
Tantost com esbahis s'escrie :
« Qu'est ce ? Las ! est morte m'amie ? »
Et la pucele sailli sus,
qui as piés du lit gisoit jus,   864

44

si dist : « Sire, ce croi je bien
que morte soit, kë autre rien
n'a demandé puis ke vint chi,
pour le courouç de son ami   868
dont ma dame l'ataïna ;
et dou cienet le ramprosna,
dont li courous li vint morteus. »
Et quant cil oï les mos teus   872
que ce qu'il dist au duc l'a morte,
sans mesure se desconforte :
« He ! Dius ! », dist il, « ma douce amor,
la plus courtoise et la millour   876
c'onques fust, et la plus loial !
Comme trecieres desloial
vous ai morte ; si fust droiture
que sour moi tournast l'aventure,   880
si que vous n'en eüssiés mal.
Mais cuer aviiés si loial
que l'avez avant de moi prise ;
mais je ferai de moi justice   884
pour la traïson ke j'ai faite ! »
Une espee du foerre a traite
qui ert pendue a un espuer,
et s'en feri parmi le cuer ;   888
chaoir se laist sour l'autre cors,   (333 vo a)
tant a sainiét quë il est mors.
Et la pucele hors sali
quant vit les deus cors mors gesir :   892
hideur a de chou qu'ele vit.
Au duc k'ele encontra a dit
chou qu'ele a oÿ et veü,
si qu'ele n'i a riens teü :   896
comment l'affaire ert commencié,
neïs dou chienet affaitié
dont la ducesse avoit parlé.
Es vous le duc adont dervé !   900

45

De maintenant en la cambre entre ;
au cevalier trait hors du ventre
l'espee dont s'estoit ochis.
Tantost s'est a la voie mis,   904
grant oirre, droit a la carole,
sans plus tenir nule parole,
de maintenant a la ducesse ;
si li a rendu la pramesse   908
quë el chief li a embatue
l'espee kë il porta nue,
sans parler, car trop fu iriés.
La ducesse chiet a ses piés   912
voiant tous cheus de la contree :
lors fu la cours toute torblee
des cevaliers qui la estoient,
qui grant joie mener devoient.   916
Et li dus tout autresi tost,
oiant tous qui oïr le volt,
dist tout l'afaire enmi la cort.
Lors n'i a celui qui ne plort,   920
et meesmement quant il voient
les deus amans qui mort gisoient,
et la ducesse d'autre part.
A doel et a courouç depart   924
la cors, et a meschief vilain.
Li dus enterer l'endemain
fist les amans en un sarqu,
et la ducesse en autre liu ;   928
mais de l'aventure ot tele ire
c'onques puis ne l'oÿ on rire.
Errant se croisa d'outremer,
u il ala sans demourer,   932
et devint illoeques Templier.

He ! Dius, trestout cest encombrier
et chius meschies por çou avint

46

c'au cevalier tant mesavint 936
qu'il dist chou ke celer devoit,
et que deffendu li avoit
s'amie, qu'il ne le deïst
tant com s'amor avoir volsist. 940
Et par cest essample doit l'en
s'amour celer, par si grant sen
c'on ait tous jors en ramenbrance
que li raconters point n'avance 944
et li celers en tous poins vaut :
qui tout çou fait ne crient assaut
des faus felons enquereours
qui enquierent d'autrui amors. 948

Explicit de la castelaine de Vergi.

TRADUCTION *

Il y a des gens qui feignent d'être loyaux, et de si bien garder les secrets qu'il semble naturel de leur faire confiance ; et quand finalement on se livre à eux et qu'ils sont au courant des détails de cet amour, ils en répandent le bruit dans tout le pays et en font l'objet de leurs plaisanteries et de leurs rires. Ainsi il arrive que celui qui a révélé le secret en perd la joie, car, plus l'amour est grand, plus les parfaits amants sont affligés, quand l'un d'eux croit que l'autre a dit ce qu'il faut tenir caché. Et c'est ainsi qu'il arrive souvent de tels malheurs que l'amour cesse dans la douleur et la honte. Ce fut le cas, en Bourgogne, d'un vaillant et hardi chevalier, et de la dame de Vergy, que ce chevalier avait priée si longtemps de son amour que la dame le lui accorda à la condition suivante : il devait savoir qu'au moment même où leur amour serait révélé par lui, il perdrait cet amour et le don total qu'elle lui avait fait d'elle-même. Et lorsqu'elle lui accorda cet amour (30) ils décidèrent que le chevalier se rendrait toujours, au moment qu'elle fixerait, dans un jardin, et ne

* Les numéros figurant entre parenthèses renvoient aux numéros des vers du texte en ancien français.

48

bougerait de son recoin avant qu'il eût vu un petit chien aller dans le jardin ; alors il devrait venir sans tarder dans sa chambre. « Il pouvait être sûr qu'à ce moment-là il n'y aurait personne d'autre qu'elle. » Longtemps tout se passa ainsi, et leur amour fut doux et secret, car personne d'autre n'en eut connaissance.

Le chevalier était beau et sage, et à cause de ses qualités il avait été admis dans le cercle des intimes du duc de Bourgogne ; il allait donc fréquemment à la cour. Il s'y rendit même si souvent que la duchesse s'éprit de lui, et lui donna de telles marques de son amour que, s'il n'avait eu le cœur ailleurs, il aurait bien pu s'apercevoir, à ces signes, qu'elle était vraiment amoureuse. Mais quelque marque qu'elle lui en donnât, le chevalier ne fit pas paraître qu'il avait remarqué peu ou prou son amour pour lui ; elle en fut tellement contrariée que, un jour, elle lui adressa la parole en lui disant :

« Seigneur, vous êtes beau et sage, tous le disent. Dieu merci ! Aussi mériteriez-vous bien d'avoir une amie si haut placée (64) que vous en auriez honneur et avantage ; une telle amie vous conviendrait bien ! »

« Madame », dit-il, « je ne me suis pas encore soucié de ces choses-là. »

« Ma foi », dit-elle, « attendre longtemps pourrait vous nuire, je crois. Je vous conseille donc de chercher l'amitié en haut lieu, si vous y trouvez bon accueil. »

Il répond : « Madame, ma foi, je ne comprends pas très bien la raison et le sens de ces paroles. Mais je ne suis ni roi ni comte pour pouvoir prétendre à un amour en si haut lieu, et je suis fort éloigné d'aimer une si haute dame, même pas si j'y consacrais tous mes efforts. »

« Oh si », dit-elle, « peut-être… ; il arrive des merveilles plus grandes. En voici encore une : dites-moi si vous savez maintenant que je vous ai donné mon amour, moi qui suis une haute dame, comblée d'honneurs ? »

Et le chevalier répond immédiatement :

« Madame, je ne le sais pas, mais je voudrais avoir votre amour en tout bien tout honneur ; que Dieu me garde pourtant d'un amour qui pourrait nous entraîner (moi ou vous) à porter atteinte à l'honneur de mon seigneur ; car à aucun prix ni en aucune façon je ne voudrais commettre la faute d'agir de manière si vilaine et si déloyale (98) à l'égard de mon suzerain légitime. »

« Fi donc ! », fit-elle, bien dépitée, « jeune sot, et qui vous en prie ? »

« Ah, dame », dit-il, « pitié ! Je le sais bien, mais ce que j'ai dit est dit. »

Elle ne lui parla pas davantage, mais était très irritée et chagrine. Voici sa pensée : si elle peut, elle se vengera bien de lui ! Elle était vraiment très fâchée !

Ce soir-là, lorsqu'elle fut couchée aux côtés du duc, elle se mit à soupirer, puis à pleurer. Le duc lui demanda aussitôt ce qu'elle avait, et lui ordonna de le lui dire immédiatement.

« Vraiment, » dit-elle, « je suis bien triste de ce que les gens haut placés ne savent qui est loyal envers eux et qui ne l'est pas ; mais ils comblent de biens et d'honneurs ceux qui les trahissent, et aucun d'eux ne s'en aperçoit ! »

« Sur ma foi, dame, » dit le duc, « je ne sais pas pourquoi vous le dites, mais cela ne s'applique pas à moi, car à aucun prix je ne garderais près de moi un traître, si j'étais au courant. »

« Haïssez donc, » dit-elle, « celui qui — et elle le nomma — aujourd'hui n'a cessé de me demander, tout au long de la journée, que je lui donne mon amour. Il m'a dit que depuis bien longtemps déjà il y pense (131) sans jamais avoir osé me l'avouer. Et j'ai décidé aussitôt, mon cher seigneur, que je vous le dirais. Sans aucun doute il y pense depuis longtemps déjà, car nous n'avons pas entendu dire qu'il aime ailleurs. Je vous demande donc que vous, de votre côté, fassiez ce qui est juste pour garder votre honneur. »

Le duc, qui est fort embarrassé, lui dit :

« Je tirerai cela au clair, et bien vite, je pense. »

Cette nuit-là le duc fut peu à l'aise, et il n'arriva pas à s'endormir, à cause du chevalier qu'il aimait, et qu'il soupçonnait d'avoir commis une faute ; ce serait alors à juste titre qu'il perdrait son amitié ! Pour cette raison il resta éveillé toute la nuit. Le lendemain il se leva de très bonne heure, et fit venir celui que sa femme lui faisait haïr sans qu'il ait fait le moindre mal. Sans tarder il lui adressa la parole, en privé, car ils étaient seuls.

« Vraiment, » dit-il, « c'est un bien grand malheur d'être beau et sage, sans être loyal ! En cela vous m'avez bien déçu, car j'ai cru très longtemps que vous étiez fidèle et loyal, en tout cas envers moi, car je vous ai toujours aimé. Je ne comprends donc pas d'où vous est venue cette idée criminelle (166) d'avoir prié la duchesse de devenir votre amie. Vous avez commis une telle perfidie qu'il ne peut en exister de plus honteuse. Quittez mes terres sans délai, car je vous en chasse irrémédiablement, et je vous en interdis et défends l'approche. N'y entrez donc jamais plus, car si, à partir d'aujourd'hui, je pouvais vous y faire prendre, sachez que je vous ferais pendre ! »

Quand le chevalier entend ces paroles il est saisi d'irritation et de dépit : il en tremble des pieds à la tête. C'est qu'il se souvient de son amie, dont il sait qu'il ne peut jouir s'il ne peut circuler librement, en restant au pays d'où le duc veut le bannir. D'autre part il éprouve bien de la peine de ce que son seigneur le considère, à tort, comme un traître déloyal. Sa détresse est si grande qu'il se croit trahi à mort.

« Seigneur, » dit-il, « pour l'amour de Dieu, ayez pitié ! Ne croyez ni ne pensez que jamais j'ai pu avoir une telle audace ! Ce dont vous m'accusez à tort, je n'y ai jamais pensé ; celui qui vous l'a dit a mal agi. »

« Il ne sert à rien de démentir, » dit le duc, « cela ne vous est pas possible. C'est elle-même qui m'a raconté de quelle façon (200) vous l'avez demandée et sollicitée, comme un traître plein de convoitise. Et peut-être même avez-vous dit des choses qu'elle préfère taire... »

« Madame a dit ce qu'il lui plaît. »

« Ah », dit le duc, bien contrarié, « nier ne vous sert à rien. »

« Rien de ce que je saurais dire ne me sert, et pourtant il n'est rien que je ne ferais pour être cru, car rien de tout cela n'a eu lieu. »

« Mais si, sur mon âme, » dit le duc, qui se souvient bien de l'habile argument de sa femme — auquel il ajoute foi : jamais on n'avait entendu dire que ce chevalier aimait une autre femme.

Alors le duc dit au chevalier :

« Si vous voulez me promettre et faire serment

que vous me direz sans mentir tout ce que je pourrais vous demander, je saurai alors, par votre parole, et de façon sûre, si vous êtes coupable ou non de ce dont je vous soupçonne. »

Le chevalier, qui désire ardemment délivrer son seigneur de la colère imméritée qu'il a contre lui, et qui redoute aussi le malheur de devoir quitter la région où se trouve celle qui lui plaît plus que toute autre, répond qu'il fera, sans s'y opposer en rien, ce que le duc a demandé ; il ne devine pas, en effet (234) les intentions du duc, et il ne saurait imaginer que son seigneur veuille s'informer d'autre chose que de cette demande d'amour. Voilà donc le serment que le duc lui proposa, et qu'il prêta. Et le duc lui dit aussitôt :

« Sachez-le, en toute sincérité, le fait que jusqu'à présent je vous ai aimé de bon cœur, m'interdit absolument de croire que vous ayez fait quelque chose d'aussi criminel et honteux que ce que me raconte la duchesse. Et je n'ajouterais pas foi à ses paroles si je n'avais été porté à les croire et à les redouter en remarquant dans votre conduite cette élégance et ces autres manières par lesquelles on comprend bien que vous aimez, même si on ignore qui. Et puisque, par ailleurs, personne ne peut deviner quelle demoiselle ou dame vous aimez, j'en viens à croire que c'est ma femme, qui m'a dit que vous la priez d'amour. Et rien au monde ne pourra me détourner de l'idée qu'il en est ainsi, si vous ne me dites que vous aimez d'amour vrai telle autre dame, et que vous me fassiez connaître toute la vérité, sans que le moindre doute puisse subsister. Et si vous n'acceptez pas ceci, quittez mes terres, sans délai, comme parjure ! »

Le chevalier ne sait que faire (269) car l'alternative est si douloureuse qu'il tient les deux termes pour mortels : en effet s'il dit la pure vérité — qu'il doit dire s'il ne veut se parjurer — il est perdu ; puisque, s'il commet la faute de ne pas tenir la promesse faite à sa dame et amie, il est sûr de la perdre si elle peut s'en apercevoir ; mais s'il ne dit pas la vérité au duc, il est parjure et traître, et perd à la fois pays et amie. Peu lui importerait de quitter le pays, s'il pouvait garder son amie, dont il redoute la perte plus que toute autre chose. Et comme il se souvient alors de la grande joie et du plaisir qu'il a connus entre ses bras, il se fait cette réflexion : s'il la trahit et la perd par sa faute, — étant donné qu'il ne peut l'emmener avec lui — comment pourra-t-il subsister sans elle ? Ainsi il se trouve exactement dans la même situation que le Châtelain de Coucy — au cœur rempli de tristesse —, qui dit dans un couplet d'une chanson :

Par Dieu, Amour, il m'est difficile de renoncer
au doux plaisir et à la présence,
et aux marques d'amour que me donnait toujours
celle qui était ma dame, ma compagne et mon
amie.
Et quand je pense à sa si douce conduite,
et aux tendres paroles qu'elle m'adressait,
comment alors mon cœur peut-il tenir dans mon
corps ?
Pourquoi ne le quitte-t-il ? Ah, vraiment, il est
bien mauvais !

(303) Le chevalier, en cette angoisse, ne sait s'il doit révéler la vérité ou mentir, et quitter le pays. Comme il se demande laquelle de ces deux choses il doit choisir, l'eau du cœur lui monte aux yeux à cause de l'angoisse qui l'étreint, et lui descend le

long du visage. Le duc pense qu'il y a quelque chose que le chevalier n'ose lui avouer. Aussitôt il lui dit :

« Je vois bien que vous n'avez pas autant confiance en moi que vous devriez. Croyez-vous que, si vous me disiez votre secret en privé, je le répéterais à qui que ce soit ? Je me laisserais plutôt, vraiment, arracher les dents l'une après l'autre ! »

« Ah, seigneur, pitié ! », dit-il. « Je ne sais ce que je pourrais dire, ni ce que je deviendrais ; mais j'aimerais mieux mourir que de perdre ce que je perdrais si je vous avais dit la vérité. Car si elle savait que je l'avais révélé à qui que ce soit… ! »

Alors le duc dit :

« Je vous promets sur mon corps et sur mon âme, et sur l'amour et sur la fidélité que je vous dois comme votre seigneur (334) que jamais de ma vie il n'en sera dit mot à âme qui vive, et que je n'en montrerai pas le moindre signe. »

Et l'autre lui répond en pleurant :

« Seigneur, voici ce que j'ai à dire. J'aime votre nièce de Vergy, et elle m'aime aussi : on ne peut s'aimer davantage. »

« Dites-moi donc, » dit le duc, « puisque vous voulez que cela reste secret, n'y a-t-il personne qui soit au courant, à part vous deux ? »

Et le chevalier lui répond :

« Non, personne au monde. »

« Mais », dit le duc, « cela ne s'est jamais vu ! Comment faites-vous donc, et comment connaissez-vous l'heure et le lieu où vous devez vous rencontrer ? »

« Ma foi, seigneur, » dit-il, « d'une façon bien adroite que je vous dirai, sans rien vous taire, puisque vous êtes déjà au courant de notre amour. »

Alors il lui a raconté toutes ses allées et venues, et la promesse faite au début, et le manège du petit chien. Le duc dit alors :

« Je vous prie de m'accorder qu'à votre prochain rendez-vous je puisse vous accompagner, et y aller avec vous, car je veux savoir sans délai si les choses se passent comme vous le dites. Ma nièce n'en saura rien. »

« Seigneur », dit-il, « je le veux bien, pourvu que cela ne vous déplaise pas. Sachez que j'irai ce soir-même. »

Et le duc déclare qu'il ira (368) et que cela ne l'ennuiera pas, mais qu'au contraire ce sera pour lui un plaisir et une distraction. Ensemble ils conviennent de l'endroit où ils se retrouveront à pied, aussitôt la nuit tombée, car la nièce du duc habitait bien près de là.

Ils s'y dirigent, et arrivent au parc. Le duc n'y est pas depuis longtemps quand il voit venir le petit chien de sa nièce au bout du jardin, où il trouve le chevalier qui l'accueille avec joie. Aussitôt le chevalier se met en route, et laisse le duc.

Ce dernier le suit pour arriver le plus près possible de la chambre ; là, il s'arrête et ne bouge plus (il s'était caché derrière un arbre bien touffu et bien large comme derrière un bouclier), et il fait de son mieux pour se cacher.

De là, il voit le chevalier aller vers la chambre, et il en voit sortir sa nièce pour aller à la rencontre du chevalier, sur la pelouse devant la chambre ; et il voit et entend le joyeux accueil qu'elle lui fait en le saluant de la voix et du geste. Aussitôt qu'elle l'aperçoit elle s'élance hors de la chambre et l'accole de ses beaux bras, et avant même d'engager la conversation elle lui donne plus de cent baisers.

56

Et lui, à son tour, l'embrasse et l'accole (403) en lui disant :

« Ma dame, mon amie, mon cœur, ma passion, mon espoir et tout ce qui m'est cher, sachez que j'ai vraiment envie d'être près de vous comme je le suis en ce moment, car je ne vous ai pas vue depuis longtemps. »

Et elle répond :

« Mon doux seigneur, mon doux ami, mon doux amour, depuis votre départ je n'ai passé jour ni heure que l'attente ne m'ennuyât ! Mais maintenant je ne me plains de rien, car j'ai auprès de moi ce que je veux, et vous êtes en bonne santé et de bonne humeur : soyez donc le bienvenu ! »

Et lui dit :

« Je suis heureux de vous retrouver. »

Le duc — il était tout près de la chambre — a entendu tout ce qui se disait à l'entrée du chevalier, et il a reconnu si bien sa nièce, à sa voix et à son attitude, qu'il n'a plus le moindre doute, et il considère que la duchesse a menti en ce qu'elle lui a dit. Et cela lui plaît beaucoup : maintenant il voit bien que le chevalier n'a aucunement commis la faute dont il l'a soupçonné.

Ainsi il est resté là, toute la nuit, tandis que la dame et le chevalier passaient la nuit dans la chambre, couchés sans dormir dans le même lit, où ils goûtaient une joie et un plaisir si grands qu'il n'est pas sage de le raconter ou d'en entendre parler, à moins de s'attendre soi-même à avoir, en récompense de ses souffrances, cette joie qu'Amour donne aux parfaits amants.

(441) Car celui qui n'attend pas une telle joie, n'ayant pas abandonné son cœur à Amour, n'y comprendra rien, s'il en entend parler ; en effet,

personne ne saurait comprendre la valeur d'une telle joie si Amour ne le lui révélait. Mais un tel bonheur n'est pas pour tout le monde, car c'est une joie sans mélange, c'est plaisir et gaieté ! Et quelle que soit la durée de cette joie, toujours est-il qu'elle dure trop peu ; c'est en tout cas l'impression de l'amant heureux. Cette douce vie lui plaît tant que, même si une nuit devenait une semaine, une semaine un mois, un mois une année, une année trois, trois années vingt et vingt cent, au moment où cette nuit s'achèverait, plutôt que de voir se lever le jour, l'amoureux voudrait que la nuit commence à tomber.

Celui que le duc attendait avait de telles pensées, car il lui fallait partir avant le lever du jour ; son amie l'accompagna jusqu'à la porte.

Lorsque les amants prirent congé, le duc vit qu'ils se couvraient de baisers, et il entendit bien des soupirs lors de l'adieu, des plaintes et des sanglots, car on y versa mainte larme ! Il les entendit également fixer le moment d'un nouveau rendez-vous.

Le chevalier s'arracha de là, et la dame ferma la porte ; mais tant qu'elle put le voir (473) elle le suivit de ses beaux yeux, ne pouvant faire mieux.

Le duc vit la porte se fermer. Aussitôt il se met en route, et rejoint le chevalier qui se plaint en lui-même de ce que la nuit, comme il l'avait dit déjà, avait duré trop peu.

(Telles furent aussi la pensée et les paroles de celle qu'il avait quittée : elle avait l'impression que la nuit ne lui avait pas apporté tout le plaisir qu'elle en avait attendu, et ne se félicitait pas de la venue du jour.)

Voilà donc ce que pense et se dit à lui-même le chevalier.

Quand le duc le rejoint il l'embrasse, lui manifeste sa joie et dit :

« Je vous promets que je vous aimerai toujours, et ne vous soupçonnerai jamais plus, car vous m'avez dit la vérité en toute chose, et vous ne m'avez menti d'un seul mot. »

« Ah seigneur », dit-il, « pitié ! Je vous demande et prie, pour l'amour de Dieu, de bien vouloir garder ce secret ; j'aurais perdu la joie et le bonheur et je mourrais à coup sûr si je savais que quelqu'un d'autre que vous en avait connaissance ! »

« N'en parlez pas », dit le duc, « sachez que cela sera très bien caché ; je n'en parlerai jamais. »

(505) Ainsi, tout en parlant, ils sont arrivés à l'endroit d'où ils étaient partis.

Ce jour-là, lors du repas, le duc fut plus aimable avec le chevalier qu'il ne l'était auparavant. Et la duchesse, en vérité, fut tellement fâchée qu'elle se leva de table, feignant un malaise. Le duc, après avoir mangé, s'être lavé les mains et avoir participé aux divertissements, est allé voir la duchesse, et l'a fait asseoir sur un lit. Il a ordonné que personne d'autre ne reste dans la chambre. On fait tout de suite ce qu'il commande ; et aussitôt le duc demande à sa femme comment ce malaise lui est venu, et ce qu'elle a au juste.

Elle répond :

« Que Dieu me vienne en aide ! Je ne croyais pas, tout à l'heure, lorsque je me suis assise à table, que vous ne fussiez pas plus intelligent et avisé que je ne voyais. En effet, vous avez encore beaucoup d'estime pour celui dont je vous ai dit qu'il cherche à me déshonorer et à m'humilier. Et quand je vis que vous étiez plus aimable avec lui qu'avant, j'en ai ressenti une telle douleur et une si grande colère que je ne pus rester à table. »

« Ah ! ma chère amie, » dit le duc, « vraiment, je ne peux croire (539) ni sur votre témoignage ni sur celui de personne d'autre que jamais ait eu lieu, en aucune façon, ce que vous m'avez raconté. Au contraire, je sais bien qu'il est innocent et qu'il n'a jamais pensé à faire cela ! J'en ai appris assez long à son sujet. Ne m'en demandez pas davantage ! »

Alors le duc sort de la chambre, et sa femme reste, plongée dans ses pensées ; jamais, tant qu'elle vivra, elle ne sera à l'aise avant d'en avoir appris davantage du secret sur lequel le duc lui a défendu de lui poser la moindre question. Mais cette interdiction ne la retiendra pas, car en son cœur elle médite déjà une ruse : elle saura bien la vérité si elle patiente jusqu'au soir, lorsqu'elle aura le duc dans ses bras. Elle sait bien qu'en de tels plaisirs elle fera de lui plus facilement ce qu'elle veut (Je n'en doute pas !) qu'en d'autres circonstances. Pour cette raison elle se tait donc.

Quand le duc vient se coucher, elle se retire à l'extrémité du lit et fait comme s'il ne lui plaît guère que le duc vienne s'étendre près d'elle, car elle sait bien qu'ainsi elle peut triompher de son mari, en feignant la colère ! Voilà pourquoi elle se comporte de façon à bien faire croire au duc qu'elle est fâchée.

Alors, pour la seule raison qu'il lui a donné un baiser, elle lui dit :

« Vous êtes bien menteur (574) tricheur et déloyal, en me donnant des marques d'amour : jamais vous ne m'avez aimée ! Et j'ai été longtemps assez folle pour croire vos paroles ; souvent vous m'avez dit que vous m'aimiez d'un cœur loyal, mais je me suis bien aperçue aujourd'hui que j'ai été trompée ! »

Le duc dit :

« En quoi donc ? »

« Vous m'avez dit, n'est-ce pas », poursuit-elle, mal intentionnée, « que je ne devais pas avoir l'audace de vous poser la moindre question au sujet de ce que vous savez bien. »

« Mon Dieu, de quoi, mon amie, parlez-vous ? »

« De ce que cet homme vous a raconté, » dit-elle, « des mensonges et des fantaisies, qu'il vous a fait accepter comme autant de vérités. Mais peu m'importe cela, car je pense que je ne gagne guère à vous aimer d'un cœur loyal ; jamais mon cœur ne vit ni ne sut rien, en bien ou en mal, que vous ne l'ayez su aussitôt ! Et maintenant je constate que vous me cachez, à votre bon plaisir, vos pensées. Sachez donc, et vous pouvez en être sûr, que désormais je ne vous porterai plus cette confiance ni ces sentiments d'amour que j'ai eus jusqu'à présent pour vous. »

Alors la duchesse se mit de nouveau à pleurer et à soupirer, et elle s'y efforça autant qu'elle le put.

(608) Le duc en eut grand-pitié et lui dit :

« Ma chère amie, je ne pourrais absolument pas supporter votre colère ou votre mécontentement, mais sachez aussi que je ne veux pas dire ce que vous me demandez : vous agissez avec vilenie. »

Elle lui dit sur-le-champ :

« Seigneur, ne me le dites pas, car je vois bien à vos façons que vous me croyez vraiment incapable de cacher votre secret. Mais sachez que je m'en étonne beaucoup, car jamais je n'ai entendu de secret, grand ou petit, que vous m'aviez confié, et que j'aie ensuite révélé. Et je vous le dis en toute bonne foi : cela n'arrivera jamais de ma vie ! »

Quand elle eut dit cela elle se remit à pleurer. Le duc la prit par le cou et lui donna un baiser ; il était fort mal à l'aise, à tel point qu'il ne put se retenir de révéler toute l'histoire.

Il lui a donc dit :

« Ma belle dame, sur mon âme, je ne sais que faire, car ma confiance en vous est si grande et je vous crois si bien que je ne dois pas vous cacher quoi que ce soit. Sachez, et je vous le dis avec insistance, que si je suis trahi par vous, vous en perdrez la vie. »

Et elle dit :

« Je l'accepte ; il me serait impossible d'agir de façon déloyale à votre égard. »

Il l'aime, et la croit donc (642) et pense qu'elle lui dit la vérité ; ainsi il lui raconte toute l'histoire de sa nièce : comment il l'avait apprise du chevalier, et comment il avait été dans le jardin, dans le coin où ils avaient attendu ensemble, et comment le petit chien était venu. Et il lui dit exactement comment la Châtelaine était sortie et le chevalier entré ; il ne tait rien de ce qu'il a entendu et vu.

Quand la duchesse entend que l'homme qui a refusé son amour aime une dame de moindre rang, elle se considère comme mortellement humiliée. Mais elle ne le montre en rien, au contraire, elle accorde et promet au duc de bien cacher cette affaire. Qu'il la pende haut et court s'il lui arrive d'en dire mot.

Et pourtant elle brûle déjà du désir de parler à la Châtelaine, qu'elle déteste à partir du moment où elle sait qu'elle est l'amie de cet homme qui lui a fait éprouver des sentiments de honte et de chagrin ; elle pense que c'est pour cette raison qu'il ne veut pas être son ami.

Elle décide donc que, si elle trouve l'occasion de s'entretenir avec la nièce du duc, elle lui en parlera aussitôt, et ne se privera pas de faire une remarque méchante. Mais ce moment ne vint pas (676) avant la Pentecôte, car ce fut la première fête à laquelle le duc tint cour plénière. Il invita donc les nobles dames de tous ses territoires, et avant toutes les autres sa nièce, la Châtelaine de Vergy.

Lorsque la duchesse la vit, son sang se mit à bouillir, parce que c'était la femme qu'elle haïssait le plus au monde, mais elle savait cacher ses sentiments et parvint à lui montrer meilleur visage que jamais. Pourtant elle eut bien envie de dire ce dont elle éprouva tant de dépit, et il lui en coûta beaucoup d'attendre, ce jour de Pentecôte.

Après le repas la duchesse a emmené les dames avec elle, dans sa chambre, pour qu'elles puissent, sans être dérangées, se faire belles pour les danses. Alors la duchesse, qui trouva le moment opportun, ne put plus se taire, mais elle dit, comme si c'était une plaisanterie :

« Châtelaine, faites-vous bien belle, car vous avez un ami élégant. »

L'autre répondit en toute simplicité :

« Je ne sais à quelle amitié vous pensez, ma dame, vraiment, car je n'ai pas envie d'avoir un ami à moins que ce ne soit tout à fait à l'honneur et de moi-même et de mon seigneur. »

« Je le veux bien », dit la duchesse (710) « mais vous avez appris, en bonne maîtresse, comment il faut dresser votre petit chien ».

Les dames ont entendu ces paroles mais n'en comprennent pas le sens; elles s'en vont avec la duchesse pour aller danser.

Mais la Châtelaine reste : elle est bouleversée par le chagrin, et son cœur se gonfle. Elle entre dans un cabinet, où se trouvait, invisible pour elle, une jeune fille, étendue au pied du lit. La Châtelaine, fort triste, s'est laissée tomber sur le lit ; elle se plaint, gémit, et dit :

« Ah, seigneur Dieu, pitié ! Que veut dire cette remarque de madame au sujet du dressage de mon petit chien ? Cela, elle ne le sait par personne d'autre, voilà qui est clair, que par celui que j'aimais, et qui m'a trahie ! Il ne le lui aurait certainement pas dit s'il ne la connaissait intimement et ne l'aimait, c'est certain, plus que moi qu'il a trahie ; je suis sûre qu'il ne m'aime pas puisqu'il manque à sa promesse envers moi.

Doux Dieu, je l'aimais autant qu'on peut aimer quelqu'un ; je ne pouvais penser à rien d'autre, à aucun moment, ni le jour ni la nuit (744) car c'était ma joie et mon plaisir, mon délice, mon réconfort, ma consolation et ma passion. Comme je restais tournée vers lui, en mes pensées, quand je ne le voyais pas !

Ah, mon ami, comment cela est-il possible ? Que s'est-il passé, pour que vous me trahissiez ? Je croyais que vous m'étiez plus fidèle — que Dieu me vienne en aide —, que Tristan ne le fut à Yseut. Je vous aimais — que Dieu ait pitié de moi —, le double de moi-même. Jamais, à aucun moment, je ne fis, en pensée, en actes ni en paroles une faute, grande ou petite, pour laquelle vous auriez dû me haïr ou me trahir de façon si vilaine, en déchirant notre amour pour en aimer une autre et m'abandonner, moi, et révéler notre secret. Hélas, mon ami ! je suis stupéfaite, car mon cœur — que Dieu m'aide —, ne fut jamais tel à votre égard. En effet, Dieu me donnerait-il le monde entier, le ciel et la terre et le paradis, que je ne l'accepterais pas si la condition était telle que je devrais vous perdre ; car vous étiez ma richesse, ma consolation et ma joie, et rien ne m'aurait été pénible tant que mon pauvre cœur aurait su que le vôtre m'aimait tant soit peu.

(778) Hélas ! parfait Amour ! qui eût cru qu'il me causerait de la peine, lui qui disait, quand il était près de moi et que je m'efforçais de faire tout ce qu'il voulait, qu'il m'appartenait, et me tenait pour celle qui pouvait commander à son corps et à son âme ? Il le disait si tendrement que je le croyais aussitôt ; et pour rien au monde je n'aurais cru qu'il eût pu trouver dans son cœur courroux ou haine contre moi, pour duchesse ni pour reine, car il m'était si doux de l'aimer que je prenais son cœur pour le mien. Je pensais que lui, de la même façon, se considérait mon ami pour la vie. Je suis certaine que, s'il était mort avant moi, je l'aurais tant aimé que je lui aurais survécu peu de temps ; car j'aurais préféré être morte avec lui plutôt que de vivre, si je n'avais pu le voir.

Ah ! parfait Amour ! est-il juste qu'il ait de cette façon dévoilé notre secret ? C'est ma mort, car lorsque je lui accordai mon amour je lui ai dit, et lui ai fait accepter, qu'il me perdrait au moment même où il dévoilerait notre amour. Et maintenant que je l'ai perdu je n'en puis plus, après un si grand malheur, car sans lui, qui est la cause de mon désespoir, je ne peux vivre, et ne le veux pas (813) car la vie me déplaît ; je prie donc Dieu qu'il m'accorde la mort, et qu'Il ait pitié de mon âme, aussi vrai que j'ai aimé loyalement celui qui m'a causé tout ce mal ; et qu'Il accorde ses bienfaits à celui qui, à tort, m'a trahie et m'a livrée à la mort. Je lui pardonne ! Ma mort est douce, je trouve,

65

puisqu'elle me vient de lui ; et quand je me rappelle son amour, il ne me pèse pas de mourir pour lui. »

Alors la Châtelaine se tait, mais elle ajoute encore, dans un dernier soupir :

« Mon doux ami, je vous recommande à Dieu. »

A ces mots elle serre les bras contre son corps : le cœur lui manque, son visage perd sa couleur ; dans la douleur, elle s'est évanouie. Elle est étendue, pâle, livide, au milieu du lit : elle est morte.

Mais son ami ne le sait pas, il est en train de s'amuser dans la grand-salle, il danse et saute, mais rien ne lui plaît, puisqu'il ne voit pas celle à qui son cœur s'est donné ; il s'en étonne, et demande au duc, en lui parlant à l'oreille :

« Seigneur, pourquoi votre nièce n'est-elle toujours pas venue aux danses ? Vous ne l'auriez pas enfermée du moins... ? » Et le duc regarde la danse ; il ne s'était aperçu de rien.

(847) Il prend le chevalier par la main, et s'en va tout droit vers la chambre ; n'y trouvant pas la Châtelaine il suggère au chevalier de la chercher dans le cabinet, ainsi le veut-il. Et le chevalier, très reconnaissant, est entré dans la pièce où son amie était étendue sur le lit, sans couleur, livide. Il a trouvé le corps, raide ; il baise sa bouche déjà froide, et constate, en regardant le corps, qu'elle est bien morte. Alors, stupéfait, il s'écrie :

« Quoi donc ? Hélas ! mon amie est morte ? »

Et la jeune fille qui était étendue au pied du lit sauta sur ses pieds et dit :

« Seigneur, je crois bien qu'elle est morte, car elle n'a cessé de prier pour que cela lui arrive depuis qu'elle est ici, à cause du chagrin que lui a causé son ami, à propos duquel madame l'a taquinée ; elle s'est

66

moquée d'elle au sujet d'un petit chien, ce qui provoqua ce chagrin mortel. »

Et quand le chevalier entendit ces mots, qui signifiaient que sa révélation faite au duc était la cause de sa mort, il s'abandonna au désespoir.

« Ah, Dieu ! » dit-il. « Mon amour, vous qui étiez la plus courtoise et la meilleure qui fût jamais, et la plus loyale, comme un traître déloyal je vous ai tuée. Il aurait été juste que la catastrophe s'abattît sur moi, et que vous fussiez épargnée.

(882) Mais vous aviez le cœur si loyal que vous avez voulu mourir avant moi : je ferai justice de moi-même pour la trahison que j'ai commise ! »

Il tira du fourreau une épée suspendue à un clou, et se la plongea dans le cœur, puis se laissa tomber sur le corps de son amie ; son sang se répand et il meurt.

La jeune fille, horrifiée par la vue de ces deux morts, se précipita hors de la pièce. Elle rencontra le duc à qui elle a dit, sans rien taire, ce qu'elle a entendu et vu ; elle lui expliqua comment l'affaire avait commencé, et parla même du petit chien dressé auquel la duchesse avait fait allusion.

Voilà le duc hors de lui ! Aussitôt il est entré dans la chambre et a retiré de la poitrine du chevalier l'épée avec laquelle il s'était tué. Sans tarder il s'est dirigé, en courant, vers la danse, et, sans un mot, est allé tout droit à la duchesse. Il s'est acquitté de sa promesse en lui assenant, de son épée nue, un coup sur la tête, sans pouvoir proférer une parole. La duchesse est tombée par terre, devant lui, aux yeux de tous les nobles de la contrée.

Alors fut bien troublée la réunion des chevaliers qui étaient venus pour se réjouir.

(917) Sans perdre un instant le duc raconta cette

histoire en pleine cour, à qui voulut l'entendre.

Alors tous pleurèrent, surtout quand ils virent les deux amants morts, ainsi que la duchesse. Tristes et bouleversés les invités partent, en grand désarroi.

Le lendemain le duc fit enterrer les deux amants dans le même cercueil, et la duchesse en un autre endroit. Il était tellement fâché de cette histoire que l'on ne l'a jamais plus entendu rire. Bien vite il prit la croix pour aller en Terre Sainte ; il s'y rendit sans tarder et s'y fit Templier.

Ah, Dieu ! ce drame et ce malheur vinrent du fait que le chevalier eut l'imprudence de dire ce qu'il devait cacher, et que son amie lui avait défendu de révéler, tant qu'il voudrait garder son amour.

Cet *exemplum* nous apprend donc qu'il faut très soigneusement garder secret son amour, et avoir toujours présente à l'esprit la pensée qu'il ne sert à rien de parler de son amour, et qu'il vaut bien mieux le cacher. Celui qui agit ainsi ne craint pas l'assaut des curieux et fourbes mal intentionnés qui cherchent à connaître les amours d'autrui.

NOTES TEXTUELLES

Dans le cas de changements plus importants nous avons indiqué lequel des mss de contrôle (C, E, Go) présente la leçon adoptée.

8   *font :* ms. *fonnt*
12   *mari :* ms. *meri*
19   Dans le ms. nous trouvons un point très net après ce vers
25   *lui :* ms. *soi* (*C, E, Go*)

132	*porpensai biaus s.* : ms. *porpens biaus dous sire* (*C, E*)
137	*oïe* : ms. *oiee*
147	*qu'il* : ms. *qui*
156	Le ms. donne : *Certes fait cest il. cest* a été intercalé plus tard (par le correcteur?).
217	*cevalier* : ms. *cevaliers*
221	*ce que je vous* : ms. *que ce que vous* (*C, E, Go*)
232	*ce que li dus* : le copiste avait d'abord écrit *cel,* mais a changé le *l* en *q̄.*
233	*qu'il* : ms. *qui*
239	Le ms. donne : *l'en fist li dus et cil l'em prist.* Les autres manuscrits donnent des leçons divergentes.
245	*de vous* : ms. *que vous* (*Go*)
305	*mence* : ms. *mennce*
329	*soit* : ms. *sont*
354	*les venues et les a* : ms. *leur v. et leur a* (*E*)
421	*contenance* : ms. *connissance* (*C, Go*)
452	*devenoit* : ms. *demouroit* (*C, Go*)
482	*fu cele* : ms. *de cele* (*E*)
493	*de tot* : ms. *de tout*
494	*de mot* : ms. *de mout*
500	*nul* : ms. *nule*
52C	*remegne* : ms. *reviegne* avec *i* surmonté d'un trait) (*C, Go*)
529	*n'eüst* : ms. *eust* (*E, Go*)
558	*k'en* : ms. *ke*
587	*rien* : ms. *bien* (*C, E, Go*)
592	*qu'il* : ms. *qui*
655	*qui* : ms. *que*
659	*a si celer* : ms. *a descouvrir* (*C, Go*)
663	*parler* : ms. *parlers*
692	*por ce* : ms. *puis ce* (*C, Go*)
702	*acointe* : ms. *et cointe* (*C, Go*)
780	*disoit* : ms. *veist* (*C, Go*)

804 *dont il me pert :* ms. *tout en apert* (*C, E, Go*)

822 Le ms. donne : *de ma mort n'est se doute non*
(*C, E*)

868 *pour le :* ms. *fors le* (*Go*)

883 Le ms. donne : *que la mors l'a ains de moi*
prise (*E*)

934 Le ms. donne : *He Dius! dist il, quel encom-*
brier (*C, Go*)

L'ISTOIRE
DE LA CHASTELAINE DU VERGIER
ET DE TRISTAN LE CHEVALIER

INTRODUCTION

Vers la fin des années 70 du xve siècle paraît *L'Istoire de la Chastelaine du Vergier et de Tristan le Chevalier,* manuscrit exécuté dans la Vallée d'Aoste, et conservé maintenant à Paris (B.N. nouv. acq. 6639).

En se basant sur la présence, dans ce manuscrit, des armes réunies des familles de Challant-Aymavilles et de La Chambre, J. Brocherel place l'exécution de ce manuscrit « vers la fin du xve siècle, après le mariage de Louis de Challant-Aymavilles avec Marguerite de La Chambre, fille d'Amédée vicomte de Maurienne, mariage qui fut conclu en mars 1477 » (Brocherel 1927:1). Selon le même auteur (p. 4) « Georges de Challant, Prieur de Saint-Ours et tuteur des six fils de Louis de Challant [aurait] choisi et commandé, à un membre de sa communauté, la transcription de la nouvelle et des pièces en vers, réunis dans notre Codex. » Vu contre cette toile de fond, le ton moralisateur et didactique de *l'Istoire...* n'étonne pas trop. Ainsi l'auteur présente d'une façon bien personnelle l'amour de la Châtelaine et de Tristan : leurs rencontres semblent être l'occasion d'interminables discussions, ponctuées seulement de quelques baisers. Ainsi donc ils « menerent ensemble en aucun temps en ce point une tres honneste vie ; et ne fust onques sceu que entre leurs amours eust chose quy fust contre Dieu et concience » (114 r).

C'est surtout dans la comparaison de cette version en prose avec le texte en vers du XIIIe siècle que nous pouvons découvrir le caractère spécifique de *l'Istoire...* En général celle-ci suit la version du XIIIe s., mais il y a quelques différences remarquables : d'une part l'introduction du nom du chevalier (anonyme dans le texte en vers), et d'autre part la description circonstanciée du début de la liaison entre les deux protagonistes. Ce qui frappe aussi dans le texte en prose est le souci de l'auteur d'être explicite : ainsi par exemple il explique pourquoi la nièce du duc est appelée « la Chastelaine du Vergier », et pourquoi il y a encore une chambrière dans « l'ostel » de la Châtelaine alors que tout le monde est allé assister à la fête à la cour.

Lorsqu'on compare la première partie des deux textes (c'est-à-dire jusqu'au passage où la duchesse va s'occuper du chevalier) on constate une importante différence quantitative : la prose est neuf fois plus longue que le texte en vers. Si l'on considère la longueur totale des deux textes (environ 48 000 signes pour la version en prose, 32 000 pour le texte en vers) on devrait s'attendre à des proportions bien différentes : 3 (prose) contre 2 (vers). Cette différence quantitative du début du texte s'explique par le souci de l'auteur de tout expliciter : il veut nous peindre la naissance de l'amour entre le chevalier et la Châtelaine, scène qui manque dans le texte en vers.

Ce n'est d'ailleurs pas seulement la différence quantitative qui saute aux yeux, c'est également le contenu qui distingue le texte du xvᵉ de celui du xiiiᵉ s. Ce dernier indique dans l'introduction qu'il faut garder secret *l'amor* (v. 6, 11-17), et l'exemple choisi ensuite (*d'un cevalier preu et hardi; et de la dame de Vregi,* 19-20), ainsi que l'emploi du terme *fin amant* (12) annonce dès le début du texte une histoire d'amour. La version en prose ne parle qu'en termes très généraux de secrets qu'il faut garder ; c'est seulement après l'introduction, au début du récit, lorsqu'on nous présente Tristan, ce parfait chevalier, que nous pouvons supposer qu'il s'agira d'une histoire d'amour : « combien qu'y fust jeulne, amoureux et parfaittement joieulx de cuer, il n'avoit mis son voulloir a amer quelque dame, pour la grant paour et doubte qu'il avoit de trouver desloyaulté en amours... » (109 r). L'entrée en matière, très rapide dans le texte en vers, se fait longue, arrosée de pleurs et entrecoupée de discours direct dans la version en prose.

La scène suivante, où nous voyons la duchesse et le chevalier ensemble, diffère d'un texte à l'autre surtout par la teneur du message. Le texte en vers part d'un présupposé courtois :

> Sire, vous estes biaus et preus,
> ce dient tuit, la Diu merci !
> Si avriiés bien deservi
> d'avoir amie en si haut leu
> qu'en eüssiés honor et preu...   (60-64)

L'emploi du terme *fin amant* dans le vers 12, et le ton de l'introduction auront sensibilisé le public :

l'atmosphère est nettement celle du 'fin'amor', et c'est contre cette toile de fond que l'histoire doit être écoutée ou lue. Nous avons l'impression que l'auteur de la prose n'a plus compris cette atmosphère courtoise ; même l'emploi d'un terme comme « la Court Amoureuse » (110 v) ne dément pas cette impression : rien dans le texte ne montre que pour l'auteur ce terme va au-delà d'une étiquette. Pour lui il ne s'agit que d'une histoire d'amour qui se termine mal parce que le secret n'a pas été gardé ; on a l'impression que c'est une question de bienséance, tandis que dans la version en vers la nécessité de garder le secret provient du fait qu'il s'agit de 'fin'amor'.

L'intention du texte en prose est nettement indiquée par certains mots forts que l'auteur emploie lorsqu'il nous parle de la scène de séduction : c'est une « diabolicque temptacion » qui prend la duchesse, et qui la pousse à vouloir « faire folie » avec Tristan « ce bon chevalier ». Une très brève mention du couple ducal mise à part, c'est ici la première fois qu'on nous parle de la duchesse : elle est ainsi condamnée dès le début de l'histoire. Le vocabulaire employé (« diabolicque t. », « faire folie », « ardaulment amoureuse », « ardeur », « eschauffoit ») semble montrer que l'auteur condamne l'amour adultère. Le caractère de la duchesse se précise d'ailleurs encore plus dans ce passage ; elle avait invité Tristan dans sa chambre et, en l'en chassant, elle le menace. Il est intéressant de constater que la duchesse, à partir du moment où elle a entendu la réponse de Tristan, se met à le tutoyer, signe de colère et de mépris.

Tandis que dans la version en vers la duchesse attend la nuit pour se plaindre du chevalier — et qu'ainsi ce n'est que le lendemain que le duc ira demander des explications à celui-ci —, la prose nous montre une duchesse furieuse qui annonce à Tristan qu'elle va le dénoncer auprès de son mari, et qui effectivement s'empresse de le faire.

La situation de départ est donc bien différente dans les deux textes.

Lorsqu'on les compare ainsi tout au long, on peut constater plusieurs différences entre la version du xiiie s. et celle du xve : il est clair que le remanieur a voulu mettre l'accent à d'autres endroits. Ainsi il aime expliquer et moderniser. Il ne modernise pas seulement la langue, mais encore l'esprit de l'histoire. Au milieu du texte en vers, lorsque le poète nous raconte la nuit d'amour de la Châtelaine et du chevalier, nous trouvons un développement sur l'amour courtois. Ces remarques sur le 'fin'amor' manquent dans la version en prose du xve. Celle-ci est d'ailleurs très discrète sur cette nuit d'amour : il n'y est question ni d'une chambre, ni d'un lit. Selon ce texte les deux amants « en telles parolles et moult d'aultres complaintes de merveilleuses consolacions, avec gracieux baisiers, passerent celle nuit en incomparables liesses, tant qu'y furent tous esbaÿs quant ilz visrent le jour esclarcy; ilz ne penssoient avoir esté ensamble que une heure... » (121 r). Le résultat de cette discrétion est que la prose est ici environ de 15 pour cent plus brève que le texte en vers : c'est la tendance moralisatrice de l'auteur du remaniement qui lui fait sauter les allusions au côté physique du rendez-vous. On peut d'autant mieux le constater lorsqu'on compare cette nuit d'amour à la scène où, dans la même version, la duchesse, très sensuelle, séduit le duc : c'est la bête contre l'ange.

Si l'on ajoute à ce refus du 'fin'amor' certains petits traits du texte (le duc va se promener dans son jardin après avoir bien fermé la porte; Tristan trouve son amie étendue « sur le tappis » ; la fête, pendant laquelle la duchesse fera comprendre à la Châtelaine qu'elle est au courant de son secret, n'est plus la Pentecôte mais une fête quelconque), on a presque l'impression que l'histoire décrite dans la prose du xvᵉ aurait pu se passer aussi bien dans la maison d'un riche bourgeois qu'à la cour d'un duc. Ce duc même a si peu d'importance pour celui qui a écrit notre texte (auteur ou copiste) qu'à plusieurs reprises nous trouvons *le roi* au lieu du *duc ;* ainsi nous lisons après la révélation du duc à la duchesse (ils sont couchés) : « Atant cesserent les parolles. Et le roy s'endormist, mais la duchesse de malle heure nee ne peult pas celler (?) ne dormir, d'annoy et de rage qu'elle avoit au cuer... » (125 r).

Tout bien considéré nous pouvons dire que notre texte présente certains traits que Doutrepont (1939:388-91) considérait comme constitutifs du genre de la mise en prose, par exemple le souci de vraisemblance et de réalisme, qui se traduit entre autres dans certaines explications de points restés dans l'ombre dans le texte du xiiiᵉ. Là où celui-ci dit que

> ... assés pres d'illoec estoit
> u la nièce le duc manoit   (373-74)

la prose nous a expliqué déjà que les demeures du duc et de la Châtelaine (ou en tout cas leurs jardins) se touchaient.

Pourtant le souci de réalisme n'appartient pas exclusivement aux mises en prose ; et le besoin de tout expliquer est un trait fréquent dans les romans originaux du xvᵉ siècle.

Le souci d'ordre et de proportion dont parle Doutrepont est une caractéristique qui s'appliquerait surtout aux longues histoires chevaleresques qu'il a étudiées : là il fallait mettre de l'ordre et écourter afin d'éviter la prolixité. Notre auteur au contraire a suivi exactement l'ordre du texte en vers et il l'a même allongé de la moitié. Le style retenu et suggestif du texte en vers a fait place à quelque verbosité. L'auteur de la prose a créé une adaptation qui laisse transparaître le récit original, mais a un esprit différent. La version du XIIIe est tout imprégnée d'amour courtois, celle du XVe siècle pourrait être caractérisée comme une histoire galante qui finit mal.

Dans les deux textes le souci didactique est évident : dans le texte en vers il est mis en lumière surtout par la structure (au début, au milieu — où se trouve le code de l'amour courtois (436-60) —, et à la fin — le texte parle même de *cest essample* (941) —). Dans *l'Istoire*, c'est surtout le ton moralisateur qui en est le signe.

Est-ce qu'en opérant de cette façon notre auteur a voulu satisfaire au goût du public de son époque ? Le fait de retrouver dans notre texte plusieurs caractéristiques des textes en prose du XVe siècle signifie en tout cas que ce remaniement a plus ou moins répondu à l'attente d'une partie du public.

Le manuscrit, exécuté pour une famille noble de la Vallée d'Aoste, nous renvoie d'ailleurs au public même des mises en prose (cf. Doutrepont 1939 : 441 et 676-78). Mais, le recueil où nous trouvons *l'Istoire* a-t-il été composé à l'expresse demande d'un de ces nobles, ou reflète-t-il seulement le goût de l'auteur ou du compilateur ? Est-ce donc seulement ce dernier qui est responsable du ton moralisateur et de l'odeur de religiosité qui s'exhale de cette version ?

Tout comme bien d'autres textes en prose de la fin du Moyen Age notre texte n'est pas toujours d'une lecture facile : les phrases sont en général assez longues et parfois même fort compliquées. Nous avons donc essayé de faciliter la lecture par une ponctuation assez dense. Le vocabulaire employé reflète les habitudes des écrivains de la deuxième moitié du XVe siècle ; nous y trouvons bien des mots nouveaux, basés ou non sur une racine latine (p. ex. *complaisement,* plaisir, satisfaction ; *désolable,* qui cause la désolation). Parfois il existe des formes modernes de ces mots, mais qui ont un autre sens : ainsi p. ex. *imfluance,* débordement ou afflux de sang. Tous ces mots-là, et d'autres qui pourraient faire obstacle à une bonne compréhension du texte, sont traduits dans le glossaire.

Notons encore quelques particularités de la langue du texte :

1. *deult* est une forme de *devoir* (il doit ou il dut) ;
2. *peult* et *peullent* viennent de *pouvoir* (formes du présent) ;
3. *qui* et *quy* sont souvent employés dans le manuscrit pour *qu'il(s)* ; dans ces cas nous avons imprimé *qu'i* ou *qu'y* ;
4. *si,* très fréquent, n'est pratiquement jamais notre *si* conditionnel moderne (rôle tenu par *se*) ; souvent *si* remplit le rôle d'une simple conjonction (et, mais, ou) ; souvent aussi on pourrait le traduire par " aussi ", " ainsi " ; parfois encore on peut le négliger sans plus dans la traduction.

Les changements apportés au texte du manuscrit sont expliqués dans les notes textuelles, placées avant le glossaire.

Remarques bibliographiques

P. Meyer donne un compte rendu de la première édition (en 50 exemplaires) de *l'Istoire*... La Bibliothèque nationale à Paris n'en possède pas d'exemplaire. (P. Meyer, dans *Romania* 19 (1890) : 340-43).

J. Brocherel (dans *Augusta Praetoria,* revue valdôtaine de pensée et d'action régionalistes, 1927, 1 : 1-17) donne sous le titre « Une chanson de geste (*sic*) du XIIIe siècle transcrite en prose par un Valdôtain du XVe siècle : *La Chastelaine du Vergier* » une brève étude et une édition de notre texte. Les remarques philologiques et littéraires accompagnant cette édition laissent parfois à désirer.

L. A. Arrathoon parle de *l'Istoire*... dans son article « The " Compte en viel langaige " Behind *Heptaméron,* LXX » (dans *Romance Philology* 30 (1976) : 192-99). Selon elle, Marguerite de Navarre se serait basée sur *l'Istoire*... en écrivant sa version de *la Châtelaine de Vergy*.

Dans *L'Istoire de la Chastelaine du Vergier*...nous avons étudié encore d'autres aspects de ce texte. Cette étude est publiée dans les *Actes du IVe Colloque sur le Moyen Français,* p.p. Anthonij Dees, Amsterdam, 1985.

Les ouvrages de G. Doutrepont (*Les mises en prose des épopées et des romans chevaleresques du XIVe au XVIe siècle,* Bruxelles, 1939) et de R. Dubuis (*Les cent nouvelles nouvelles et la tradition de la* *nouvelle en France au Moyen Age,* Grenoble, 1973), ainsi que le récent *Précis de littérature française du Moyen Age,* sous la direction de Daniel Poirion (Paris, 1983), aideront à mieux comprendre le climat littéraire de l'époque.

L'ISTOIRE
DE LA CHASTELAINE DU VERGIER
ET DE TRISTAN LE CHEVALIER

<small>TEXTE</small> (B.N.n.a.fr. 6639. f. 108 r.)

Aucunes gens sont quy tant s'apellent loiaulx et
secreps et moustrent samblant de donner bon
conceil [que] par celles raisons et pour leur bel
parller tres decevant, les gens se fient en eulx, si que
par droitte foy, amour et charité les gens s'i fient. Et
ceulx les destruisent de leur intencion — parce que
ceulx quy le veullent savoir promettent de les celler
—, et eulx, par leur courage trahistre et failly,
tantost qu'ilz ont la pocession s'efforcent de les
descouvrir et desceller, a la grant blasme, comfusion
et honte de ceulx quy feablement s'i fient et leur ont
ouvert et desclos leur pencees. Et les langues de
telles gens sont comparees aux langues des serpens
qui souvent tout se qu'elles touchent nasvrent a
mort. Si seroit moult profitable sagesse de savoir
celler (108 v) son secret contre telles gens, quy les
pourroit congnoistre. Dont pour les grans perilz quy
s'en peullent enssuivir, et que faulceté n'est pas
apperceue partout ou elle habite mais se cache
souvent soubz la couverture de Biau Samblant, bon
seroit de croirre le conceil d'ung acteur quy dist en
ceste magniere : « Tant que ton secret as en ton

81

cuer sans l'avoir descouvert, tu le tiens en ta prison ; mais si tost que tu l'as desclos a aultre il le tient en la scienne. » Et la raison principalle pour quoy je conceille a chascun garder et celler son secrept contre tous, c'est pour ce que mainttes personnes nobles et vaillans ont esté menees a povretté, a honte et a mort pour avoir dit leurs secreps aux mauvais ypocriptes desloyeux et decevans ; dont a ce propos veuil racompter une ystoire de merveilleuse pitié.

Ung puissant duc de Bourgoigne fust, lequel avoit en sa court plusieurs nobles princes, contes, barons, chevaliers et escuiers. Et entre les aultres ung nommé Tristan, son premier chevalier, quy tant estoit noble, vaillant et plain (109 r) de toute biaulté, que riens ne luy failloit quy se appartenist a noblesse ; et mesmes estoit tant bel de personne que c'estoit merveilles, et de si bel service et si gracieulx en ses affaires que tous ceulx de la court quy tan doient a honneur prenoient exemple a luy et a ses euvres, par quoy il estoit moult cherement amé du duc et de la duchesse. Et si le prisoient et amoient merveilleusement tous les nobles de la court, ensamble les dames et les damoiselles ; mais combien qu'y fust jeulne, amoureux et parfaittement joieulx de cuer, il n'avoit mis son voulloir a amer quelque dame, pour la grant paour et doubte qu'il avoit de trouver desloyaulté en amours ; car il se sentoit tant acomply en la vertu de loyaulté que s'il se donnast a la vertu de amer loyaulment et il trouvast faulceté en amours, samblant luy estoit que ja mais n'aroit racine de liesse en son cuer.

Or avoit iceluy duc de Bourgoigne en aucunes parties une niepce jeulne, joieuse et tant belle dame que de la biaulté et bonté ne puis donner louange sufisant, (109 v) laquelle il envoia querir pour estre en sa court. Et luy bailla ung tres exellant lieu pour tenir son estast, lequel estoit apellé " le Vergier ", et estoit joignant au palais du duc, pour quoy elle fust tourjours apellee depuis " la chastelainne du Vergier " ; laquelle pour sa biauté et bonté fust tant amee et honoree du duc, de la duchesse et de tous les nobles que a toutes les solempnittés, festes et esbastemens qu'on faisoit a la court, la chastelaine estoit tourjours premiere appellee. Laquelle tant bien se savoit porter en toutes honnestes et joieuses comppaignies, que sur tout elle emportoit la louenge, le pris et la fleur, combien qu'elle fust encores moult tendre et jeulne.

Si fust ainssi que Tristan, le gracieux et vaillant chevalier quy c'estoit longuement gardé d'amer par amours — pour doubte des baratz que plusieurs tiennent en l'amoureuse vie —, ne sceult metre remede en son fait qu'y ne fust pris et enlaxé estroictement en l'amour de la gentille chastelayne du Vergier. Si le commenssa Amours a lancer et versser de ses dars amoureulx si angoiseusement (110 r) et si continuellement qu'i ne povoist prendre de jour ne de nuit reppos, mais pour paour d'estre refusé, et aussi qu'elle estoit de si hault lieu, il ne luy osoit descouvrir sa pencee. Si se meurdrissoit le cuer et se cruxiffioit a part soy en plainttes, soupirs, regretz et lamentacions, par quoy tant fust afoibly et traveillié qu'i ne peult plus souffrir le martire, mais se destermina qu'y prendroit en luy vertu et courage de raconter a celle qu'il amoit tant, les angoisses [et] travaulx qu'y soustenoit pour l'amour d'elle.

Dont une foys, a ung tres honorable esbastement qui se faisoit a la court, apres ce qu'il eust gracieusement menee a la dance, il trouva achoison de parler a elle quant il vist son lieu. Et fist sa complaintte le plus humblement qu'i peult en ceste magniere : « Tres haulte et tres honoree dame et ma tres

83

exellant et redoubtee maistresse, je supplie a la largesse de vostre debonnairetté [et] pitié amoureuse qu'il soit de vostre plaisir de ouïr ma piteuse requeste. Noble dame, verité est que, nonostant ma jeulnesse et l'abondance de joye ou j'ay esté nourry tout mon vivant (110 v) en ceste noble court au service de mon tresredoubté seigneur monseigneur vostre oncle, je me suis continuelment gardé, selon tout mon povoir, de mon cuer : je suis tout certain que, se je trouvoye desloiaulté en amours, que par moy ne seroit joye recouvree. Et pour ce j'ay tour jours esté maistre de mon cuer juques a nagueres, que la volenté de Dieu vous a amenee en ceste court, pour mon tres heureux advencement ou pour ma piteuse destruccion : car, tres haulte et tres honoree dame, depuis que j'eux choisi vostre riche et honoree biaulté tres exellant, ensemble vostre doubz parler et grant maintien, et que vous estes le meilleur tresor et complaisement de toute richesse quy peult estre desiree et aquise en la Court Amoureuse, Amour n'a plus voullu laissier mon cuer en ma pocession, mais l'a [chassé] tant qu'i l'a pris et ravy es tres haulx pointtes de ses dars, et l'a mis du tout en vostre singulliere obeissance, moy constraignant et obligent a vivre mon temps en vostre service. Et moy, feru et nasvré irevocablement de vostre biaulté non compareille, ay depuis vostre gracieux advenement souffert et porté, (111 r) souffre et porte tel et si rigoureux martire que bouche humaine ne [le] pourroit raconter ne main escripre. Mais pour concideracion de vostre biaulté, haulte noblesse et seignorie, et pour timeur d'estre esconduit de vostre amour, j'ay cellé mes angoisses destreceuses sans les vous descouvrir et sans oser requerre le don de vostre amoureuse pitié. Mais le feu de vostre amour a tant enbrasé mon cuer qu'i me

y gracieux et plaisant », dit elle,
s bien. Si vous respons a celuy
ung petit chiennet quy porte ung
clochettes, lequel chiennet je intro-
rce que le lieu deu Vergier que
on oncle m'a donné joint au palais,
uvent voir et regarder ; en celuy jour
és le mien petit chien faire le tour
on jardin, vous pourrés venir seure-
moy (114 r) sans doubter chose quy

» dit Tristan, « vous avés trouvé la
e magniere quy peult estre. Si vous prie
qu'i soit fait en ceste guise. »
rolles s'entredonnerent ung amoureux
uis par ung gracieux congié se departi-
l'autre, affin que aucung ne s'aperceult
clusion. Et quant la feste fust faillie le
ist remener la chastelayne moult honora-
ome il avoit acoustumé. Laquelle fist
d'endotriner son petit chien en telle
que Tristan le bon chevalier le vist venir
effois faire le tour, comme dit estoit. Et
signe alla souvent vers la gracieuse dame
. Et menerent ensamble en aucung temps
nt une tres honneste vie ; et ne fust onques
entre leurs amours eust chose quy fust
ieu et concience.
celles choses advint que par diabolicque
ion la duchesse devint moult ardaulment
use de Tristan celuy bon chevalier, et desira
tes riens avec luy faire folie ; pour quoy elle
plusieurs (114 v) atraiemens, tant par bel
nt que par amoureuses parolles, et [par] luy
r aucung gracieulx don. Pour lesquelles choses
meult, car il estoit chevalier loyal et amoit

convient morir martireusement se vostre grace ne
m'est misericordieuse en pitié. Et j'ay concideré puis
que Dieu et nature vous ont donné telle perfeccion
de tous biens, que telle fontaine de largesse ne peult
estre sans habondance de loyaulté, pitié et charité,
pour quoy j'ay pris en moy hardiesse de venir
requerir le souverain bien de sa misericorde, si que
par mort ou par vie puisse avoir fin de mes inumerables travaulx ; car s'il plaist a Amour vous mouvoir a
pitié, et que me recepvés a mercy, ma fortune sera
plus grande et noble en toute beneurté que toutes les
aultres graces qui peullent estre au monde aquises.
Et se vostre amour me refusés (111 v) je mourray de
la plus martireuse mort c'onques soufrist loyal amou
reux ; et ainssi aray la fin de mes douloureuses
destresses. Pour quoy, haulte dame, en tant que
vous tenés ma mort ou ma vie du tout a vostre
ordonnance, je vous supplie que pour charitable
comppassion me recepvés pour vostre loyal serviteur, en moy octroiant le don de vostre amiable
mercy, sans souffrir que pour vous bien voulloir je
perisse a telle comfusion. »

Doulces parolles et piteuses complaintes fist Tristan le bon chevalier a la vaillant dame, en plourant
moult amerement et getant soupirs tres parfons, quy
luy entrerompoient sa voix et ses parolles, en telle
magniere que la dame peult bien appercevoir qu'il
estoit pris en l'amour d'elle sans rappel.

Et elle par avent, pource qu'il estoit le plus
gracieulx et vaillant de tous aultres, avoit parfaictement mis son cuer en luy, et pour nul aultre ne le
changast, combien que elle onques n'en avoit fait
chere ne samblant, car elle amoit honneur sur toutes
riens. Pour quoy, quant elle eust entandue sa piteuse
(112 r) et amoureuse requeste, et congnu les grans
angoisses qu'il souffroit pour loyalment servir et

amer, elle fust moult de legier meue a pitié, et luy donna responce doucement et en grant cremeur par telles parolles : « Tristan, tres noble chevalier, j'ay entandu vos tres amoureuses complainttes ; si ay bien par avent veu aucuns signes et magnieres, lesquelles concideree je croy certainement estre vray tout se que m'avés dit de vous mesmes. Mon cuer ne fust onques octroyé, ne mes amours, a home qui les decelast ; tantost que sa desloyaulté vendroit a ma congnoissance j'en prendroye la mort pour annoy et amere doulleur. Et se je vous congnoissoie vraiement estre loyal et secrept pour entierement et deligenment garder tel tresor que c'est de loiaulx amours, je me veuil bien de tant fier en vous de vous dire qu'i n'est home pour quy je vous changasse. »

« O », dist Tristan, « ma tres honoree dame et maistresse, je vous mercy de vostre gracieusse responce, pour laquelle je puis avoir grant esperance en vostre misericordieuse grace. Tres noble dame, vous plaise a savoir (112 v) qu'y n'est riens plus impocible que mon cuer estre separé de vostre amour ; et au regard de ma loyaulté, s'il vous plaist vous tant humilier a moy octroier le riche don de pitié et moy pour vostre humble servant recevoir et retenir, je vous fais promesse come loyal chevalier de vous aymer, honorer et servir et obeir, gardant vostre honneur en toutes choses, et de nos amours maintenir et celler si loyaulment et entierement que, pour perdre ma vie, [elles] ne seroient descouvertes de ma part. »

Adonques respondit la chastelaine : « Tres noble chevalier et mon loial amy ; il me sufit vostre bon voulloir, et espere en vous tant de franchise, loyaulté et bonté que pour riens ne voudroye faire trahison ne faulcer ma promesse, et pour ce suis je contente, et desire que puissons ensamble mener tres joieuse

vie et an
moy et
m'amour
celler, soy
qui soient
vouldrés de
certainemen
dance de des
perdu vostre

« Aa, tres e
dist Tristan, «
reverance le ric
[regraciant] de
ceste heure me c
voudroye perdre
Si vous promet de
que mieulx voudr
corps et de mon
desloyaulté ; mais fe
povre povoir tout se
esjoïr et plaire. »

A ces parolles s'en
doucement. Et en sign
rent la foy l'un a l'autre
ceste magniere : « Ma s
tres honoree, (113 v) m
esperance, ma vie et ma j
tous mes desirs ; puis qu
humble debonnairetté vou
soit ung cuer, une voullenté
que nous regardons par q
congnoistre quant il sera tem
devers vous pour vous trouve
rablement, joieusement et a
ensamble du consolable plaisir
nul ne puisse apercevoir nostre

« Mon bel am
« vous conseillé
propos que j'ay
petit [collier] de
duiray. Et pou
monseigneur m
vous pourrés s
que vous verr
environ de m
ment devers
soit. »

« Madame.
plus gracieus
humblement

A ses pa
regard ; et p
rent l'un de
de leur cor
noble duc f
blement,
diligence
magniere
par maint
par celuy
d'amours
en ce poi
sceu qu
contre D

Entre
temptac
amoure
sur tou
luy fis
sambl
donne
il se

l'amour et l'onneur du duc son droitturier seigneur tres entierement. Et quant la duchesse vist que pour chose qu'elle fist, ne pour bel samblant qu'elle luy moustrat, il ne la prioist d'amours, elle en fust moult couroucee. Dont pour l'ardeur de la temptacion quy l'eschauffoit de plus en plus, elle prist hardiesse et courage de parler a luy en ceste magniere :

« Tristan, » dit la duchesse, « je me donne bien grant merveille de vostre fait ; vous estes le plus bel, le plus vaillant et le plus gracieulx quy soit en nostre court, et si n'est aucun qui se peult appercevoir de vostre amour. Comment povez vous trouver ne aymer si secreptement que nul ne s'en peult prendre garde ? »

« Certes, ma tres redoubtee dame, » dist Tristan, « je ayme chascung, et si me samble — la mercy a chascung — que je suis aymé de tous. » « Or n'est pas responce qui sufise, » dit (115 r) la duchesse, « car estre ne peult que vous soyés sans dame par amours que vous amés sur toutes aultres, et quy sur tous aultres vous ayme. » « Certes, dame duchesse, » dit il, « j'ayme chascung en general, et si say bien que de dame quy vive ne suis aymé en especial. » « Tristan, » dit la duchesse, « vous ne debvés pas afermer que de dame quy vive ne soyés aymé, car vous ne le povés savoir. » « Sauf vostre honneur, » dit il, « madame, car je n'ay pas deservy ne requeru ne pourchassé d'estre aymé especialment d'aucune dame. Et pour ce je scay bien que je ne le suis pas. » « Vous dictes chose moult merveilleuse ; » dit la duchesse, « et savés vous se je vous ayme de tout mon cuer, et se j'ay desir que vous soyés mon seul et loyal amoureulx ? » « Dame, » dit Tristan, « je scay bien que non, car je ne voy aucune chose ne raison pour quoy vous me doyés amer en telle magniere ; et aussi j'ayme bien monseigneur le duc de si loyalle amour que je ne voudroye, pour chose quy fust, amer ne pencer en lieu dont il fust, ne qu'i peult par mon fait avoir deshonneur. »

(115 v) De celle responce fust la duchesse moult confuse et merveilleuse, et eust grant vergoigne ; et pour la couvrir, et sa grant honte, elle fust plaine d'ire et de male voullenté, et dist a Tristan ses parolles : « O », dit elle, « faulx trahistre desloyal ! Il sembleroit selon ton parler que je te priasse d'amour, au deshonneur de mon seigneur. Vuide tantost hors de ma chambre, et t'en va si loings que ja mais ne te voye, ou je te feray faire tel desplaisir que ja mais ne le verras amender. » « Haa », dit Tristan, « tres noble dame, je vous crie mercy, car certes en se que j'ay dit n'ay pencé que bien et honneur. » « A tant paix ! » dit la duchesse, « et gardes de plus dire mot devant moy, car tu es ung faulx trahistre desloial, et saches que sans plus atendre m'en vois racompter au duc ta grant desloyaulté et trahison. » Alors Tristan demoura tout seul en grant soucy et descomffort de se que sans ocasion et pour aymer loyaulté et l'onneur de son prince estoit si subitement cheu au malvoulloir de la duchesse.

Laquelle s'en vint au duc son mary et en plorant moult faintement (116 r) et faisant moult admirable deuil luy dist ses parolles : « Tres redoubté et puissant seigneur ; je suis tant troublee et couroucee que presque juques au morir. Et pource que vous estes celluy en quy je doy trouver comfort contre toutes advercités, je viens vers vous a remede ; car se vous ne relevés en moy consolacion, je croy que je mourray subitement d'angoisse et de dueil. » Adonc le roy, quy l'amoit tendrement, en eust pitié, mesmement quant il la vist tant triste et esplouree. Si luy demanda moult doucement quelle chose estoit

achoison de son courroux, luy promettant qu'il feroit
son debvoir d'elle esjoïr. « Certes », dit elle, « mon
redoubté sire, je ne seray ja mais recomfortee tant
que soit en vostre court ung faulx trahistre, auquel
vous avés moult grant amour et fiance. Et se tantost
ne me vengiés de la honte qu'il a voullu pourchasser
a vous et a moy, je ne croiray ja mais estre de vous
amee. » « Dame duchesse », dit le duc, « puis que le
fait [est] tant grant, donnés moy clerement a entendre la verité de la chose ; et au (116 v) plaisir de Dieu
je y metray remede convenable. » « Sire », dit elle,
« c'est de Tristan vostre chevalier, quy nagueres m'a
requise de folie. Et se je ne me fusse vertueusement
deffendue, il m'eust ahontee ; de laquelle offence
j'ay tant grant abhominacion que ja mais ne le
pourroye voir sans qu'il me soit trop grief. Et se vous
luy faictes raison, il est digne de morir sans aultre
jugement ; pour quoy, se vous le supportés contre
moy, ja mais en vous ne aray fiance. » « Certes
dame », dit il, « je suis moult esmerveillié se ce que
vous dictes est vray, car Tristan mon chevalier n'a pas
trouvé en moy quy me deust trahir. Et si ne vis onques
en luy chose quy fust contre loyaulté et bonté de chevalier parfait et vaillant. Si vous souffrés ung peu ; et je
saray la verité du fait au plus subtillement que je
pourray ; puis en ordonneray come il appartendra. »

Adonc se partist le duc de sa chambre. Et la
duchesse demoura tres mal conptente de sa responce, car selon ce qu'elle vousist, il n'avoit pas par
ses parolles mis legerement (117 r) cuer a ire contre
[le bon chevalier. Le duc fit venir] Tristan si le prist
par la main, et en faisant joieuse chere le mena en
son jardin ; puis ferma moult bien la porte. Et
Tristan avoit moult grant paour en son cuer, car il
doubtoit bien que la duchesse l'avoit faulcement
imformé contre luy.

Et adonc parla le duc a luy en ceste magniere :
« Tristan, ne vous troublés aucunement en vostre
courage de chose que je vous die, car je veuil savoir
de vous une chose ; dont, se ja mais voullés estre
mon amy, gardés que ne me cellés verité de se que je
vous demanderay. » « Certes, mon tresredoubté
seigneur », dist Tristan, « demandés moy, et je vous
donneray responce veritable, s'i avent que par raison
le pourray faire de vray. » « Il me plaist », dit le
duc ; « or veuil savoir en quel lieu vous aymés par
amours. Et que tant vous fyés en moy que me diés la
pure verité. » « O monseigneur », dist Tristan,
« vous me demandés chose dont en brief vous puis
faire assés legiere responce, car certes, je ayme
chascun egalment de tout mon povoir, fors tant que
j'ayme vous et vostre hostel par (117 v) dessus
tous. » « Tristan », dit le duc, « je vous croy, mais il
ne peult pas estre que chevalier tant bel, jeulne et
gracieulx, noble, vaillant et parfait come vous estes,
soit sans avoir une dame par amour par dessus
toutes. Si vous prie que vous le me diés. » « Hellas !
mon redoubté seigneur », dit Tristan, « se je vous en
ay respondu autant que je vous en puis respondre, je
suplie a vostre noble franchise que vous demourés a
tant comptant. » « Certes », dit le duc, « vous
m'avés promis de dire verité. Si vous dy que vers
moy vous en aquittés vostre foy, se ja mais voullés
estre amé de moy ». « Monseigneur », dit il, « quant
vous me requerés tant estroictement, je comfesse
que j'ayme par amours en certain lieu tant loyalment
come de toute ma puissance, et tellement qu'il ne
seroit en ma posibilité de mestre mon cuer en aultre
lieu. Si vous prie que a tant soyés comptent, car plus
avent ne vous en puis dire par raison. »

« Treschier amy », dit le duc, « vous vallés bien de
amer loyalment, mais je vous prie que feablement

me descouvrés le lieu, ou autrement (118 r) n'arés ja paix a moy. » « O monseigneur », dit le bon chevalier, « je vous prie que me pardonnés, car pour riens ne le diroye a creature quy vive; et aussi il me samble que vous ne le me debvés pas demander. »

« Tristan », dit le duc, « bien vous povés tant fier en moy de moy descouvrir en quel lieu vous aymés. Si vous octroye que de deux choses vous choisissés laquelle qu'il vous plaira; c'est que me desclairés premier ce que je demande, ou que vous vuidiés ma terre et toute ma seignorie sans jamais retourner. Et je vous promet comme loyal et vaillant chevalier, se de vostres amours me donnés congnoissance, de les celler et garder en telle magniere que vous et vostre dame n'en aurés ja villennie ne desplaisir. » « Monseigneur », dist Tristan, « je suis content, et je vous prie que vous m'envoiés sur les Sarrazins mestre mon corps contre la puissance de tous les adverssaires de Jhesucrist, ou que vous me faictes combastre contre quatre de vos plus fors et crueulx lions, ou me tramettés en aultre peril tel qu'il vous plaira, affin que, se je n'en puis eschaper par ma vaillance, que au moins je meure (118 v) a honneur, sans moy exillier a honte de vos terres et pays. Mais de mes amours ne m'en veuillés plus avent requerir, car j'ayme mieulx a morir que le desceller, et suis certain que se je le vous dis, que moy et celle que j'ayme en perdrons la vie. »

« Tristan », dit le duc, « vecy la derniere requeste que je vous en feray. Je vous commande que se dire ne le me vollés, que presentement vous partés et exilliés de ma court et de toute ma seignorie pour ja mais, car après la promesse que je vous ay faicte de loyalment garder et seller vous ne le me deussiés pas contredire. Et je vous promet encore plus avent que, en quelque lieu que vous amés, et fust ma mere, ma fille ou ma femme, que je le vous pardonne, mais que me diés toute la verité. »

Sur ses parolles fust Tristan moult pencif, car il doubtoit moins la mort que descouvrir sa tres chere dame et maistresse ; et en oultre il regardoit que s'il se partoit exillié du pays, il ne la verroit ja mais et aroit perdu sans recouvrer la consolacion de ses loyalles amours. Si avoit en son cuer tant grande contradiccion (119 r) et si divers regretz qu'il ne savoit qu'il devoit faire. Mais en conclusion de ses pencees la fiance qu'il avoit en la parfaitte loyaulté qui devoit estre au duc, luy donna courage de rendre responce telle : « Monseigneur, vous me constraignés tant estroictement, que metre me convient en vostre ordonnance la mort ou la vie de ma dame par amours et de moy. Et mesmes me constraignés a faulcer ma foy vers elle. Or plust a Dieu mon createur, que ma bouche ne fust onques faicte pour dire chose dont mon cuer [est] si estraint, et dont la mort est et sera en brief donnee a moy et a aultre que vous aymés moult. Et pource que celler ne le vous puis plus, je vous dy que c'est vostre niepce du Vergier. Si vous supplie humblement que le me pardonnés, et que ja ne le me descellés, si cher que vous aymés et tenés vostre foy, et de garder la vie d'elle et de moy. »

Adonc fust le duc merveilleusement joieulx, et entandit bien que la duchesse luy avoit menty faulcement, et qu'elle n'estoit (119 v) pas celle qu'il amoit par amours. Si acolla son chevalier estroictement par grande amiabletté, disant : « Franc chevalier et mon cher amy ; vous ne m'avés en nulle magniere courcé ne offendu pour avoir prises aliances de loialles amours avec ma niepce du Vergier, car je croy que on ne pourroit au monde trouver amours mieulx parties de toute biaulté, bonté, gracieuseté et noblesse d'une part et d'aultre. Mais je vous prie que me diés en quelle magniere vous povés savoir lieu et temps de parler l'un a l'autre, s'il est ainssi que nul ne sache l'estat de vos amours que vous deulx. »

« Monseigneur », dist il, « la franche dame a ung chiennet qu'elle a endotriné, lequel se vient jouer aucuneffois entour de se jardin quant il est temps que je voise voir ma maistresse. Et par ainssi say je tourjours l'eure que nous povons avoir opportunitté de parler ensamble. » « Or par mon ame », dit le duc, « c'est une tres belle magniere. Si vous prie que a la premiere fois que vous irés je vous fasse comppaignie, car ma niepce n'en sara (120 r) riens ; et si seray vostre comppaignon d'armes loyal tout mon vivant. » « Monseigneur », dit Tristan, « je y doy aller ceste presente nuit ; dont, affin que puissiés voir que je me fye en vous parfaitement, vous vendrés avec moy, et vous pourrés escondre dessoubz les abres vers, que vostre niepce ja ne vous apercevera. Et verrés se je vous ay dit verité. » « Mon cher frere et amy », dit le duc, « je vous en mercie, et vous promet que je desire moult l'eure pour voir vostre gracieuse et amoureuse vie. »

Le jour passa et la nuyt vint. Si s'en alla Tristan le bon chevalier devers sa maistresse. Et le duc le suivist de loing, si se mussa pres du lieu dessoubz ung bel rosier vert et flory, en telle magniere qu'il ne povoist pas estre apperceu ; et il povoist bien voir tout l'estat d'eulx. Le bon chevalier vint a sa dame et maistresse laquelle il atendoit en grant affeccion de desir ; il la salua en tres amoureuse reverance, et elle luy vint encontre a moult humble et joieuse chere, en le recevant et le acueillant tant bel que plus dire ne puis. Et apprés se qu'i se furent entrebaisiés et (120 v) acollés moult honorablement et par magniere tres ordonnee, ilz commencerent a parler ensamble moult gracieusement de plaisantes parrolles. Et dist Tristan en ceste maniere : « Ma treschere maistresse et ma tres exellante dame, mon joieulx desir et mon souvenir amoureux, comment vous estes vous portee puis que derniere fois partis de vostre joieuse pencee ? Avés vous eu tourjours tous vos grés et plaisirs ? Avés vous eu annoy, soulcy ou aultre riens quy vous ait aucunement despleu ? Puis je pour toute ma pocibillité faire chose quy vous puisse esjoïr et plaire ? Commandés moy vostre voulloir tourjours, a toutes heures, et vous pourrés apercevoir comme de vous complaire et servir suis ardaulment desirant. »

Adont la dame respondit moult amiablement : « Tres noble chevalier et mon seul et parffait amy, mon cuer, ma vie et toute ma joieuse esperance, je n'ay eu — la mercy Dieu — grief ; ne se j'avoye eu toutes les fortunes et discors quy peullent estre, si seroient a vostre joieuse venue toutes mes doulleurs acomplies, et converties en habondance de parfaicte (121 r) liesse ; car entre ciel et terre n'est chose quy me peult grever tant que Dieu vous tiengne en prosperité, et que nos amours soient entierement et honnestement gardees. Si vous mercie de vostre joieuse visitacion, moy offrant a tout se qu'il vous plaira et que me vouldrés demander, car je congnoys nos amours de si entiere loyaulté fermee, que moy et vous ne voudrions demander chose quy soit contre l'onneur de l'un et de l'autre. »

« Haulte dame et treshonoree princesse d'amours », dit Tristan, « je vous mercie tant come je puis, vous acertiffiant loyalment que je ne doubteroie mort ne aultre peril quy peult estre, pour vostre honneur maintenir et garder. »

En telles parolles et moult d'aultres complaintes

de merveilleuses consolacions avec gracieux baisiers passerent celle nuit en incomparables liesses, tant qu'y furent tous esbaÿs quant ilz visrent le jour esclarcy; ilz ne penssoient avoir esté ensamble que une heure, car il leur estoit moult grief a eulx departir de sy consolable plaisir, mais force estoit de eulx departir pour garder leurs honneurs. (121 v) Pour quoy ilz prisrent le plus gracieulx congié quy fust onques veu, requerant et octroiant l'ung l'autre d'eulx entrevoir tant souvent et diligenment que faire se pourroit. Adonc se partist le bon chevalier de la. Si trouva le duc quy estoit ja ung peu retrait affin qu'il ne fust apperceu de sa niepce la chastelaine, et tantost qu'il vist son loyal chevalier il luy vint au devant et l'acolla moult estroitement, disant : « Certes, mon cher frere et loyal comppaignon, ores suis je maintenant tout asseuré que vous me estes loyal, et que aucuns quy vous ont cuidié blasmer et oculper vers moy ont eu tord de vous. Si povés bien estre certain que d'ores en avent seray vostre, de corps d'amis et de chevance et puissance, cent mil fois plus que onques ne fus. Et mercie Dieu quy tant de grace a fait a vous et a ma niepce qu'y de vos deux cuers a fait une voullenté, car je croy que onques ne furent amours tant acomplies en perfeccion de vraye loyaulté, plaisir, gracieuseté et honneur come celle de vous deux; car en voiant vostre amoureux et honorable deport, et oyant vos consolables et amoureuses parolles (122 r) j'ay passé ceste nuit en la plus gracieuse liesse que je sentis onques en mon vivant au cuer. » « Haa, monseigneur », dist Tristan, « je vous remercie de l'onneur que me faictes et dictes, et des biens que vous me presentés, mais pour tous bons services et guerredon je vous demande une seulle requeste : c'est si cher que vous aymés la vie de ma dame et de moy, qu'il vous plaise

97

celler entierement se que je vous ay donné a congnoistre de nos amours. » « Cher frerre et comppaignon », dit le duc, « ostés vostre cuer de toute doubtance, car mieulx ameroye avoir perdu tous les biens que Dieu m'a prestés que ja mais personne par moy en sceult aucune[s] nouvelles. »

Ces choses dictes le duc et le chevalier misrent fin en leurs parolles, et se departirent l'ung de l'autre. Toute celle journee fust la duchesse moult troublee ; et fist tant mal samblant que le duc et tous ceulx de la court ne peurent d'elle avoir ung biau samblant ne une parolle consolative, car elle veoist Tristan le chevalier aller et venir parmy la court comme il avoit acoustumé, et servir le duc, qui plus luy faisoit (122 v) d'onneur et de bel samblant c'onques mais n'avoit fait. Si passa se jour en moult grant amertume de cuer, juques a la nuit que le duc et elle furent ensamble couchiés. Et quant le duc se voulust dormir — quy toute la nuit avoit veillié, comme vous avés ouÿ —, la duchesse se degetoit et tournoit d'ung costé sur aultre, en elle detordant et getant souspirs par si merveilleuses fainttes que le duc en eust grant pitié, et luy demanda qu'elle avoit.

« Sire », dist la duchesse, « vous savés bien l'achoison de ma desplaisance, mais il ne vous en chault gueres. Je congnoys bien que se j'estoye mòrte ou deshonoree pour ja mais, que riens ne vous en seroit grief. » « Duchesse », dit il, « pour quoy dictes vous ses parolles ? Ne savés vous pas que je vous ayme autant comme prince vivant peult amer sa loyalle espouse ? » « Certes, monseigneur », dit elle, « vous monstrés mal qu'i soit verité se que vous dictes, car vous tenés avec vous et en vostre court le trahistre quy vous et moy a voullu desheriter d'onneur, dont j'ay pour l'amour de vous tant grant despit que quant je le regarde devant moy, advis m'est que le cuer me deult partir (123 r) de deuil et d'angoisses. Et vous le soutenés malgré moy, pour moy faire despiter, et luy faictes plus d'onneur et de bel samblant c'onques mais. N'esse pas bonne chose ? » « Dame », dit le duc, ne me parllés plus de ses choses, car je scay bien que Tristan le bon chevalier ne penssa onques desloiaulté contre moy. »

« O moy, tres maleureuse et meschante », dit la duchesse, « je doy bien haïr ma vie et maudire tous ceulx et celles quy onques furent consentans et causes de nostre mariage, quant, pour vous avoir dit la verité et vous avoir gardé loyaulté et foy, vous me reputés pour janglerresse et mensongiere. Et si deussiés bien croirre que Tristan m'a voullu deshonorer, car vous ne persone quy vive n'avés congnoissance qu'il ait dame par amours en quelque lieu. » « Duchesse », dit le duc, « ne m'en parllés ja mais, se courroucer ne me voullés, car je scay bien que Tristan ayme dame par amours plus belle, plus jeulne, plus gracieuse et plus plaisant que vous n'estes, et qu'y ne penssa onques en vous a deshonneur. » « Voyre », dit la duchesse, « certes, je croy que, sauf vostre honneur, qu'y n'en soit riens, car onques creature n'en eust congnoissance ! Et se vous me savés (123 v) dire quy sont ses amours je seray contente, et ne vous en parleray ja mais. » « Dame, » dit le duc, « ne me surquerés point de le vous dire, car a vous ne a aultre, pour chose qui puisse advenir, ne le decelleray. »

Par ses parolles entandit la duchesse que elle avoit failly a sa faulce emprise, et qu'elle ne pourroit mestre malle voullenté entre le duc et Tristan. Si desira moult de savoir quelle dame Tristan amoit, affin qu'en aucune magniere leur peult a tous deux porter deshonneur et desplaisir ; car elle avoit le cuer plain de moult despiteuse rage, pour ce que [il] l'avoit refusee quant elle par parolles couvertes c'estoit a luy presentee, come devant [est] dit. Si dist au duc ses parolles : « Certes, monseigneur, se vous savés qu'il ayme aultre femme vous le me poés bien dire, car adonc je croiray que se qu'y m'a dist a esté par esbastement, et en seray plus contente de vous et de luy, et plus appaisié mon cuer. » « Dame », dit le duc, « atant paix ! Car pour riens ne le deceleroye, et se vous me voullés faire plaisir grant, c'est de ja mais en ouvrir vostre bouche pour en parler en ma (124 r) presence. » Et atant cessa le duc d'en parler.

Et la duchesse fust moult comfuse de se que sa malle voullenté ne povoist a fin traire. Si penssa environ partie de la nuit qu'elle ne cessa onques de plaindre, soupirer et plourer, mais pour ce ne se disposoit pas le duc a luy en dire aultre chose, pour quoy elle s'apenssa d'ung aultre barat. Et s'aprocha du duc, lequel elle acolla moult doucement, disant en ceste magniere : « Hellas, mon tres redoubté seigneur ! Je suis bien esbaÿe et trahie, quy vous ayme, craing et croy, prise et honneure tant comme loyalle femme peult amer son seigneur et mary. Et ne seroit secrept tant fust grant que je vous peusse celler, fust pour ma mort ou pour ma vie. Et vous ne m'aymés riens et ne me creés pas et ne vous fiez riens en moy. Hellas ! quelz secreps ay je descellés de se que me dicttes onques ? Quelle chose vous ay je sellé, que je ne vous aye dit tous mes secreps ? Quy debvés vous selon verité mieulx amer que moy ? Quelle chose doit estre en vostre cuer que le mien ne le doye savoir ? Et ou sera mais trouvee loyaulté se le mary et la femme se deffient ? (124 v) Je vous suplie par amoureuse comppaignie que tant vous fiez en moy, que me diés se que je vous requier, car bien savés que jamais apprés n'en sera parllé, et que plus possible seroit la mer monter au ciel que ja ma bouche fust ouverte pour descouvrir a creature vivant chose que me eussiés dit en secrept. »

Adont elle l'acolla plus estroit que devant, luy joygnant pres de ses tetins et luy baisant la bouche et les yeulx, plourant a lermes, destournans et soupirans moult parfondement et en faisant les trahistres fainctes qu'elle peult, tant que le roy en prist pitié et luy dist : « Dame, je ne puis plus vous voir tant couroucee, pour quoy je vous diray se que vous demendés, se je savoye que le voulsissés celler, et le garder parfaictement et entierement. » « O monseigneur, » dit elle, « je vous jure sur Dieu et sur ma conscience et en foy de toute gentillesse, de le celler si estroitement et si discreptement que jamais n'en aura personne par mon fait congnoissance. »

« Dame, » dit il, « et pour mestre vostre cuer en paiz je le vous diray. Sachés que Tristan mon chevalier loyal ayme ma niepce du (125 r) Vergier, et elle luy, tant que je croy qu'y ne furent amours de si grande consolacion ne si parfaicte. Et la dame du Vergier a introduit son chiennet, lequel vient gentilment faire son tour entour de son jardin devant le chevalier quand il est temps qu'y voise vers elle. Et j'avoye promis a Tristan non le deceller ; donc pour ce que vous estes femme en quy doit estre loyaulté, je vous l'ay descouvert pour vous apaisier, mais vrayement, se vous ne le cellés et gardés moult discreptement vous en arés de moy la mort. » « O monseigneur, » dit elle, « certes, vous ne debvés point doubter que jamais par moy en soit parllé. »

Atant cesserent les parolles. Et le roy s'endormist, mais la duchesse de malle heure nee ne peult pas celler ne dormir, d'annoy et de rage qu'elle avoit au cuer par envie de se que Tristan amoit aultre dame qu'elle, et avoit moult grant desir qu'il fust jour,

pour voir comme elle luy porroit faire honte et aussi
a la chastelayne.

L'endemain fust une grant feste, et tind le duc
grant court, ou furent fais aprés disner plusieurs
esbastemens de dances, jouxtes et tournois. (125 v)
Et y fust la chastelaine, que le duc avoit fait venir,
avec plusieurs seigneurs, dames et damoiselles quy
danssoient moult joieusement.

Et la duchesse dit a la chastelaine : « Soyés
joieuse et faictes bonne chere, car femme pourveue
de tant bel amy et gracieux come vous estes, doit
estre habille et legiere a tous esbastemens. » De ses
parolles fust la chastelaine merveilleusement esbaÿe,
et respondit moult humblement a la duchesse :
« Dame, je voudroye bien faire [a vostre] command
bonne chere et joieuse feste ; mais au regard des
amours dont vous parllés, je vous dy bien que tallent
n'ay d'avoir amy, sinon a l'ordonnance de mon
tresredoubté seigneur et de vous, et a l'amour de
chascun. » Atant cessa la duchesse ung peu son
parler. Et quant elle eust dancé encore ung tour elle
dist en danssant et chantoist ses quatre vers :

> Chastelayne, soyés bien joincte,
> Car bel amy avés et cointte,
> Et si savés bien le mestier
> Du petit chiennet affaictier. »

Alors que fust chantee ceste douloureuse chans-
son plaine de venin mortel par (126 r) la duchesse,
Tristan le bon chevalier n'estoit pas en la place, car
le duc l'avoit mené pour soulacier en son jardin,
pour joieusement passer temps. Et la chastellaine,
tantost qu'elle eust ouÿe et entandue ladite chans-
son, elle congnust qu'elle estoit trahie et que ses
amours estoient descellees : si fust son cuer nasvré a

mort. Et se departist de la feste piteusement et subitement, et s'en alla au Vergier et entra en sa chambre, plorant et soupirant moult desolablement. En celle heure estoient toutes les gens du Vergier allés voir la feste a la court, fors une petite chamberiere quy estoit demouree a l'ostel pource qu'elle trambloist les fievres, laquelle s'esmerveilla moult quant elle vist la chastelayne sa maistresse revenir de la court, seulle et plourant si tres piteusement ; pour quoy elle ne l'osa araisonner, mais se asist au dehors de l'uys pour entendre se qu'elle diroit. Laquelle tout a part soy commenssa a plaindre moult doucement en ceste magniere :

« Helas, vray Dieu glorieux, moy tres angoiseuse et dolante descomfortee ; aujourd'uy ay bien trouvé la fin de ma liesse, quant madame (126 v) m'a reprochié que j'ay affaittié mon chiennet, car par ce je puis clerement apercevoir que elle scet tout l'estat de nos amours, lesquelles ne peullent estre decellees sinon par celuy que j'amoye de tout mon cuer, et il m'a trahie ! Hellas, moy tres imfortunee, la plus malheureuse et miserable que la terre aujourd'uy soustiengne. Certes, il n'est pas pocible que ja mais, pour chose que je fasse, je peusse recouvrer consolacion, car je sens mon cuer disposé a soy habandonner au plus desolable descomfort quy puisse estre. Hellas, noble chevalier tres vaillant, comment tu soyes le plus gracieulx, debonnaire, amiable, amoureulx de tous les aultres, je ne cuidasse que jamais loyaulté deult en toy defaillir, mais penssoie que tu deusses aussi avoir largesse de tous les aultres biens de grace et de nature, par dessus tous aultres, et loyaulté plus qu'en home vivant. Et pour ce je m'estoye donnee a toy si entierement que mieulx estoye tiengne que miengne, et ne te changasse pour tous les biens que la terre contient, ne pour morir ne pensasse desloiaulté en toy; et tu m'as [trahie] si piteusement !

(127 r) Hellas, mon amy gracieux, treschier amé, quant tu parloyes a moy tant doucement come ung angle, de condicion et de magniere tant ordonnee, et que nous prenions tel plaisir en nos amours tres honnestes que nous passions ensamble le jour et la nuit plus tost que oysel ne volle, je ne cuidasse pas adonc que tu pensasses desloyaulté vers moy, et que tu me voulsisses trahir a la mort. Hellas, mon amy, je cuidoye que tu me amasses aprés Dieu sur toutes riens, come je faisoye toy; mais bien appert que tu amoyes mieulx la duchesse, et que je n'estoye pas digne de pocider si riche tresor come d'avoir seulle le don de tes amours. Hellas, ou sera plus trouvee loyaulté, quant la fleur de tous les chevaliers parfais et vaillans a si desloyalment faulcé sa promesse en descouvrant amours, pour moy deffendre de la Court Amoureuse? Hellas, Fortune, je n'ay pas grant cause de moy plaindre de toy, car tu as usé de ton office quy ne tind onques ordre ne regle ne mesure, mais je me doy bien plaindre d'amours quy ont souffert a mon amy penser desloyaulté. (127 v) Hellas, Amours, j'ay tord de faire de toy complaintte, car se je veuil verité regarder je doy humblement regracier ta noble seignorie quant tu m'as garnie de si grande loyaulté que mon cuer n'eust pour riens enffraint tes regles; et pour loyalment amer veuil je morir, laquelle mort sera honorable, combien que dommagable me soit. Si ne me say de quy plaindre, sinon de mon parffait amy, lequel j'ayme tant loyalment que pour trahison qu'il ait faicte vers moy ne le puis oublier ne haïr.

Hellas mon amy ! Certes, quant je regarde que mon cuer ne puis oster de toy et je sens que tu as donné tes amours a aultre qu'a moy en descouvrant nostre amoureuse aliance, je sens multiplier en moy la grande destresse et le desesperable descommfort, quy si grefment me tourmente que plus ne puis porter ceste martireuse doulleur quy mon chetif cuer desollé fait miserablement fendre et partir. Et ne veuil plus vivre aprés se que j'ay perdu le hault bien d'amours que je cuidoye garder toute ma vie. Et quant tu me saras estre morte pour l'amour de toy, ores congnoistras tu ma loyaulté. Hellas ! Engoisse (128 r) me court sus, le cueur me part, la parolle me fault, tous mes membres labourent a la fin ; et la mort me constraint et chace, dont je la regracie, car on doit tenir la mort pour heureuse quy fait finer telles destresses que je porte. »

La dame avoit le cuer si serré pour l'amour qu'elle languissoit, qu'elle ung peu aprés ses complainttes gesta ung soupir du cueur si parfont et merveilleux, en disant ses dernieres parolles : « Mort angoiseuse, de tous haÿe et despitee, bien soyes tu venue, quy veulx mestre fin au plus rigoureux martire quy onques fust veu ne que onq cueur humain soustint. Sire Dieu glorieux, je rens a toy mon ame, priant a l'imfinitté de ta misericorde que tu la reçoyves a mercy. A Dieu te commant, mon bon amy ; je meurs pour toy loyalment amer, si que ja mais ne te verray et ja mais vive ne me verras. »

Belles piteuses complainttes et aultres inumerables lamentacions fist la franche dame en grant habondance de pleurs et soupirs, et en tant admirable descommfort qu'i n'est si dur cuer s'i la regardast, qu'i se peult tenir de (128 v) plourer tres amerement. Et en telles complaintes faisant, deromppant ses robes et ses biaux cheveulx, par trop grant imfluance et efusion de desolable et angoiseuse destresse le cueur luy fendit et esclatta, et fust ilec subitement morte.

105

Ung peu aprés que la chastelaine se fust partie de la dance par les parolles de la duchesse, come dit est dessus, le duc et le chevalier vindrent de l'esbastement, et furent esmerveillés de se que la chastelaine n'y estoit pas. Si dist le duc a Tristan qu'il alast vers elle et la menast a la feste, lequel tout seul y alla moult joieulx. Et comme il entra en la chambre et il la vist gesir a terre sur le tappis — elle estant morte —, il fust moult esmerveillié, encores quant il la vist tant desolablement esplouree et eschevellee, mais il ne cuidoit pas qu'elle fust morte, car elle avoit encores sa biaulté vermeille et coulouree pour la grant habondance quy luy avoit esmeu le sanc. Si l'apella, mais elle ne parlla point. Et adonc il araisonna la chamberiere qui la estoit, laquelle luy (129 r) racompta comment elle estoit venue seulle de la court, merveilleusement esplouree, et comme elle c'estoit complaintte de la duchesse, quy luy avoit reprochié d'avoir affaittié son chiennet, et les gresves complainttes qu'elle faisoit de son amy quy l'avoit trahie, en disant que elle voulloit morir, et que en commandant son ame a Dieu elle c'estoit laissee choir a terre.

Quant le chevalier entandist ses parolles il fust a merveilles descomforté ; si vint vers sa maistresse et quant il congnust que elle estoit morte il fust moult outrageusement nasvré a mort.

« Hellas ! » dit il, « moy dolant et miserable, pour quoy vint onques le jour de ma nativitté, et pour quoy me donna onques Dieu estre humain ? Pour trahir a mort ma tres loyalle Dame et maistresse, laquelle estoit le tresor et l'acomplicement de tous mes biens et loyaulté que Amours peureust onques amasser... ! Hellas, ma tres honoree maistresse, le miroer et l'exemplaire de toute beaulté, bonté, honneur et loyaulté : comment peult Dieu et nature avoir souffert que vous, quy seule estiés remplie de tous (129 v) biens et graces que tous les autres du monde ne peullent ensamble atendre, [soiés] morte tant subitement, et que je voye vostre gent corps sans vie? Et comment me peult la justice de Dieu soustenir; pour quoy ne meurs sans avoir puissance ne vertu de parler? Comme tant exelante soit morte par mon deffault, quelle chose peult deffendre mon cuer de rompre et partir, quant je voy morte la fleur des fleurs et la plus loyalle Dame que la terre soustenist, qui m'avoit fait seigneur de ses amours et c'estoit donnee a moy tant entierement, quy pour l'amour de moy a voullu morir. Hellas, ma tres amiable Dame, j'ay bien cause de multiplier en moy le plus rigoreux deuil que cuer humain peult porter, quant aujourd'uy la fleur de toute noblesse [est] perie et morte, par quoy la Court Amoureuse a perdu tout son povoir et sa vaillance. Ce dommage ne peult estre jamais recouvré, mais puis que c'est advenu par moy, je veuil morir pour elle, combien que se ne soit pas condigne sathiffacion, car aprés sa mort ne veuil (130 r) ja mais vie possider. Hellas, ma tres loyalle dame, Dieu scet bien que quant je descouvris nos amours au duc, que se fust en grant feableté, et affin que je ne perdice le pays, pource que ja mais ne vous eusse veue. Hellas, tres noble duc, la fiance que j'avoye en toy te deult bien avoir tenu et gardé en loyaulté, et toy avoir deffendu de nous avoir descouvert a la duchesse, laquelle par faulce envie a tout d'ung coup nafvré a mort ma maistresse et moy. O duchesse, se j'eusse voullu acomplir ton plaisir — au deshonneur de monseigneur le duc — tu ne m'eusses pas pourchassié ceste malle fortune; mais j'amoye mieulx loyaulté que vain delit contre mon prince. O franche chastelaine et ma tres loyalle dame en amours, plust a Dieu que vous sceussiés comment j'ay eu tourjours le cuer loyal vers vous. »

Adonc le chevalier gentil, regardant continuellement sa dame gisant morte a ses piés, trait une espee clere tranchant qu'y portoit a son costé, puis dist : « Ma seulle Dame, la loyaulté que vous avés envers moy eue a voulloir pour moy morir, me constraint a morir pour vous. Vray Dieu, roy (130 v) de tous les roys, tout puissant, je te commande en tes mains mon esperist, en toy priant que tu ayes misericordieusement mercy de ma dame et de moy et que nous mettes ensamble en ta gloire. » Et se disant il adressa la pointte de son espee contre son cuer et le mist en deux parties, et chaÿ mort emprés le corps de sa Dame.

De laquelle inumerable pitié la chamberiere, quy vist tout le fait, fust moult esbaÿe, et s'en vint devers le duc moult piteusement effroye[e], auquel elle racompta tout le fait de la mort de l'ung et de l'autre au mieulx qu'elle peult, et toutes leurs parolles et complaintes. Par quoy le duc entandit bien que la duchesse avoit pourchassié tout se meffait par couroulx et envie qu'elle n'avoit eu son plaisir de Tristan. Puis se remenbra que tout estoit venu pour sa parolle, car il avoit descouvert le fait a la duchesse sans mal pencer, laquelle pour habondance de malice et d'envie estoit cause principal de tout celuy piteux meurtre. Si vint au lieu et vist la douloureuse adventure, dont il fust estroittement courroucé.

Et adonc subitement (131 r) mena grant ire, et trait l'espee hors du corps du chevalier toute rouge du sanc, si vint a la feste ; et comme tout forcené et habandonné a toute desesperance il escria la duchesse a mort, laquelle s'en cuida bien fuir. Mais il la suivist roidement et luy dist : « Duchesse, or est vostre malicieux malice descouvert, car parce que vous n'avés peu joïr a vostre plaisir de Tristan mon chevalier, vous avés par envie et par vos faulces jangles aujourd'uy descouvertes les amours de luy et de ma niepce du Vergier, tant qu'y sont tous deux mors l'ung pour l'autre. Et je fais veu a Dieu que vous en perdrés la vie. » Et adonc, sans nulle mercy d'elle ne sans voulloir avoir [escouté] excusacion qu'elle vousist dire, il luy trancha la teste publicquement.

Quant le duc eust occis la duchesse, il se prist a complaindre piteusement en ceste magniere : « Helas, moy povre dollant et descomforté, je suis cause de la mort des plus loyalles amoureuses creatures qui fussent au monde et que j'amoye le plus, lesquelz sont mors par ma parolle, combien que je n'y eusse onques penssé mal. Puis, par courroulx, (131 v) ay mis mon espouse a mort, qui par faulce envie et janglerie avoit perpetré tout se meschief. Si suis ores tout seul et sans comfort, et useray tout le plus de ma vie en habondance de tristesses ; dont, affin que Dieu ait mercy de moy, je propose laissier le monde et toutes ses vanittés et entrer en religion, pour contempler a servir Dieu en penitance, et priant a Dieu qu'y se meuve a pitié et qu'y pardonne aux ames des deux loyaulx amoureulx. »

Lequel Dieu glorieux nous doint a tous et a toutes ainssi vivre et finer qu'en la fin nous fasse heritiers de son glorieulx royaulme, en participacion de vision divine et de perdurable paix. Amen.

Cy finist l'istoire de la Chastelaine
du Vergier et de Tristan le chevalier.

Pour celluy qui m'a escript
Ave Maria soit dit.

Les changements apportés au texte du manuscrit se trouvent entre crochets dans le texte imprimé.

f. 108 r *que :* ms. *quy*

f. 109 v Le ms. donne deux fois de suite le mot *festes*

f. 110 r *et :* manque dans le ms. (2x)

f. 110 v *tres haulte et :* répété dans le ms.

f. 110 v *chassé :* ms. *laissé*

f. 111 r *le :* ms. *la*

f. 112 v *elles :* manque dans le ms.

f. 113 r *regraciant :* ms. *regracient*

f. 113 v *collier :* le ms. donne *clochier,* qui ne semble pas avoir trop de sens ici.

f. 114 v *par :* ms. *pour*

f. 115 r Le ms. donne « *et que savés vous se je vous ayme de tout mon cuer...* »

f. 116 r *est :* ms. *et*

f. 117 r *le bon chevalier. Le duc fit venir :* nous avons ajouté ces quelques mots pour donner un sens acceptable à la phrase, qui semble être incomplète. Le copiste a sans doute sauté une ou plusieurs lignes.

f. 117 v Le ms. donne « *Certes* », dit le duc, « *vous m'avés promis de vous dire verité.* »

f. 119 r Le ms. donne « *la parfaitte loyaulté de qui devoit estre au duc...* » Le copiste a biffé *de.*

f. 119 r *est :* ms. *et*

f. 119 v Le copiste commence cette page ainsi : « *pas celle qu'il amoit par amours que la duchesse.* » Nous avons supprimé les trois derniers mots.

f. 120 v (vers la fin). Le ms. donne « *si seroient ilz a vostre joieuse venue toutes mes doulleurs acomplies.* »

f. 122 r *aucunes* : ms. *aucune nouvelles*

f. 123 v Le ms. donne, à la fin de la réplique du duc : « *ne v le decelleray.* » Le copiste a biffé *v*.

f. 123 v *il* : ms. *elle*

f. 123 v *est* : ms. *et*

f. 125 r Le ms. donne : « *faire son tour entour de son jardin faire son tour.* »

f. 125 v *a vostre* : ms. *vostre a*

f. 126 r Le copiste a écrit d'abord « fors une petite chamberiere quy estoit demouree a la court » ; il a remplacé *la court* par *l'ostel*.

f. 126 v *trahie* : ms. *trahiee*

f. 128 v (au milieu). Ici encore le copiste a fait preuve d'inattention : il a écrit d'abord : « *et furent esmerveillés de se que la duc* ». S'apercevant de son erreur il a biffé *duc* et continué par *chastelaine*.

f. 129 v *soiés* : ms. *soit*

f. 129 v *est* : ms. *et*

f. 130 v Le copiste avait écrit : « *il adressa la pointte de son espee contre son cuer et la mist en deux parties* ». Il a changé *la* en *le*.

f. 130 v *effroyee* : le ms. donne *effroye*. Le copiste continue par *auquell* : il a biffé le second *l*.

f. 131 r *escouté* : ms. *executé*.

GLOSSAIRE

abhominacion : horreur, répugnance
acertiffier : assurer
achoison : occasion, cause
acolla : embrassa
acomplir : achever
acteur : auteur
adonc, adonques, adont : alors
advenement : arrivée

111

advis : avis ; *estre a.* : sembler
affaictier : dresser, instruire
ahontee : déshonorée
angle : ange
angoiseusement : violemment
annoy : ennui, chagrin
s'apensser de : inventer, imaginer
appartenir : convenir
appert : il apparaît
araisonner : adresser la parole à
ardaulment : ardemment
arés : vous aurez
aroit : il aurait
atant : maintenant, alors
atendre : atteindre
atraiemens : manières séductrices : *atraiemens faire* :
   faire du charme
aucun : a un sens positif : *en aucune magniere* :
   d'une façon ou d'une autre
avant (plus a.) : davantage
avent (par a.) : déjà, auparavant
avent, avendra < avenir/advenir; v. impers. : il
   arrive
bailler : donner
barat : tromperie, ruse
beneurté : félicité
biaulté : beauté
brief (en b.) : rapidement
celer, celler : cacher, garder secret
chaÿ : passé simple de *choir* : tomber
chere : mine
chetif : malheureux
cheu : part. passé de *choir* : tomber
choir : tomber
chevance : biens matériels
choisir : remarquer

combien que : quoique
comfort : réconfort
commander : recommander
comme : = parfois comment
comment (+ subj.) : bien que
complaisement : satisfaction, plaisir
comptant, conptent : graphies de *content*
conclusion : pacte
condigne : approprié aux circonstances
consolable : réconfortant, agréable
consolative : agréable
constraignés < constraindre : presser
courage : intention, cœur
courcé : p. passé de *courcer* : irriter
Court Amoureuse : l'ensemble des amants
cremeur : timidité
cuidasse : imp. du subj. de *cuidier* : penser
cuidier : penser
dars : plur. de *dard*
decevant : trompeur
degeter : se remuer, bouger
deligenment : avec soin, diligemment
delit : plaisir
departir : se séparer de, quitter
deport : manière d'être
deceler, descetler : révéler
desclairer : déclarer
desclore : communiquer
descouvrir : révéler
deservir : mériter
desesperable : qui cause le désespoir
desolable : déplorable
desolablement : à cœur fendre
despiter : mépriser
despiteus : insolent
destreceuses : poignantes

detordre : (se) tordre
deu : du
devers : vers
die, dies : prés. subj. de dire
diligenment : avec soin, diligemment
discors, plur. de *discord :* contrariété
divers : opposé
doint : subj. de donner
dolant, dollant : malheureux, désolé
doyés : subj. prés. de devoir
droitturier : légitime
emprise : entreprise
endotriner : dresser (un animal)
enlaxer : enlacer
ensamble : ainsi que
entre : entre celles choses : vers ce moment
entrerompre : interrompre
esbastement : divertissement
esclarcy : p. passé d'*esclarcir :* faire jour, apparaître
escondre : (se) cacher
escripre : écrire
esjoïr : réjouir
estraint : étreint
estroictement : rigoureusement ; avec insistance
exemplaire : exemple
faillir : manquer, terminer
failly : faux, méchant
faintement : artificiellement
feablement : en toute confiance
feableté : confiance
fermer : observer fermement, fidèlement
feru : p. passé de *ferir :* frapper
fortune : accident, malheur
finer : finir, mourir
gent : beau, joli
gesir : être étendu, couché

114

gesta : passé simple de *geter*

grefment : grièvement

gresves : adj. fém., voir *grief*

grever : nuire, affliger

grief : subst. : peine

grief : adj. : désagréable, pénible, douloureux

guerredon : récompense

ilec : alors

imfluance : afflux (de sang), débordement

intencion (de leur i.) : intentionnellement

introduire : instruire

inumerable : innombrable

ire : colère ; *mener ire* : se mettre en colère

ja : renforce la négation. Signifie aussi : jamais (sens positif)

jangle : médisance

jangleresse : bavarde, médisante

janglerie : bavardage

jouxte : joute

juques a : jusqu'à

legier (de l.) : facilement

mais que : pourvu que, à condition que

martireus(ement) : cruel(lement)

mener ire : se mettre en colère

meschant : infortuné, malchanceux

meschief : malheur, calamité

mesmement : surtout

meult : passé simple de *se movoir* : se troubler

meurdrir (se) : se meurtrir

miroer : parangon, modèle

misrent : passé simple de mettre

musser (se) : se cacher

nasvrer : blesser

ne : ni

nonostant : malgré

occis : p. passé d'*occire* : tuer

oculper : accuser

offendu : p. passé d'*offendre* : offenser

office : *user de son office* : exercer sa fonction

onq : jamais (positif)

onques, onques mais : jamais (sens positif)

opportunitté : occasion

ordonnee : sage, convenable

or : maintenant

ores : alors, maintenant

ouïr (p. passé *ouÿ*) : entendre, écouter

oyant : entendant

oysel : oiseau

paour : peur

part (a part soy) : tout seul

partir : rompre

partir de : pourvoir de, doter de

perdurable : éternel

peureust : pourrait

piteusement : adv., voir *piteux*

piteux : malheureux, qui inspire la pitié

pocider : graphie de posséder

pour : a plusieurs significations :

    pour + infinitif : a souvent une nuance concessive, en particulier dans une phrase négative :

    pour perdre ma vie : même si je devais en perdre la vie

    pour moy deffendre..., indiquerait la conséquence

presentement : immédiatement

prisrent : passé simple de prendre

puis : depuis

quy : signifie parfois « si l'on »

rappel (sans r.) : irrévocablement

regraciant : remerciant

requerir, requerre : demander

116

requeru : p. passé de requerir/requerre
retrait : p. passé de *retraire* : se retirer
riens : peut fonctionner comme adv. : aucunement
roidement : rapidement
samblant : expression du visage
            (monstrer s.) : faire mine
            (estre s.) : avoir l'impression
saras : tu sauras
sceult : passé simple de savoir
secreps : discret
seller : graphie de *celler*
si que : de sorte que
souffrir (se) : avoir patience
souffrir : permettre
soulacier : se délasser
surquerir : forcer
sus (courir sus) : attaquer
tallent (avoir t.) : avoir envie
timeur : crainte
trahistre : traître (adj. et subst.)
traire (a fin) : faire réussir, aboutir
trait : p. passé de *traire*
tramettés : vous envoyez
travaulx : peines
uys : porte
vendrés : vous viendrez
veuil : je veux
villennie : infamie
visitacion : visite
visrent : passé simple de *veoir* : voir
vois : prés. ind. d'aller (je)
voise : prés. subj. d'aller (je)
voulsisses : imp. subj. de vouloir
vousist : imp. subj. de vouloir
vuide : impér. de *vuidier* : vider, quitter
vuidiés : voir *vuide*

LA CHASTELAINE DU VERGIER
LIVRE D'AMOURS DU CHEVALIER ET DE LA DAME CHASTELLAINE DU VERGIER

INTRODUCTION

Dans l'introduction à son édition de *la Chastelaine de Vergi*, Gaston Raynaud parle de la version imprimée de 1540 environ sans trop s'attarder sur les traits qui caractérisent le contenu : « Un auteur aujourd'hui inconnu [...] tout en conservant le fond, changea complètement la forme de l'original. Ce nouveau petit poème, en vers de 8 syllabes, est coupé en dialogues... » (1892 : 159). Les remarques qu'il y consacre semblent être destinées surtout à corriger une remarque faite en 1830 par Francisque Michel, qui avait parlé d'une version en prose éditée au xvie siècle. Lorenz, dans sa thèse de 1909, cite Raynaud, ajoute une remarque sur une mention plus ancienne de cette édition de 1540, et signale ensuite une « moralité » sous le titre *la Chastellene du Vergier,* mentionnée dans le catalogue d'un libraire de Tours au xve siècle (Lorenz 1909 : 62). Il suggère la possibilité que cette moralité, dont on n'a pas retrouvé le texte, ait été la (ou une) source de l'imprimé de 1540. Dans un article paru en 1976, L. A. Arrathoon reprend avec enthousiasme cette suggestion de Lorenz ; elle parle du texte de 1540 comme d'une pièce de théâtre (« a playlet ») et ajoute en note la remarque que l'hypothèse de Lorenz « was almost certainly correct » (p. 193).

C'est sans doute la forme dialoguée du texte qui a fait croire qu'il s'agit ici d'une pièce de théâtre ; les lignes en prose qui se trouvent dans le texte pourraient être expliquées comme des indications scéniques. Mais on pourrait les expliquer aussi d'une autre façon : dans les remaniements en prose produits au xve siècle, les chapitres sont indiqués très souvent par *un titre* commençant par « Comment... » (dans notre texte par exemple : « Comment la Duchesse envoye son messagier querir le Chevalier »). Souvent aussi ces titres se doublent, dans ces remaniements manuscrits, de miniatures ; dans l'imprimé de 1540, nous trouvons au lieu de miniatures des gravures sur bois. Mais est-il courant, au xvie siècle, d'éditer des textes de théâtre dans ces livrets de petit format (pas encore 7 sur 10 cm), avec illustrations ? Et est-ce que le sous-titre (*Livre* d'amours du Chevalier et de la Dame Chastellaine du Vergier) est courant pour une pièce de théâtre ? A-t-on retrouvé des traces d'une représentation théâtrale de ce texte ? Autant de questions auxquelles il faudrait donner une réponse avant de pouvoir être sûr qu'il s'agit dans ce cas d'une pièce de théâtre.

Le texte lui-même est bien différent de la version en prose : le caractère didactique de celle-ci est ici absent : le but semble être de raconter une tragique histoire d'amour.

Il est surprenant d'ailleurs de constater que, ici encore, le texte commence par les hésitations du chevalier qui n'ose avouer son amour à la Châtelaine : il lui faut presque 250 vers pour enfin se déclarer à la jeune femme, et ce n'est qu'au vers 400 environ que l'action commence. A titre de comparaison, dans ce texte la duchesse adresse la parole au chevalier au vers 448 — sur un total d'environ 1570 vers —, dans la version du xiiie siècle — environ 950 vers — elle le fait au vers 60. L'attitude de la Châtelaine dans ce premier fragment n'est d'ailleurs pas sans rappeler certains textes du début du xve siècle : là où elle dit « allez ailleurs… » (v. 144-5 et 287) on croit entendre l'écho de *la Belle Dame sans Merci* d'Alain Chartier (v. 489-96) ; les vers 250-52 de notre texte rappellent certains vers de *l'Epistre au Dieu d'Amours* et des *Cent Ballades d'Amant et de Dame* de Christine de Pizan. Il y a encore d'autres points communs entre la version en prose et le texte de 1540 : ainsi la Châtelaine est une jeune fille dans les deux cas (cf. les vers 338 et 1097 où elle est appelée « Damoyselle ») ; elle a reçu, dans les deux cas, « le Vergier » de son oncle, le duc (v. 1468-9), qui semble être jaloux de la bonne conduite de sa nièce (cf. les vers 125-31 ; moins marqué dans la version en prose, f. 114 r).

Il n'est pas nécessaire de conclure sans plus à une filiation directe entre ces deux textes, il y a aussi la possibilité toute classique d'un « ancêtre commun » (solution acceptée par Mme Arrathoon qui fait venir la version en prose et le texte de 1540 de la Moralité perdue du xve siècle).

Toute la dernière partie du texte semble être un peu confuse : comment le chevalier apprend-il la cause de la mort de son amie (cf. la prose avant le v. 1325) ? Comment expliquer l'absence du duc (v. 1400-01) lors de la mort du chevalier (cf. la prose avant le v. 1336) ? Faudrait-il voir dans ces failles du texte, ainsi que dans l'absence de scènes d'amour et de séduction (châtelaine-chevalier, duchesse-chevalier, duchesse-duc) une indication qu'il s'agirait bien d'un texte dramatique ? Ou s'agit-il tout simplement d'un texte « châtié », destiné à un public qui n'aurait pas accepté les allusions aux aspects physiques de l'amour, mais aurait fort goûté au contraire les pieuses façons de s'exprimer des personnages ? La virulente condamnation de la duchesse par le duc (il l'appelle « mauldicte puterelle », v. 1455) pourrait, par contraste, confirmer cette dernière vision.

Cette attitude envers la femme curieuse, qui cherche à connaître les secrets de son mari, n'est pas sans rappeler *le Roman de la Rose*. La scène, importante dans le déroulement de l'histoire de la Châtelaine, où la duchesse arrive à extorquer à son mari le secret du chevalier, a son parallèle dans le discours qu'adresse, dans *le Roman de la Rose,* Genius à Nature. La situation est la même : une femme veut profiter de l'intimité du lit conjugal pour savoir ce qui préoccupe son mari.

A partir du vers 1032 nous pouvons juxtaposer le texte de l'imprimé de 1540 et *le Roman de la Rose* (v. 16435 éd. Poirion, v. 16405 éd. Lecoy). La correspondance parfois littérale semble indiquer que le remanieur s'est servi d'une copie du *Roman de la Rose*. L'auteur de la version de 1540 ne sera sans doute pas le premier venu : il savait où trouver, dans la littérature en ancien français, une scène parallèle à celle qu'il avait déjà devant lui dans *la Chastelaine de Vergi.*

Le texte que nous donnons se trouve dans un tout petit livre (68 sur 96 mm.), conservé à Paris (B. N. Imprimés, Réserve, Ye 2963). Selon Brunet (1860) le livre daterait d'environ 1540, date acceptée par tous ceux qui ont parlé de ce texte. D'après la page de titre le livre fut vendu « à Paris en la rue neufve

Nostre dame a l'enseigne Sainct Jehan Baptiste, près Saincte Geneviefve des Ardans ». Cette adresse précise ne donne pas encore la réponse à toutes les questions que l'on pourrait se poser sur l'éditeur et la date de parution : en effet, différents éditeurs ont été établis à l'adresse indiquée, à partir de 1501. Pourtant, tenant compte du format, des vignettes et du sujet du livre, on pourrait avancer peut-être le nom de Denis Jannot, établi à l'enseigne Sainct Jehan Baptiste à partir de 1532, qui édite vers 1540 certaines œuvres de Gilles Corrozet dans le même format et avec des bois rappelant ceux de notre texte.

L'exemplaire de la Bibliothèque nationale n'est pas complet : il y manque le feuillet central du cahier D (f. 4-5), ce qui signifie qu'une centaine de vers au maximum ont été perdus. (Les pages comptent 25 lignes ; il faudrait compter pour ce passage quelques changements de personnages, probablement quelques lignes de prose, et peut-être une gravure. Le nombre de vers perdus sera donc de (4×25) — $(3 + 3 + 12 ?) = 82$ à 94.) Les grandes lignes du passage peuvent être facilement reconstruites à l'aide des autres versions.

Le texte est écrit en vers octosyllabiques, tout comme la version du XIIIe siècle. Souvent il est question d'une reprise textuelle de cette dernière. Parfois le poète du XVIe donne un vers de 7 ou de 9 syllabes ; nous n'avons pas tenu à « corriger » tous ces vers. Pour la lecture il ne faut pas oublier que le « *e* muet » compte très souvent pour une syllabe, la terminaison « — *ion* » souvent pour deux.

Pour cette édition nous avons suivi fidèlement le texte de l'imprimé de 1540. Les imprimeurs du début du XVIe siècle ne font pas le plus souvent la distinction moderne entre *u* voyelle et *v* consonne, ni entre *i* et *j*; leur emploi des majuscules ne correspond pas non plus à l'emploi moderne; nous avons adapté la graphie du texte, seulement dans ces cas-ci, à la langue moderne. Ensuite nous avons résolu les rares abréviations dans le texte, ajouté quelques lettres ou fins de mots qui manquaient, corrigé les coquilles et changé un ou deux mots : le relevé complet de tous ces changements se trouve dans le paragraphe *Notes textuelles* avant le glossaire. Nous y avons ajouté une brève description des gravures.

Dans l'édition de 1540 la succession des feuillets est indiquée par les signatures Ai à iiii, Bi à iiii, etc. Nous avons complété (par A 5 à 8, B 5 à 8, etc., et par *v* (verso)) ces indications, afin d'obtenir une pagination continue. Nous avons ajouté également la numérotation des vers.

Remarques bibliographiques

L'édition de 1540 est mentionnée dans le *Manuel du Libraire* [...] (T.I, Paris, 1860; col. 1820-21) de J.-Ch. Brunet. Lorenz 1909 : 61 fait remarquer que De Bure l'a signalée déjà en 1756.

Gaston Raynaud a édité *la Chastelaine de Vergi* en 1892, dans la *Romania* (21 : 145-93); dans son introduction il parle de toutes les versions connues du texte (p. 159-60 pour l'imprimé de 1540).

Dans *Die altfranzösische Versnovelle von der Kästellanin von Vergi in spätern Bearbeitungen* (Thèse, Halle a. S., 1909) Emil Lorenz parle du texte qui nous occupe aux pages 60-62. En fait il cite Raynaud 1892, en y ajoutant deux nouvelles observations.

Jean Frappier mentionne l'imprimé de 1540 dans son grand article sur « *la Chastelaine de Vergi,*

Marguerite de Navarre et Bandello » (1946 : 112).
Cf. ici p. 188.

Leigh A. Arrathoon parle de l'édition de 1540
dans son article de 1976, mentionné déjà à la page
79.

LA CHASTELAINE DU VERGIER

(Aii) La complainte et louenge que faict le Chevalier
de sa Dame Chastellaine du Verger.

Entré suis en melencollye
D'amours et de leur doulce vie,
Car jamais en nulle saison
Ne veis que gens ayans raison,
5   Comme Dames et Chevaliers,
Jolys Clers, et beaux Escuyers,
Fillettes moult bien gracieuses,
(v)   Et Pucellettes amoureuses,
Remplis de responces, et beaulx ditz.
10   Par eulx ne sont point nulz lais ditz;
En eulx est toute courtoisie,
Toute doulceur sans villennie
En acomplissant leur advis
Par leurs beaulx regardz et doulx ris,
15   Car doulx regard et ris joyeulx
Sont aux Amantz delicieux.
Mais il fault tout premierement
Que ce soit faict celeement,
Car vray Amant perd bien sa mye
20   Par faulx rapport et plains d'envye,
Qui envenime et qui embouche

Par jalousie et male bouche,
Tant qu'il convient par desconfort
Aux vrays Amantz souffrir la mort.
25 Pour tant supplie au Dieu d'amours
Qu'il confonde tous faulx jaloux,
Tous envieulx, tous mesdisans
Qui vont sur Amantz mesdisans
Et leur font souffrir trop d'ennuytz
30 Par leur faulx parler, jours et nuytz;
Aux vrays Amantz face secours
Et leur doint joye de leurs amours,
(Aiii) Car sans ce vivre ne pourroit
Nul vray Amant qui aymeroit
35 Dames de cueur loyallement,
Sans penser en mal nullement.
Amours les vrays Amantz faict vivre
Par l'esperance qu'il leur livre,
Car l'esperance les conforte
40 Et le vray talent leur apporte
De leurs cueurs a martyre offrir;
Esperance les faict souffrir
Les maulx dont on ne scet le compte,
Pour la joye qui les surmonte.
45 Si vouldroye doresnavant
Le dieu d'Amours entierement
Craindre, servir, aymer, querir,
Honnorer, doubter, requerir
Qu'il me vueille joye donner
50 De mes amours, et consoler,
Car point n'a soubz le firmament
Plus belle, ne plus advenant
Qu'est celle en qui j'ay mon cueur mis.
A la servir me suis submis,
55 Comme a elle bien appartient;
En elle tout bien se contient,
Tout honneur, et toute beaulté,

(v) Loyalle en cueur, en feaulté,
     Les cheveulx blondeletz et longz,
60   Aussi doulcette que coulons,
     Front reluysant, sourcilz voultiz,
     Les yeulx luysantz, beaulx et petis ;
     Elle a les joues vermeillettes
     Et si a riante bouchette,
65   Le corps bien faict, et par droicture,
     Elle est assez grand par mesure ;
     Je ne scauroye en nulle terre
     De plus beau corps de femme querre.
     Quant d'elle bien je me remembre,
70   De la façon de chascun membre,
     Je croy que soubz le firmament
     On ne scauroit aucunement
     Trouver plus belle et gratieuse ;
     En tous ses faictz elle est joyeuse
75   Plus que nulle qui soit au monde,
     En elle trestout bien habonde.
     Haulte Dame est, et honnoree,
     De toute Noblesse paree,
     Elle est niepce de mon seignour.
80   Prier ne l'oseroye d'Amour
     De paour que ne soye esconduyt,
(Aiiii) Mais touteffoys, sans contredit,
     Il fault que mon cas elle sache,
     Ou autrement je seroye lasche
85   Se a elle ne me declairoye.
     Helas, vray Dieu, je n'oseroye
     Parler a elle, par mon ame !
     S'esconduyt suis je suis infame
     Et en dangier de desespoir ;
90   Non pourtant, certes j'ay espoir
     Que d'elle receu je seray,
     Tout droict a elle m'en iray ;
     Quant certes mourir j'en debvroye,

128

A elle m'en voys droicte voye.
95 J'ay mainteffoys ouÿ compter
Que nul homme ne doibt doubter
A prier d'amours, ou de jeux,
Dames d'honneur ou de haulx lieux,
Car tant est de plus noble affaire
100 Et plus tost luy doibt il plaire
De descouvrir sa volunté
A son amy ; en verité,
A elle m'en voys vistement.

Comment le Chevalier entra dedans le vergier,
et comment il salua la Dame, la requerant
d'estre sa loyalle amy sans deshonneur.

Le Chevalier
(v) Celluy qui fist le firmament
105 Vous doint honneur et vie saine,
Ma chere Dame souveraine,
Joyeulx je suis quant je vous voy.

La Dame du Verger
Trop hardy estes, en bonne foy,
D'avoir entré en ce vergier,
110 Pourtant ce estes, Chevalier ;
Se mon oncle vous y trouvoit
Vistement pendre vous feroit.
Mis vous estes en grand dangier,
(A5) Car Dame suis de ce vergier ;
115 Je vous prie, pour Dieu mercy,
Que vistement saillez d'icy
Et que tantost vous en allez.

Le Chevalier
Madame, puis que le voulez
Tresvoluntiers je m'en iray,
120 Mais s'il vous plaist, je vous diray

129

Avant que parte, ma pensee,
Ma chere Dame honnoree,
Mais qu'il ne vous vueille desplaire.

La Dame
Voluntiers vous vouldroye plaire,
125 Mais a vous je n'ose parler,
Perdue seroye sans tarder
S'a vous parlant trouvee estoye,
De mon Oncle grand noyse auroye,
Car nuict et jour me faict garder
130 Que nul ne puisse a moy parler,
Mais je vous prie doulcement
Que me vueillez dire comment
Icy dedans vous estes entré.

Le Chevalier
(v)   Helas Madame, en verité,
135 Voluntiers je le vous diroye,
Mais, par ma foy, je n'oseroye.
Vous estes si tres belle Dame
Que vous passez beaulté de femme,
Dame vous estes du vergier
140 Dont vous estes moult a priser ;
Sur toutes estes advenant,
Saige, courtoyse, et bien scavant
De doulceur, et de bonnaireté,
De grand valeur, et de bonté.
145 Et moy je suis ung triste homs
Qui ay des maulx a millions ;
Bien scay que tost perdray la vie,
Car fortune me contarie.
Je vis en tresgrand desconfort,
150 Bien souvent regretant la mort ;
Pieça feusse mort sans doubtance,
Se ce ne fust bonne esperance
Qui mon paovre cueur tient en vie

Et diffiner ne laisse mye.
155 Si redoubte fort l'esconduyre,
Parquoy je ne vous ose dire
La volunté de mon couraige ;
Helas, Dame de hault paraige,
(A6) En rien ne vous vueille desplaire.

La Dame

160   Pour certain, Chevalier, desplaire
Ne m'en pourroit aucunement.
Mais que je sceusse vrayement
Que mon oncle vostre venue
Ne sceust, et que ne feusse veue.
165 Vous dictes que ne me osez dire
Vostre pensee, car l'esconduyre
Vous craignez, et ne scay pourquoy ;
Congé vous donne en bonne foy
De me dire vostre couraige,
170 De moy vous n'en aurez dommaige,
Dictes tout a vostre loysir.

Le Chevalier

Madame, et puis que a plaisir
Vous vient, de vostre noblesse,
Tout vous diray ce qui me blesse,
175 Dont au cueur me touche forment ;
Je vous supplie humblement
Chere Dame, par courtoysie,
Que me pardonnez ma follie
Et que n'en ayez aucune yre,
(v) Force d'Amours le me faict dire.
181 Il y a sept ans acomplis
Que de vostre Amour suis remplis,
Et me destruict si rudement
Que bien vous dy certainement :
185 Se je n'ay aucun bon confort
Faillir je ne peultz a la mort.

Helas ! souffrez que je vous ayme,
Et que pour ma Dame vous clame ;
De ce ne me povez desdire
190 Ne deffendre, ne contredire.
Certes, Madame, bien scavez
Que despriser ne m'en debvez,
Car, par tous les corps sainctz du monde,
Dame, qui estes nette et munde,
195 Vous jure et prometz loyallement
D'acomplir tout vostre comment.
Comme vray Amant vous supply
Que me recepvez pour Amy,
Ou vostre homme a tout le moins
200 Prest suis de vous jurer sur sainctz
Que la vostre amour sans faulcer
Loyaulment vouldroye garder.
Pourquoy, las, ne la garderoye,
Car je n'ay nul soulas ne joye
(A7) Fors de vostre amour ; doulce amye,
206 En vostre main tenez ma vie,
Toute ma joye et mon confort,
Et d'autre part tenez ma mort :
J'auray lequel qu'il vous plaira.
210 Mais se Dieu plaist point n'adviendra
Que si tres belle Dame face
Chose dont le monde le sache ;
Se la mort vous m'aviez donnee
A droict vous en seriez blasmee,
215 Car on diroit en verité
Que trop avez grand cruaulté
De laisser mourir vostre amy
Sans le vouloir prendre a mercy.
Mon cueur, mon corps, ma volunté
220 Je submetz a vostre bonté ;
Vous estes mon cueur, mon confort,
Mon desduyt, et tout mon desport,

132

Ma joye, aussi ma lyesse,
M'amour, mon plaisir. Ma maistresse,
225 Quant je pense a vostre doulx viz,
Vos doulx regardz et vos doulx ris,
En mon cueur j'ay si tresgrand joye
Qu'a nul dire ne l'oseroye.
Et pour ce sa peine perdroit
(v) L'amant qui dechassé seroit
231 De l'amour qui fort le tourmente ;
Par quoy vous dy, Madame gente,
Que se de vous je n'ay confort
Briefvement j'en recepvray mort,
235 Dont après serez dolente.

La Dame

Chevalier, oyez mon entente :
De me parler ce langaige
Point je ne vous trouve saige,
Car on ne doibt mye muser
240 En lieu ou l'on veult abuser ;
Pour ce vous pry par courtoysie :
Ne me requerez villennie,
Allez ailleurs vous enquerir
Ou vous pourrez amye querir,
245 Point en moy ne l'avez trouvee,
Car je seroys deshonnoree ;
Trop je redoubte le parler
D'aucuns, qui se veullent vanter,
Car incontinent que faict ont
250 Tout leur plaisir, tantost le vont
Reveller a l'ung et a l'autre ;
Par quoy vous dy sans nulle faulte
Qu'on ne ce scet en qui fier.

(A8)   Le Chevalier
Madame, voulez vous cuider
255 Que envers vous face ne die

133

Chose qui vienne a villennie,
A blasmer, ny a reprocher?
Plustost me laisseroye noyer!
De telz, certes, je ne suis mye,
260 Qui se vantent de leurs follies
Quant ilz ont faict leur volunté
De leurs Dames, plains de bonté.
Pensez qu'il est plain de rudesse
Qui trahist ainsi sa maistresse.
265 Par ung desloyal sont mescruz
Cent loyaulx, et par luy perdus
Leur temps, leur sens, et leur avoir;
A vous le puis je bien scavoir.
Dame, jamais ne le feroye,
270 Faulx vanteur certes je seroye
Quant je vouldroye cela faire.
Plustost mes dentz laisseroys traire
Que de vous, certes, me ventasse
Ne envers vous d'amours jenglasse.
275 Sachez pour certain, sans faulcer,
Que de ce ne vous fault doubter,
J'aymeroye plus cher mourir
(v) Que aucunement descouvrir
Le secret d'entre vous et moy;
280 Par quoi vous pry en bonne foy
Qu'il vous plaise moy esprouver.
Vostre amour vouldroye recouvrer,
Et estre vostre doulx amy.

La Dame

Beau Chevalier, je vous em pry,
285 Ne me requerez villennie,
Mais faictes d'autre part amye,
Car tantost l'aurez belle et gente
Se mettre y voulez vostre entente;
Vous estes beau, doulx, et poly,

290　Saige, courtoys, et bien joly,
　　　Digne vous estes d'estre aymé
　　　Et aussi d'estre amy clamé ;
　　　Par quoy je vous vouldroye prier
　　　Que ne me vueillez enginer,
295　S'ainsi est que m'amour vous donne.

Le Chevalier
　　Helas, Madame chere et bonne,
　　De certain croyez fermement :
　　Mourir vouldroys cruellement
　　Avant que je vous feisse tort.
300　Vous estes mon cueur, mon confort,
(Bi)　Mon soulas, et toute joye.

La Dame
　　Chevalier, mon cueur si larmoye
　　Quant vous entendz ainsi parler,
　　Ne pensez point a vous galler
305　Envers moy, puis vous en mocquer,
　　Se vostre amour veulx colloquer
　　En mon cueur pour vostre plaisir.
　　Je vous prie que desplaisir
　　Ne m'en advienne aucunement,
310　Car je vous jure bon serment
　　Et le sacrement de baptesme,
　　Autant vous ayme que moymesme !
　　Longtemps a que vous ay donné
　　Tout mon cueur, et habandonné,
315　Mais je ne m'osoye descouvrir
　　A vous, de paour d'encourir
　　A la vostre indignation ;
　　J'ay de vous grand compassion
　　Car en amour a doulce vie,
320　Plaisir, deduyt, et courtoysie,
　　Et toute doulceur, sans mentir,
　　Fors quant se vient au departir.

Toutes les foys qu'il m'en souvient
Grand desplaisance au cueur me vient,
(v) Car sans aymer je ne pourroye
326 Avoir au cueur soulas et joye ;
Si n'euz oncques amy par amour,
Dont j'ay au cueur fort grand doulour
Et en suis malade forment
330 Et nuict et jour certainement,
Fors vous, je vous jure mon ame,
Dont bien souvent le cueur me pasme.
Et si ne fust le doulx espoir
Qui me garde de son povoir,
335 Et tous les vrays Amantz conforte,
Certes je feusse pieça morte :
Plus de moy il ne fust nouvelle.

Le Chevalier

Ma gratieuse Damoyselle,
Joyeulx suis de vostre parler,
340 Si vous requiers que appeller
Me vueillez pour le vostre Amy.

La Dame

Le cueur seroit bien endormy
Qui a ce vous reffuseroit,
Mais dictes moy s'il vous plaisoit
345 Que je feusse la vostre Amye ;
Et je vous promectz que en ma vie
Je n'aymeray autre que vous.

Le Chevalier

(Bii) Certes, Madame, a tousjours
Seray vostre loyal servant ;
350 Mais tenez moy vray convenant,
Et je vous promectz sur ma vie
Que jamais n'auray autre Amye.
Je vous le promectz, et le jure.

La Dame

Pour Dieu, point ne soyez parjure,
₃₅₅ Monstrez vous estre noble en cueur.
De m'amour estes possesseur
Sans nulle contrarieté.
Faictes a vostre volunté ;
Certes a vous je suis donnee.

Le Chevalier

₃₆₀ Ma chere Dame honnoree
Je vous mercye humblement ;
Mon cueur, mon corps, tout en present
Je vous donne sans nul diffame,
Et si vous jure sur mon ame
₃₆₅ Que loyaulment vous serviray
A tousjours, tant que je vivray ;
Je vous promectz par mon serment.

La Dame

Je vous prie amoureusement
Que nostre amour ne revelez
_(v) A nulluy, mais bien le celez,
₃₇₁ Car je vous faitz serment loyal
Que ce vous estes desloyal
Vers moy, par Dieu, le filz Marie,
Vous aurez perdu vostre amye.
₃₇₅ Et si sachez, par desconfort,
Que recepvoir m'en fauldra mort ;
Je vous pry ne le dictes mye.

Le Chevalier

Ma treschere Dame et amye,
Voicy ma foy, je la vous baille.
₃₈₀ Je vous promectz, comment qu'il aille,
Que mieulx aymeroye mourir
Que point nostre amour descouvrir,
Par quoy ne soyez en doubtance
Que jamais en face semblance ;

385 Il nous fauldra trouver la voye
Comment demenrons nostre joye,
Et a quelle heure je viendray.

La Dame
J'ay ung chiennet que j'apprendray ;
Quant le verrez en ce vergier
390 Venez tost vers-moy, sans dangier ;
Adoncques vous pourrez scavoir
Qu'avecq moy ne peult nul avoir.
(Biii) Ainsi deduyrons noz amours,
Mon bel amy, le voulez vous,
395 Est ce bien vostre volunté ?

Le Chevalier
Ouy Madame, en verité,
Vostre vouloir si est le mien,
Vous ne dictes sinon que bien.
Il seroit temps de s'en aller
400 Madame, car j'ay a parler
A la Duchesse en cestuy jour ;
Je vous supply par doulce amour
Que me donnez ung doulx baiser.
Le soleil se prend a baisser,
405 Et que j'aye congé de vous.

La Dame
A Dieu, mon amy, soyez vous ;
Souvienne vous souvent de moy.

Le Chevalier
Ma chere Dame, je l'octroy,
Jamais en mon cueur n'auray joye
410 Jusques a tant que vous revoye ;
A Dieu, Madame, vous comment.

Comment la Duchesse envoye son messagier
querir le Chevalier.

Sa Messagier, venez avant,
Allez tost, sans faire sejour,
Parler au Chevalier d'honnour,
415 Et luy dictes sans demeure
Qu'a moy vienne parler en l'heure ;
Et faictes tost vostre messaige.

Le Messager
Dame, j'entendz vostre couraige,
Par quoy en scauray mieulx parler ;
420 Advancer me veulx d'y aller,
Vistement me voys mettre en voye.

Se Dieu me donne au cueur joye,
Je le voy, sans point varier :
Sire, Jesus le droicturier
(Biiii) Vous doint aujourd'huy tres bon jour !
426 Madame, sans point de sejour,
A vous, sire, se recommande,
Et aussi de par moy vous mande
Que venez a elle parler.

Le Chevalier
430 Je ne le doy pas reffuser,
Aller y veulx sans nul demeure ;
Mais se vous scavez en bonne heure
- Qu'elle me veult, dictes le moy.

Le Messagier
Je ne scay sire, par ma foy,
435 Elle vous mande vistement.

Le Chevalier
A elle voys appertement,
Messagier, allez luy tost dire.

Le Messagier
Je le feray sans contredire.
Chevalier, a Dieu vous command,

440 Aller me fault diligemment
Sans point faire aucun arrest.

Dame, le Chevalier est prest,
Tost sera icy, sans demeure.

Le Chevalier
Honneur vous doint Dieu, et bon jour
(v) Dame ; devers vous suis venu
446 Pour entendre le contenu
De tout ce qu'avez a plaisir.

Comment la Duchesse prie le Chevalier
d'amour desordonnee, lequel s'excuse honnestement.

Certes, j'avoye grand desir
De parler a vous de secret,
450 Et de vous dire tout mon faict.
Il est vray que ja longtemps a
Que aucunement parlé on m'a
De vous mettre en mariage ;
Vous estes homme de hault paraige,
(B5) Doulx, gratieulx, bien advenant,
456 Comme l'on dit communement,
Dont je loue Dieu et mercy ;
Si avez moult bien desservy
D'avoir en ung hault lieu amye.

Le Chevalier
460 Madame, certes, je n'ay mye
Encore a ce mise mon entente.

La Duchesse
Chevalier, certes, longue attente
Vous pourroit nuyre, a mon advis.
Se me croyez vous serez mis
465 En ung hault lieu (se vous voulez)

140

Ou vous serez tres bien aymez;
Je le vous dy en bonne foy.

Le Chevalier
Madame, je ne scay pourquoy
Le me dictes, ne que ce monte,
470 Car je ne suis ne Duc ne Conte
Qui si haultement aymer doye.
Ne je ne suis point homs qui doye
Dame avoir si tressouveraine.

La Duchesse
Se vous y eussiez mise peine
475 Bien eussiez eue ma pareille.
(v) Il advient bien plus grand merveille,
Et telles viendront bien encores!
Or escoutez en brief parolles :
Se je vous ay m'amour donnee,
480 Qui suis haulte Dame honnoree,
Seriez vous pas bien esbahy?

Le Chevalier
Certes, ma chere Dame, ouy.
Bien je vouldroye vostre amour
Avoir, pour bien et pour honnour;
485 Mais Dieu de faulce amour me gard,
Et que je n'ayme nulle part
Ou la honte mon seigneur gise;
Car a nul feur n'en nulle guise
Je ne prendroys nulle achoyson
490 Que de faire telle mesprison
Envers mon seigneur natural :
Tousjours luy veulx estre loyal.
Jesus m'en gard, le filz Marie.

La Duchesse
Edea, musard, qui vous en prie?
495 Vuydez tantost appertement

Et vous en allez vistement,
Car vous estes faulx Chevalier.

Le Chevalier

(B6)   Dame, mercy je vous requier,
Point ne le disoye pour mal.

La Duchesse

500   Traystre vous estes et desloyal,
Allez hors de ma compaignie ;
Vous ne pensez qu'a villennie,
Dont je suis fort desconfortee.
Mais devant qu'il soit la nuictee
505   Serez en vostre cueur marry,
Dire le voys a mon mary ;
Bien je scay, quant il le scaura
En son cueur courroucé sera
Quant me verra ainsi troublee.

Comment la Duchesse se va complaindre au
Duc son mary que le chevalier l'a requise de
deshonneur, dont le Duc sera marry.

(v)   Honneur ayez celle journée,
511   Mon loyal seigneur et amy.
Eussiez vous pensé qu'ennemy
Vous fust ung de vostre maison,
Lequel est plain de desraison,
515   De deshonneur, et villennie ?

Le Duc

Or me dictes, ma doulce amye,
Qui est celluy dont me parlez ?
Dictes le, point ne le celez,
Et ne soyez plus courroucee.

La Duchesse

(B7)   Certes, je vous dy que couchee
521   Vouldroys estre au lict de la mort ;

Trayson on vous faict a tort,
Dont ne vous appercevez mye.

Le Duc

Et comment doncq, ma doulce amye ?
525 Je ne scay pourquoy vous le dictes,
De ses parolles je suis triste ;
Jamais certes je ne tiendroye
Nulz traystres, se je le scavoye,
Ne je ne me firoye en luy.

La Duchesse

530 Vous debvez scavoir que celluy
Qui m'a priee au long du jour
N'ayme vostre bien ny honnour,
Et m'a dit qu'il y a longtemps
Qu'il a esté en ce pourpens,
535 Ne jamais ne me l'osa dire.
Si me suis pourpensee, beau sire,
Que certes je le vous diroye.
Certainement, mieulx aymeroye
Mourir plustost cruellement,
540 Que de vous faulcer mon serment.
Par quoy, mon doulx amy loyal,
Faictes que le tresdeloyal
(v) Soit pugny bien amerement.
Offencé il a faulcement
545 Envers vous, je vous certifie.

Le Duc

Or me nommez sans tricherie
Celluy de quoy vous me parlez ;
Dictes le moy, plus ne le celez,
Car j'en ay au cueur grand tristesse.

La Duchesse

550 Monseigneur plain de grand haulte[sse],
C'est bien raison que le vous die
Et que envers vous ne contredie

Chose contre vostre plaisir.
Le Chevalier a qui plaisir
555 Tous les jours pretendez de faire,
Le jeu d'Amours m'a voulu faire,
Et souventeffoys m'a requise
Que m'abandonnasse a sa guise
Et a la sienne volunté.
560 Par quoy, monseigneur redoubté,
Vous y debvez remedier.

Le Duc
Comment cecy, jamais cuydé
Je n'eusse en jour de ma vie
Qu'il m'eust pourchassé telle follie !
(B8) En luy si treffort me fioye
566 Que le jour que ne le veoye
Mon cueur estoit plein de tristesse ;
Eslevé l'avoys en haultesse
Plus que nul qui fust en ma court.
570 Enragé suis, a dire court,
S'il est vray ce que allez disant.

La Duchesse
Estre n'en peult contredisant ;
Je vous promectz Dieu et mon ame,
Mettre m'a voulu a diffame,
575 S'a luy me feusse habandonnee.
Mais plus cher mourir la journee
Eusse voulu, qu'a luy complaire
Ne que de sa volunté faire,
Je vous promectz certainement.

Le Duc
580 Par le vray Dieu du firmament,
De ce cas je suis esbahy,
M'a il ainsi voulu trahyr ?
Je prie a Dieu qu'il me confonde,
Que plus l'aymoye que nul du monde,

585 En luy du tout je me fioye
Et mon secret tout luy disoye :
Pourchassé il m'a trahyson !
(v) Mais bien en feray la raison :
Point ne me trouvera si nice
590 Que de luy ne face justice,
Remedier je veulx au cas.

Comment le Duc appella ses conseilliers pour
prendre conseil du cas imposé sur le Chevalier.

Sa, mon conseil, plus que le pas,
Escoutez que je vous vueil dire :
Le cueur si me fend de grand yre
595 Tant que bien pres suis de la mort.
(Ci) Aucun m'a voulu faire tort,
Deshonneur, et grand villennie.
Je ne scay se je le vous die,
Et se secret me le tiendrez.

Le premier conseiller
600 Ha ! monseigneur, et ou direz
Vostre secret, sinon a nous ?
Vous scavez bien que sommes tous
A vostre noblesse obligez ;
Pour nulle chose ne laissez
605 De nous dire vostre vouloir.
Mon frere (comme j'ay espoir)
Comme moy secret le tiendra.

Le second conseiller
Monseigneur, point il n'adviendra
Que maintenez ung tel courroux.
610 Prenez vigueur et force en vous,
Et faictes comme Duc doibt faire ;
Mais qu'il ne vous vueille desplaire,
Vostre faict a nous descouvrez.

Le Duc

Chers amys, puis que le voulez
615 De mot en mot le vous diray.
Jamais de tel cueur je n'aymay
Homme, comme mon chevalier,
(v) Souvent l'avez bien peu cuyder
Au semblant que je luy monstroye.
620 Par mon baptesme, plus l'aymoye
Que nul sur la terre vivant !
Pardonnez moy se j'en dy tant,
Il a faict trop grand mesprison
Envers moy, car par trahyson
625 Ma femme a voulu decepvoir
Pour sa compaignie avoir,
Faulcement et mauvaisement ;
Par quoy je jure bon serment
Qu'en mon cueur j'en ay grand destresse.
630 Ma femme, la noble Duchesse,
Si m'a trestout le faict compté,
Et de mot a mot racompté
Comme tressaige et bien apprise,
Affin qu'elle ne fust reprise,
635 Car aussi le droict si le veult.
Helas ! et se le cueur m'en deult
Point n'en debvez avoir merveille :
N'est ce pas chose nompareille
Que celluy en qui me fioye
640 Et a qui tout mon cas disoye
M'a voulu decepvoir ainsi ?
Il n'y a point ne ça ne cy,
(Cii) Par la raison mourir en doibt.

Le premier conseiller
Ha ! monseigneur, pour Dieu ne soit !
645 Ne vueillez faire tel oultraige,
Se vous seroit trop grand dommaige

146

D'ung si beau chevalier destruyre.
Ayder luy debvez, non pas nuyre,
Car il est gratieulx et gent,
650 Honneste, courtoys, diligent,
De lignee bien renommee,
Toute en est vostre court paree.
Certainement, je ne croy mie
Que pensé il ait telle follie
655 Que de Madame requerir
De deshonneur ; plus cher mourir
Il auroit, je vous certifie.
Il est doulx, plein de courtoysie,
Servy il vous a longuement,
660 Des sa jeunesse honnestement
Sans point de nul reproche avoir.
Premierement vous fault scavoir
Qu'il vous a juré loyaulté
Sans point vous faire faulceté,
665 Et que vostre honneur garderoit
En tous les lieux ou il seroit,
(v) Par quoy, monsieur, ne debvez mye
Luy faire si tost villennie
Sans estre du cas informé ;
670 Pour cruel vous seriez nommé
Se aucun mal luy voulez faire.

Le second conseiller
    Bien congnoys que dictes au contraire
De tout vostre entendement,
Et bien parleriez autrement
675 (Se vous vouliez) pour tout certain.
Point ne fault querir si loingtain
Les passages que alleguez.
Vous scavez bien que vous trouvez :
« Qui est traystre a son seigneur
680 Doibt mourir a grand deshonneur

147

Sans nulle contradition ».
Par quoy eschet pugnition
Au chevalier, sans point mentir,
Et se vous voulez soubstenir
685 Le contraire, de ce que dis,
Je dy, moy, sans nulz contreditz,
Que le voulez favoriser
Et son grand deshonneur priser,
Par quoy je dy a mon advis
690 Que l'homme en ung tel cas surpris
(Ciii) Trop endurer mal ne pourroit,
Car qui tout vif l'escorcheroit
Des maulx ne souffreroit assez.
Pour tant doncques, plus n'en parlez
695 Et ne soubstenez que raison.

Le Duc
Or venons a conclusion.
Plus attendre je ne pourroye
Se vengeance de luy n'avoye ;
Voulez vous plus riens replicquer
700 Ny autre raison appliquer,
Qui soubstenez le chevalier ?

Le premier conseiller
Certes, mon seigneur droicturier,
Envers vous ne veulx contredire,
Mais mon advis si est, de dire
705 Que cestuy certes luy veult mal.
Je parle amont et aval
Pour celluy qui n'est pas icy ;
Je cuyde s'il scavoit cecy
Que bien se scauroit excuser
710 Du cas qu'on le veult accuser.
Il me semble que bon seroit
Qu'a vous venir on le feroit :
S'il y vient bon signe sera,

(v)   S'il n'y vient adoncq apperra
715   Qu'il a devers vous aucun tort ;
      Meure s'il a gaigné la mort.
      Quant par devant vous le verrez
      Tout vostre courroux luy direz,
      S'il se excuse justement
720   Ayez y bon entendement,
      Et s'il ne [se] scait excuser
      Adoncq le pourrez accuser
      A droict, et le faire mourir.

                  Le Duc
          Par mon serment, j'ay grand plaisir
725   Que m'avez ainsi conseillé.
      De ce cas suis esmerveillé ;
      Point je ne cuyde, par mon ame,
      Qu'il ait pensé cestuy diffame
      Ne contre moy tel deshonneur,
730   Qui suis son naturel seigneur.
      Pour tant vostre conseil prendray :
      Mon messaiger appelleray
      Pour aller faire le messaige.

      Comment le Duc envoye son messagier devers
      le Chevalier, qu'il vienne parler a luy.

(Ciiii)   Sa, Jacquemin, sans long langaige,
735   Aller te fault sans delayer
      Dire tost a mon Chevalier
      Qu'il vienne soubdain devers moy,
      Et ne luy parle point pourquoy.
      Despesche toy legierement.

      Comment le Duc envoye querir son Chevalier
      pour le interroguer du cas sur luy imposé.

                                              149

Le Messager

740   A luy m'en voys appertement
Monseigneur, car je suis tout prest ;
Point ne me fault faire d'arrest
Que tantost ne soye au retour.

Chevalier, Dieu vous doint bon jour,
745   Incontinent vous fault aller
(v)   A monseigneur le Duc parler.
Et vous hastez legierement.

Le Chevalier

Dy moy amy, par ton serment,
Scez tu point pourquoy m'a mandé ?

Le Messager

750   Non, Chevalier, en verité.
Je vous pry, point ne demourez ;
Je voys dire que vous venez.

Sire, voicy le Chevalier
Qui tantost, sans point deslayer,
755   A vostre mandement est venu,
Pour scavoir tout le contenu
De vostre desir et pensee.

Comment le noble Chevalier arriva devers son
seigneur et maistre le Duc, pour luy obeyr en
tout ce qu'il luy plairoit commander.

(C5)   ### Le Chevalier

Monseigneur, tres bonne journee
Si vous doint la Vierge Marie.
760   Je suis a vostre seigneurie
Venu obeyr vrayement.

Le Duc

On m'a donné entendement
Que vous n'estes pas si feal
Comme cuidoys, ne si loyal,

765 Dont j'ay au cueur grand marrison ;
Joué m'avez de trahyson !
La chose en est toute prouvee.
Que mauldicte soit la journee
(v) Que jamais je vous ay congneu !
770 En estat vous ay maintenu
Et eslevé en grand haultesse.
Deshonneur a vostre maistresse
Luy faire, avez pretendu,
Mais je pry Dieu que confondu
775 Je puisse estre avant la nuictee
Se n'en avez malle journee.
Desservy l'avez loyaulment ;
Faulcé m'avez vostre serment,
Quant par pensee tristeresse
780 Me vouliez jouer telle finesse.
Allez viste hors de ma terre
Jusques a tant que vous mande querre ;
Congié je vous donne sans doubte
Et ma terre vous deffendz toute,
785 N'y arrestez ne tant ne quant.
Se depuis icy en avant
Vous y povoye faire prendre,
Par le col je vous feroys pendre,
Quant faulcement m'avez trahy.

Le Chevalier

790 Ha ! monseigneur, pour Dieu, mercy !
Ne croyez point, et ne pensez
Que je feusse point si osez
(C6) Que je pensasse trahyson
Envers vous ! Trop grand mesprison
795 A faict celluy qui ce a dit.

Le Duc

Riens ne vous vault vostre esconduyt,
Car cecy est assez prouvé :

Elle mesme si m'a compté
En quelle maniere, et quelle guise
800 Vous l'avez priee et requise
Comme faulx et traystre envieulx ;
Telle chose avez faict vous deux,
Peult estre, dont elle se taist.

Le Chevalier
Madame dit ce qui luy plaist,
805 Dont en mon cueur j'ay grand tristesse.
Je ne scay dont procede ce
Descombrier qu'on me pourchasse.
Je prie a Dieu qu'il me defface
Se jamais en jour de ma vie
810 Envers vous pensay villennie.
Je le vous jure par mon ame.

Le Duc
Chevalier, quant est de ma femme,
Je cuyde bien sans faulceté
Qu'elle m'a dit la verité,
(v) Car je n'ouÿs oncques parler
816 Que d'autres voulsissez aymer ;
Et si n'eustes oncques amye,
Dont la chose est plus mal partie :
Vous estes mignon, et joly,
820 Bien parlant, advenant, poly,
Plus que nul qui soit en ma terre.
Envers vous je me veulx enquerre
Se point dame avez ou non ;
J'en seray hors de souspesson
825 Et en osteray ma pensee.

Le Chevalier
Sire, par la Vierge honnoree,
Je vous prometz par mon serment
Que je vous ayme loyaulment,
Et si vous diray verité.

152

Le Duc

830   C'est bien dit, par la Trinité,
Dictes le moy de tres bon cueur.
Point ne croy, par le Createur,
Que vous m'aiez faict si grand honte
Comme la Duchesse me compte.
835 Nonpourtant j'en suis en doubtance :
Quant je voy vostre contenance
L'on peult certes moult bien scavoir
(C7) — Sans aucun souspesson avoir —
Que vous aymez, ou que ce soit,
840 Mais nul si ne s'en apperçoit.
Damoyselle aymez, ou dame.
J'ay paour que ce ne soit ma femme,
Qui m'a dit que l'avez priee.
Si n'en puis oster ma pensee
845 Se ne me dictes sans demour
Se ailleurs aymez par amour.
Dictes moy, sans avoir nul doubte,
De ce la verité trestoute ;
Et ce faire ne le voulez
850 Comme traystre vous allez
Hors de ma terre, sans delay.

Le Chevalier

    Helas ! tresdoulx Dieu, que feray ?
J'aymeroys mieulx perdre la vie
Que descouvrir ma doulce amye.
855 Ja ne scay si me parjure
Ou se die verité pure ;
Je me tiens mort se meffaictz tant
Que je trespasse convenant
Las ! qu'a m'amye faicte j'ay.
860 Je suis seur que je la perdray
Se elle s'en peult appercevoir.
(v) Parjure je seray, pour voir !

Dont fauldra le pays laisser
Et a tout mon faict renoncer,
865 Mais de tout ce ne m'en chaulsist
Se ma Dame me remansist,
Laquelle perdre me convient.
Helas ! quant d'elle me souvient,
De la grand joye, et du soulas
870 Que j'ay eu entre ses deux bras,
Las ! comment pourray je durer
Quant je ne la puis emmener :
Certes mourir me conviendra
Quant delaisser la me fauldra.
875 Comment me peult durer le cueur ?
Qu'il ne part par trop grand langueur ?
Le cueur me fault certainement.
Ha ! vray Dieu, je ne scay comment
En cecy je doibve penser,
880 Ne en quel moyen commencer.
Se je dis ma desconvenue
Nostre amour si sera congneue,
Par quoy je seray desloyal.

Le Duc
Envers moy n'estes point feal.
885 Vuydez d'icy plus que le pas,
(C8) Bien voy que ne vous fiez pas
En moy, tant que vous deussiez.
Se vostre conseil me deissiez
Sachez de moy certainement,
890 Bien je le tiendray celeement.
Plustost me laisseroys sans faulte
Tirer les dentz l'une apres l'autre
Que vostre secret deceller.

Le Chevalier
Vray Dieu, vueillez moy consoler !
895 Helas ! monseigneur, je vous prie

Que de ce n'aye villennie.
Je vous jure Dieu, sans mentir,
Que plus cher j'auroye mourir
Que perdre ce que je perdroye.
900 C'est tout mon soulas et ma joye,
Toute ma lyesse et plaisir ;
Se je luy faisoys desplaisir
Je seroye certes mauldit.
Au convencier elle me dit
905 Que tantost mourir se lairroit
Quant nostre amour sceue seroit
De nul homme qui fust vivant.

Le Duc
Chevalier, je fais convenant
(v) Sus l'ame et le corps de moy,
910 Et sus l'amour, aussi la foy
Que je vous doibtz de vostre hommage
Et aussi a tout mon lignaige,
Que point a creature nee
N'en sera parolle comptee,
915 Ne semblant a grand ne petit.

Le Chevalier
Cher seigneur, vous avez bien dit.
Puis qu'ainsi va vous le scaurez ;
Vostre convenant me tiendrez
Ainsi comme l'avez promis.

Le Duc
920 Puis que me suis a ce submis
Ma convenance veulx tenir,
Et devant tous la maintenir
Sans la faulcer aucunement.

Le Chevalier
Croyez seigneurs, certainement,
925 Que vous diray sans menterie
Tout mon cas, sans nul tricherie :

J'ayme Madame du Vergier,
Vostre niepce, seigneur trescher,
Loyaulment et par bonne amour
930 Sans penser a nul deshonnour,
(Di) Et elle moy, tant que peult plus.

Le Duc
Or me dictes doncque au surplus,
Comment voulez vous que vous croye :
Scet nul fors vous deux la voye ?
935 Je vous prie, dites le moy.

Le Chevalier
Certes monseigneur, par ma foy,
Creature qui soit nee.

Le Duc
Comment est doncques vostre allee,
Ne comment avez lieu et temps ?

Le Chevalier
940 Par ma foy, mon seigneur, par sens.
Quant il est temps que a elle aille
Ung petit chien si vient sans faille
Cheminant du long du vergier,
Lors y puis entrer sans dangier.
945 Vela ainsi que nous faisons.

Le Duc
Vous me dictes bonnes raisons.
Mais par bonne amour je vous prie
Que me menez sans villennye
Avec vous, que mieulx seur soye.
950 Plus cher mourir certes vouldroye
(v) Que nulle personne en sceut rien.

Le Chevalier
Monseigneur, je le veulx tres bien
Vostre vouloir je veulx parfaire ;
Je vous prie que point desplaire

955 Ne vous vueille de cestuy faict.

Le Duc
Vous estes mon amy parfaict,
Je le vous prometz sur mon ame.
Ne craingnez point d'avoir diffame
De moy mener avecques vous ;
960 Bien joyeulx suis de voz amours
Puis qu'ils sont en honnesteté.

Comment le Chevalier monstre au Duc la
maniere du revisitement de sa dame par
amours.

(Dii)
Le Chevalier
Venez a vostre volunté,
Et vous verrés sans demouree
Le desir de vostre pensee.

965 Jesus bonne journee vous donne,
Ma chere dame belle et bonne ;
Le Dieu qui fist le firmament
Vous doint joye sans finement,
Bonne paix, et prosperiter.
970 Je vous suis venu visiter,
Ma tresdoulce loyalle amye ;
Or me baisez, je vous en prie,
(v) Mais que se soit vostre plaisir.

La Dame
Voluntiers, sans nul desplaisir,
975 Mon loyal amy et seigneur,
Sans penser a nul deshonneur.
Sachiez qu'il ne fut depuis l'heure
Que ne me durast la demeure,
Mais de present point ne m'en deulx
980 Puis qu'ay pres de moy ce que veulx.
Le tresbien venu vous soyez :

Baisez moy, et si m'acollez,
Mon tresdoulx amy et loyal.

                    Le Chevalier
          Voluntiers, de cueur cordial.
985   Helas ! pourquoy ne le feroye ?
      Vous estez mon soulas, ma joye,
      Mon esbatement, mon plaisir ;
      Jamais mon cueur n'a desplaisir
      Quant entre mes bras je vous tiens.
990   Par le vray Dieu qui tout soustient,
      Tant plus vous voy et plus vous ayme,
      Car se nuict devenoit sepmaine,
      Et sepmaine devenoit moys,
      Et moys ung an, et ung an troys,
995   Et troys ans vingt, et les vingt cent,
(Diii) Quant viendroit au depertement
      De la nuict, ains qu'il adjournast,
      Si vouldroie qu'il anuitast,
      Ma tresdoulce dame honnoree.

                    La Dame
1000   Vous avez tres bonne pensee.
      Mais au plus tost que vous pourés
      Devers moy vous retournerés,
      Mon cher amy, je vous en prie.

                    Le Chevalier
          Si feray je, n'en doubtez mye,
1005 Je vous prometz certainement.
      Il m'en fault aller vistement
      A la court, car trop je demeure.

                    La Dame
          Allez amy, a la bonne heure
      Que Dieu vous donne, et le bon jour.

                    Le Chevalier
1010   Adieu mon soulas, et m'amour,
      Mon plaisir, et toute ma liesse.

Baisez moy, ma doulce maistresse,
Avant que face departie.

La Dame

Voluntiers, et de chere lye,
1015 Mon loyal amy gratieulx.
(v) De vous voir ay le cueur joyeulx,
Je vous prometz par mon serment.

Le Chevalier

Ma dame, a Dieu vous comment
Jusques a tant que vous revoye.

Comment le Chevalier, après qu'il eut prind
congié de sa dame, retourna devers son seigneur.

Le Duc

1020 Plus vous ayme que ne faisoye.
J'ay veu la verité toute,
Maintenant je suis hors de doubte

. . . .

La Duchesse

1023 . . . .
(D6) Pas je ne doibs estre joyeuse
1025 Quant de moy vous vous deffiez :
Vostre secret vous me deubsiez
Dire plus tost qu'a nul vivant.
Jamais nul jour de mon vivant
Ne vous vouluz desdire en rien,
1030 Mais maintenant je congnois bien
Que vous ne m'aymez nullement.
Quant vous et moy premierement
Fusmes espousez a l'eglise
M'aviez vous pas la foy promise,
1035 Et moy a vous, de la tenir
Et loyaulment la maintenir ?

Vous scaviez bien, mon amy cher,
Que Dieu nous mist en une chair
Et si nous assembla en une.
1040 Par le droit de la loy commune,
Nul ne peult en une chair estre
Fors ung seul cueur en la senestre,
Comme doncques c'est le cueur nostre :
Le mien avez, et j'ay le vostre,
1045 Rien ne doibt doncque au vostre avoir
Que le mien ne doibve scavoir.
Pour ce vous pry que me le dictes,
Et envers moy ne contredictes.
(v) Jamais joye au cueur n'auray
1050 Jusques a tant que le scauray
Se dire ne me voulez
Bien scauray que point ne m'aymez ;
Jamais ne vous decellay chose
Qui dedans mon cueur fust enclose.
1055 Je laisse pour vous pere et mere,
Oncles, parens, et seur, et frere,
Dont j'ay faict ung tresmauvais change
Quant envers moy vous trouve estrange.
Autreffoys m'avez esprouvee :
1060 M'avez vous en faulte trouvee ?
Certes, pas bien vous ne gardez
Envers moy, ne contregardez
Vostre foy, dont suis bien dolente
En mon cueur, et fort desplaisante.
1065 Trop grandement me mesprisez
Quant vostre secret ne m'osez
Dire, moy qui suis vostre femme.
Je vous jure Dieu et mon ame,
Pas bien ne tenez vostre foy
1070 Quant vous vous meffiez de moy ;
Je vous pry amyablement
Que vous me deissiez hardiment

Vostre cas et vostre secret,
(D7) Et je vous jure que secret
1075 Le tiendray jusques a la mort.

Le Duc

Las ! conscience me remort,
Je ne scay que je doibtz faire.
Se je le dy, je suis faulcere
Et parjure de convenance.
1080 Aussi en mon cueur ay doubtance
Que se je le dy a ma femme,
Que ma niepce tantost diffame ;
Touteffoys il fault que luy die.

Or venez ça, ma doulce amye,
1085 Dire vous veulx sans point tarder
Tout mon secret ; contregarder
Le vueillez bien celeement,
Ou je vous jure grand serment
Que, s'il m'en vient aucun reprouche,
1090 Pendue serez a une fourche
Et estranglee a une corde.

La Duchesse

Mon cher seigneur, je m'y accorde,
Et plus encores tourmentee.

Le Duc

Dame, je vous dy ma pensee :
1095 Certes, le joly Chevalier
(v) Ayme ma niepce du Vergier.
La damoyselle a affecté
Ung petit chien, par amitié,
Lequel va querir son amy
1100 Quant il est temps qu'il vienne a luy.
Je vous pry ne le dictes mie.

La Duchesse

Non feray ge, je vous affie,
Mon cher seigneur, je vous prometz.

La châtelaine de Vergy. 6.

Mal il joue de cestuy metz
1105 Qui j'aymoye perfaictement :
Je vous jure mon sacrement
Que, se je puis, je luy nuiray.
Trestout le cas descouvreray
Avant qu'il soit ung moys passé ;
1110 Mon vouloir a oultrepassé
Et ne m'a voulu obeyr.
La niepce au Duc feray trahyr
Se je puis, en quelque maniere,
La faulce villaine loudiere
1115 Et desloyalle triteresse.

Le Duc
Par le filz de Dieu qui ne cesse
Nous sommes pres de Panthecouste.
Mander il nous fault, quoy qu'il couste,
Trestous noz amis et parens
(D8) Pour faire feste liemens
1121 Tous ensemble avecques nous.
Or ma femme, qu'en dictes vous,
N'en estes vous pas bien contente ?

La Duchesse
Mandez les en l'heure presente,
1125 Sans plus longuement sejourner.

Le Duc
Tout le cas me fault ordonner.
Sa, delivre toy, Jaquemin,
Il te fault mettre en chemin
Vistement, pour aller tost querre
1130 Tous les Chevaliers de ma terre,
Toutes Dames et Damoyselles,
Mariees, aussi pucelles,
Et ma niepce de beaulté pleine
Qui du Vergier est chasteleine.
1135 Va vitement et te delivre.

162

Comment le messagier se met en chemin
pour acomplir son messaige.

(v) J'en vouldroys ja estre delivre.
Je vous jure Dieu et mon ame,
Boire il me fault une dragme
De ce vin de ma bouteillette,
1140 Grand bien me faict a la gorgette.
Je vous promectz par mon serment,
Despescher me fault vistement
D'aller parfaire mon messaige.
Je voy la Madame tressaige
1145 Qui est niepce de mon seigneur;
Saluer la fault par honneur,
Car tres bien a elle appartient
    Le vray Dieu qui trestout soubstient
(Ei) Vous doint honneur, soulas, et joye.
1150 Monseigneur devers vous m'envoye,
Qu'il vous plaise tost de venir
A la feste qu'il veult tenir,
Et vous en prie cherement.
Pour tant ne vueillez nullement
1155 Faillir que tantost n'y soyez.

La Dame
    Amy, de par moy luy direz
Que tantost a luy je seray;
Tout son plaisir acompliray
Sans differer en nulle rien.

Comment après que le messaigier eut annoncees
les nouvelles a la dame du Vergier luy declaira
ce qui s'ensuyt.

Le Messagier
(v)   Vous estes dame de hault bien,
1161 Digne d'avoir honneur et pris.

Affin que je ne soye repris :
Il mande dames et damoyselles,
Seigneurs, chevaliers et pucelles,
1165 Que tous viennent sans arrester
Au bancquet qu'il faict apprester,
Et vous luy ferez grand plaisir.

La Dame du Vergier
J'acompliray tost son desir,
Messaigier, je vous certiffie.
1170 Allez devant, je vous en prie,
A luy m'en vois sans demouree.
Trescher oncle, bonne journee
Vous doint Jesus le droicturier.

(Eii) Comment le Duc receu amyablement sa niepce,
la dame du Vergier.

Le Duc
Dieu vous gard de mal encombrier,
1175 Ma niepce pleine de beaulté ;
Joyeulx suis, par ma loyaulté,
Qu'estes venu au mandement
Que vous ay faict ; par mon serment,
De vous veoir j'ay tresgrand plaisir !

La Dame
1180 Preste suis de vostre desir
Acomplir, mon trescher seigneur.

Le Duc
(v) Je vous remercy de bon cueur,
Ma niepce, faictes bonne chere.
Je vous donne m'amour entiere,
1185 Je vous promets Dieu et mon ame.
Venez avant, ma chere femme,
Allez passer vostre jeunesse
Avecques m'amye ma niepce,
Et vous me ferez grand plaisir.

La Duchesse

1190 J'acompliray vostre desir
Et feray vostre volunté.
    Sa, Dame pleine de beaulté,
Venez dancer la basse dance.

La Dame

    Rendre vous veulx obeyssance
1195 Madame, car c'est bien raison.

La Duchesse

    Avez vous veu vostre mignon,
Le gentil galant Chevalier ?
Dictes, Madame du Vergier,
Affaicté avez le chiennet,
1200 Dont vostre cas n'est pas trop net.
Je le vous dy priveement.

La Chastellaine

    Je ne scay quel affaictement
(Eiii) Vous pensez, Madame, pour voir.
Talent je n'ay d'amy avoir
1205 Qui ne soit du tout a l'honneur
De mon oncle, mon cher seigneur ;
Autrement je seroys traystresse.

La Duchesse

    Vous estes tres bonne maistresse
Qui avez apris le mestier
1210 Du petit chiennet affaictier,
Chastellaine, tant vous en dy.

La Chastellaine

    Helas ! vray Dieu, dont vient cecy ?
Maintenant je suis bien trahye.
Dont procede la villennie
1215 Qui sur moy a esté gectee ?
Las ! chetive desconfortee !
Or congnoys je bien maintenant

Que failly a au convenant
Mon amy, que tant fort j'aymoye.
1220 Helas ! mon soulas et ma joye,
Mon plaisir, toute ma lyesse,
Pas bien n'avez tenu promesse !
Quel desplaisir vous ay je faict,
Ne en quoy vous ay je forfaict ?
1225 Certainement jour de ma vie
(v) Envers vous ne feis villennie.
Quant dedans le vergier entraste
Foy et loyaulté me juraste
Que la tiendriez entierement,
1230 Et maintenant voy clerement
Que vous avez faict le contraire.
Las ! chetive, que doibtz tu faire,
Quant tu as perdu ton desir,
Ton soulas, et tout ton plaisir,
1235 Tout ton cueur, ton esbatement ?
Certes, je m'esbahys comment
Il m'a esté si desloyal ;
Plus le maintenoye feal
Que trestous les hommes du monde.
1240 Helas ! quelle douleur parfonde
Il a mis a mon paovre cueur.
Helas ! vray Dieu et vray seigneur !
Comment avez le cueur si fier
De ma mort querir et cercher ?
1245 Dont vous procede ce couraige
De m'avoir faict si grand oultraige ?
Bien scavez que jour de ma vie
Envers vous ne feis villennie
Ne chose qui vint a reproche.
1250 Vous jurastes de vostre bouche
(Eiiii) Que me tiendrez le compromis
Que vous et moy avions promis,
Mais or congnoys je maintenant

166

Que faulcé avez faulcement
1255 Vostre serment, dont avez tort.
Mais je considere au fort
Que de ce faire avez raison,
Car je croy qu'en autre maison
Plus belle dame avez conquise
1260 Que moy, et aussi mieulx apprise.
Je suis seure que la Duchesse
Si est vostre dame et maistresse :
Bien je congnoys et apperçoy
Que vous l'aymez trop plus que moy.
1265 Se Dieu ait de m'ame pitié,
Plus vous aymoye la moytié
Que moy, je vous jure mon ame.
Vous m'avez faict trop grant diffame
De m'avoir ainsi dessellee.
1270 Mon amour vous avoys donnee
Comme celluy qui tant j'aymoye,
Boire ne manger ne povoye
Se je n'estoye avecq vous.
Helas ! mon cueur, mon amy doulx,
1275 Et que vous ay je faict ne dit ?
(v) Envers vous aucun contredit
Jamais ne feis, certainement.
Je vous aymoye si loyaulment
Qu'il n'est possible a creature
1280 De plus aymer, je vous asseure.
Quant avecq moy vous estiez
En me baisant vous me disiez
Que m'aimiez de bon cueur et d'ame,
Et que j'estoye vostre dame ;
1285 Vous le disiez si doulcement !
Et je vous croyois fermement… !
Point n'eusse cuidé a nul feur
Que eussiez tourné vostre cueur
Ne pour Royne, ne pour Duchesse,

1290 Ne pour Dame de grand haultesse
Comme avez faict, dont suis dolente.
En vous j'avoye mon entente
Plus qu'en tous les hommes du monde.
S'il n'est ainsi, Dieu me confonde,
1295 Et que meure cruellement.
Helas! mon amy, et comment
Avez vous eu si faulx couraige?
Ung chascun vous tenoit si saige,
Si doulx, si courtoys, si begnin;
1300 On ne sceut jamais que venin
(E5) Vous portissiez en jour de vie,
Mais maintenant m'avez trahye.
Helas, helas! pour Dieu, mercy!
Pourquoy suis je trahye ainsi?
1305 J'ay esté si treslonguement
Sans avoir amy nullement,
Et si faulcement m'a deceue...
Helas! pourquoy suis je venue
A ceste langueur orendroit?
1310 Las! que feray? est ce doncq droict
Que j'aye mal contre le bien?
C'estoit tout mon cueur et mon bien,
Tout mon soulas et mon amour,
Je suis pleine de grand doulour.
1315 Or puis je bien crier: He! lasse!
Que fera ceste paovre lasse?
Si grand courroux au cueur en ay
Que de plus vivre cure n'ay,
Ne ma vie ne me plaist point.
1320 Je pry Dieu que la mort me doint,
Et que, tout ainsi vrayement
Comme j'ay aymé loyallement
Celluy qui ce m'a pourchassé,
Ait Dieu de mon ame pitié.

Comment la Dame du Vergier print congé
devant sa mort des seigneurs et Dames, et de
son loyal amy le noble Chevalier, puis demoura
transie.

1325   Adieu mon cueur, adieu m'amour,
Mourir me convient sans sejour,
De vous je fais departement.
Je pry Dieu que benignement
Vueille conduyre ma paovre ame.
1330 Je meurs icy en grand diffame
Sans faire nul tort a pucelles.
Adieu Dames, et Damoyselles.
Helas ! le cueur me fend parmy,
A Dieu vous command, mon amy ;
1335 Le cueur me fault, plus ne voy goutte.

Comment après que le Chevalier eut congneu
que sa Dame par amours estoit morte a cause de
sa convenance, laquelle n'avoit tenue, remons-
tre au Duc sa faulceté, et du desplaisir qu'il a se
tue devant tous.

Le Chevalier

Helas ! je voy bien que sans doub[te]
Pour bien faire me vient le mal.
Ha ! Duc, es tu si desloyal
Que as failly de convenance !
1340 Mon ame s'en va en balance
(E6) Pour ton faulx et mauvais parler,
Pour tant que ne voulz accorder
Ne consentir a la Duchesse,
Qui vouloit estre ma maistresse
1345 Et m'amye par grand desir.
Je ne voulz faire a son plaisir,
Dont elle fut si eschauffee

Que tost comme desesperee
Donna a son mary entendre
1350 Que par force la voulois prendre,
Et que je l'avoye requise
De peché faire a ma guise.
Helas ! et pour moy excuser
Et le contraire mieulx prouver
1355 Luy monstray ma tresdoulce amie.
Las ! m'as tu celle compaignie
Faicte, et celle trahyson !
Helas, helas ! Dieu, luy pardon !
Faulx Duc, tu es trop desloyal.
1360 Las ! je pensoye que feal
Tu feusses par ta convenance ;
Par ta mauldicte decepvance
Ton ame si sera dampnee.
Faulcement tu l'as desellee
1365 Comme traystre et desloyal.
Plus te cuidoys estre loyal
(v) Que trestous les hommes du monde.
Helas ! quelle douleur parfonde
M'est aujourd'huy mesadvenu !
1370 Convenance n'ay pas tenu
A elle, dont j'ay trop grand tort.
Pour moy elle receu la mort,
Pour elle la veulx recepvoir.
Helas, Amours ! quel desespoir
1375 Vous est venu, ne quel tourment.
Je n'eusse creu certainement
Que sans moy si tost mourussiez,
Au moins que vous ne me dissiez
Premierement vostre couraige.
1380 Helas ! ceste mort m'est sauvaige
Et a mon paovre cueur amere,
Plus que celle qui est a mere.
Je doibs mourir, c'est bien raison :

170

J'ay envers vous faict mesprison
1385 Qui point ne sera reparee,
Tant fut longue la demouree.
Sans plus attendre monstrer[ay]
Que plus de vivre cure n'ay.
Je prie a Dieu le Toutpuissant
1390 Qu'il nous garde de dampnement,
A la doulce Vierge Marie
Qu'elle nous soit dame et amye ;
(E7) Et se peine debvois porter,
Doulx Dieu, je veulx supporter.
1395 Plus certes ne pourroye attendre
De la mort recepvoir et prendre.
Doulx amans, priez tous pour moy,
Car pour aymer la mort reçoy.
Adieu m'amour, adieu ma mye,
1400 Adieu la noble compaignie.

Comment les nouvelles furent annoncees au duc
que sa niepce et son chevalier estoient mors.

Ha ! cher seigneur, pour Dieu, mercy !
On a faict trop grand meudre icy,
C'est assavoir du chevalier
Et de Madame du Vergier.
1405 Tous deux sont mors presentement.

Le Duc
Helas ! doulx Dieu omnipotent !
Comment leur est il advenu ?

L'escuier
Le chevalier estoit venu
Après sa mye dernier,
1410 Mais vostre niepce vint premier,
Se complaignant de son amy
Lequel l'avoit traÿe ainsi

Et descouverte leurs amours ;
Si trespassa par grand douleurs,
1415 Pour Madame, qui la tansa
(v) D'ung petit chien qu'afaité a.
Et depuis vint le chevalier
Qui la courut tantost baiser :
Adonc vit bien qu'elle estoit morte.
1420 Par grand douleur se desconforte,
Et disoit qu'il l'avoit perdue
Pour avoir dit sa convenue
A son tresredoubté seigneur,
Par grant affinité d'amour.
1425 Et puis s'amie salua
Et print l'espee et se tua :
Ainsi deffinerent leur vie.

Le Duc

Bien je t'en croy, c'est par envie.
Et tout ce faict la Duchesse :
1430 Elle en mourra comme tristesse,
Sa foy faulcement a faulcee.
A elle vois, de ceste espee
La turay sans point varier,
Car elle m'a faict encombrier.

1435 Plus icy je n'arresteray
Car vistement je la turay,
Tout a present de ceste espee
Tuee sera, et decollee.
Or tien, tu l'as bien deservy !
(E8) Helas ! je vifz en grand ennuy
1441 Quant mon amy est trespassé,
Tout mon soulas si est passé.
Il m'avoit [dit] par grand honnour
Tout le conseil de son amour,
1445 Et je le dictz a la Duchesse.
Mais par pensee tristesse

172

Vistement ma niepce mocqua
D'ung petit chien qu'afaicté a,
Et en mourut desconfortee.
1450 Or n'est il rien au monde nee
D'icy en avant qui me plaise.
Helas! amy, tout ton affaire
Tu m'aviez doulcement monstré :
En moy trahyson as trouvé
1455 Par la mauldicte puterelle,
La faulce Duchesse cruelle,
Qui en trahison me disoit
Que le cas ne decelleroit,
Mais faulcement elle m'a deceu.
1460 Bien je doibs estre confondu,
Quant doulcement monstré tu m'as
La belle que tant aymee as.
He! Duchesse tant desloyalle,
Je te pensois estre fealle
(v) Plus que nulle qui fust au monde.
1466 Por ta luxure tant immunde
As faict mourir mon chevalier
Et ma niepce, qui du Vergier
J'avoye faicte chasteleine.
1470 Halas! bien je doibtz souffrir peine :
Mon amy est mort, et m'amye,
Halas! tant doulce compaignie
Sont mors par si treffaulx langaige ;
Je meurs de dueil en mon couraige.
1475 Aller m'en veulx sans plus tarder
— Pour ma penitence alleger —
Oultremer faire mon repaire,
Du monde je n'ay plus que faire :
Hospitalier je deviendray,
1480 Et la les paovres serviray
Tant qu'au monde seray vivant.
Je prie a Dieu le Toutpuissant

Que leurs ames ne soient perdues :
Doulx Dieu, a toy ilz soient rendues.
1485 Donne moy faire penitance,
Qu'a leurs ames soit allegence.
Demourer plus ne veulx icy :
Seigneurs et Dames, adieu vous dy.

DEO GRATIAS.

NOTES TEXTUELLES

Dans ces Notes nous mentionnons les corrections de coquilles et les changements que nous avons apportés au texte original.

38   *qu'il* : impr. *qui.* Nous avons corrigé de la même façon le *qui* des vers 323, 504, 961, 977, 1100, 1118, 1152 et 1390.

61   *front* : impr. *fronc*

65   Dans le texte nous trouvons ici trois vers rimant sur *-ure.* Etant donné le sens de ces vers nous en avons supprimé le deuxième : *Tres bien faict par bonne mesure.*

207-8 Dans l'imprimé ces deux vers se trouvent dans l'ordre inverse.

375   *desconfort* : impr. *descoufort*

455   *advenant* : impr. *adnenant*

540 et 542 Les dernières lettres de *serment* et *desloyal* manquent d'encre.

550   *haultesse* : impr. *haulte*

596   *Aucun* : impr. *Aucuu*

662   *fault* : impr. *sault*

721   *ne se scait* : *se* manque dans l'imprimé

739   La rubrique *Le messager* ne se trouve pas dans l'imprimé.

786   *se* : impr. *sa*

174

799	*guise* : la dernière lettre manque d'encre
922	*tous* : *t* renversé
945	*faisons* : impr. *faisous*
954	*desplaire* : impr. *desplaise*
1015	*gratieulx* : impr. *gratteulx*
1019	*Jusques* : impr. *Jnsques*
1022	Entre 1022 et 1023 se trouve la lacune causée par la perte du feuillet médian du cahier D. Nous avons ajouté la rubrique *La Duchesse*.
1026	*vostre* : impr. *vestre*
1045	*ne* : impr. *me*
1067	*femme* : *f* renversé
1091	*a une* : impr. *rdne*
1098	*Ung* : impr. *Nug*
1101	*le* : impr. *ie*
1105	*j'aymoye* : impr. *laymoye*
1110	*oultrepassé* : impr. *oultrepasser*
1124	*mandez* : impr. *maudez*
1132	*mariees* : impr. *maries*
1152	*qu'il veult* : impr. *qui veulx*
1158	*acompliray* : impr. *acompliry*
1172	*journee* : impr. *iournnee*
1248	*vous* : impr. *vons*
1288	*tourné* : impr. *tourner*
entre	1335 et 1336 : *laquelle* : impr. *laqnelle*
1336	*doubte* : impr. *doub*
1368	*douleur* : impr. *douceur*
1379	*premierement* : impr. *premieremnnt*
1387	*monstreray* : impr. *monstrer*
1393	*debvois* : impr. *debvez*
1422	*dit* : impr. *de*
1440	*ennuy* : impr. *enuny*
1442	*tout* : impr. *tont*
1443	*dit* : manque dans l'imprimé
1461	*monstré* : impr. *monstrer*
1473	*Sont* : impr. *Sout.*

1. f. Ai recto (la page de titre). Vignette de 32 sur 54 mm, représentant un chevalier (à droite) saluant une dame qui lui fait signe. La dame se trouve à la fenêtre d'une tour de château.

2. f. Aii recto. Vignette de 38 sur 54 mm : scribe au travail.

3. f. Aiiii verso. Vignette de 33 sur 54 mm : scène dans un jardin. Deux hommes à gauche, dont l'un montre à l'autre une dame qui se trouve à droite et qui lui fait signe.

4. f. Biii verso. 33 sur 54 mm. Scène d'intérieur : à gauche une dame en train d'écrire ; à droite un messager (?) qui entre.

5. f. Biiii verso. 33 sur 53 mm. Scène d'intérieur. Une femme (à gauche) et un homme (à droite), assis sur un rebord de fenêtre, en train de parler.

6. f. B6 recto. 32 sur 54 mm. Scène d'intérieur : un homme et une femme (à gauche) reçoivent (?) une jeune femme (à droite).

7. f. B6 verso. 32 sur 54 mm. Groupe dans un paysage. Deux femmes à gauche parlent avec un chevalier. Un deuxième chevalier, se trouvant à droite, tourne la tête.

8. f. B8 verso. 39 sur 54 mm. Scène d'intérieur. Au milieu un homme, assis dans un fauteuil, discute avec un homme à gauche. Un deuxième homme à gauche est en train de discuter avec deux hommes qui se trouvent à droite du fauteuil.

9. f. Ciiii recto. 32 sur 55 mm. Scène d'intérieur. Un homme couronné, assis sur un trône, remet une lettre à un messager qui est agenouillé devant lui (sur la droite). Deux hommes se trouvent à l'arrière-plan.

10. f. C5 recto. 32 sur 55 mm. Rencontre devant une tour. Un homme, arrivant sur la droite, salue deux autres qui se trouvent à gauche.

11. f. Dii recto. Même bois que 3 (f. Aiiii verso).

12. f. Diii verso. 32 sur 54 mm. Deux amants dans un jardin. Scène d'adieu? L'homme est à gauche, la femme à droite.

13. f. D8 verso. 33 sur 54 mm. Deux hommes sous un grand portail attendent un troisième homme qui accourt à gauche.

14. f. Ei verso. 33 sur 54 mm. Scène d'intérieur. Une jeune femme à genoux (à gauche) salue un homme et une femme qui se trouvent au centre de l'image; une troisième femme (sur la droite) regarde les autres.

15. f. Eii recto. 32 sur 54 mm. Groupe dans un paysage. Deux femmes (sur la gauche) reçoivent trois hommes venant de droite. Deux figures à genoux (à l'extrême droite).

GLOSSAIRE

a : il y a (p. ex. dans l'expression *longtemps a* : il y a longtemps)

achoyson : occasion

affaictement : dressage

affaictier, affecter : dresser (le petit chien)

ains que : avant que

allegence : allégement

anuitast (anuiter) : la nuit tombe

apperra (apparoir) : il sera clair

appertement : promptement

apprendre (a. un chiennet) : dresser (un petit chien)

aucun : quelque, quelqu'un

bailler : donner

begnin : doux, bienveillant

benignement : doucement

bonnaireté : bonté, douceur

ça : Il n'y a point ne ça ne cy : il n'y a pas de discussion

celeement : en secret

celer : cacher

chaulcist : (il m')importerait

chetif : malheureux

colloquer : placer

comment : (subst.) volonté : (vb.) de *commander :* recommander

confort : réconfort

convenance, convenant : promesse

convencier : (infin. subst.) échange des promesses

convenue : promesse

coulons : pigeons

couraige : cœur, sentiment

cuider, cuyder : croire

dampnement : damnation

deceller, deseller : divulguer, découvrir

decepvance : tromperie

deduire : (d. ses amours) : jouir de son amour

(soy) delivrer : se hâter

demener : (d. sa joye) : jouir de son amour

demeure : attente

departement : (faire d.) : quitter

depertement : fin

desconfort : désolation, désespoir

desconfortee : désolée, inconsolable

desport : délice

desservir : mériter

deult, deulx : (de doloir) : souffrir, pleurer

diffame : déshonneur, honte

diffiner : terminer

doint : (de *donner*) : qu'il donne

178

dont : d'où

dragme : petite quantité (de vin)

(par) droicture : légitimement, de droit

droicturier : équitable

emboucher : alimenter, nourrir

encombrier : ennui, peine

enginer : tromper

entendement : opinion

entente : pensée

envenimer : empoisonner

esbatement : agrément

eschet : il convient, est nécessaire

estrange : étranger

faulcere : traître, trompeur

fault : (il) manque

feal : fidèle, loyal

feur (dans : *a nul feur*) : (à aucun) prix

feaulté : fidélité, attachement loyal

fors de : hors de

fort (au fort) : après tout

galler, se galler : s'amuser, se divertir

gard (de *garder*) : qu'il garde

gise (de *jesir*) : se trouver, reposer

heure (en bonne h.) : par hasard (?)

Hospitalier : Hospitalier (chevalier de l'ordre de l'Hôpital de Saint-Jean à Jérusalem). Les textes plus anciens mettent ici *Templier* (autre ordre religieux militaire, établi à Jérusalem, supprimé en 1311)

infame : honteux

ja : particule de renforcement ; vraiment

jengler : plaisanter, mentir

las : malheureux

legierement : rapidement

liemens : joyeusement

loudiere : femme débauchée

loyaulment : selon la loi ; de façon loyale
mais que : pourvu que, à moins que
marrison : peine, tristesse
mesadvenir : (vb.) arriver malheur
mesprison : tort, injustice
meudre : meurtre
monter : signifier
munde : pur
mye (ne... m.) : (ne...) pas
nonpourtant : néanmoins
oncques : jamais
orendroit : maintenant
ouÿs (passé défini d'*ouÿr*) : entendre
oyez (de *oÿr*) : écouter, entendre
partir : fendre
pieça : depuis quelque temps déjà
puterelle : putain
quant : puisque
que : signifie parfois « car »
querir : chercher
qui : signifie parfois « si l'on »
remansist : (qu'il) restât
requerir : demander
revisitement : visite
se : signifie souvent « si » (conjonction)
semblance (dans : *faire s.*) : donner signe, faire apparaître
semblant : apparence
senestre : côté gauche
sens : moyen ingénieux
si : a plusieurs sens : et, et aussi, aussi
souffrir : supporter
tant : *pour tant* : pour cette raison
transi : trépassé, mort
treffaulx : très faux, méchant
trespasser : violer, désobéir à

180

tri(s)teresse, tristesse : traîtresse
varier, dans : *sans point v. :* sans manquer
viz : visage
voir, dans : *pour voir :* vrai, vraiment
voultiz : voûtés
voulz : je voulus
voys : je vais
vuyder : quitter, s'en aller

MARGUERITE DE NAVARRE :
L'HEPTAMÉRON. NOUVELLE 70.

INTRODUCTION

A la fin septembre de l'année 1540 environ, le hasard réunit une dizaine de personnes (cinq femmes et cinq hommes) à l'abbaye de Notre-Dame de Sarrance (Htes-Pyrénées). Venant des bains de Cauterets et ne pouvant poursuivre leur chemin à cause du mauvais temps qui a sévi, les voyageurs se décident à passer ensemble les dix jours nécessaires à la construction d'un pont sur le Gave d'Aspe. Lorsqu'on discute la question de savoir comment passer le temps, la dame la plus âgée de la compagnie — Oysille — propose que l'on s'occupe à lire et à méditer ensemble la Bible : Parlamente, plus jeune qu'Oysille, fait état d'un projet qu'avait eu le roi François Ier : réunir dix personnes qui raconteraient toutes dix nouvelles, pour imiter en quelque sorte « les cent Nouvelles de Boccace ». On est dix, alors...? On accepte les deux propositions, et le programme de la journée sera donc le suivant : lever, leçon d'Oysille sur la Bible, messe, dîner (à dix heures), rassemblement sur le pré (« la, assiz à noz aises, dira chascun quelque histoire qu'il aura veue ou bien oÿ dire a quelque homme digne de foy.

Au bout de dix jours aurons parachevé la centaine »), vêpres, souper, coucher.

C'est ainsi qu'est présentée la naissance de *l'Heptaméron,* le recueil de nouvelles écrites par Marguerite de Navarre, la sœur du roi François Ier. Née en 1492 elle eut une existence inquiète et tourmentée : elle fut mêlée aux affaires importantes du royaume, essaya de racheter son frère, prisonnier de Charles-Quint après la défaite de Pavie en 1525, et fut impliquée plus ou moins dans les mouvements « évangéliques » et réformateurs de l'époque. Vers 1542 elle se montra de moins en moins à la cour et séjourna pendant de longs mois dans ses terres (à Nérac, Mont-de-Marsan, et Pau). C'est probablement dans cette période de sa vie qu'elle commença à rédiger ses nouvelles ; sans doute avait-elle déjà accumulé depuis quelque temps des sujets.

Il nous reste dans les éditions courantes 72 nouvelles, au lieu des 100 qu'elle aurait voulu écrire selon le prologue. 72 nouvelles, racontées par 10 personnes différentes : la question se pose évidemment de savoir si nous sommes en présence d'une collection de contes disparates, ou si, au contraire, il y a unité ?

Lors de la mise en forme Marguerite veille à ce que femmes et hommes alternent comme conteurs, et que les sujets gais succèdent aux sujets tristes, les contes brefs aux contes plus longs. Il y a donc un souci net de construction. Les dix personnages ont tous une personnalité bien distincte : ainsi Madame Oysille contera presque toujours des nouvelles de ton grave, dont les situations émeuvent et qui frappent la sensibilité — elle veut avant tout instruire. Aussi n'est-il pas étonnant que ce soit Oysille qui raconte la nouvelle de *la Chastellaine du Vergier.* Une particularité du recueil de Marguerite (et qui l'oppose par exemple aux *Cent Nouvelles Nouvelles* du XVe siècle) est que la compagnie commente toutes les nouvelles. Les leçons de morale qui se trouvent dans ces débats passent avec les nouvelles, sans que l'on s'en aperçoive. Pour Marguerite de Navarre cette morale semble être la suivante : elle condamne la pure adoration de la beauté, l'amour pour l'amour. « J'appelle parfaicts amans ceulx qui cherchent, en ce qu'ilz aiment, quelque perfection, soit beaulté, bonté ou bonne grace ; toujours tendans à la vertu, et qui ont le cueur si hault et si honneste, qu'ilz ne veulent, pour mourir [dussent-ils en mourir], mettre leur fin aux choses basses que l'honneur et la conscience reprouvent : car l'ame, qui n'est creée que pour retourner à son souverain bien, ne faict, tant qu'elle est dedans ce corps, que desirer d'y parvenir. » (Débat qui suit la nouv. 19.) Ces mots s'appliquent bien à la nouvelle 70. Nous y voyons une duchesse qui cherche « ung contentement bestial » et une châtelaine qui, au moment de mourir, constate que « par trop avoir adoré la creature [son âme a] oblié le Createur ». La valeur exemplaire de ce conte est accentuée encore dans la discussion qui suit. Etant donné que cette nouvelle est la dernière de la septième journée c'est sur cette histoire que les devisants vont aux vêpres, « n'obliant en leur bonnes prieres les ames des vraiz amans, pour lesquelz les religieux, de leur bonne volunté, dirent ung *de Profundis*. »

La 70e nouvelle a un statut spécial dans le livre ; comme nous le voyons dans la discussion qui précède ce conte, Oysille (ce serait Louise de Savoie, la mère de Marguerite) s'excuse de la longueur (il n'y a qu'un seul conte de Parlamente qui soit plus long) et du caractère littéraire de l'histoire : c'est alors Parlamente qui l'engage à la raconter quand même. Il nous semble que Marguerite de Navarre (Parlamente) a tenu à l'insérer dans son recueil à cause de la valeur exemplaire de l'histoire. Déjà le texte du XIIIe siècle disait à la fin qu'il s'agissait d'un exemple (*exemplum !*) :

> « Et par cest essample doit l'en
> s'amour celer [cacher]… »
>
> (v.941-2).

Le texte de Marguerite mettra l'accent sur le fait qu'il faut avant tout aimer parfaitement, et se rapprocher ainsi de l'amour de Dieu. Dans la discussion qui avait suivi la nouvelle 19 Parlamente avait fait remarquer que « jamais homme n'aymera parfaictement Dieu, qu'il n'ait parfaictement aymé quelque creature en ce monde. » A la lumière de cette affirmation, l'insertion de notre nouvelle dans l'ensemble de ce recueil se comprend très bien.

C'est sans doute cette perspective nouvelle qui a été à l'origine de certains changements apportés au texte tel que nous le présentent les versions du XIIIe siècle. Une étude comparative des différents textes révèle des concordances entre le texte de Marguerite, le texte de 1540, la version en prose et les vieux textes en vers. Les différences qui, d'autre part, existent entre ces quatre versions, ont fait dire à Gaston Paris et à Jean Frappier que Marguerite a dû se baser sur un texte en prose du XVe que nous n'avons plus.

Il est intéressant de signaler que les vieilles éditions de *l'Heptaméron* donnent un texte qui diffère en plusieurs lieux du texte tel qu'il se trouve dans les manuscrits. La première édition parut en 1558 ; elle était de la main de Pierre Boaistuau, était intitulée *Histoires des Amans fortunez,* et ne comportait que 67 nouvelles. En 1559 parut une deuxième édition, sous le titre *l'Heptaméron des Nouvelles* [...], « par Claude Gruget, Parisien ». Cet auteur a rétabli l'ordre des nouvelles et leur distribution sur les différentes journées, sans doute en se basant sur certains manuscrits ; il a également arrangé le texte, afin de le rendre plus digne de la mémoire de « la feue Royne » Marguerite. Ainsi il a fait disparaître dans la nouvelle qui nous occupe jusqu'au nom de la Châtelaine ; elle reste la nièce du duc de Bourgogne, mais Gruget gomme même les noms des châteaux qui se trouvent dans les versions manuscrites. Il n'est pas exclu qu'il l'ait fait pour épargner les membres de la famille de Vergy, encore influents à l'époque. Un autre changement significatif se trouve dans la scène du rendez-vous nocturne ; dans le texte des manuscrits on lit que la Châtelaine, après avoir embrassé le chevalier sur le pas de la porte, se retire avec lui dans sa chambre, en fermant la porte sur eux. Gruget a sans doute jugé trop dangereuse une telle situation ; il change donc ce passage de la façon suivante : « Et à l'heure entrerent dedans la chambre qu'ils laisserent ouverte, ou le Duc entra secretement après eux, car il n'y avoit aucune lumiere ; lequel entendant tout le discours de leur chaste amitié se tint plus que satisfaict, et attendit la non trop longuement [...] ».

Etant donné que ces changements de Gruget semblent trop souvent porter atteinte au texte de Marguerite, on choisit en général pour une édition qui ne trahisse pas trop la pensée de l'auteur le manuscrit Paris, B.N.fr.1512, un magnifique volume du milieu du XVIe siècle, que nous reproduisons pour la 70e nouvelle d'après l'édition de P.L. Jacob, Bibliophile (= Paul Lacroix), de 1858. Nous avons expliqué au Glossaire les quelques termes qui pourraient poser des problèmes de compréhension. Lors de la lecture du texte il ne faut pas oublier que le – *e* – devant voyelle, et le – *s* – devant consonne ne sont le plus souvent pas prononcés ; en général ces lettres disparaissent dans la graphie moderne. Ainsi *il feit* = il fit, *il commencea* = il commença, et *elle eust* = elle eut, ou elle eût.

Remarques bibliographiques

Editions : *L'Heptaméron des nouvelles, de très-haute et très-illustre princesse Marguerite d'Angoulême, Royne de Navarre.* Nouvelle édition, publiée d'après le texte des manuscrits avec des notes et une notice par P. L. Jacob, bibliophile. Paris, 1858.

L'édition courante est celle de Michel François, *Marguerite de Navarre, l'Heptaméron.* Paris, Garnier Frères, plusieurs impressions à partir de 1943.

L'étude de loin la plus importante de ce texte de Marguerite, et qui le rapproche de la version du XIIIe siècle de *la Châtelaine de Vergy,* est de la main de Jean Frappier, « *la Chastelaine de Vergi,* Marguerite de Navarre et Bandello » (*Publications de la Faculté de Lettres de Strasbourg,* fasc. 105 (1946) : 89-150). Cette étude a été reproduite dans Jean Frappier, *Du Moyen Age à la Renaissance. Etudes d'histoire et de critique littéraire.* Paris, 1976 : 393-473.

Gaston Paris (*Mélanges de littérature française du Moyen Age,* 1912 : 650), en parlant de la nouvelle, suggère que la source de Marguerite a été dans ce cas un texte en prose que nous n'avons plus.

L. A. Arrathoon affirme dans son article « The " Compte en viel langaige " Behind *Heptaméron,* LXX » (dans *Romance Philology* 30 (1976) : 192-99) que « the " compte en viel langaige " behind *Hepta-*

méron 70 was *l'Istoire de la Chastelaine du Vergier et de Tristan le chevalier,* enriched by the *Odyssey,* Biblical material such as Gen. 39 and Dan. 13, an Old French narrative of the Lanval story type, and Marguerites memory of a lost play whose subject was the Chastelaine de Vergi » (p. 199).

L'HEPTAMÉRON 70

[...]

— Les femmes de bien, dist Longarine, n'ont besoing d'autre chose que de l'amour de leurs mariz, qui seullement les peuvent contenter ; mais celles qui cherchent ung contentement bestial ne le trouveront jamais ou honnesteté le commande. — Appelez-vous contentement bestial, dist Geburon, si la femme veult avoir de son mary ce qui luy apartient ? » Longarine lui respondit : « Je dis que la femme chaste, qui a le cueur remply de vray amour, est plus satisfaicte d'estre aymee parfaitement, que de tous les plaisirs que le corps peut desirer. — Je suis de vostre oppinion, dist Dagoucin, mais ces seigneurs icy ne le veullent entendre ny confesser. Je pense que, si l'amour reciproque ne contente pas une femme, le mary seul ne la contentera pas ; car, en vivant de l'honneste amour des femmes, fault qu'elle soit tentee de l'infernale cupidité des bestes. — Vrayement, dist Oisille, vous me faictes souvenir d'une dame belle et bien maryee, qui, par faulte de vivre de ceste honneste amitié, devint plus charnelle que les pourceaulx et plus cruelle que les lyons. — Je vous requiers, ma dame, ce dist Simontault, pour metre fin a ceste journée, la nous vouloir compter. — Je ne puis, dist Oisille, pour deux raisons : l'une, pour sa grande longueur ; l'autre, pour ce que n'est pas de nostre temps ; et si a esté escripte par ung autheur, qui est bien croyable, et nous avons juré de ne rien mectre icy qui ait esté escript. — Il est vray, dist Parlamente, mais me doubtant du compte que c'est, il a esté escript en si viel langaige, que je croy que, hors mis nous deux, il n'y a icy homme ne femme qui en ait ouÿ parler ; parquoy sera tenu pour nouveau. » Et, a sa parolle, toute la compaignye la pria de le voloir dire, et qu'elle ne craingnist la longueur, car encores une bonne heure pouvoient demorer avant vespres. Madame Oisille a leur requeste commencea ainsy :

(SOIXANTE DIXIESME NOUVELLE)

En la duché de Bourgongne, y avoit ung duc, tres honneste et beau prince, aiant espousé une femme, dont la beaulté le contentoit si fort, qu'elle luy faisoit ignorer ses conditions, tant, qu'il ne regardoit que a luy complaire ; ce qu'elle faingnoit tres bien luy rendre. Or avoit le duc en sa maison ung gentil homme, tant accomply de toutes les perfections que l'on peut demander a l'homme, qu'il estoit de tous aymé, et principallement du duc, qui des son enfance l'avoit nourry pres sa personne ; et, le voiant si bien conditionné, l'aymoit parfaictement et se confyoit en luy de toutes les affaires, que selon son aage il povoit entendre. La duchesse, qui n'avoit pas le cueur de femme et princesse vertueuse, ne se contantant de l'amour que son mary luy portoit, et du bon traictement qu'elle avoit de luy, regardoit souvent ce gentil homme, et le trovoit tant a son gré, qu'elle l'aymoit oultre raison ; ce que a toute heure mectoit peyne de luy faire entendre, tant par regardz piteux et doulx, que par souspirs et contenances passionnés. Mais le gentil homme, qui jamais n'avoit estudyé que a la vertu, ne povoit congnoistre le vice en une dame qui en avoit si peu d'occasion ; tellement que œillades et mynes de ceste pauvre folle n'apportoient aultre fruict que ung furieux desespoir, lequel, ung jour, la poussa tant, que, obliant qu'elle estoit femme qui debvoit estre priee et refuser, princesse qui debvoit estre adoree, desdaignant telz serviteurs, print le cueur d'un homme transporté, pour descharger le feu qui estoit importable. Et, ainsy que son mary alloit au conseil, ou le gentil homme, pour sa jeunesse, n'estoit point, luy fit signe qu'il vint devers elle ; ce qu'il feit, pensant qu'elle eust a luy commander quelque chose. Mais, en s'appuyant sur son bras, comme femme lasse de trop de repos, le mena pourmener en une gallerie, ou elle luy dist : « Je m'esbahys de vous, qui estes tant beau, jeune et tant plain de toute bonne grace, comme vous avez vescu en ceste compaignye, ou il y a si grand nombre de belles dames, sans que jamais vous ayez esté amoureux ou serviteur d'aucune ? » Et en le regardant du meilleur œil qu'elle povoit, se teut, pour luy donner lieu de dire : « Madame, si j'estois digne que vostre haultesse se peust abbaisser a penser a moy, ce vous seroit plus d'occasion d'esbahissement de veoir ung homme, si indigne d'estre aymé que moy, presenter son service, pour en avoir refuz ou mocquerie. » La duchesse, ayant oÿ ceste sage response, l'ayma plus fort que paravant, et luy jura qu'il n'y avoit dame en sa court, qui ne fut trop heureuse d'avoir ung tel serviteur ; et qu'il se povoit bien essayer telle advanture, car sans

192

peril il en sortiroit a son honneur. Le gentil homme tenoit tousjours les œilz baissez, n'osant regarder ses contenances qui estoient assez ardantes pour faire brusler une glace ; et ainsy qu'il se vouloit excuser, le duc demanda la duchesse pour quelque affaire, au conseil, qui luy touchoit, ou avec grand regret elle alla. Mais le gentil homme ne feit jamais ung seul semblant d'avoir entendu parolle qu'elle luy eust dicte ; dont elle estoit si troublee et faschee, qu'elle n'en sçavoit a qui donner le tort de son ennuy, sinon a la sotte craincte, dont elle estimoit le gentil homme trop plain. Peu de jours après, voyant qu'il n'entendoit point son langaige, se delibera de ne regarder craincte ny honte, mais luy declarer sa fantaisye, se tenant seure, que une telle beaulté que la sienne ne porroit estre que bien receue ; mais elle eust bien desiré d'avoir eu l'honneur d'estre priee. Toutes-fois, laissa l'honneur a part, pour le plaisir ; et, après avoir tenté par plusieurs foys de luy tenir semblables propos que le premier, et n'y trouvant nulle res-ponse a son gré, le tira ung jour par la manche et luy dist qu'elle avoit a parler a luy d'affaires d'impor-tance. Le gentil homme, avec l'humilité et reverance qu'il luy debvoit, s'en va devers elle en une profonde fenestre ou elle s'estoit retiree. Et, quand elle veid que nul de la chambre ne la povoit veoir, avecq une voix tremblante, contraincte entre le desir et la craincte, luy va continuer les premiers propos, le reprenant de ce qu'il n'avoit encores choisy quelque dame en sa compaigyne, l'asseurant que, en quelque lieu que ce fust, luy ayderoit d'avoir bon traicte-ment. Le gentil homme, non moins fasché que estonné de ses parolles, luy respondit : « Ma dame, j'ay le cueur si bon, que, si j'estois une foys refusé, je n'aurois jamais joye en ce monde : et je me sens tel, qu'il n'y a dame en ceste court qui daignast

193

accepter mon service. » La duchesse, rougissant, pensant qu'il ne tenoit plus à rien qu'il ne fust vaincu, luy jura que, s'il voulloit, elle sçavoit la plus belle dame de sa compaignye qui le recepvroit a grand joye et dont il auroit parfaict contentement. « Helas, ma dame, je ne croy pas qu'il y ait si malheureuse et aveugle femme en ceste compaignye, qui me ait trouvé a son gré ! » La duchesse, voyant qu'il n'y vouloit entendre, luy va entreouvrir le voille de sa passion ; et, pour la craincte que luy donnoit la vertu du gentil homme, parla par maniere d'interrogation, luy disant : « Si Fortune vous avoit tant favorisé que ce fut moy qui vous portast ceste bonne volunté, que diriez-vous ? » Le gentil homme, qui pensoit songer, d'oÿr une telle parolle, luy dist, le genoulx a terre : « Madame, quand Dieu me fera la grace d'avoir celle du duc mon maistre et de vous, je me tiendray le plus heureux du monde, car c'est la recompense que je demande de mon loial service, comme celluy qui plus que nul autre est obligé a mectre la vie pour le service de vous deux ; estant seur, ma dame, que l'amour que vous portez a mon dict seigneur est accompagnee de telle chasteté et grandeur, que non pas moy qui ne suis que ung ver de terre, mais le plus grand prince et parfaict homme que l'on sçauroit trouver ne sçauroit empescher l'unyon de vous et de mon dict seigneur. Et quant a moy, il m'a nourry des mon enfance et m'a faict tel que je suis ; parquoy il ne sçauroit avoir femme, fille, seur ou mere, desquelles, pour mourir, je voulsisse avoir autre pensee que doibt a son maistre ung loial et fidele serviteur. » La duchesse ne le laissa pas passer oultre, et, voyant qu'elle estoit en danger d'un refuz deshonorable, lui rompit soubdain son propos, en luy disant : « O meschant, glorieux et fol, et qui est-ce qui vous en prie ? Cuydez-vous, par vostre beaulté, estre aymé des mouches qui vollent ? Mais, si vous estiez si oultrecuydé de vous addresser a moy, je vous monstrerois que je n'ayme et ne veulx aymer aultre que mon mary : et les propos que je vous ay tenu n'ont esté que pour passer mon temps a sçavoir de voz nouvelles, et m'en mocquer comme je fais des sotz amoureux. — Ma dame, dist le gentil homme, je l'ay creu et croy comme vous le dictes. » Lors, sans l'escouter plus avant, s'en alla hastivement en sa chambre, et voiant qu'elle estoit suivye de ses dames, entra en son cabinet ou elle feit ung deuil qui ne se peut racompter ; car, d'ung costé, l'amour ou elle avoit failly luy donna une tristesse mortelle ; d'autre costé, le despit, tant contre elle d'avoir commencé ung si sot propos, que contre luy d'avoir si saigement respondu, la mectoit en une telle furie, que une heure se vouloit deffaire, l'autre elle vouloit vivre pour se venger de celluy qu'elle tenoit son mortel ennemy.

Après qu'elle eut longuement pleuré, faingnit d'estre mallade, pour n'aller point au souper du duc, auquel ordinairement le gentil homme servoit. Le duc, qui plus aymoit sa femme que luymesmes, la vint visiter ; mais, pour mieulx venir a la fin qu'elle pretendoit, luy dist qu'elle pensoit estre grosse et que sa grossesse luy avoit faict tomber ung rume dessus les œilz, dont elle estoit en fort grand peyne. Ainsy passerent deux ou trois jours, que la duchesse garda le lict, tant triste et melancolicque, que le duc pensa bien qu'il y avoit autre chose que la grossesse. Et vint coucher la nuyct avecq elle, et luy faisant toutes les bonnes cheres qu'il luy estoit possible, congnoissant qu'il n'empeschoit en riens ses continuels souspirs, luy dist : « M'amie, vous sçavez que je vous porte autant d'amour que a ma propre vie ; et que, defaillant la vostre, la mienne ne peut durer ;

parquoy, si vous voulez conserver ma santé, je vous prie, dictes moy la cause qui vous faict ainsy souspirer, car je ne puis croire que tel mal vous vienne seullement de la grossesse. » La duchesse, voiant son mary tel envers elle qu'elle l'eut sceu demander, pensa qu'il estoit temps de se venger de son despit, et, en embrassant son mary, se print à pleurer, luy disant : « Helas, monsieur, le plus grand mal que j'aye, c'est de vous veoir trompé de ceulx qui sont tant obligez a garder vostre bien et honneur. » Le duc, entendant ceste parolle, eut grand desir de sçavoir pourquoy elle luy disoit ce propos, et la pria fort de luy declarer sans craincte la verité. Et, après en avoir faict plusieurs refuz, luy dist : « Je ne m'esbahiray jamais, monsieur, si les estrangiers font guerre aux princes, quand ceulx qui sont les plus obligez l'osent entreprendre si cruelle, que la perte des biens n'est rien au prix. Je le dis, monsieur, pour ung tel gentil homme (nommant celluy qu'elle haÿssoit) lequel, estant nourry de vostre main, et traicté plus en parent et en filz que en serviteur, a osé entreprendre chose si cruelle et miserable, que de pourchasser a faire perdre l'honneur de vostre femme ou gist celluy de vostre maison et de vos enfanz. Et, combien que longuement m'ait faict des mynes tendant a sa meschante intention, si est ce que mon cueur, qui n'a regard que a vous, n'y povoit rien entendre ; dont a la fin s'est declaré par parolle. A quoy je luy ay faict telle responce, que mon estat et ma chasteté devoient. Ce neantmoins, je luy porte telle hayne, que je ne le puis regarder : qui est la cause de m'avoir faict demorer en ma chambre et perdre le bien de vostre compaignye, vous supliant, monsieur, de ne tenir une telle peste auprès de vostre personne ; car, après ung tel crime, craignant que je le vous dye, pourroit bien entreprendre pis.

Voyla, monsieur, la cause de ma douleur qui me semble estre tres juste et digne que promptement y donniez ordre. » Le duc, qui d'un costé aymoit sa femme et se sentoit fort injurié, d'autre costé aymant son serviteur duquel il avoit tant experimenté la fidelité, que a peyne povoit-il croyre ceste mensonge estre verité, fut en grand peyne et remply de colere : s'en alla en sa chambre, et manda au gentil homme, qu'il n'eut plus a se trouver devant luy, mais qu'il se retirast en son logis pour quelque temps. Le gentil homme, ignorant de ce l'occasion, fut tant ennuyé qu'il n'estoit possible de plus, sçachant avoir merité le contraire d'ung si mauvais traictement. Et, comme celluy qui estoit asseuré de son cueur et de ses œuvres, envoya ung sien compaignon parler au duc et porter une lettre, le supliant tres humblement que, si par mauvais rapport il estoit esloigné de sa presence, il luy pleut suspendre son jugement jusques après avoir entendu de lui la verité du faict ; et qu'il troveroit que, en nulle sorte, il ne l'avoit offensé. Voiant ceste lettre, le duc rapaisa ung peu sa collere et secretement l'envoia querir en sa chambre, auquel il dist d'un visaige furieux : « Je n'eusse jamais pensé que la peyne que j'ay prins de vous nourrir, comme enfant, se deut convertir en repentance de vous avoir tant advancé, veu que vous m'avez pourchassé ce qui m'a esté plus dommageable que la perte de la vie et des biens, d'avoir voulu toucher à l'honneur de celle qui est la moictié de moy, pour rendre ma maison et ma lignee infame a jamais. Vous pouvez penser que telle injure me touche si avant au cueur, que, si ce n'estoit le doubte que je fais s'il est vray ou non, vous fussiez desja au fond de l'eaue, pour vous rendre en secret la pugnition du mal que en secret m'avez pourchassé. » Le gentil homme ne fut point estonné de ces propos, car son ignorance le faisoit constamment parler ; et luy suplia luy vouloir dire qui estoit son accusateur, car telles parolles se doibvent plus justifier avecq la lance, que avecq la langue. « Vostre accusateur, dist le duc, ne porte autres armes que la chasteté ; vous asseurant que nul autre que ma femme mesmes ne me l'a declaré, me priant la venger de vous. » Le pauvre gentil homme, voyant la tresgrande malice de la dame, ne la voulut toutesfois accuser, mais respondit : « Mon seigneur, ma dame peut dire ce qui lui plaist. Vous la congnoissez mieulx que moy ; et sçavez si jamais je l'ay veue hors de vostre compaignie, sinon une foys qu'elle parla bien peu a moy. Vous avez aussy bon jugement que prince qui soit ; parquoy je vous suplie, mon seigneur, juger si jamais vous avez veu en moy contenance qui vous ait peu engendrer quelque soupson. Si est-ce un feu qui ne se peut si longuement couvrir, que quelquefois ne soit congneu de ceulx qui ont pareille malladye. Vous supliant, mon seigneur, croire deux choses de moy : l'une que je vous suis si loial, que, quand madame vostre femme seroit la plus belle creature du monde, si n'auroit amour la puissance de mectre tache a mon honneur et fidelité ; l'autre est que, quand elle ne seroit point vostre femme, c'est celle que je veis oncques, dont je serois aussi peu amoureux ; et y en a assez d'aultres, ou je mectrois plus tost ma fiance. » Le duc commencea a s'adoulcir, oyant ce veritable propos, et luy dist : « Je vous asseure aussy que je ne l'ay pas creue ; parquoy faictes comme vous aviez accoustumé, vous asseurant que, si je congnois la verité de vostre costé, vous aymeray mieulx que je ne feiz oncques ; aussi, par le contraire, vostre vie est en ma main. » Dont le gentil homme le mercia, se soubmectant a toute peyne et punition, s'il estoit trouvé coulpable.

La duchesse, voiant le gentil homme servir comme il avoit accoustumé, ne le peut porter en patience, mais dist à son mary : « Ce seroit bien employé, monsieur, si vous estiez empoisonné, veu que vous avez plus de fiance en vos ennemys mortelz, que en voz amys. — Je vous prie, m'amye, ne vous tormentez point de ceste affaire ; car, si je congnois que ce que vous m'avez dict soit vray, je vous asseure qu'il ne demeurera pas en vie vingt-quatre heures ; mais il m'a tant juré le contraire, veu aussy que jamais ne m'en suis aparceu, que je ne le puis croire sans grand preuve. — En bonne foy, monsieur, luy dist elle, vostre bonté rend sa meschanceté plus grande. Voulez-vous plus grande preuve, que de veoir ung homme tel que luy, sans jamais avoir bruict d'estre amoureux ? Croiez, monsieur, que, sans la grande entreprinse qu'il avoit mise en sa teste de me servir, il n'eut tant demeuré a trouver maistresse, car oncques jeune homme ne vesquit, en si bonne compaignye, ainsy solitaire comme il faict, sinon qu'il ait le cueur en si hault lieu, qu'il se contante de sa vaine esperance. Et, puis que vous pensez qu'il ne vous cele verité, je vous supplye, mectez le a serment de son amour, car, s'il en aymoit une aultre, je suis contente que vous le croyez ; et sinon, pensez que je vous dis verité. » Le duc trouva les raisons de sa femme tresbonnes, et mena le gentil homme aux champs, auquel il dist : « Ma femme me continue toujours ceste oppinion et m'allegue une raison qui me cause ung grand soupson contre vous ; c'est que l'on s'esbahit que, vous estant si honneste et jeune, n'avez jamais aymé, que l'on ayt sceu : qui me faict penser que vous avez l'oppinion qu'elle dict, de laquelle l'esperance vous rend si content, que vous ne povez penser en une autre femme. Parquoy je vous prie, comme amy, et vous commande, comme

maistre, que vous aiez a me dire si vous estes
serviteur de nulle dame de ce monde. » Le pauvre
gentil homme, combien qu'il eut voulu dissimuller
son affection autant qu'il tenoit chere sa vie, fut
contrainct, voiant la jalousie de son maistre, luy
jurer que veritablement il en aymoit une, de laquelle
la beaulté estoit telle, que celle de la duchesse ne
toute sa compaignye n'estoit que laydeur auprès, le
supliant ne le contraindre jamais de la nommer ; car
l'accord de luy et de s'amye estoit de telle sorte, qu'il
ne se povoit rompre, sinon par celluy qui premier le
declareroit. Le duc luy promist de ne l'en presser
point, et fut tant content de luy, qu'il luy feit
meilleure chere qu'il n'avoit point encore faict. Dont
la duchesse s'aperceut tresbien, et, usant de finesse
accoustumee, mist peyne d'entendre l'occasion. Ce
que le duc ne lui cela : d'ou avecques sa vengeance
s'engendra une forte jalousie, qui la feit supplier le
duc de commander au gentil homme de luy nommer
ceste amye, l'asseurant que c'estoit ung mensonge et
le meilleur moien que l'on pourroit trouver pour
l'asseurer de son dire, mais que, s'il ne luy nommoit
celle qu'il estimoit tant belle, il estoit le plus sot
prince du monde, s'il adjoustoit foy a sa parolle. Le
pauvre seigneur, duquel la femme tournoit l'oppinion comme il lui plaisoit, s'en alla promener tout
seul avec ce gentil homme, luy disant qu'il estoit
encores en plus grande peyne qu'il n'avoit esté, car il
se doubtoit fort qu'il luy avoit baillé une excuse pour
le garder de soupsonner la verité, qui le tormentoit
plus que jamais ; pourquoy luy pria autant qu'il
estoit possible de luy declarer celle qu'il aymoit si
fort. Le pauvre gentil homme le suplia de ne luy
faire faire une telle faulte envers celle qu'il aymoit,
que de luy faire rompre la promesse qu'il luy avoit
faicte et tenue si long temps ; et de luy faire perdre

[en] ung jour ce qu'il avoit conservé plus de sept ans ; et qu'il aymoit mieulx endurer la mort, que de faire ung tel tort à celle qui luy estoit si loiale. Le duc, voiant qu'il ne luy voulloit dire, entra en une si forte jalousie, que avecq ung visaige furieux luy dist : « Or, choisissez de deux choses l'une : ou de me dire celle que vous aymez plus que toutes, ou de vous en aller banny des terres ou j'ay auctorité, a la charge que, si je vous y trouve huict jours passez, je vous feray morir de cruelle mort. » Si jamais douleur saisit cueur de loial serviteur, elle print celuy de ce pauvre gentil homme, lequel povoit bien dire *Angustiae sunt mihi undique*[1], car d'un costé il voyoit que en disant verité il perdroit s'amye, si elle sçavoit que par sa faulte luy failloit de promesse ; aussy, en ne la confessant, il estoit banny du pays ou elle demoroit et n'avoit plus de moien de la veoir. Ainsy pressé des deux costez, luy vint une sueur froide comme celle qui par tristesse approchoit de la mort. Le duc, voiant sa contenance, jugea qu'il n'aymoit nulle dame, fors que la sienne, et que, pour n'en povoir nommer d'autre, il enduroit telle passion ; parquoy luy dist assez durement : « Si vostre dire estoit veritable, vous n'auriez tant de peyne à la me declarer, mais je croy que vostre offence vous tourmente. » Le gentil homme, picqué de ceste parolle et poulsé de l'amour qu'il luy portoit, se delibera de luy dire verité, se confiant que son maistre estoit tant homme de bien, que pour rien ne le vouldroit reveler. Se mectant a genoulx, devant luy, et les mains joinctes, luy dist : « Monseigneur, l'obligation que j'ay a vous et la grand amour que je vous porte me force plus que la paour de nulle mort, car je vous voy telle fantaisye et faulse oppinion de moy, que, pour vous oster d'une si grande peyne, je suis deliberé de faire ce que pour nul torment je

n'eusse faict ; vous supliant, monseigneur, en l'honneur de Dieu, me jurer et promectre en foy de prince et de chrestien, que jamais vous ne revelerez le secret que, puisqu'il vous plaist, je suis contrainct de dire. » A l'heure, le duc luy jura tous les sermens qu'il se peut adviser, de jamais a creature du monde n'en reveler riens, ne par parolles, ne par escript, ne par contenance. Le jeune homme, se tenant asseuré d'un si vertueux prince, comme il le congnoissoit, alla bastir le commencement de son malheur, en luy disant : « Il y a sept ans passez, monseigneur, que, aiant congneu vostre niepce, la dame du Verger, estre vefve et sans parens, mys peyne d'acquerir sa bonne grace. Et, pour ce que n'estois de maison pour l'espouser, je me contentois d'estre receu pour serviteur ; ce que j'ay esté. Et a voulu Dieu que nostre affaire jusques icy fut conduicte si saigement, que jamais homme ou femme qu'elle et moy n'en a rien entendu ; sinon maintenant, vous, monseigneur, entre les mains duquel je mectz ma vie et mon honneur ; vous supliant le tenir secret et n'en avoir en moindre estime madame vostre niepce, car je ne pense soubz le ciel une plus parfaicte creature. » Qui fut bien aise, ce fut le duc ; car, congnoissant la tresgrande beaulté de sa niepce, ne doubtant plus qu'elle ne fust plus agreable que sa femme, mais ne povant entendre que ung tel mistere se peust conduire sans moien, luy pria de luy dire comment il la pourroit veoir. Le gentil homme luy compta comme la chambre de sa dame sailloit dans ung jardin ; et que, le jour qu'il y debvoit aller, on luy laissoit une petite porte ouverte, par ou il entroit a pied, jusques a ce qu'il ouÿt japper ung petit chien que sa dame laissoit aller au jardin, quand toutes ses femmes estoient retirees. A l'heure, il s'en alloit parler a elle toute la nuict ; et, au partir, luy assignoit le jour qu'il debvoit retourner ; ou, sans trop grande excuse, n'avoit encores failly. Le duc, qui estoit le plus curieux homme du monde, et qui en son temps avoit fort bien mené l'amour, tant pour satisfaire a son soupson, que pour entandre une si estrange histoire, le pria de le vouloir mener avecq luy la premiere foys qu'il iroit, non comme maistre, mais comme compaignon. Le gentil homme, pour en estre si avant, luy accorda et luy dist comme ce jour-la mesme estoit son assignation ; dont le duc fut plus ayse que s'il eut gaigné ung royaulme. Et, faingnant s'en aller reposer en sa garderobbe, feit venir deux chevaulx pour luy et le gentil homme, et toute la nuyct se mirent en chemyn pour aller depuis Argilly ou le duc demoroit, jusques au Vergier². Et laissans leurs chevaulx hors l'enclosture, le gentil homme feit entrer le duc au jardin par le petit huys, le priant demorer derriere ung noyer, duquel lieu il povoit veoir s'il disoit vray ou non. Il n'eut gueres demeuré au jardin, que le petit chien commencea a japper, et le gentil homme marcha devers la tour ou sa dame ne failloit a venir au devant de luy, et, le saluant, luy dist qu'il luy sembloit avoir esté mille ans sans le veoir, et a l'heure entrerent dans la chambre et fermerent la porte sur eulx. Le duc, ayant veu tout ce mistere, se tint pour plus que satisfaict et attendit la non trop longuement, car le gentil homme dist a sa dame qu'il estoit contrainct de retourner plus tost qu'il n'avoit accoustumé, pour ce que le duc debvoit aller des quatre heures a la chasse, ou il n'osoit faillir. La dame, qui aymoit plus son honneur que son plaisir, ne le voulloit retarder de faire son debvoir, car la chose que plus elle estimoit en leur honneste amitié estoit qu'elle estoit secrete devant tous les hommes. Ainsy partyt ce gentil homme, a une heure après minuict ; et sa dame, en manteau et en couvrechef, le conduisit, non si loing qu'elle vouloit, car il la contraignoit de retourner, de paour qu'elle ne trouvast le duc ; avecq lequel il monta a cheval et s'en retourna au chasteau d'Argilly. Et, par les chemyns, le duc juroit incessamment au gentil homme mieulx aymer morir, que de jamais reveler son secret ; et print telle fiance et amour en luy, qu'il n'y avoit nul en sa court, qui fut plus en sa bonne grace ; dont la duchesse devint toute enragée. Mais le duc luy defendit de jamais plus luy en parler ; et qu'il en sçavoit la verité, dont il se tenoit contant, car la dame qu'il aymoit estoit plus aimable qu'elle. Ceste parolle navra si avant le cueur de la duchesse, qu'elle en print une malladie pire que la fiebvre. Le duc l'alla veoir, pour la consoler, mais il n'y avoit ordre, s'il ne luy disoit qui estoit ceste belle dame tant aymee ; dont elle luy faisoit une importunee presse, tant que le duc s'en alla hors de sa chambre, en luy disant : « Si vous me tenez plus de telz propos, nous nous separerons d'ensemble. » Ces parolles augmenterent la malladie de la duchesse, qu'elle faingnyt sentir bouger son enfant : dont le duc fut si joieux, qu'il s'en alla coucher auprès d'elle. Mais, a l'heure qu'elle le veid plus amoureux d'elle, se tournoit de l'autre costé, luy disant : « Je vous suplye, monsieur, puisque vous n'avez amour ne a femme ne a enfant, laissez nous morir tous deux. » Et, avecq ces parolles, geta tant de larmes et de criz, que le duc eut grand paour, qu'elle ne perdist son fruict. Parquoy, la prenant entre ses bras, la pria de luy dire que c'estoit qu'elle vouloit ; et qu'il n'avoit rien que ce ne fust pour elle. « Ha, monsieur, ce luy respondit elle en pleurant, quelle esperance puis je avoir que vous fassiez pour moy une chose difficile, quand la plus facile et raisonnable du monde, vous ne la voulez pas faire, qui est de me dire l'amye du

plus meschant serviteur que vous eustes oncques ? Je
pensois que vous et moy n'eussions que ung cueur,
une ame et une chair. Mais maintenant je congnois
bien que vous me tenez pour une estrangiere, veu
que vos secretz qui ne me doibvent estre celez, vous
les cachez, comme a personne estrange. Helas,
monsieur, vous m'avez dict tant de choses grandes et
secrettes, desquelles jamais n'avez entendu que j'en
aye parlé ; vous avez tant experimenté ma volunté
estre esgale a la vostre, que vous ne povez doubter
que je ne sois plus vous mesme que moy. Et, si vous
avez juré de ne dire a aultruy le secret du gentil
homme, en le me disant ne faillez a vostre serment,
car je ne suis ny ne puis estre aultre que vous : je
vous ay en mon cueur, je vous tiens entre mes bras,
j'ay ung enfant en mon ventre, auquel vous vivez, et
ne puis avoir vostre cueur, comme vous avez le
mien ! Mais tant plus je vous suis loiale et fidelle,
plus vous m'estes cruel et austere : qui me faict mille
foys le jour desirer, par une soubdaine mort, delivrer vostre enfant d'ung tel pere, et moy, d'ung tel
mary ; ce que j'espere bien tost, puisque preferez
ung serviteur infidelle a vostre femme telle que je
vous suis, et a la vie de la mere d'ung fruict qui est
vostre, lequel s'en va perir, ne pouvant obtenir de
vous ce que plus desire de sçavoir. » En ce disant,
embrassa et baisa son mary, arrousant son visaige de
ses larmes, avec telz criz et souspirs, que le bon
prince, craingnant de perdre sa femme et son enfant
ensemble, se delibera de luy dire vray du tout ; mais,
avant, luy jura que, si jamais elle le reveloit a
creature du monde, elle ne mourroit d'autre main
que de la sienne : a quoy elle se condamna et
accepta la pugnition. A l'heure, le pauvre deceu
mary luy racompta tout ce qu'il avoit veu, depuis
ung bout jusques a l'aultre : dont elle feit semblant

d'estre contente ; mais en son cueur pensoit bien le contraire. Toutesfois, pour la crainte du duc, dissimulla le plus qu'elle peut sa passion.

Et le jour d'une grande feste, que le duc tenoit sa court, ou il avoit mandé toutes les dames du pays, et entre aultres sa niepce, les dances commencerent, ou chacun feit son debvoir. Mais la duchesse, qui estoit tormentee, voiant la beaulté et bonne grace de sa niepce du Vergier, ne se povoit resjoyr ny moins garder son despit d'aparoistre. Car, ayant appelé toutes les dames qu'elle feit asseoir a l'entour d'elle, commencea a relever propos d'amour, et, voyant que madame du Vergier n'en parloit point, luy dist, avecq ung cueur creu de jalousie : « Et vous, belle niepce, est-il possible que vostre beaulté soit sans amy ou serviteur ? — Ma dame, ce luy respondit la dame du Vergier, ma beaulté ne m'a point faict de tel acquest, car, depuis la mort de mon mary, n'ay voulu autres amys que ses enfans dont je me tiens pour contante. — Belle niepce, belle niepce, ce luy respondit madame la duchesse par ung execrable despit, il n'y a amour si secrette, qu'il ne soit sceue, ne petit chien si affaité et faict a la main, duquel on n'entende le japper. » Je vous laisse penser, mes dames, quelle doulleur sentyt au cueur ceste pauvre dame du Vergier, voiant une chose tant longuement couverte estre a son grand deshonneur declaree ; l'honneur, si soingneusement gardé et si malheureusement perdu, la tormentoit, mais encores plus le soupson qu'elle avoit que son amy luy eust failly de promesse ; ce qu'elle ne pensoit jamais qu'il peust faire, sinon par aymer quelque dame plus belle qu'elle, a laquelle la force d'amour auroit faict declarer tout son faict. Toutesfois sa vertu fut si grande, qu'elle n'en feit ung seul semblant, et respondit en riant, a la duchesse, qu'elle ne se congnoissoit point au langaige des bestes. Et, soubz ceste saige dissimullation, son cueur fut si plein de tristesse, qu'elle se leva, et, passant par la chambre de la duchese, entra en une garderobbe ou le duc qui se pourmenoit la veid entrer. Et, quand la pauvre dame se trouva au lieu ou elle pensoit estre seulle, se laissa tumber sur ung lict avecq si grande foiblesse, que une damoiselle, qui estoit assise en la ruelle pour dormir, se leva, regardant par a travers le rideau qui ce povoit estre ; mais, voiant que c'estoit madame du Vergier, laquelle pensoit estre seulle, n'osa luy dire riens, et escouta le plus paisiblement qu'elle peut. Et la pauvre dame, avecq une voix demye morte, commencea a plaindre et dire : « O malheureuse, quelle parolle est-ce que j'ay ouÿe ? Quel arrest de ma mort ay je entendu ? Quelle sentence de ma fin ay je receue ? O le plus aymé qui oncques fut, est ce la recompense de ma chaste, honneste et vertueuse amour ! O mon cueur, avez vous faict une si perilleuse election et choisy pour le plus loial le plus infidelle, pour le plus veritable le plus fainct, et pour le plus secret le plus mesdisant ? Helas ! est il possible que une chose cachée aux yeux de tous les humains ait esté revelee a madame la duchesse ? Helas ! mon petit chien tant bien aprins, le seul moien de ma longue et vertueuse amitié, ce n'a pas esté vous, qui m'avez decelé, mais celluy qui a la voix plus criante que le chien abbayant, et le cueur plus ingrat que nulle beste. C'est luy qui contre son serment et sa promesse a descouvert l'heureuse vie, sans tenir tort a personne, que nous avons longuement menee ! O mon amy, l'amour duquel seul est entree dedans mon cueur, avecq lequel ma vie a esté conservee, faut il maintenant que, en vous declarant mon mortel ennemy, mon honneur soit mis au vent, mon corps en la terre, et mon ame ou eternellement elle demorera! La beaulté de la duchesse est-elle si extresme, qu'elle vous a transmué comme faisoit celle de Circee? Vous a-t-elle faict venir de vertueux vicieux, de bon mauvays, et d'homme beste cruelle? O mon amy, combien que vous me faillez de promesse, si vous tiendray de la mienne, c'est de jamais ne vous veoir, après la divulgation de nostre amitié; mais, aussy ne povant vivre sans vostre veue, je m'accorde voluntiers a l'extresme douleur que je sens, a laquelle ne veulx chercher remede ne par raison ne par mede-cine; car la mort seulle mectra la fin, qui me sera trop plus plaisante, que demorer au monde sans amy, sans honneur et sans contentement. La guerre ne la mort ne m'ont pas osté mon amy; mon peché ne ma coulpe ne m'ont pas osté mon honneur; ma faulte et mon demerite ne m'ont point faict perdre mon contantement; mais c'est l'infortune cruelle, qui rendant ingrat le plus obligé de tous les hommes, me faict recepvoir le contraire de ce que j'ay deservy. Ha! madame la duchesse, quel plaisir ce vous a esté, quand par mocquerye m'avez allegué mon petit chien! Or joyssez vous du bien qui a moy seule appartient! Or vous mocquez de celle qui pense par bien celer et vertueusement aymer estre exempte de toute mocquerye! O! que ce mot m'a serré le cueur, qui m'a faict rougir de honte et paslir de jalousye. Helas! mon cueur, je sens bien que vous n'en povez plus: l'amour qui m'a recongneue vous brusle; la jalousie et le tort que l'on vous tient, vous glace et admortit, et le despit et le regret ne me permectent de vous donner consolation. Helas! ma pauvre ame, qui, par trop avoir adoré la creature, avez oblié le Createur, il fault retourner entre les mains de Celluy duquel l'amour vaine vous avoit ravie. Prenez confiance, mon ame, de le trover meilleur pere que n'avez trouvé amy celluy pour lequel l'avez souvent oblié. O mon Dieu, mon createur, qui estes le vray et parfaict amour, par la grace duquel l'amour que j'ay portee a mon amy n'a esté tachee de nul vice, sinon de trop aymer, je suplye vostre misericorde de recepvoir l'ame et l'esperit de celle qui se repent avoir failly a vostre premier et tresjuste commandement ; et, par le merite de Celluy duquel l'amour est incomprehensible, excusez la faulte que trop d'amour m'a faict faire ; car en vous seul j'ay ma parfaicte confiance. Et adieu, amy, duquel [le] nom sans effect me creve le cueur ! » A ceste parolle, se laissa tumber tout a l'envers, et lui devint la couleur blesme, les levres bleues et les extremitez froides. En cest instant, arriva en la salle le gentil homme qu'elle aymoit ; et, voyant la duchesse qui dansoit avecq les dames, regarda partout ou estoit s'amye ; mais, ne la voiant point, entra en la chambre de la duchesse ; et trouva le duc qui se pourmenoit, lequel, devinant sa pensee, luy dist en l'oreille : « Elle est allee en ceste garderobbe, et sembloit qu'elle se trouvoit mal. » Le gentil homme luy demanda s'il luy plaisoit bien qu'il y allast : le duc l'en pria. Ainsy qu'il entra dedans la garderobbe, trouva madame du Vergier, qui estoit au dernier pas de sa mortelle vie ; laquelle il embrassa, luy disant : « Qu'est cecy, m'amye ? Me voulez vous laisser ? » La pauvre dame, oiant la voix que tant bien elle congnoissoit, print un peu de vigueur ; et ouvrit l'œil, regardant celluy qui estoit cause de sa mort ; mais, en ce regard, l'amour et le despit creurent si fort, que avecq ung piteux souspir rendit son ame a Dieu. Le gentil homme, plus mort que la morte, demanda a la damoiselle comme ceste malladie luy estoit prinse. Elle luy compta du long les parolles qu'elle luy avoit oÿ dire. A l'heure, il

209

congneut que le duc avoit revelé son secret a sa femme ; dont il sentit une telle fureur, que, embrassant le corps de s'amye, l'arrousa longuement de ses larmes, en disant : « O moy, traistre, meschant et malheureux amy, pourquoy est ce que la pugnition de ma trahison n'est tumbee sur moy, et non sur elle qui est innocente ? Pourquoy le ciel ne me fouldroya il pas le jour que ma langue revela la secrette et vertueuse amitié de noz deux ? Pourquoy la terre nè s'ouvrit pour engloutir ce faulseur de foy ? O ma langue, pugnye sois tu comme celle du mauvays riche en enfer [3] ! O mon cueur, trop crainctif de mort et de banissement, deschiré sois tu des aigles perpetuellement comme celluy de Ixion ! Helas ! m'amye, le malheur des malheurs, le plus malheureux qui oncques fut, m'est advenu ! Vous cuydant garder, je vous ay perdue ; vous cuydant veoir longuement vivre avec honneste et plaisant contentement, je vous embrasse morte, mal content de moy, de mon cueur et de ma langue jusques a l'extremité ! O la plus loialle et fidelle femme qui oncques fut, je passe condamnation d'estre le plus deloyal, muable et infidelle de tous les hommes ! Je me vouldrois voluntiers plaindre du duc, soubz la promesse duquel me suis confié, esperant par là faire durer nostre heureuse vie ; mais, helas ! je debvois sçavoir que nul ne povoit garder mon secret mieulx que moy mesmes. Le duc a plus de raison de dire le sien a sa femme que moy à luy. Je n'accuse que moy seul de la plus grande meschanceté qui oncques fut commise entre amys. Je debvois endurer estre jecté en la riviere, comme il me menassoit ; au moins, m'amye, vous fussiez demoree [vive] et moy glorieusement mort, observant la loy que vraye amitié commande ; mais, l'ayant rompue, je demeure vif ; et, vous, par aymer parfaictement, estes morte, car vostre cueur tant pur et nect n'a sceu porter, sans mort, de sçavoir le vice qui estoit en vostre amy. O mon Dieu ! pourquoy me creastes vous homme, aiant l'amour si legiere et cueur tant ignorant ? Pourquoy ne me creastes vous le petit chien, qui a fidellement servy sa maistresse ? Helas, mon petit amy, la joye que me donnoit vostre japper est tournee en mortelle tristesse, puis que aultre que nous deux a oÿe vostre voix ! Si est ce, m'amye, que l'amour de la duchesse ne de femme vivant ne m'a faict varier, combien que par plusieurs foys la meschante m'en ait requis et pryé ; mais ignorance m'a vaincu, pensant a jamais asseurer nostre amitié. Toutesfois, pour estre ignorant, je ne laisse d'estre coulpable, car j'ay revelé le secret de m'amye ; j'ay faulsé ma promesse, qui est la seulle cause dont je la voy morte devant mes œilz. Helas ! m'amye, me sera la mort moins cruelle que a vous, qui par amour avez mis fin a vostre innocente vie. Je croy qu'elle ne daigneroit toucher a mon infidelle et miserable cueur, car la vie deshonoree et la memoire de ma perte, par ma faulte, est plus importable que dix mille mortz. Helas, m'amye, si quelqu'un, par malheur ou malice, vous eust osé tuer, promptement j'eusse mis la main a l'espée pour vous venger. C'est doncques raison que je ne pardonne a ce meurtrier, qui est cause de vostre mort par ung acte plus meschant que de vous donner ung coup d'espée. Si je sçavois un plus infame bourreau que moy mesmes, je le prierois d'executer vostre traistre amy. O amour ! par ignoramment aymer, je vous ay offensé : aussy vous ne me voulez secourir comme vous avez faict celle qui a gardé toutes vos loix. Ce n'est pas raison, que, par si honneste moyen, je define, mais raisonnable que ce soit par ma propre main. Puisque avecq mes larmes j'ay lavé vostre visaige et avecq ma langue vous ay requis pardon, il ne reste plus qu'avecq ma main je rende mon corps semblable au vostre et laisse aller mon ame ou la vostre ira, sçachant que ung amour vertueux et honneste n'a jamais fin en ce monde ne en l'aultre. » Et, a l'heure, se levant de dessus le corps, comme ung homme forcené et hors du sens, tira son poignard, et, par grande violence, s'en donna au travers du cueur ; et de rechef print s'amye entre ses bras, la baisant par telle affection, qu'il sembloit plus estre attainct d'amour que de la mort. La damoiselle, voiant ce coup, s'en courut a la porte cryer a l'ayde. Le duc, oiant ce cry, doubtant le mal de ceulx qu'il aymoit, entra le premier dedans la garderobbe ; et, voiant ce piteux couple, s'essaya de les separer, pour saulver s'il eust esté possible le gentil homme. Mais il tenoit s'amye si fortement, qu'il ne fut possible de la luy oster jusques ad ce qu'il fut trespassé. Toutesfois, entendant le duc qui parloit a luy, disant : « Helas ! qui est cause de cecy ? » avecq ung regard furieux, luy respondit : « Ma langue et la vostre, monsieur. » Et, en ce disant, trespassa, son visaige joint a celluy de s'amye. Le duc, desirant en sçavoir plus avant, contraingnit la damoiselle de luy dire ce qu'elle en avoit veu et entendu ; ce qu'elle feit tout du long, sans en espargner rien. A l'heure, le duc, congnoissant qu'il estoit cause de tout le mal, se gecta sur les deux amans mortz ; et, avecq grandz criz et pleurs, leur demanda pardon de sa faulte, en les baisant tous deux par plusieurs foys. Et, puis, tout furieux, se leva, tira le poignard du corps du gentil homme, et, tout ainsy que ung sanglier estant navré d'un espieu court d'une impetuosité contre celluy qui a faict le coup, ainsy s'en alla le duc chercher celle qui l'avoit navré jusques au fond de son ame ; laquelle il trouva dansant dans la salle, plus joieuse qu'elle n'avoit accoustumé, comme celle qui pensoit estre bien vengee de la dame du Vergier. Le duc la print au milieu de la dance et luy dist : « Vous avez prins le secret sur vostre vie, et sur vostre vie tombera la pugnition. » En ce disant, la print par la coeffure et luy donna ung coup de poignard dedans la gorge, dont toute la compaignie fut si estonnee, que l'on pensoit que le duc fut hors de sens. Mais, après qu'il eut parachevé ce qu'il voulloit, assembla en la salle tous ses serviteurs et leur compta l'honneste et piteuse histoire de sa niepce et le meschant tour que luy avoit faict sa femme, qui ne fut sans faire pleurer les assistans. Après, le duc ordonna que sa femme fust enterree en une abbaye qu'il fonda en partye pour satisfaire au peché qu'il avoit faict de tuer sa femme ; et feit faire une belle sepulture ou les corps de sa niepce et du gentil homme furent mys ensemble, avecq ung epitaphe declarant la tragedie de leur histoire. Et le duc entreprint ung voiage sur les Turcs, ou Dieu le favorisa tant, qu'il en rapporta honneur et proffict, et trouva a son retour son filz aisné suffisant de gouverner son bien, luy laissa tout, et s'en alla rendre religieux en l'abbaye ou estoit enterree sa femme et les deux amans : et là passa sa vieillesse heureusement avecq Dieu.

« Voyla, mes dames, l'histoire que vous m'avez priee de vous racompter ; que je congnois bien a vos œilz n'avoir esté entendue sans compassion. Il me semble que vous debvez tirer exemple de cecy, pour vous garder de mectre vostre affection aux hommes, car, quelque honneste ou vertueuse qu'elle soit, elle a tousjours a la fin quelque mauvais desboire. Et vous voiez que sainct Pol encores, aux gens mariez, ne veult qu'ilz aient ceste grande amour ensemble[4]. Car, d'autant que nostre cueur est affectionné a

213

quelque chose terrienne, d'autant s'esloigne il de l'affection celeste ; et plus difficile en est a rompre le lien, qui me faict vous prier, mes dames, de demander a Dieu son Sainct Esperit, par lequel vostre amour soit tant enflambee en l'amour de Dieu, que vous n'aiez point de peyne, a la mort, de laisser ce que vous aymez trop en ce monde. — Puisque l'amour estoit si honneste, dist Geburon, comme vous nous la paignez, pourquoy la falloit il tenir si secrette ? — Pour ce, dist Parlamente, que la malice des hommes est telle, que jamais ne pensent que grande amour soyt joincte a honnesteté ; car ilz jugent les hommes et les femmes vitieux, selon leurs passions. Et, pour ceste occasion, il est besoing, si une femme a quelque bon amy, oultre ses plus grands prochains parens, qu'elle parle a luy secretement, si elle y veult parler longuement ; car l'honneur d'une femme est aussi bien mys en dispute, pour aymer par vertu, comme par vice, veu que l'on ne se prent que ad ce que l'on voyt. — Mais, dist Geburon, quand ce secret la est decelé, l'on pense beaucoup pis. — Je le vous confesse, dist Longarine ; parquoy, c'est le meilleur du tout de n'aymer point. — Nous appellons de ceste sentence, dist Dagoucin, car, si nous pensions les dames sans amour, nous vouldrions estre sans vie. J'entendz de ceux qui ne vivent que pour l'acquerir ; et, encores qu'ilz n'y adviennent, l'esperance les soustient et leur faict faire mille choses honnorables jusques ad ce que la vieillesse change ces honnestes passions en autres peynes. Mais qui penseroit que les dames n'aymassent point, il fauldroit, en lieu d'hommes d'armes, faire des marchans ; et, en lieu d'acquerir honneur, ne penser que a amasser du bien. — Doncques, dist Hircan, s'il n'y avoit point de femmes, vous vouldriez dire que nous serions tous meschans ? Comme si nous n'avions cueur que celluy qu'elles nous donnent ! Mais je suis bien de contraire oppinion, qu'il n'est rien qui plus abate le cueur d'un homme que de hanter ou trop aymer les femmes. Et, pour ceste occasion, defendoient les Hebrieux, que, l'année que l'homme estoit marié, il n'allast point a la guerre, de paour que l'amour de sa femme ne le retirast des hazardz que l'on y doibt sercher. — Je trouve, dist Saffredent, ceste loy sans grande raison, car il n'y a rien qui face plustost sortir l'homme hors de sa maison, que d'estre marié, pource que la guerre du dehors n'est pas plus importable que celle de dedans ; et croy que, pour donner envye aux hommes d'aller en pays estranges et ne se amuser en leurs foyers, il les fauldroit marier. — Il est vray, dist Ennasuitte, que le mariage leur oste le soing de leur maison ; car ilz s'en fyent a leurs femmes et ne pensent que a acquerir honneur, estans seurs que leurs femmes auront assez de soing du proffict. » Saffredent luy respondist : « En quelque sorte que ce soit, je suis bien ayse que vous estes de mon oppinion. — Mais, ce dist Parlamente, vous ne debatez de ce qui est le plus a considerer : c'est pourquoy le gentil homme qui estoit cause de tout le mal ne mourut aussi tost de desplaisir, comme celle qui estoit innocente ? » Nomerfide luy dist : « C'est pource que les femmes ayment mieulx que les hommes. — Mais c'est, ce dist Simontault, pource que la jalousie des femmes et le despit les faict crever, sans sçavoir pourquoy ; et la prudence des hommes les faict enquerir de la verité : laquelle congneue, par bon sens, monstrent leur grand cueur, comme feit ce gentil homme, et, après avoir entendu qu'il estoit l'occasion du mal de s'amye, monstra combien il l'aymoit, sans espargner sa propre vie. — Toutesfois, dist Ennasuitte, elle morut par vraye amour, car son ferme et loial cueur ne povoit endurer d'estre si villainement trompee. — Ce fut sa jalousie, dist Simontault, qui ne donna lieu a la raison ; et creut le mal qui n'estoit point en son amy, tel comme elle le pensoit ; et fut sa mort contraincte, car elle n'y povoit remedier ; mais celle de son amy fut voluntaire, après avoir congneu son tort. — Si fault il, dist Nomerfide, que l'amour soyt grande, qui cause une telle douleur. — N'en ayez point de paour, dist Hircan, car vous ne morrez point d'une telle fiebvre. — Non plus, dist Nomerfide, que vous ne vous tuerez, après avoir congneu vostre offence. » Parlamente, qui se doubtoit le debat estre a ses despens, leur dist, en riant : « C'est assez que deux soient mortz d'amour, sans que l'amour en face battre deux autres, car voyla le dernier son de vespres qui nous departira, veuillez ou non. » Par son conseil, la compaignie se leva, et allerent oÿr vespres, n'obliant en leurs bonnes prieres les ames des vraiz amans, pour lesquelz les religieux, de leur bonne volunté, dirent ung *de Profundis*. Et, tant que le soupé dura, n'eurent aultres propos que de madame du Vergier ; et, après ung peu passé leur temps ensemble, chascun se retira en sa chambre, et ainsi meirent fin a la septiesme journee.

FIN DE LA SEPTIESME JOURNEE.

NOTES

1. Cf. Daniel 13 : 22.
2. Argilly : Côte-d'Or, arr. Beaune, canton Nuits-Saint-Georges.
   Le Vergier = Vergy : Côte-d'Or, arr. Dijon, canton Gevrey-Chambertin.

216

3. Il est probable que Marguerite renvoie ici au texte de Saint Luc 16.
4. Peut-être un renvoi à la première lettre aux Corinthiens 7 : 29.

GLOSSAIRE

acquest : acquisition
admortir : étouffer
affaité : dressé
asseuré de : sans crainte en ce qui concerne
assignation : rendez-vous
cel(l)er : cacher
conditions : nature, caprices
constamment : avec courage
coulpe : faute
creu : gonflé
decel(l)er : trahir, révéler
(se) deffaire : (se) donner la mort
definer : mourir
departir : séparer
deservir : mériter
enclosture : enclos
entendre : comprendre
espieu : épieu
estrange : étranger
faillir : manquer
fouyer : foyer
garderobbe : alcôve
hazard : danger, risque
huys : porte
ignorance : candeur
ignorant : candide
importable : insupportable
main (faict à la m.) : dressé

muable : inconstant, changeant

navrer : blesser

ne : ni

nect : sans tache

ordre (avoir o.) : moyen

oÿr (oïant, ouÿ) : entendre, écouter

piteulx : mélancolique

pour (pour mourir) : même si je devais en mourir

prix (au p.) : en comparaison

qui : signifie parfois 'ce qui'

rechef (de r.) : de nouveau

relever propos : parler

saillir : donner sur

semblant : signe

suffisant : capable

transmuer : métamorphoser

va : Employé souvent avec un infinitif pour indiquer une action dans le passé. Parfois aussi cette combinaison est employée pour le futur.

venir (vicieux etc.) *:* devenir

vertu : maîtrise de soi

vif : vivant

voulsisse : je voulusse, aurais voulu.

TABLE DES MATIÈRES

Achevé d'imprimer en mars 1985
sur les presses de l'Imprimerie Bussière
à Saint-Amand-Montrond (Cher)

Nº d'édition : 1575. Nº d'impression : 2899.
Dépôt légal : mars 1985.

Imprimé en France